MW01166606

Link by Link

M. Dalto
Candace Robinson
Jess Moore
C. Vonzale Lewis
Pam S. Dunn
Elle Beaumont
Leslie Rush
Kristin Jacques
Lauren Emily Whalen

Link by Link

M. Dalto, Pam S. Dunn, Kristin Jacques, C. Vonzale Lewis, Jess Moore, Candace Robinson, Leslie Rush, Lauren Emily Whalen

Edited by Meg Dailey

LINK BY LINK.

Published by Midnight Tide Publishing.
www.midnighttidepublishing.com
Edited by Meg Dailey
Cover Art and Design by Jessica Dueck of StarsColdNight
Interior Formatting by Elissa Carr/Book Savvy Services

AN ANTHOLOGY OF
HAUNTED HOLIDAYS
LINK
BY
LINK
EDITED BY MEG DAILEY

Foreword by Meg Dailey

Foreword

Here's a fun fact about me: I was in college before I knew that there was only one Marley in *A Christmas Carol*. Why? Well, Gonzo the Great started his version of the tale with, "The Marleys were dead to begin with," implying there were at least two, and he'd never lied to me before!

I've never been one to read the classics for fun. There were a few over the years that I read for one class or another that I liked—and more that I sloughed through as if they were my own personal Statler and Waldorf, heckling me from every page like my not knowing *why* the curtains were blue was the biggest sin of them all.

The thing is, I still ended up learning about the classics, just in other ways, by seeing them in different mediums I could relate to infinitely better than the original source material. They weren't always sung to me by Muppets—though I believe to this day that's the best way to tell ANY story—but I was not missing out these well-known tales. I was just experiencing them with a different narrative spin.

Today, I'm a big proponent of modern fairy tales. The more inundated with information we get, the harder it can be to relate to stories we've already heard. Information is old hours after it's released. There's always something new the moment we refresh the page, and it can be difficult as writers to keep up with that.

Modern authors, especially those who are a part of

anthologies like this one, write to combat the idea that it's all been written already, that there's nothing new to be said.

This is not a book of *A Christmas Carol* retellings; it's a collection of new and unique stories exploring an old theme from a fresh point of view. And, haunted though they are, these stories are also often... hopeful.

What you take away from these holiday tales is up to you. It may be different than what we took away, and it may be different for you now than it would have been a few years ago or will be years in the future. Things are constantly changing, updating, upgrading, moving on—and these stories will move with you, if you let them.

Happy Holidays, all!

Meg Dailey

Lead Editor, Link by Link Anthology

Between the Quiet

Candace Robinson

ONE

2001

Hand. Invisible brick. Hand. Invisible brick. Slide hand, and twirl. Tuesday Collins pressed her hands against an invisible brick wall that she imagined was a bright, blazing yellow. Tilting her head at a young woman with red hair pulled into two braids, Tuesday lowered herself in a crouched position and felt around an illusioned box. The redhead arched a brow at Tuesday, paused, and scrambled on by. Tuesday sighed and slumped her shoulders in mock disappointment.

As a man with salt-and-pepper hair walked her way, Tuesday's fingers fumbled up inside her black-and-white striped sleeves and plucked out a glittery pink orchid. She hopped off the stairstep in front of the man and held the flower out to him.

The corners of the man's eyes wrinkled into a smile. "No thanks."

Tuesday gestured to her dark bowler hat resting on the ground, filled with mostly pennies.

"Oh." He dug into his pocket and pulled out two crisp one-dollar bills, dropping them into her hat.

That's what I'm talking about. She gave the man a widening smile and a hasty bow in thanks. Behind her came the soft clinks of a few more coins being released into her hat.

Every Saturday, and most Sundays, Tuesday spent her weekends performing mime tricks right outside the edge of the subway at Grand Central Station. In the background, the subway swished on by, gathering passengers as bagpipes, a saxophone, and a violin were played. Other entertainers inside were breakdancing, painting portraits, doing anything they could to break out and get noticed.

All Tuesday wanted was to be the next great mime artist, like Marcel Marceau. However, she felt as though she'd been born decades, or even centuries, too late. It was a mostly dead trade. But she didn't care, because this was the weekend, *her* weekend. And one day, she would get that Broadway play, or that film, or even join Cirque du Soleil.

The morning sun was already beating down on her heavily-painted face. Not breaking character, she pretended to pick up heavy boxes as she searched around the walking civilians, the leafless trees of autumn, the glass buildings. Her pantomime partner was nowhere to be found. Where the hell was Francis? Francis was always late for *everything*. She was late every Saturday. Hell, half the time Francis forgot the day was Saturday and didn't show up. It was as though she didn't take this as seriously as Tuesday, even though it had been Francis's idea to start coming out here on the weekends in the first place.

Tuesday bet it had to do with Francis's new boyfriend, or possibly an old one... She placed her hand in position, as if she was holding a glass, and chugged the invisible drink. As her head lowered back down, she wiped a gloved hand across her mouth and her heart stopped. Literally stopped. There was a microsecond where she broke character, but no one noticed except for her.

Before her stood a boy, a boy she knew incredibly well, one from school. Maybe not "knew" in a close friend sense, but he was Francis's cousin. Her very, *very* cute cousin. Becker Barber. *Beck.* Why was he here? His bleached hair hung right at his pitch-black brows. He wore a long-sleeved Guns N' Roses shirt paired with tight black jeans and checkerboard Vans.

She wanted to topple over and die right there. Seriously, just vanish. But she kept miming, hoping he wouldn't notice that the mime was indeed her.

Tuesday's heart karate kicked her sternum, bringing her back to the present. Beck wouldn't recognize her. Not in her costume. Not with her face painted, beret, scarf, striped top, her skirt, the suspenders, black and white pantyhose, the boots, and her bob hair pulled back in braids. He barely gave her a nod when passing her at school, even though he'd moved across the street at the beginning of the year. She'd known him since kindergarten, but had only seen him at Francis's annual birthday parties—until this year.

Tuesday tapped her knees and shot up, realizing she probably looked like a damn monkey instead of a toy jack popping out of its box. She side-stepped and attempted to focus her gaze on any other passing faces. There were none. Of course there weren't. *Stupid in-between subway times.*

Seriously, where is Francis?

Tuesday pulled a fake gold coin from her hidden skirt pocket and tossed it up and down in her gloved hand. Beck didn't move on. Instead, his dark brown eyes watched the coin. As it struck her palm, she held her hand up—now empty. Then she moved to her bowler hat and scooped up the gold coin before placing it back into her pocket. She turned around and breathed in a calming breath.

When she faced Beck again, he gave her a small smile and dipped his hand into his pocket. He pulled out two quarters, tossed them inside her hat, and strolled away.

She could finally relax again.

Then he glanced over his shoulder and said, "Nice moves, Tuesday." He smiled again and walked toward the subway. "Tell Francis I dropped the two quarters in the hat."

Tuesday cringed and stared up at the sky and nodded. She bet Francis had invited him here and told him they were desperate for people to stop by. So why didn't she show up? Tuesday was not going to break her silence while in character, even for a cute boy. But she did watch his toned body as he moved down the stone path toward the tunnel.

The day stayed chilly as Tuesday continued to work through her routine, moving with the music from a trumpet not too far in the distance. Winter was still a little over a month away, but she'd need to add a jacket during her routine soon. At the end of the day, Tuesday had made thirty-four dollars, two condoms, a pack of bubblegum, and two dice. This was a win; sometimes she'd come away with only a few coins and condoms. The collection there was growing.

Tuesday gathered her things, hopped into her Ford Focus, and prepared for the tedious drive back home.

Tuesday turned down her street, flickers of red, yellow, and orange leaves from trees catching her attention. Most of the yards were scattered with leaves that needed to be raked —she'd do her yard tomorrow with her brothers.

As she pulled into the driveway of the brick two-story home, she thought about Francis not showing up and decided she'd try to call her as soon as she got inside. After she stepped out of the car, Tuesday kicked away a few leaves from the porch and entered the house. She found her mother and three younger brothers playing a game of Clue at the dining room table. Tuesday's dad was on a business trip to California for the next week with his law firm. This would mean lots of board games, movies, and her mom over-cleaning everything because she got bored when he was gone on these trips.

"You wanna play Clue?" her mom asked.

"Um, how about I'll play something tomorrow?" Tuesday said. "I'm going to wind down for a bit."

"All right, you can pick tomorrow."

"Battleship." She preferred the old-school one without the annoying sounds.

"Great!"

"Any phone calls for me?"

"Nope."

Francis must be really busy then...

Tuesday's younger brother, Jackson, rolled the dice and let out a "muahaha" as though he'd just won a million bucks. She smiled at that as she went up the stairs to her room, glad that she'd been born a girl so she didn't have to share a room with any of the boys. Jackson and Lincoln both had to share, and neither one knew how to keep their room clean.

She walked down the hall, past the family portraits, to her room in the back. Setting down her bag and accessories, she picked up the phone and dialed Francis. Her voice mail picked up after the fourth ring, a recording of her usual chipper self. "Hey, it's Francis, leave me a message and I'll call you back... if I feel like it."

"Francis, you little vixen, call me back after you get this. I'm annoyed and have something to discuss. But don't worry, all will be forgiven." Tuesday hung up the phone and rotated her shoulders.

Removing her costume, she threw on comfy black sweatpants and an oversized Nine Inch Nails T-shirt, then went to wash the makeup from her face in the bathroom she shared with her three brothers.

The night was still young, so she turned on an old Charlie Chaplin film and hopped on the computer. She signed into AOL Instant Messenger while checking her email. Nothing from Francis, and her screen name was offline. The only person on was Tuesday's cousin from Georgia, and she didn't feel like talking to her. So she focused on other things: searching online sites for pantomime music and gestures to improve her miming skills.

Somehow, she'd landed on pictures of Marcel Marceau and Michael Jackson, and an article about their friendship. Michael had apparently mastered his moonwalk by using Marcel's techniques. Tuesday stood from her chair and flexed and unflexed her feet along the carpet, attempting to walk against the wind. She didn't go anywhere. "Still needs work." She sighed. Or maybe she needed different shoes.

Jamie Lee Curtis's *Halloween* scream came from Tuesday's computer, causing her to jump a fraction. Sometimes she forgot that she'd chosen the Messenger alerts to be horror movie screams—much better than a doorbell or the other options though. She glanced at the computer screen and found a message had popped up.

"Finally, Francis!" She knew Francis would apologize. And then all would be forgiven.

But when she plopped down in her hard desk chair, it wasn't Francis. It was a screen name she didn't recognize.

BBRock4Life: Hey

Tuesday narrowed her eyes at the screen, wondering if this was another pervert who'd read her profile thinking she'd be interested in his banana. Most of the time, it was someone double her age, and she'd have to block them.

TheMimingFairy85: Who art thou?

BBRock4Life: Tis a secret.

TheMimingFairy85: Mmm, I don't like dirty little secrets. Sorry!

BBRock4Life: Good. Neither do I. But I do know you like wearing little black mime skirts.

What the hell?

TheMimingFairy85: Seriously, Francis, quit using new screen names.

Francis had done it four other times, trying to freak Tuesday out. It never worked.

BBRock4Life: I'm not Francis.

Shit, it's like Scream *up in here tonight.* It wasn't as if she was alone here—her mom and brothers were somewhere, probably already asleep. There were butcher knives in the kitchen, but those were far away. Tuesday searched around the comfort of her room for anything she could use in case the doorbell rang. There was a heavy black-and-white magician wand in the corner—it would do the trick if she needed it.

TheMimingFairy85: Who the hell is this?

Nothing.

TheMimingFairy85: Waiting...

She was done messing around and was about to hit the block button when her computer screamed.

BBRock4Life: It's Beck.

Tuesday's eyes popped forward and she leaned back too hard, causing her rickety chair to flip backward. She crashed onto the carpet with a heavy thump.

"I'm okay," she said to no one, or maybe to herself as her face flushed. Tuesday's head remained hidden beneath the desk as though if she rose, Beck would see her there. But maybe he could, since his window was across the street from hers. Her heart pounded at the thought.

Jamie Lee Curtis screamed again.

BBRock4Life: Francis gave me your screen name and told me you wanted me to message you tonight.

Freaking Francis! She didn't want to say that Francis was lying because Tuesday did want to keep talking to him. So, she figured would spin a lie of her own.

TheMimingFairy85: Yeah, I wanted to see if you were available to mime... Since Francis can't make it all the time.

She should've thought about having an alternate sooner.

BBRock4Life: I know nothing about miming.

Tuesday smiled at the screen. She could've easily guessed that.

TheMimingFairy85: That's too bad.

BBRock4Life: You could come over and show me though.

Was he serious? She almost fell out of her chair again as she broke out into a smile.

TheMimingFairy85: Now?

She glanced at the clock. It was 10:30 PM. It wasn't *that* late, and it was a Saturday.

BBRock4Life: Sure

TheMimingFairy85: Where?

BBRock4Life: My window's open.

Tuesday peered around her computer, out the window, and could see just past Beck's deformed-looking oak tree that his window was indeed open. She'd never been in his room, hadn't ever really been in any boy's room. She was sixteen, turning seventeen in a couple of months—she desperately needed to be able to say she'd stepped inside a boy's room. Most girls her age had already been to numerous bases and hit the homerun already.

Why was she thinking about sex and sports? It was going into his bedroom for God's sake. At night. To discuss mimes. That was it.

Collecting two Marcel Marceau DVDs, a history book on the father of pantomime, John Rich, and her tote bag of mime goodies, Tuesday tiptoed down the stairs. She froze when she saw the TV was still on. Staying quiet, she moved farther into the room, and her shoulders relaxed. Tuesday's fourteen-year-old brother, Kyle, sat sprawled out on the couch.

His head turned to her as she approached him. "Where do you think you're going?" he asked, shoving popcorn into his mouth.

"Across the street." Tuesday adjusted her backpack.

"What do I get for not telling Mom?"

"Not getting a punch in the face."

"Fine, you win." He chuckled. "I'll leave the door unlocked for you."

She was relieved her brothers were easy to get along with. Francis's brother and sister could be real jerks.

Tuesday ducked out of her house and into the cool night. Trying to not shake from nervousness, she followed the shadows across the dimly-lit street and stopped in front of Beck's gray-bricked two-story. Maybe it would've been better to ask him to have the front door open, but this had seemed more *Romeo & Juliet*.

She tightened her backpack and climbed his deformed tree. It was rotting in a few areas. The bark scraped her hands as she tried to be nimble and scale her way up. She hadn't been in a tree since she was maybe nine, so she was a tad rusty.

When she got to the branch leading to his window, she called out in a low voice, "Hey!"

Beck moved the curtain aside and came into view, wearing a tight black T-shirt and jeans. "I was kidding, Collins." With a smile, he closed the window.

Her eyes widened in horror, and she was about to go into full-on panic mode. "Are you serious?" she whisper-shouted.

Then he pushed the window up. "Kidding again. Get in here." He reached out, grabbed her hand, and tugged her through his window. His skin was warm against hers, and as he released her, his calloused fingers brushed against her palm, sending tingles down her spine.

"So how did you recognize me today at the subway?" she asked after she straightened.

"Duh." He smiled and scratched the back of his neck. "How would I not know it's you? I see your face every day at school and you live right across the street. Besides, Francis said you two were going to be there and asked me to stop by on my way to see about my band doing a gig."

Beck was in a rock band, and she'd seen them live with Francis a couple times over the past few months. They were better than good.

"Makes sense." Maybe she'd let the subway situation slide with Francis. But she still should've warned her that she was going to tell Beck to message her.

"So, why don't you ever talk to me at school?" he asked and took a seat on his bed. Movie and band posters covered every inch of his wall. Two guitar cases took up space in the corner. A desk and computer rested beside his bed with a TV and stand on the opposite side.

She sat down next to him, maybe a little too close. "I wave. But you don't talk to me."

"I nod." Beck bit his lip, looking almost shy for a moment. Before she could ask something else, he arched one of his dark brows and peered down at her bag. "*So*," he drawled. "Miming techniques? Show me what you got."

Tuesday pulled out a book on the history of pantomime with an illustration of John Rich on the cover. "You can borrow this." Then she fished out one of the Marcel Marceau DVDs and handed it to him. Marcel's arms were spread wide, and one hand held a top hat. Beck eyed the mime on the cover as he popped the DVD into his player before sitting on the bed. He scooted back and propped his back against the headboard. She didn't know whether she was supposed to linger at the edge of the bed or move to where he was. But then he patted the spot beside him and she slid back, her shoulder only a few inches from brushing his. It was strange, it was awesome, and it was hormonally frustrating when all she wanted to do was press her lips to his instead of watching Marcel.

This one time in her life, it felt as if the movie would never end. She didn't want it to end, but then it did. Beck got up from the bed and took the DVD out from the player. As he came back toward her, he lifted and curved his feet so it looked as though he was walking toward her but being pulled backward. Her jaw dropped as he perfectly performed the walking against the wind movement as he handed her the DVD.

"Shut up. You did not just do that."

"Shut up? I wasn't even talking." He chuckled. "I was in mime mode. Plus, I was a huge Michael Jackson fan when I was younger."

"Figures. I still can't do it." Tuesday glanced at the clock radio and saw that it was close to one in the morning. "It's getting late. I'd better jet." Her mom would throw a fit if she knew she'd snuck out.

"We should do this again." He leaned forward. "I don't have the white gloves just yet, but I do have some mittens."

"In the meantime, go ahead and practice, and read the book if you have time." She put on her backpack and took a step backward.

They both awkwardly stared at each other, or at least she did. He didn't look even a little awkward.

"Well, goodnight," he said, smiling.

"Goodnight," she said and scurried out the window and onto the branch.

"You might want to practice the moonwalk while you're at it," he called down as he closed the window and her feet struck the earth.

Tuesday shook her fist at him while she could still see him chuckling behind the glass. She couldn't help smiling as she crossed the street, the air chillier now, sending goose-bumps across her flesh.

Slowly turning the knob, she slipped back into her dark house. The only light came from the TV in the living room, where her brother lay fast asleep, softly snoring, with an old game show playing. Kyle always did this on the weekends, and sometimes she'd fall asleep beside him. He looked funny when he slept, like a cute little old man. She covered him with a flannel blanket from the back of the couch and went up the stairs to her room.

As she slipped out of her Converse, Jamie Lee Curtis screamed from her computer. With the mouse, she shook away the bouncy ball screensaver and checked Messenger. Still nothing from Francis, but Beck had sent her a message.

All her nerves seemed to dance and come to life in that moment.

BBRock4Life: Thanks for the miming lesson.

TheMimingFairy85: :)

Francis still wasn't on AIM, so Tuesday shot her a quick email.

So I just came from your cousin's house! Not like that! But you told him I wanted him to message me, so I told him I needed a miming alternative. Seriously, hurry up and get back to me!

Before she lay down to sleep, like every night, she turned on Charlie Chaplin's music and set the instrumental sounds for low, letting the violins and trombones do the talking. Christmas wasn't that far away, and she and Francis would need to discuss a routine for the winter season. Closing her eyes, she fell asleep dreaming about a winter wonderland where she and Francis were twirling large metal hoops on a stage covered in multi-colored Christmas lights. An audience filled with people with unclear faces watched Tuesday and Francis in their matching black slacks, suspenders, striped shirts, and painted faces. In the background, a piano played, quickly pulling her deeper and deeper into it.

Tuesday's door flew open and she bolted up in bed, her dream already becoming a distant memory. It took a moment for her eyes to adjust to the morning light before they settled on her mom's disheveled hair. She stood there in her silky PJs with a quivering hand on her cheek, and her eyes were rimmed with red as though she'd just been crying. Something was wrong.

"What is it?" Tuesday asked hurriedly. "Is something the matter with Dad?" She had always secretly feared that when her dad was gone, something could happen to him. Ever since a shaky flight with lights flickering on a plane's landing when she was younger, she'd harbored a fear of flying.

"No, Dad's fine." Her mom shook her head. "It's—it's Francis."

Tuesday tore the blankets from her legs and jumped up, her body trembling with worry "What about Francis? Is she here?"

"Tuesday, I'm so sorry." Tears slipped from her mother's eyes and ran down her cheeks.

"What?" Tuesday's heart beat rapidly, too rapidly, in her chest. "Where is she?"

"Her parents got a call this morning. They thought she'd been over here." Tuesday's mom closed her eyes. "She was found dead in the woods."

Tuesday sat in front of her bedroom mirror as though it was her greatest performance to put on. It was, because she had to hold herself together. She was so incredibly close to completely shattering. Tonight was Francis's viewing, the last time she'd see her friend before the funeral. Everyone would be wearing black—she'd be wearing black. But tonight, for Francis, she'd dress the way her friend would've wanted her to.

Hot tears slid down her face, but Tuesday had to stop, not break, for the makeup to go on, for it to stay on. It still didn't feel real. None of it did.

Francis had gone for her morning jog in the woods before going to meet up with Tuesday. Apparently, she had a heart abnormality—hypertrophic cardiomyopathy—that no one knew about. Not until it was too late, not until she was already dead and had been alone in the woods for hours before a stranger discovered her. All day, she had to have lay there... cold. It was bullshit. Life was bullshit.

She applied the thick white makeup, the eyeliner, the

lipstick. Then she studied herself in the mirror, wondering if she could really see her friend like this.

A tap-tap sounded at the door. "Are you ready?"

"Yes, Mom." Tuesday stood from her chair and brushed her hands down her skirt.

The door squeaked open, and Tuesday's mom leaned against the frame, her hand covering her mouth.

"Is it too much?" Tuesday cringed. "I know it is, but it's for Francis."

"I think Francis would find it perfect."

The wake had already been going on for several hours, and when she entered the funeral parlor with her mom and three brothers, people inside stared at her oddly. As though they'd never seen a mime before. She knew they didn't understand why she was dressed like this, and she didn't care —it was for Francis.

Tuesday searched for Beck, but he wasn't there. She wasn't sure if he'd already come by earlier, but it would've been comforting to see his face. Francis's mom, dad, brother, and sister were huddled in a corner talking to an elderly man with balding gray hair.

"Can I have a moment alone with Francis first, Mom?" Tuesday asked, knowing that Francis would be in the next room, exposed, in a coffin for all to see. She wanted to have a few words with her without anyone else hearing.

"If you need us, we're here." Her mom wrapped Tuesday in a hug before stepping across the hall to go talk to Francis's parents.

Tuesday inhaled and held her breath as she entered the

green-carpeted room filled with too many floral arrangements. She knew Francis didn't like flowers.

Blue paint coated the walls along with a thin strip of wallpaper with gold crosses near the ceiling. In the center of the room lay an open ivory coffin—Francis.

Tuesday didn't walk to her, she ran, gripping the edges of the coffin. There rested her best friend. Dark hair cascading down her shoulders, eyes closed. She looked small, she looked young, she looked... dead.

"I'm so sorry, Francis." Tuesday choked back a sob. "I'm sorry I wasn't there."

Francis didn't answer. There was pink eyeshadow painted on her eyelids, and Tuesday wanted to wipe it away. She should be wearing her thick black eyeliner.

"I have something for you to take with you so you don't get bored, in case there isn't enough entertainment where you are." She unbuckled her satchel and pulled out the Marcel Marceau DVD case.

She touched Francis's cold hand and tucked the DVD inside.

"I'll miss you more than you'll ever know, my pantomime friend." She couldn't stop the tears from falling.

THREE

Tuesday spent the next month in a fog of grief, unable to do the things she'd once loved. It had been a repetitive cycle of Tuesday going to school, talking to no one, and then coming home. There was one person she still talked to—Beck—but it was online, between the quiet. Maybe because it was easier that way.

Every Saturday night, Beck would climb up her tree and knock on her window. She didn't go to see who it was, even though she knew it was him. Tuesday knew he felt sorry for her, and that was exactly what she didn't want. She hadn't gone to the subway to do any of her performances since that last day when Francis was supposed to show up. That was the day Tuesday had been at Beck's instead of being home, when Francis had needed her best friend to find her.

Christmas would be here soon, and this year it wouldn't be a real one at all. She and Francis would always exchange presents the Saturday before the holiday, but not this year.

After Tuesday stepped out of the shower and dried her hair with a towel, she got dressed and sat down in front of her computer. There was a message waiting for her from an hour ago.

BBRock4Life: Go check your window.

Tuesday pulled back the lacy curtain and didn't see anyone. But there was a folded white piece of paper tucked into the side of the window. She lifted the glass and a rush of cold breeze slapped her in the face. Hurriedly, she snatched the paper before it went tumbling to the grass.

Her heart grew anxious as her fingers fumbled while unfolding the note.

I have a show tonight at Fitz if you want to come.

She closed her eyes and folded the note. He was being nice again. Beck had never asked her to do anything before, and the one time they'd hung out was because of Francis. Beck would be okay. At the funeral, he'd looked visibly upset, but Francis had been Tuesday's best friend since kindergarten. They'd shared everything together.

At school, Beck would give her the same little nod, surrounded by the same group of girls and friends. She didn't need another friend—she wanted him to be more than that. The smartest thing she could do was just not go.

"Sorry, Beck." She placed the paper in the wastebasket beside her desk.

Jamie Lee Curtis screamed from her computer, and Tuesday whirled around, thinking he'd somehow heard her. But it wasn't Beck who'd sent the message. Tuesday blinked and her lips slowly parted when she read the screen name.

YesFrancisIsAwesome: Come on, Tuesday. Stop feeling sorry for yourself. We both know you've liked Beck forever.

Tuesday's fingers shook, her hand clasping her mouth. She took several stumbling steps away from the computer. Someone was messing with her in the worst way possible. Why? Why would someone do something so awful? Tears pricked at her eyes as Francis's death washed over her again as though it had just happened. She thought about the message again and swiped at her eyes. At that moment, her fear was drowned out by anger as she stomped back toward the computer.

TheMimingFairy85: Who is this? This isn't funny.

YesFrancisIsAwesome: Who do you think it is, Miss Day Before Wednesday?

Tuesday gasped. That was what Francis always called her. She fumbled with the mouse as she blocked the screen name and exited out of the chat window. Someone was using her dead friend's screen name, but the fact that they'd known the nickname Francis had used was creepy.

"Tuesday, can you not take a joke anymore?" a familiar voice teased from behind her.

Tuesday whirled around toward the speaker, that familiar voice, one she would recognize anywhere. Francis stood in the middle of her room in full-on mime makeup—white face paint, black diamonds colored around her hazel eyes, pink cheeks and a crimson heart drawn over her lips. She wore a black-and-red striped shirt with dark overalls and boots. A scarlet beret sat snuggly over her long dark braid.

Tuesday's hand flew up to her mouth. She could barely breathe. "How are—"

"How am I dressed like this?" Francis interrupted,

holding up her hands and smiling. "Why am I dead and dressed like a mime?"

Tuesday didn't respond. Her nostrils flared as her breaths came out ragged and tears filled her eyes.

"Because I was supposed to meet you after my run." She shrugged. "Better to put it on late than never."

"But..." Words were starting to form, but still not fully, as Francis took a step closer. The room grew chillier, and the scent of winter frost permeated the air.

"Why am I here? That's what you want to know, right? Because, I got tired of watching you screw up everything I'd put into motion."

What in the world was she talking about?

"Beck!" she continued. "You've always thought he was cute, but when he moved onto your street and he came to our school, I thought you'd get on the ball and make a move. Well, you didn't! So I had to get that ball rolling."

Tuesday's brows lowered. All she'd wanted this whole month was to have her friend back, to wrap her arms around her. "Do you think I care about a boy?" she whisper-shouted so her family wouldn't stumble into her bedroom thinking she was a looney. "Do you think I could go and hang out with a boy after my best friend died?"

Francis tapped her chin and stepped over Tuesday's backpack and two books on the carpet. "Yes, I find that hanging out with others can help the healing process."

"Anyway, he was only being nice in that note. Things are the same at school as they've always been. It isn't like he's sat down with me at lunch."

"Mmm. Have you thought that maybe he wonders the same thing, but about you?" Francis paused and bounced on the bed. "It's almost Christmas, snow is about to fall, decorations are out, so what better way to get you prepared for moving on than to be your own personal ghost like Scrooge had."

"There were three ghosts..." Tuesday rolled her eyes.

"Yeah, so about that... I'm only going to be able to combine two and show you the past and present." She smiled her crooked grin. "But by the end, I promise you, it will be like I'm Santa Claus, so maybe it will be like I'm three. Speaking of Santa Claus, thank you for the DVD you left with me. You truly did understand me."

Tuesday fell to the bed, letting her back strike the mattress as she stared up at her dusty ceiling fan. "I'm dreaming, aren't I?"

"Or maybe I'm the one dreaming?" Francis shrugged and lay down next to her, pressing a hand against Tuesday's.

Tuesday took in a sharp breath as a chill ran up her spine from the intense coldness. "I-I can feel you. You're so cold."

"Only because I'm here. In the afterlife, I'm in a freaking warm paradise unless I choose otherwise. Ready?"

"Still seems like a waste for you to come back just to try to get two people together. Couldn't you just come to visit?" Tuesday wouldn't mind seeing Francis every night, even if it was only here.

"No, only this one night." Francis stood from the bed. "Besides, can't deny the greatness that could come of you and my cousin together. You two may happen to birth the one person who can save the entire world from suffering."

"Really?" Tuesday sat up, her interest piqued.

"Hell if I know, but wouldn't that be amazing?" Francis laughed. "Now, take hold of my hand."

Tuesday hesitated for a moment before pressing her palm out, feeling the chill of Francis's hand once more. "So why can't you do the future?"

"Because it can ruin your path, and I can't see it anyway

or you know I'd tell you." Francis tightened her hold on Tuesday, colder than ice. "Anyway, this will make the story a bit more original. Close your eyes."

Tuesday did as she was told because she'd always trusted Francis. And she knew it was her—she had to believe that. A frosty wind surrounded her. Tiny icicles seemed to thrum a rhythm against her flesh as chill bumps rose. A sound like the swish of skirts enveloped her, causing her to feel dizzy.

"You can open your eyes now." Francis shook Tuesday's shoulders eagerly.

Tuesday hesitated before slowly opening her eyes. It took her a moment to adjust to the new fluorescent lighting. She peered around, taking stock of her surroundings. The two large staircases, the cafeteria with long tables and several students in chairs, the rectangular benches in the open area. They were at her school. Francis had taken her to *school*?

Tuesday's gaze swept across the benches and locked on a familiar girl with a short, angled brown bob and blue eyes. It was *Tuesday*. She sat alone with her legs crossed, back relaxed against a tall pole, wearing a tight black vest over a hot pink shirt, paired with knee-length baggy shorts and Converse. In her hands rested a book on Cirque du Soleil. She knew that book by heart from start to finish. It was strange seeing herself and her movements like this, flipping through pages. A mirror couldn't show everything.

"Can we go somewhere else?" Tuesday asked, feeling too weird monitoring herself.

"Just watch." Francis sank onto the nearest bench and patted the wooden seat.

Tuesday slumped down beside her and avoided looking at her own face. "Watch *myself*?"

Two cold hands touched Tuesday's cheeks and tilted her head in the direction of the cafeteria. Her eyes stopped on the middle table nearest the walkway. There sat Beck, wearing a three-quarter sleeve shirt and chatting with his friends. He was laughing at something one of the guys with dreadlocks had said, then his head angled in the direction of Tuesday, as if he'd known she'd been there all along. He looked at her for several seconds before turning back to his friends.

"And?" Tuesday asked, not seeing the big deal as she watched her past self look up from her book and peer over at Beck, who was back to talking to his friends.

"And!" Francis stood up and shouted. "He was looking at you, and then you were looking at him, and you both missed glancing at each other at the same time."

"But we all look at people—it's in our nature. You and I people-watch all the time!" She paused, a sinking feeling erupting in her chest. "Or did."

"Keep watching!" Francis grabbed Tuesday's head again as if she might ignore her friend's order.

Beck got up from the table and adjusted his backpack. He took something white and square from his pocket. While moving in Tuesday's direction, his fingers clutched the paper. But right as he walked past Tuesday, he slid the mystery paper back into his pocket and continued in the opposite direction.

"Did you see it?" Francis waved her hands in front of Tuesday's face.

"See what?" If this was why Francis had brought her here, Tuesday could've thought of better things to do.

"He was going to hand you a note!"

Tuesday crinkled her nose. "No, I don't think so." He hadn't even looked at her as he passed by.

"I know so, because I wrote the note!" Francis's brows flew up and she looked so excited it seemed she might burst like an overinflated balloon.

"What the hell did you do?" Tuesday grumbled.

"Follow me." Francis ticked her finger at Tuesday then plopped her elbow on Tuesday's shoulder. "Close your eyes."

As she did as Francis requested, a whoosh of cold air ruffled Tuesday's bob, making her feel almost dizzy. The scent of snow filled her nostrils as she shivered.

"Open your eyes."

Tuesday's eyelids flicked open, and it took her a second to recognize the art room. The class was filled with Greek-God-inspired ceramics on the back counter. From the ceiling hung painted flags of all the different countries of the world. Along the back wall were several prints of Picasso's famous colorful paintings.

The only other person inside the classroom was Francis, who was shaping a bowtie from clay. Her long blue-black hair cascaded all the way to her waist, and Tuesday wanted to cry right then. Because without the mime makeup, only the dark eyeliner, that was her friend, the one who was always so strong, yet possessed the most vulnerable heart, a heart only Tuesday had known about. She wore a fishnet skirt under a button-up shirt, both her signature black. Francis had always claimed she was so Goth she was dead. Now it seemed to ring true.

"If I'm fine, you can be fine, Tuesday," Francis murmured near her ear.

Tuesday nodded and held back a sob while watching the old Francis continue to shape the clay. She would always head to class to get an early start on her art. That was why Tuesday sat alone most mornings. Tuesday would drive to school with Francis and walk her to class before heading to the lobby to study her own art form.

A shuffle of feet sounded behind her, and Tuesday glanced over her shoulder to see Beck stroll in. He sat down at the table across from Francis, and she immediately looked up. Francis stood from her table and, with a bright smile, dropped down beside Beck.

"So, did you give Tuesday the note?" she asked.

"No..."

"You can play the guitar with a band on stage while girls ogle you, but you can't even do this?"

"That's not how it is, and I don't know..." He ran a hand through his bleached hair. "I don't think she's interested in me like that."

"Look, just do it so you can get her nose out of that book. She needs it."

"*What?*" Tuesday whirled around to face Francis's ghost. If her friend hadn't been dead, Tuesday would've shoved her through the wall right then.

Francis held her hands up. "All right, so sometimes love needs a little push."

"You aren't Cupid." Tuesday wanted to die, right then and there, of embarrassment. This was all a pity thing, just as she'd thought.

"No, Miss Day Before Wednesday, I'm better than that winged baby."

Tuesday couldn't help but sigh and groan and sigh again, all while wanting to sink right into the floor as a puddle of Tuesday goo.

"We may not be close, but I know you well enough." The old Francis grinned. "I've seen you watching her—you like her."

Another girl with crimped auburn hair walked into the classroom and sat across from Beck. Francis shrugged when Beck waved her away and went back to her art table.

"I didn't know you were into Goth chicks now," the girl said.

Beck looked over his shoulder at Francis and rubbed the back of his neck. "That's my *cousin*."

"He didn't like me, Francis!" Tuesday exclaimed. "At least not in that way!" Beck was a good guy, but he could have anyone—and she was only Tuesday, one of the worst days of the week.

"I know how it looks, but just trust me on this." Francis pressed her frigid hand against Tuesday's wrist. "Now, close your eyes again." Tuesday followed the familiar instruction.

The chilly wind kicked up, wintry bliss caressed her nostrils, then stopped as soon as it had started. Tuesday opened her eyes, finding herself and Francis no longer in the school, but outside. The back of the school building was covered in red and brown brick—several places had lovers' names written in Sharpie. Two dumpsters and a recycling bin sat in the narrow road across from the school in front of a matching brick wall. An alive Francis stood alone, sifting through her backpack.

A moment later, Beck slipped out the back door. It shut with a loud clang.

"You wanted me to meet you out here..." he started. "I don't smoke and I'm not going to make out with you. So..."

"Since you're too chicken shit with this note situation, I have a better idea," Francis said. "First, here's Tuesday's screen name. She needs you to message her."

"Geez. Come on!" Tuesday moaned.

"What does she want to ask me?" He looked as though he knew Francis was fibbing.

"You'll have to message her to find out." Francis's spine straightened, her expression growing serious. "Now this is the important part, and I swear, if you don't show up, I'll leave you alone. Tuesday and I perform every weekend at the subway, and I know you go that way sometimes for your band. Look for a mime in a skirt, and if you like her, drop two quarters into her hat. She'll know what it means because I'm going to tell her when I meet up with her."

"And what if I don't drop them in, or what if I don't go?"

"Then I won't bug you about it anymore, and I'll know I've been wrong this whole time."

"If you weren't my cousin, I swear to God I'd be pissed right now." Beck stuffed the note with Tuesday's screen name into his pocket.

Francis cocked her head and batted her lashes. "Have you thought about the winter dance at least?"

"I've had two other girls ask me about it." Tuesday's heart dropped at his words. And then she was curious as to which girls he was talking about. Was one of them the girl from art class?

"Nooooooooooo." Francis closed her eyes and shook her fist at him.

"I didn't say yes."

"Because there's someone else..." She waggled her eyebrows at him. "Hint. Hint."

Tuesday did it then. She smacked Ghost Francis on the arm for blabbing in her past. Dead or not, her friend was there and appeared alive, and Tuesday couldn't hold back. Francis only grinned at Tuesday.

"You're my cousin..." Beck wrinkled his nose.

"Don't be gross."

"I swear, she doesn't like me."

Francis shrugged. "Everyone likes you."

"But she doesn't."

"How do you know?"

"You would tell me if she did." He pressed his back against the wall and looked over his shoulder at the door. "She's your best friend."

"Life is a labyrinth, and some things we must do on our own. Go listen to some Prince. You both have the guitar in common, and his words will help you with life."

"Seriously?" Tuesday said at the same time Beck did.

"Well, it's true." Ghost Francis arched a dark eyebrow at Tuesday.

"What did you do with the letter, anyway?" Francis asked Beck.

He pulled it out from his pocket but didn't unfold it. "I still have it."

"Just hold onto it, and if you toss her the coins, then give the note to her on Monday at school." She grabbed his arm. "You usually don't have a problem talking to anyone, so quit being stupid." With her eyes narrowed, Francis pushed off from the wall. "Now remember. Look for a mime in a skirt."

"I know... I'll be seeing you there."

Tuesday blinked, remembering that day, the one that felt like it had been longer than only a month ago. He'd dropped in two quarters that day. She hadn't thought anything about it because Francis wasn't there. Francis hadn't told her what it would mean.

"He dropped in the two quarters..." she whispered.

"Of course he did. Now you're pulling the pieces together." Ghost Francis slung her cold arm around Tuesday's shoulders. "How could anyone not like you? You are your own worst enemy, my dear."

"No one's ever seemed interested before."

"The school is full of idiots. You're beautiful. It's just that you have this face you walk around with where you look mad all the time. But I've always loved your natural expression."

"I don't know whether to take that as a compliment or not..." She tried to smile.

"Now that is unnatural." Francis laughed. "How about we go check out the present?"

"All right."

"You know what to do. Close your eyes." Francis's icy hand clasped Tuesday's.

Tuesday couldn't help but wish she could read what was going on in Beck's head that day behind the school, but she didn't think Francis was that magical. Plus, thoughts were private anyway—she wouldn't want someone inside her brain, picking apart memories. And was it awful to feel hope for a relationship with Beck when her best friend was still dead? But even with Francis being a ghost, with her back by her side, her friend felt more real than anything. Tuesday had missed her so much, more than life itself.

The cool, biting breeze swayed around her, as though seeping all the way to her bones. The wintry smell vanished, and the wind came to a halt, her hair collapsing against her cheeks. Tuesday opened her eyes. It wasn't a place she'd expected—though she actually didn't know where she expected to wind up this time. But she stood with Francis in a spacious room filled with a couple hundred people. It reeked of cigarettes and stale beer and body odor. A band played on the Christmas-lighted stage. She knew that band, that sound. Beck strummed on his guitar, his bleached hair falling right over his brows. Tuesday had seen his band twice with Francis, but she'd never talked to him, only waved, while Francis had told him what could be improved. *Stage presence is key,* Francis had said. *Look back at Freddie Mercury.*

Beck peered straight out at the crowd, his expression relaxed, as though he could see Tuesday. She ducked.

"Don't worry." Francis smiled widely. "He can't see you, silly."

They watched through two of the band's original rock

songs before Beck stepped up to the singer's mic. "This one's for my cousin, Francis, who constantly gave us shit for not being Freddie Mercury enough. I miss seeing you in the halls at school."

Tuesday turned to Francis, whose eyes glistened as she watched Beck start to strum Queen's "I Want To Break Free" on his guitar. If Tuesday hadn't already fallen for Beck, she would've right then.

As soon as the final note of the iconic song ended, the band went off the stage, and a few minutes later, Beck and the other three guys came out the side door. A group of four smiling girls was already waiting for them, wearing T-shirts printed with the band's name. Tuesday's heart beat double-time as she rolled her eyes to try and look as though she didn't care.

"Is this why you brought me here?" she finally said. "To show me that other girls are interested in Beck and that he's going to go home with one of them?"

"No..." Francis rubbed her jaw, her tell-tale sign of not really knowing. "I mean, I don't know. This is the present, so I don't know exactly what's going to happen."

"Then let's go somewhere else." Tuesday sighed, focusing on the next band that came on stage. A chick singer in a plaid skirt performed with her band that had a ska sort of sound with trumpets.

"Just a little longer. Please?" Francis stuck out her bottom lip. How could Tuesday say no to that?

"Fine... But I swear, if any kissing goes down, we're outta here." Tuesday knew that she was too late. A month had gone by. Beck had asked her to come tonight, and she hadn't.

"Come on then." Francis waved her on to the back patio of the second floor where Beck and the group were heading.

"You know, I don't mind going home and spending the rest of my life missing you."

"What the hell kind of life would that be?" Francis spun around, and for the first time that night, she appeared truly angry. "I told you, I'm more than fine in the afterlife, and one day we're going to see each other again. As long as you don't become an axe murderer or anything. Besides, you're going to do this for me. He's my cousin. You're my best friend. Please make me happy, get married, and have lots of babies."

"I don't want babies," Tuesday muttered as they stepped outside onto the dinky lime-green painted patio, where several people were smoking or sitting around talking over the loud music in the background.

"Get married then."

"I'm going to ignore that statement." Tuesday watched as Beck pressed his hands onto the wooden rails and studied whatever it was he was looking at below.

A girl with short spiky hair and a tank top sauntered up to Beck. "Do you want to go to the party?"

Tuesday stepped to the other side of him and placed her arms beside his.

Beck blew out a breath. "I'm actually calling it a night."

"This is good." Francis rubbed her palms together as though she was warming herself up. "Let's see what happens next."

Feeling like a stalker and slightly uncomfortable, Tuesday followed Francis and Beck out of the building and toward his car in the back parking lot. One bright light lit up the gravelly lot as Beck loaded his guitar into the trunk of his Civic. The night sky was filled with more twinkling stars than usual as she hopped into the back of his car beside Francis. After Beck started the engine, he took a CD out of his stereo and popped in a new one. It was the band she'd recommended when she'd talked to him online the week before.

TheMimingFairy85: You should check out Pure Rubbish.

BBRock4Life: Haven't heard of them.

TheMimingFairy85: And you usually have such good taste in music. :)

Tuesday rested her head on Francis's cool shoulder and closed her eyes while listening to the guitar's fast rifts, the quick drum beats, the lead singer's raspy voice.

Beck finally pulled to a stop in front of his driveway, and she opened her eyes to the porchlight illuminating his front door.

Tuesday and Francis watched as Beck grabbed his guitar before following him inside the darkened house. Francis guided Tuesday down the hallway to Beck's room. As he entered, he flipped on the light, set down his guitar case in the corner, and tossed his keys and wallet on the side table before sitting down in front of his computer screen.

Beck stretched his back and lifted his shirt over his head.

Tuesday's eyebrows shot up as she glanced toward Francis. "Maybe we shouldn't stay here."

"If the pants come off, we're leaving. I can't look at my cousin naked. But you can..."

"Shut up."

As Beck signed into his email and AIM, the pants stayed on, and Tuesday may have been a little disappointed about that. As she leaned over his bare shoulder, she couldn't help but notice the curve of his jaw, the tiny mole beside his left eye, his plump bottom lip. She'd never looked at anyone this closely before. Her gaze flicked away from him to the list of people online—she noticed she was still signed into Messenger.

Beck clicked her screen name and started typing into the box. She leaned closer, feeling his warmth; she wondered if he could feel hers.

Do you want to come over? He erased it. *I wish you'd come tonight.* He erased it. *How have you been?* He erased it. *Do you want to go to the winter dance next Saturday?* He erased it. "I'm an idiot." Exiting out of the window, he stepped away from the computer.

Tuesday whirled around to face Francis. "He was going to ask me to the dance?"

Francis only smirked.

Beck stood from his desk and looked out the window, across the street, toward her bedroom. He then collapsed on his bed and reached into his drawer at the side table before pulling out a small folded paper.

It was the same paper he'd been carrying around with him! The one from Francis.

He unfolded the note. *Do you want to go to the winter dance with me?*

Tuesday's eyes widened. "You're smirking because you knew about the dance! You were going to have him ask me that?"

Francis sat beside her cousin on the bed and wrapped her arm around his shoulders. Beck shivered, but didn't look around, as though it was just his room making him cold. "He needed the nudge since he was just too chicken shit to ask. Still is, apparently. But see, he does like you."

As Beck reached for the button of his jeans, and Tuesday was about to see what kind of underwear he wore, Francis grabbed her wrist. She shut Tuesday's eyes with her fingers and the brisk wind tickled her skin as its coldness surrounded her.

The soft swishing sounds came to an end, and Tuesday opened her eyes. They were back where they'd started: in her mostly-clean room.

"Sorry," Francis started, "the higher power wouldn't want you spying on people naked who didn't know you were watching. Although, I don't think Beck would've minded you watching him."

Tuesday could feel her cheeks growing hot.

"As I said before," Francis continued, "I can't show you the future because I'm not that powerful, but I think my business is now officially done."

"Wait!" Tuesday screamed, reaching out to clasp her friend's arm. "Don't leave."

Francis sighed and placed her hands on Tuesday's shoulders, meeting her gaze. "Are you really trying to make me spend all eternity in this crap hole when I can be having a blast in the afterlife? Although, I'm going to miss you for a long time until I see you again."

"How do you know I'll even end up there if you can't see the future?" Tuesday could be selfish at times, she could want things a certain way, she could be greedy.

"Because I know your heart, Tuesday. None of us are perfect, but you have a wonderful organ tucked away inside that ribcage of yours." Tuesday attempted to speak, but Francis placed a cold hand over her mouth. "The one thing I want to leave you with is that you should always have confidence. And even if things might not end up the way you want, at least try going for it."

"I..." She wanted to have confidence, she really did, but she didn't know how to make it happen.

"My question is, are you going to go for it? Or are you going to wallow around over me? You can miss me, just as I'll miss you, but we have each other's hearts wherever we are. Now, make the decision." Francis placed her palms on either side of Tuesday's head and pressed a cool kiss to her forehead. Tuesday wrapped her arms around her friend, not caring that it felt as though she was bathing in snow—she didn't want to see Francis go.

"Merry Christmas, Miss Day Before Wednesday," Francis whispered and took a step back. "This was my one last gift to you this year." Tears streamed down Tuesday's face as she watched her friend fade and fade until Francis was no longer standing in the room. She was back to being alone.

Tuesday dropped to her bed and picked up her favorite miming book, *Pantomimes 101*. Francis had given it to her for her last birthday. The spine was severely creased and a few pages were slipping out. She opened it to the first page.

Always go for what you want.
Your best friend,
Francis

The words had originally been to encourage Tuesday to start miming at the subway, but the words felt like more than that now. They were words that could be used for anything when Tuesday didn't believe in herself.

And right now, it may have been something as minuscule as a boy, but this wasn't just any ordinary boy. Tuesday rushed to her computer and wiggled the mouse, impatiently waiting for the bouncy ball screensaver to clear. Her chest tightened when she saw Beck's screen name was offline. So she wrote him a note instead.

Hey Beck,
How about meeting me tomorrow at noon at the subway? If you want to go with me to the winter dance, then drop two quarters in my hat. If not, then that's okay.
Tuesday (Hopefully your favorite day of the week)

She tiptoed down the stairs and out of the house into the freezing night. Remaining quiet, she scaled up the crooked tree and slid her note into the corner of the window. Tuesday tapped her knuckles on the glass, then hurried down the tree and rushed across the street. Unable to control herself, she glanced over her shoulder, seeing the light on in Beck's bedroom and a shadowed silhouette at the window.

As Tuesday walked back into the house, she wondered about Francis, thinking how it really had been a Christmas gift that she got to have a final goodbye that most people never got.

FOUR

Tuesday woke with a yawn and released a groan when she remembered the note she'd left for Beck. *No. No. No.* Why did she do that? Oh yes, because her friend had wanted her to be more confident. Maybe he hadn't gotten it. Maybe it had fallen from the window. Maybe he didn't read it. Maybe he *did* read it...

Tossing back the blankets, Tuesday opened her closet and stared at her mime outfit hanging in the back. Did she really want to do this? Yes. Even if Beck didn't show up, she wanted to do it for herself, for Francis. It would be her first time miming at all since her best friend's death, and she couldn't help but be nervous about it.

She took the clothes from the hanger and slid on her shirt, her skirt, her suspenders, her pantyhose, and her hat. Taking a seat at her vanity, Tuesday painted on her face, starting with the thick white clown makeup. Her hands shook as she drew on the black liner, and it came out crooked. She wiped it off before sketching on the black again, this time smoothly. Then came the diamonds, the pink circles on her cheeks, and the red lipstick. The costume makeup from the small party store a few blocks over always held on the longest.

After finishing getting ready, Tuesday headed outside. It already felt like winter with frost covering the ground and a nipping wind. She tugged her coat tight as she got into her Focus and drove toward the subway.

The thirty-minute drive was without the usual traffic. Tuesday parked her car near a curb and made her way down the uneven sidewalk and up the graffitied steps. Her palms were sweating beneath the gloves, but she didn't hesitate. In the distance, the melodic beats of a saxophone danced invisibly in the air, and the quick steps of people pounded by as they headed to their destinations.

To her right, silver and gold ball ornaments covered every single branch of a tree, and two women in green and red elf leotards stretched their arms and legs in willowy movements beneath it. Three young kids in puffy coats stood watching their gentle swaying.

Tuesday smiled as she moved past the ticket booth to her spot on the corner. She halted. In her place sat another mime in black slacks, a gray button-up sweater, and full face paint, along with a top hat on the ground in front of him. This was her territory, and she didn't care if she'd been gone for a month—it was hers and Francis's. Tightening her fists, she inched closer until she caught sight of the mime's profile, his strong jaw. A boy she recognized: Beck.

Her heart thump-thumped as his gaze caught hers. She gave him a bow, unable to hide the giddiness stirring inside her. Him being there, dressed like this as if he'd done it just for her, which she knew he had.

Neither spoke—they let the quietness between them do all the talking as they remained in character. He started stacking pretend glasses, just like in the book she'd left with him to study. Her heart seemed as though it would burst when he waved her to join him. Tuesday pretended to stroll and leap across a tight rope as passers strolled by. They worked together as she blew imaginary balloons and he tied their ends, pretending he was being lifted away. Beck was good for his first time as he produced a deck of cards, maybe even better than good because he could walk against the wind practically as good as Marcel Marceau. Tuesday had always been great with Francis, but something about performing with Beck felt different, like they understood each other's movements, as though everything was all entwined on a molecular level.

As their chests heaved up and down after hours had passed, Beck's dark brown eyes locked on hers. The cool breeze blew his bangs against his forehead while his empty hand dipped into the pocket of his trousers. He fished two coins from inside, causing her breath to catch. Cocking his head, he smiled as the quarters released from his palm into her bowler hat. Her heart hammered against her rib cage, almost cracking it in half. He still wanted to go with her to the winter dance.

Around the two of them, as though they were the only ones standing outside the subway, specks of white started to fall. Snow. The first fall of snow had begun. Tuesday opened her mouth and let a flake hit her tongue. When she tilted her head back down, Beck was looking at her with his mouth curved into a smile. He strode toward her, letting his gloves fall to the icy pavement as he closed the gap between them, his eyes never leaving hers. Tuesday held her breath as he brought his calloused fingers to her cold cheeks, his skin like fire, his touch warming her from head to toe. And then his lips were on hers. Standing on tiptoes, she wrapped her arms around his neck and kissed him back.

She liked the way his lips felt, as though they were shaped for hers.

"I should've done that a long time ago," he murmured as he pressed his forehead to hers.

"I'm sorry. That's partially my fault." She should've stepped out of her comfort zone earlier.

"I understand, Tuesday. I would've waited however long you needed."

"I wish I'd known, wish I knew what the quarters had meant." Francis had done all this for her, even left the after-life for a bit to see her best friend happy.

"Francis knew." Beck wiped a tear from her cheek, smudging her makeup.

"She knew about me liking you too."

He lowered his head and kissed her one more time. "By the way, Tuesday is my favorite day of the week."

Five

Present Day

"Maybe I *am* in charge of the future since things turned out just as I said they would." Francis blew against her black nails.

She stared out at the cloud-covered ballroom, glistening with sparkly snow.

Marcel shrugged and ran a hand along his felt top hat with a red flower attached.

"Marriage, yep. Babies, yep. Mime-inspired family touring the world, yep."

He withdrew a white handkerchief from his silky shirt pocket and waved it in front of her face.

"Just wait until you get to meet Tuesday yourself. She'll flip her lid."

Reclining backward, Marcel pressed his hand to his bright white forehead as though swooning.

"Now, time for you to finally teach me how to walk against the wind, because I still can't do it!"

Marcel hopped in the air and waved Francis to follow, to

the main court, through the clouds and snow. She promised herself that she would learn this before she met with Tuesday again one day. For now, Francis would continue to hold on to the time she and Tuesday did have together while dancing not only against the wind, but also the snow.

Between the Quiet

By Candace Robinson

Candace Robinson spends her days consumed by words and hoping to one day find her own DeLorean time machine. Her life consists of avoiding migraines, admiring Bonsai trees, watching classic movies, and living with her husband and daughter in Texas—where it can be forty degrees one day and eighty the next.

Cursed Hearts Duology

Lyrics & Curses

Music & Mirrors (coming soon)

Faeries of Oz

Lion

Tin

Crow (coming soon)

Ozma (coming soon)

Glass Vault Duology

Quinsey Wolfe's Glass Vault

The Bride of Glass

Laith Trilogy

Clouded by Envy

Veiled by Desire

Shadowed by Despair

Short Stories

Dearest Clementine

Dearest Dorin

Lullaby of Flames

A Layer Hidden

Bacon Pie

Avocado Bliss

Hearts Are Like Balloons

authorcandacerobinson.wordpress.com

instagram.com/literarydust

facebook.com/literarydust

twitter.com/literarydust

The Spirit of You

Elle Beaumont

ONE

Dustin's fingers slid up the guitar's strings, eliciting a shriek from the amplifier. He grinned wildly at Koryn, who scrunched up her nose in response. He was trying to make her laugh, to break through the jitters coursing through her. Her voice shook as she sang her heart out into the microphone, eyes closed, hands clenched together. The haunting melody spilled from her lungs, even as Dustin's guitar screamed in dismay.

In a few days it would be Thanksgiving, which meant there were only four weeks until their battle of the bands, where agents would be there to judge. For three years, this is what they'd been working so hard for. It was how Koryn had met Dustin, back before his pierced lip and eyebrow, long before deciding to dye his growing hair blue. Dustin, being Dustin, had posted in the school's forum requesting a talented, self-motivated singer and guitarist. Koryn hadn't taken the leap of faith. Her friend Caitlin took it for her, posting under her name and giving Dustin her number in private.

After that, Koryn had no choice but to meet him. It was awkward at first, but talking with him was easy. So was being around him.

Koryn fell in love with the gangly guitarist with a voice as smooth as silk and fingers as quick as lightning.

It was a mutual tumbling down the musical scale. At least that's what he'd said. She was weird, and he liked weird things. Koryn was his "all things strange and beautiful" kind of girl.

"Kor, stop that." Dustin crossed the distance, booping her nose. "Get out of your head and into my arms."

Every time anxiety threatened to devour her, Dustin pulled her away from the darkness. She laughed at him, swatting his hand away. He caught her, pulling her to him so his lips could place a soft kiss against the corner of her mouth.

"I didn't say 'hit me.'" He laughed, slipping the guitar strap over his head. "I said, into my arms, girl." Dustin tightened his grip on her, squeezing, then moved his hand to her sides. Before Koryn knew it, he was tickling her, assaulting her sides with quick pokes and strokes.

"Dus–ty!" she gasped, tumbling back onto her bed with him on top of her. His fingers jabbed, moved, danced all over her torso. Breathless and thrashing, Koryn's worries drifted away until Dustin was the only thing she could think of.

He must have sensed it because his tickling relented.

"There she is," he murmured, hovering over her. "My beautiful babe." Dipping his head down, he placed soft kisses along Koryn's lips, like he was savoring each one.

"Careful, dummy, I can't breathe still," Koryn panted, staring up at him through orange and red bangs.

"Now is my chance. You're defenseless!" Winking, Dustin lowered his head for another kiss.

Koryn had other ideas. She pushed against his chest, and

he willingly tumbled to the side, allowing her to climb on top of him and pin his arms down. "I don't think so!"

He smirked at her, teasing his lip ring with his teeth. "Oh, dear... What ever shall I do." His long lashes fluttered shut, fanning against his olive cheeks.

How could Koryn love someone this much? So much her heart twisted in place. She wanted to cling to him, to this very moment, and never let go.

"I love you." She looked down at him, committing every inch of his face to memory. When his eyes opened, the light hit them in such a way that it made the amber tones in the hazel-green pop.

"I love you too." Dustin's brows furrowed, his gaze flicking toward her window. "Which is why you need to get off me now. I think your mom is home."

Sure enough, the front door shut with a telltale groaning thud, and keys clattered onto the counter.

Koryn stole a kiss, letting her tongue graze Dustin's, then she leaped off the bed and fiddled with the amp.

"Koryn, that door better be open!" Mom's voice carried upstairs. "Hi Dustin! It'd be nice to see you. Why don't you come downstairs?"

It was her way of making sure they were abstaining. Truth be told, it was too late for that, and they didn't need a room for it. Just Dustin's pickup truck, some stargazing at the lighthouse, and sinfully delicious tacos. That's all it took to woo Koryn—and, of course, Dustin's crooked smile.

Koryn rolled her eyes. "Guess we're done practicing for today."

"Like we'd be practicing anyway." He waggled his brows and rolled off the bed. "You'd just take advantage of me."

She grinned. Shutting the amp off, she twisted on her

heels and walked up behind him. She spanked his butt, grabbing a handful. "I would, because this is mine."

"Oof..." His hand darted out, returning the gesture.

Heat flooded her instantly, but Koryn's mother was waiting for them, no doubt timing how long it took them to hurry down. Luckily, neither one of them appeared disheveled or had kiss-swollen lips.

"Hey, Mom. What are we having for dinner?"

"I had a great day, Koryn, how about you?"

Dustin chuckled, sitting down at the island in the kitchen. "How are you, Mrs. T?"

She hummed in response, flicking through the mail pile. "I was thinking about ordering from Wicked Soups. I could go for some of their soup and bread."

Koryn's stomach rumbled in agreement. "Um, yes. Their garlic and herb bread is the cure to any ailment. It's also the perfect day for clam chowder." It was gray out, and while it wasn't the kind of cold that sunk into her bones, it was definitely sweater weather.

"How's practice coming along for you two? You guys must be getting pretty excited." Koryn's mother looked between them, lifting her eyebrows in question. Like her daughter, her eyes were crystal blue, and her hair a glossy, dark brown—which was why Koryn dyed her hair frequently. She didn't want to look like anyone except herself.

"Good."

Dustin drummed his fingers on the countertop and shook his head. "What she means is, good, but..." He paused dramatically, propping his chin up with his fist. "Koryn doesn't want to use the song she wrote, and I think she should. Everyone does covers; few write and sing their own songs." Dustin shifted on the barstool, grimacing as Koryn huffed in exasperation.

"Hm. I see. I think it'd be unique if you went with your own. The both of you, you're a team."

Dustin glanced in Koryn's direction, lifting an eyebrow as if to say, *See? Told you so.*

"Koryn! You *should* use your song. But I know you won't listen to me." She sighed, picking up her cellphone. "I'll just be a minute, I'm going to order dinner. Are you staying, Dustin?"

"Oh yeah. I'm not missing dinner, not with Koryn in the hot seat and squirming." He waggled his eyebrows at Koryn, who promptly sighed.

"Mmkay. I'm going to order the usual then. Dad should be home by the time I get back from picking it up."

Koryn's mother ducked out of the kitchen, leaving her alone with Dustin again. She scrunched her nose and reached over, squeezing his upper thigh. "Thanks for throwing me under the bus."

He shifted at the contact, lowering his eyes to her hand, and grinned devilishly. "I didn't. I just got a second opinion, that's all. And you can keep your hand there if you please, just go a little higher."

"Dustin..." Koryn's voice lowered, but even she felt a familiar tension rippling between them. She wanted him, just as much as he wanted her, and they wouldn't even have time to fool around before her mother got home.

His phone dinged, breaking the moment.

When he pulled it out, Koryn waited for him to meet her eyes. "It's Tyler." He shook his head and quickly texted back. "His excuse for ditching practice is girlfriend troubles. I guess I should thank you for being a pretty easy girlfriend."

"Easy? I'll show you easy."

The moment dissolved as her mother walked back into

the kitchen, cutting off any other teasing touches or words that might have occurred.

"Want us to grab the food instead, Mom?"

"Actually, that would be perfect. Drive safely, okay Dustin? Seatbelts."

Dustin saluted. "You have my word. I'll strap her in myself if I have to."

It was snowing by the time they got to Wicked Soups. White flakes peppered the ground, clinging to Koryn's vibrant hair. Ocean-effect snow at its finest, but it was scenic, and it made the historic district of town look like something out of a Hallmark movie.

Dustin spun her around, dipping her before he moved in for a kiss that was fit for the silver screen.

She melted in his arms, flinging an arm back as she gazed up at him through lidded eyes. Several snowflakes settled in his thick lashes, melting quickly. "You're kinda cheesy. I love it." Koryn held her lips against his, lifting her hands to pull on the collar of his jacket.

Dustin sighed, loosening his hold on her as if he were going to let her fall. "Soup calls." At the last minute, he tightened his arms, pulling her upright.

"Dummy."

"Forever your dummy."

Koryn hoped so.

Sometimes her mother worried they were getting too serious too soon, but what could she say when she'd married her high school sweetheart?

"Typical," Koryn groused as he pulled away, leaving her cold and wanting more of the kiss.

Dustin waved his hand like a conductor, signaling an invisible orchestra that Koryn only assumed was her whining. "Soup," he repeated.

"Say it one more time."

"Soouuuppp."

She leaned down, scooped up a handful of slush, and lobbed it at him; he quickly took refuge inside the soup shop. Koryn stuck her tongue out at him, then followed him inside.

Warmth rushed at her face, while cold air tickled her neck from the door shutting. An array of scents hung in the air: garlic, fresh bread, and a handful of spices she wasn't able to name. Together, it smelled like a pot of goodness.

At the counter, Dustin grabbed the food while Koryn grabbed oyster crackers. It was a terrible habit, an addiction really, to the salty little crackers. She blamed her Nana for giving them to her as busy food, and she also blamed being a New Englander.

"You have a problem."

"There are worse things than oyster crackers. How about liver and onions? Pickled pigs' feet? Head cheese?"

Dustin's lip curled, his face contorting in disgust. "You got me there..."

"Leave me to my packets!" She curled around her hands, laughing the entire way outside.

The snow fell steadily, sticking to the slush covering the ground instead of melting on contact.

A familiar voice from across the street caught Koryn's attention. Tall, blond, built like a linebacker: it was Tyler with his girlfriend. Oh, he wasn't getting off that easily.

"Dusty, Tyler is across the street with what's her face..." Koryn shoved the crackers into the bag once it was in the truck. "Should we stir shit up with him or let them be?" She watched as they walked hand in hand, smiling at one another. It burned Koryn up inside. He hadn't shown up to practice—*again*—and she wanted to beat him for it. It wasn't as if he just skipped today. Since he'd started dating the cheerleader, it happened all the time. Koryn wondered how serious Tyler even was about the event, but Dustin didn't seem to mind.

Dustin watched the pair for a moment. Then, "Let them be. We've got hot food." His hazel eyes caught her blue gaze, and he motioned for her to hop in the truck. Once he was in and the door closed, he stared at his friend and bandmate walking away. "I know what it's like to want to have special moments with someone you love. Those moments are never enough, Kor. I think a lifetime wouldn't be enough, but I want that, and I know that. What about you?" He didn't turn the key or buckle up. Instead, Dustin turned his body and waited for an answer.

What could Koryn say to that? She felt like a heel, and more than that, felt ashamed for wanting to disrupt someone else's special moment. But it was his last few words that struck a chord deep within, tugged at her heart and soul, then made her want to sing. They'd talked about their feelings, expressed their love, made love even, but this wasn't a subject they'd ever touched base on. Marriage. Forever.

"Kor, I didn't mean to—"

"No. I'm fine. I just needed a moment. We've just never talked about stuff like that, and I'm okay with talking about it. I... I want that too. I don't know where life is going to take us or how this event will go. But I know I never want to be without you because I love you with everything." She sucked in a breath and reached forward, grasping onto his hands. "After graduation, our lives will be open, options laid at our feet, but I want you in all of my options."

Koryn glanced down at her hand, noting a ring on her thumb. It was a simple black ring which had originally belonged to Dustin, but she'd commandeered it. Plucking it off, she took up his left hand and slid the ring onto his ring finger. "This is my promise to you." When she looked up at him, she wasn't prepared to see his eyes shimmering with happiness and unshed tears.

"Till death do us part," Dustin murmured. He leaned forward and pressed his lips against hers in a tender kiss.

"And beyond."

"Suppose we should get back to the house." The truck started with a rumble.

Koryn smiled, touching her lips softly. What did this mean for them? Were they almost engaged, or pre-engaged? Was there even such a thing? Whatever it was, happiness filled every nook and cranny of her body.

Life could toss whatever it had in store at her as long as she had Dustin.

Two

On Thanksgiving morning, Koryn woke up to the sound of her phone buzzing on her nightstand. She reached for it, answering it still half-asleep.

"Mmmph? Hello?" she croaked, voice rough from a night of disuse. Koryn blinked when no answer came, then squinted at the screen, realizing it was a text.

Dustin: *Good morning, beautiful. Dinner is earlier today, since my cousins are here visiting from Puerto Rico.*

Koryn: *Oook. What time?*

Dustin: 2... *I'll come get you.*

Koryn: *K. Love you.*

Dustin: *Love you most.*

The clock on her phone said it was ten, which meant she

needed to shower and make herself look presentable. With a grunt, Koryn rolled out of bed and headed for the bathroom down the hall. She knew her parents weren't home. Her father was a medic, and usually worked holidays, and her mother was a nurse at the local hospital. Sometimes their schedules allowed for normal holidays, but not always.

Ever since Koryn and Dustin started dating, the Serranos had welcomed her over for every holiday, big and small. She didn't complain, because their food was a wonderful assortment of traditional American food and Puerto Rican food. There was always so much to choose from and so many leftovers, sometimes Koryn thought she'd have to roll home.

Truth be told, she could do away with the turkey dinner, green bean casserole, and turnips if it meant having triple the amount of arroz con gandules, jamón con piña, and mofongo, the latter of which she preferred as an alternative to bread stuffing.

Once she was out of the shower, she dressed in a pair of skinny dark-wash jeans, a flannel button up, and a jean vest. The Doc Martens would come in handy today, since snow had piled up last night. When she looked out the window, it appeared to be around four inches. Enough to build a small snowman.

Koryn hopped downstairs to grab a quick bite to eat. Knowing a big dinner awaited her, she opted for a Pop-Tart. Her phone buzzed, lighting up as another text came in.

Mom: *Happy Thanksgiving, Koryn. Bring home some leftovers! Wish the Serranos a happy day.*

Dad: *Happy Turkey Day, Punk. Please bring home all the mofongo stuffing. Pass on my best wishes. Wish we could all be together.*

She smiled at the group text and typed back to them.

Koryn: *Nope... All mine. Love you guys.*

Dad: *Love you too*

Mom: *Love you too*

As she sat down at the island in the kitchen, Koryn opened iNotes on her phone and started to type the words that had suddenly come to mind. It was something that happened frequently; lyrics popped into her head, and she had to get them down before they disappeared entirely.

Chewing on the s'mores Pop-Tart, she tapped out the words as they flowed from her mind to her fingers.

The part of you that lives in me
Chases away the monsters inside
A wind that blows away the storms
And silences the mounting tide
The Spirit of You
Yeah, that's the part I love most
A strength that can bring me through
The Spirit of You

Painted black nails paused mid-word. Koryn's eyes narrowed as a tune struck her. She immediately cast aside the notes and set to writing down chords, humming the phantom tune as it evolved in her head.

By the time the chorus chords made it into the phone, Dustin's truck had pulled down the driveway. She knew it was him by the telltale rumble of his muffler. Somehow time had sped up—it was no longer morning, but closer to one o'clock. It wasn't the first time she'd been so absorbed in writing, nor would it be the last.

Quickly, she locked her phone, wanting to keep this song a surprise until she finished it. The song was for him, after all.

"Well, aren't you a sight for sore eyes?" Dustin strolled into the kitchen, blue hair styled so that it swept over to one side, revealing the shaved portion of his head. He wore dark jeans and a blue flannel button up.

They matched, and it wasn't even planned. *How disgustingly cute*, Koryn mused.

"Likewise!" She grinned, hopping off the stool to greet him.

"The lady's chariot awaits!" Dustin bowed, clicking his boots together.

Koryn laughed. "What a glorious chariot it is!" She grabbed her house key and phone, then headed out the door. Her mouth already watered in anticipation of the feast she was about to pig out on.

Little Mills, Massachusetts was known for cranberry bogs, and the town consisted of mostly that and livestock. It was a small farm town with a claim to fame for hosting cranberry festivals and renaissance faires.

The back roads, during a snowstorm or after one, were always fun. Koryn wasn't worried—Dustin was a good driver, unlike her. She'd flunked the road test twice already, largely because of her anxiety about being behind the wheel. Thankfully, Dustin didn't judge her for that.

By the time they arrived at the Serranos' house, the driveway was packed with cars. The aroma of dinner snaked from the house and directly toward the truck. Koryn's mouth watered as she slid from the truck.

Inside the house, a perfect blend of families mingled. Dustin's cousin Thomas leaned in the corner, waving. His mother was Mr. Serrano's sister, and she looked like a female version of him with wild black curls and deep brown eyes. Thomas's father, on the other hand, was blond, tall, and had green eyes. If someone told Koryn he was related to Fabio, she might have believed it.

Thomas's little sister sat in the corner, coloring in a Lisa Frank book. Koryn wanted to join her.

The perfect blend of cultures didn't stop there. Mrs. Serrano's sister had married a man from Germany, who often brought his own holiday food to add to the delightful feast. And Mrs. Serrano's brother sat with his long-term girlfriend on his lap—Roseline, Koryn remembered. Most of Roseline's family was from Haiti, but she had been born and raised in Massachusetts. Koryn typically begged for her wonderful food.

This, Koryn thought, *is what family is about.*

"Koryn! Happy Thanksgiving. Come, we haven't started dinner yet. Everyone came early, we were just catching up. How are your parents, by the way?" Mrs. Serrano squeezed through the throng of people, only embracing Koryn once there was enough elbow room. Then, looking at her son, she winked and pulled Koryn deeper into the house.

Carolyn Serrano was as nice as someone got. Dirty blonde wavy hair, sun-kissed cheeks, and hazel eyes, she looked as though she belonged on a beach somewhere. But then again, so did Mr. Daniel Serrano.

Typically, his hair was slicked back for work, but today, Mr. Serrano's tight curls were allowed their freedom. Expressive, dark brown eyes smiled as much as his lips did, and his complexion, which was darker than Dustin's, was flawless.

"Feliz día del pavo, Koryn! We already made to-go bags

for your parents. They'll have a feast of their own when they get home. Extra mofongo for your dad."

Dinner was loud but enjoyable. Everyone talked over each other, but they did it in excitement. Some talk went over Koryn's head, since Spanish had never been her strong point, even though she had been taking classes and learning from Dustin.

She absorbed the energy of the family, the togetherness, the abundant love they had for one another. Maybe someday she could have this with her family too.

"Now that everyone is spread out a little more..." Thomas moved in for a hug, wrapping his arms around Koryn. He laid a loud kiss against the top of her head and chuckled. When he was done squishing Koryn, he moved in to hug Dustin, pounding his back as he did. "Hey, brother."

Dustin grinned. "Hey yourself. Happy Turkey Day."

"Likewise." Thomas jerked his head to the stairwell. "You guys better run before Abuela Lucia hunts you down and questions you about marrying Koryn again."

Cringing, Dustin swept his gaze around the room, then took Thomas's cue to haul Koryn upstairs to his room. He shut the door, sighing softly.

"I thought you might need a break."

Koryn glanced at the door, then laughed. "I don't mind it. Your family is beautiful. Okay, minus your abuela questioning our non-existent wedding plans."

He chuckled. "Loud, but beautiful, yeah." He rubbed the back of his neck. "She wants all her grandchildren to be happy, but happy doesn't mean getting married." Dustin plucked a flyer off his bureau and shook his head, changing the subject. "I can't believe we're doing this. If we win—"

Taking the hint at the change of topic, Koryn smiled. "Our lives will change for the better," she assured him, leaning against his shoulder once he sat down. Less than a month from now, they'd be performing in front of agents, and hopefully they'd win the chance to impress Subliminal Records. The actual prize was the chance to write half a record of songs, then perform them in front of prospective managers. If they loved it, they'd garner a deal. It would be beyond a dream come true for the both of them.

Dustin poked Koryn in the side. "Hey."

Koryn's lip curled. Her full belly protested. "Do it again and I'll puke all over you, your bed, and the floor."

"You looked like you were getting lost again."

He had a knack for noticing that. He also always knew how to pull her out of the chaos inside her mind. "I was."

"I'll always find you." Dustin's fingers brushed orange and red strands of hair from Koryn's face. His lips pressed a tender kiss to her brow, then he laid back on his mattress, taking her with him.

He would; Koryn knew that. She sighed heavily, willing herself to calm down as she thought of the upcoming performance. Her skin prickled with anxiety, but Dustin nosed her neck, kissing it softly. The simple gesture was enough to tug her back to the now, with him, in his room.

"Would it make you feel better if we practiced? Tyler is available tomorrow. He said he'd be coming over to binge on leftovers and play. Or I can hook up now, and you can go over the lyrics of your song."

"I don't want to sing that one, Dust. I mean, what if they hate it? It's new, and no one knows it."

"Yeah, but everyone sings a cover. Very few play their own music. You wrote the lyrics *and* music. That's pretty amazing, Kor."

She shrugged. "I guess." Koryn's hands ran over her face, willing the tension to fade away. "Buuuut..."

Dustin eased her hands away, smiling. "Promise me you'll think about it?"

"You're kidding, right? You know all I do is think, right?" She scoffed, nudging his shoulder with hers.

"Not like that. Not worrying. But consider it, okay? You're more than a singer, you're a talented writer and musician too. You should show them that." Dustin rolled off the bed, crossing the room to his amp and guitar.

While Koryn knew it, she didn't believe it. But maybe with Dustin she could. Maybe it was time to believe in herself. "I'll think about it."

"You're braver than you know."

Koryn only hoped he was right.

At eight o'clock, Koryn's parents texted, begging her to come home with the food. She laughed, taking it as her cue to pack up and head out.

"It was great seeing you, Koryn. Let your parents know I wish them a Happy Turkey Day." Mr. Serrano smiled, handing one full bag to Dustin and the other to Koryn.

"Gracias!" Koryn grinned, showing off the *one* phrase she couldn't botch.

It took almost forty minutes to make her way through the family, wishing them well and a Happy Thanksgiving.

The ride home was a silent one, mostly because Koryn's mind was blaring every single anxiety at her. Doubt screamed while her heart wailed. It was hard to listen to both at once, let alone focus on an actual conversation.

When Dustin pulled into the driveway, it took a moment for her to realize they'd arrived.

"Earth to Koryn..." Dustin teased.

Koryn blinked, unbuckling herself automatically. "Sorry. You know me."

"I do. Which is why I never want you to apologize for being yourself." He jerked his head toward the front porch. "I'll walk you to the door, but I have to go back." He walked with her up to the house, carrying the extra bag and placing it down by the door.

"Give me a kiss that'll last the night." Koryn waggled her eyebrows.

Dustin eyed the door skeptically, but when no one opened it, he leaned in, pressing his lips to hers softly. His arm slid around her waist, tugging Koryn against his chest. Tentatively, his tongue flicked along her lips—then he pulled away. "I'll leave you wanting more for tomorrow." He winked.

Breathless and flushed, Koryn rolled her eyes. "Tease."

"Always. I'll pick you up tomorrow."

"Dustin, I love you."

"I love you too."

THREE

The next morning, Koryn's phone rang, startling her awake. There was no gentle buzzing to annoy her into wakefulness, just the obnoxious trilling of the ringer. She missed it, but as she picked it up, it rang again.

She grunted. "Hello?

A woman's voice rushed forward. "Koryn! Oh God, Koryn... Dustin—it's Dustin!" It was Mrs. Serrano. Panic shot through Koryn immediately.

She bolted upright. "What?"

"Dustin. We don't know... He didn't wake up. I'm so sorry." Carolyn's voice broke. "He's dead." Sobs filled the other end of the line, and in that moment, Koryn's heart shattered for Carolyn and for herself.

Everything that was supposed to be... Everything that could have been... all shattered into oblivion.

"No!" Koryn wailed. "Dustin... Oh God, no."

"I have to let you go... I'll be in touch, okay? I'll let you... I can't believe this."

The phone went dead, leaving Koryn to her personal hell. She shook violently, tears streaming down her face. This surely was a nightmare that she'd wake from, and her beautiful, smiling Dustin would walk through her front door again.

Emotions bubbled up within, too much for her to handle, and she jumped out of bed, making a beeline for the bathroom. She vomited bile in between sobs.

Dustin was dead.

"Koryn?" Her mother's voice cut through her crying. "Are you okay?"

The question didn't help her calm down any because it meant she had to say it out loud. Saying it out loud made it real, made it permanent.

Her mother's arms encircled her, rocking her like she had when Koryn had been little and had a bad dream.

Unfortunately, this was reality, and she'd never have her Dustin again.

"I'm so sorry, baby girl. I'm so sorry," Koryn's mother whispered over and over, but even her voice shook with tears.

Life came to a screeching halt for Koryn. As much as she didn't want it to happen, the Serranos held a wake, which was as awful as she'd expected it to be.

Somehow, after a week of crying every day and night, Koryn still had tears to offer. She was grateful the Serranos had opted for a closed casket because she didn't think she could manage keeping it together otherwise. Not that she did anyway.

The Serrano family stood in the receiving line, trying

their best to not dissolve into tears. Koryn knew the moment she faced them, that would be it.

She was right.

When it was her turn to embrace them, offer her condolences, and wish that Dustin was still there, Koryn's body shook violently.

"I don't know what to do," she murmured. "I'm so sorry."

Mr. Serrano embraced Koryn tightly. "We know, Koryn." His voice trembled as he spoke, fighting off his emotions. "Live, because you know that's what he'd want. Live for Dustin."

How? How could she? When he would miss everything.

She nodded and made it through the rest of the line, offering her sincerest condolences. All the while, she felt like crumbling into the floor.

As if that wasn't bad enough, they then played a recording of Dustin singing, and there wasn't a dry eye in the room. His smooth voice reverberated off the walls, shattering everyone's heart all over with each note he sang. It was one of his earlier recordings, from before Dustin perfected his *sound.* This was raw and powerful; it was from his soul.

Why did you leave me? she thought miserably.

I didn't. I'm still here, Koryn could swear she heard him say, but she decided it was her mind playing tricks on her.

He was gone, and it wasn't fair.

After the wake, everyone drove to the cemetery, and it struck Koryn how final this was. Permanent. Forever.

She endured the ceremony for the sake of the Serrano family, but every moment that ticked by, she wanted to bolt. Koryn wanted to run, hide, and sleep until this nightmare ended, or at the very least until she didn't feel like this.

When the funeral finished, Koryn was hollow, devoid of

any remaining emotion. She went home and slept the day away.

An entire week passed.

When Koryn returned to school, the guidance counselor suggested therapy to help her through. It was the last thing she wanted to do, talking about the gaping hole inside of her. Talking about how the life she'd imagined with Dustin would never happen now.

She glanced down at her thumb, twisting and toying with the ring she'd given back to Dustin, only to now have it again. Koryn wished she didn't have it, because that would mean he was still alive, but the Serranos said they wanted her to have a tangible piece of him.

"Koryn, before all of this, Dustin and you had plans, didn't you?" Dr. Kelly inquired gently.

"Yeah..." Koryn fidgeted with the ring.

"Something to do with the band?"

Koryn's gaze shifted to the window behind Dr. Kelly. She shrugged, not wanting to think of the plans, not wanting to feel the anguish swelling inside. "We did, but I don't. Without him, I can't do it."

"I understand. But maybe it would be good if you continued and strove toward something positive."

"I don't want to!" Koryn snapped. "What's the point if he isn't here? It was *our* dream."

Quiet filled the room. Then Dr. Kelly spoke up. "It was a dream you shared. It was both your dream and Dustin's dream. He isn't here to experience it, and for that you have my deepest sympathies. But I think it would be a good thing for you to complete the task for yourself, and for Dustin."

Koryn's teeth gnashed together. There was nothing about doing the show alone that appealed to her. Tyler didn't even know how to handle Koryn. He'd tried to reach out, but when she'd brushed him off too many times, he stopped.

"At least consider it." Dr. Kelly closed her notebook, smiling. "Until next week, Koryn."

"I'll think about it." She stood from the chair, quickly exiting the room before she broke down.

Those were the exact words she'd said to Dustin. The memory twisted her heart, wringing out whatever emotion it had left inside.

When she slid into the passenger seat, her mother looked at her expectantly. "How'd it go?"

"Fine." Koryn bit her bottom lip, turning away so her mother wouldn't see tears shimmering in her eyes.

"Okay, baby. When you're ready to talk, I'm ready to listen."

Koryn was grateful her mother didn't prod. It still was too fresh, too unreal that this had truly happened.

Neither spoke a word on the drive home.

"I just want to sleep, Mom."

"You need to eat something."

Koryn sighed. Her stomach churned away with hunger and anxiety. Stress always made it difficult to eat, especially when coupled with emotional distress. She feared any actual food would end up in the toilet bowl.

"I'll grab a Pop-Tart." It'd be enough to hold her over.

"All right. I love you, Koryn."

"Love you too, Mom."

Koryn plodded upstairs, neglecting the Pop-Tart and opting to curl up in bed instead.

"I'm not doing the stupid show," she murmured, burying her head under her pillow. With her mind full of dismay, she fell into a deep sleep.

Until she felt lips grazing her cheek. She assumed it was her mother checking on her, but when she peeked from under her pillow, she yelped.

Dustin's hazel eyes stared back at her, his crooked grin tugging at his lips. "Hey, beautiful."

"Dustin?" she squeaked. "No... you're..."

"Dead." He crawled over her and laid against the wall, forcing Koryn to roll and look at him. "I am, and I'm sorry for leaving you. I didn't want to."

"But how... Why?" Koryn was dreaming. She had to be. One of those dream-within-a-dream things, where it felt real but was actually a trick of the mind. "This isn't real."

He booped her nose. "It is. To sound like every lame movie ever, I guess I have some unfinished business to attend to."

Koryn would bite. She'd endure this dream because it was the closest thing she'd get to having her Dustin back.

"Like what?"

Dustin was by Koryn one moment, then at her desk the next, holding the event flyer. "Could it be this?" He waved it in the air like a banner. "I think it is, anyway. I remember going to bed that night thinking of a way I could help you find your confidence." He shrugged, placing the paper down. "Other than that, I don't know." He scrubbed at his face, threading his fingers through his hair.

Koryn glanced at her phone. The time glared at her,

proclaiming it was one o'clock in the morning. A sob choked her; this was surely a dream teasing her senses.

"This isn't real. I'll wake up and you'll be gone again."

The not-real-Dustin frowned. He crossed the distance and sat beside her again. "I'm not sure how long I have here, but I promise I'm real, baby."

Koryn's hands moved to her face, hiding the fact she was crying.

"I'm sorry," he whispered, touching her hand lightly. "I didn't want to leave."

"I know, but you did, and I'm a mess. I can't do anything without you."

Dustin's fingers curled around Koryn's wrist, pulling her hand away. "That's bullshit. You can do anything you put your mind to. I've been trying to tell you that for years."

"Not without you." She fought to keep quiet, not trusting her voice to not rise into hysteria.

"Oh yes, without me. You don't need me to do anything."

Koryn didn't believe that for one minute. She needed Dustin to level her out, keep her calm, and be her confidence. Without him, she was nothing.

"Especially that show you're going to." Dustin left the bed, folding his arms across his chest. "I know I threw a wrench in the plans, but I promise you've got this. Thomas always said he'd step in for me if need be; you should take him up on that."

Thomas also played bass guitar, and anything with strings. He always mentioned if there was ever room for another, he'd be happy to join, but Koryn always skirted around answering.

"No. I'm not doing it without you! What is the point?" she snapped, then turned her back to the apparition haunting her. "You're not here, and it was our dream."

"Now it's your dream, Koryn. And you're right, I'm not here. That's why you should live it for the both of us. Just promise me you'll think about it?"

He always did that. Dustin always ensured she'd think about it, which meant she'd usually give in, because he was typically right.

"Fine. I'll think about it."

"That's all I ask."

FOUR

For the next several days, Koryn assumed it'd been a dream, just wishful thinking that she'd seen Dustin. But still, she thought of what had transpired in that dreamland, considered dream-Dustin's words about the show.

The song she'd started a few weeks ago tickled the back of her mind during class. She'd finished the music, but the lyrics still needed attention. Not that she'd felt inspired to finish them since Dustin's death. Every once in a while, the lyrics would pop into her mind, begging her to return, to complete the song.

Frustration rippled through her. Luckily, the teachers had been amazing during her struggles, and understood the situation, but life still felt like it had slid to a halt.

After the last bell rang, Koryn collected her belongings and left the room, only to run directly into Thomas. It was strange seeing him; Thomas looked so much like Dustin, except his eyes were golden and his skin creamy. He also didn't have blue hair. But the way he smiled, how the laughter touched his eyes and made her want to smile too, that was all Dustin.

"Hey... I've been texting you. Are you all right?"

Koryn paled. She didn't want this confrontation right now. "Yeah, I'm okay."

"No, I mean, really..."

"No, I'm not." Koryn tried to walk by him, but he jogged backward and barred her path.

Those damn Serrano genes. She narrowed her eyes at him, seeing the same playfulness that Mr. Serrano and Dustin had.

"I know this is going to sound weird but... I had a dream about Dustin, and I really want to help out with the event. I think you should still do it."

"A dream?" Koryn's heart pounded wildly.

"Yeah, but it felt real. In the dream, he woke me up and told me he'd haunt me for the rest of my days if I didn't help you." Thomas snorted.

Koryn moved to the side to let the other students push by her. She wanted to cry and laugh at the same time. "That's dramatic."

"And so was Dustin," they said at the same time.

"I don't know, Thomas. I don't even know how to feel or think..." Her voice trailed, and the moment she allowed herself to dwell on Dustin, her eyes filled with tears.

Thomas moved in, wrapping an arm around her shoulder to pull her in for a hug. "It's okay to feel that way. I feel the same way. He might as well have been my brother." He leaned against the wall, sighing. "But you know as well as I do—"

"Dustin would've wanted me to continue. He would have wanted me to sing my own damn song and sing my heart out."

Thomas smiled. "You know it. Come on, I'll drive you home if you'd like." His dirty blond eyebrows lifted, waiting for Koryn to answer.

"All right." As much as she didn't want to be in Thomas's company, the bus didn't appeal to her either. "Just... please don't bother me about this again?"

"You got it. Well, unless I'm visited by Dustin kicking my ass; then I won't have a choice."

Koryn tried not to think about whether it had been a dream or if it really was the spirit of Dustin trying to team up with Thomas, and she let the topic dissolve on the ride home.

That night after dinner, Koryn hid away in her room, pulling her phone out to glance over the neglected song. The lyrics held a new meaning now; they'd transformed since November into a song that felt like the truth. The spirit of Dustin that lived inside her *was* the best part of her.

Blue polish coated Koryn's nails, chipping away here and there. She closed her eyes, listening to the melody in her head, letting the lyrics flow through her.

Before she knew it, the song surged from her fingertips again, scrolling on the screen as she typed the rest.

Time froze as her emotions poured outward, misting Koryn's eyes with longing and misery. She exhaled as she finished, tossing her phone aside.

A minute later, she felt cool fingers against her cheek as Dustin appeared.

Koryn yelped and fell off the bed when he solidified. The noise prompted her father to stick his head into the room.

"You okay?" He glanced around, then down at her.

Koryn looked to her father and then to where Dustin sat. His blue hair shifted, covering one of his eyes, but the uncovered one peered up at the door.

He couldn't see him? Dustin was as solid as the wall, and moving on the bed, and her father couldn't see him?

Nothing. No reaction.

"Yeah, I'm okay. I just fell."

"Just checking. Get some rest, you look exhausted." He ducked out, leaving Koryn to stare at Dustin.

Eventually, he spoke. "You should play that song," he murmured, holding the phone in his grasp. "I didn't know you were writing this."

Koryn laid down on the carpet in her room, staring up at the slowly spinning fan. "You weren't supposed to. It was going to be a Christmas surprise. I wrote it before..." She choked, stopping herself. "It was meant for you."

"Then sing it for me, please? I want to hear it."

Koryn glanced at the door, rolled over, and stood. Her palm rested against the back of it, pushing it shut. "Since I'll never get another chance, even if you're a figment of my imagination... here we go."

She took it from the top, snapping her fingers in time with the music playing in her head, and sang her song. Koryn had wanted to sing softly, so as not to disturb her parents down the hall, but when she closed her eyes and felt the emotions flooding every piece of her, she belted it.

The spirit of Dustin surrounded her, filled her lungs with air, soothed her troubled soul and aching heart.

When the last note fell from her lips, Koryn trembled. She knew then, no matter what, she had to sing this song. As if Dustin could hear her thoughts, he nodded his head and scooted off the bed.

"Thank you." He crossed the room to embrace her. "God, I wish I was really here. I'm proud of you."

"Do you really think I should sing that song?" Koryn pulled back, searching his hazel eyes, which were full of tears.

Dustin grinned. "I know you should. I've told you all along that I thought you should sing an original song, but this one... I selfishly want to hear and see you kick ass with this song."

Without thinking, she moved around Dustin, picking up her phone to text Thomas. He'd be the stand-in, and he needed to practice the chords just as much as Tyler needed to practice the drums now.

Excitement wove with dread as she put down the phone. "But I can't..."

"Yes, you can. We'll sing it together."

Questions regarding how bubbled up within. How, when no one could hear his beautiful voice? Koryn rubbed her chest, knowing it would be inside of her. The sound of his melodies echoing in her head, his playful laughter against her neck, they would always be there in her memories.

She sighed. "You'll do this with me like you promised?"

"Cross my heart, baby."

"Okay. We can do this." Even as the words left her lips, doubt swirled in her mind. Koryn had to believe in herself, and if Dustin always had, she supposed there was no time like the present to start.

But why was she so terrified?

Five

Thomas arrived promptly at eleven o'clock in the morning. He didn't have a rumbling truck like Dustin, but a black Jeep Wrangler instead.

Koryn loaded her guitar into the back with his and plopped into the passenger seat. Anxiety snaked through her, as did doubt. *This isn't the right song. This isn't what we're meant to do*, the voice of doubt snarled at her.

"This is what you're supposed to do." Dustin's voice cut through doubt's venomous lies.

Koryn jumped, staring over her shoulder at his smiling face. Beside her, Thomas leaped too.

"What?" His eyes flicked the rearview mirror, but his furrowed brows told Koryn he saw nothing.

"I'm losing it, that's all."

"Nah, you're not." Dustin wrinkled his nose, then ran his fingers up his cousin's neck playfully, eliciting a shiver.

Koryn didn't know the terms of his ghost abilities. She didn't know why only a few people could see him, but maybe it had to do with who he *wanted* to see him. If Dustin was here for her, or to help with the event, it would explain why Thomas could suddenly see him.

Thomas's eyes flicked to the side. He yelped at the sight of a man's arm snaking forward, but when his gaze met a familiar pair in the rearview, Thomas lost his composure. "Shit. Fuck. Dustin?" His voice cracked.

"Not quite in the flesh." Dustin leaned back, sighing.

"So, you're real... I saw you for real the other night?"

Dustin dipped his head. "I don't know why, but here I am. All I know is I'm hell-bent on making sure Koryn, and you guys, pull this battle off while singing her song. Got it?"

"Uh, yeah, got it."

Koryn screwed her eyes shut. Earlier, she'd called her therapist and asked if it was normal to see and hear things. She'd been assured it was, in fact, a normal coping mechanism for immense stress as well as loss. That if, come the New Year, things weren't getting better, they'd need to have another talk.

She listened to the steady thrum of her heart, felt the cool window against her cheek, grounding herself before she had the chance to slip away into an attack.

Dustin and Thomas bickered like they used to. It seemed some things never changed, even when all that remained was the spirit of Dustin.

Koryn laughed. She opened her eyes, casting a look in Thomas's direction. He was tense, gripping the steering wheel tightly, but etched on his face was a grin.

By the time they reached Tyler's house, Koryn felt her skin buzzing with nervous energy. But instead of fading into it, she used it as fuel.

In front of the Jeep, the two-story garage towered over them. Inside, heat blasted and music played in the background. The scent of food hung heavy in the air, sending

Koryn's belly into a rumbling fest. She hadn't eaten yet, but thankfully, Tyler's mother always knew to supply enough food for an army.

"Today, we're going to try something new." Koryn glanced in Dustin's direction, wondering if he'd make himself known to Tyler. Just as she was ready to speak, Tyler swore and leaped backward.

"I'm seeing things," Tyler said, then repeated himself, threading his fingers through his hair. It took a full five minutes for him to relax enough to sit down behind his drum set.

"I wrote a song for Dustin a few weeks ago, and I want us to play it at the event. Dus... I think it would be a good move, since no one typically plays originals. It would show we're creative, flexible, and... yeah." Koryn fidgeted with her guitar strap, chewing on her bottom lip.

"Sure! I think that's a great idea. Play it for us, and I'll meet you there?" Tyler twirled his drumsticks, nodding to her.

"Y-yeah, let me give it a go." Plugging her guitar into the amp, Koryn twisted and turned the microphone on. "Okay... I can do this."

"Yes, you can." Dustin stood next to her, waiting for her cue.

Koryn's fingers strummed the opening chords to the song smoothly. Her voice flowed out, haunting and slow. Tyler picked up the beat she laid out for him, then Thomas filled in the void with his voice and bass guitar.

It was Dustin's voice that stood out the most to her, encouraging her, twining with her own as they sang his song.

Something shifted into place for Koryn. She let go of her doubts and fears, the absence of Dustin, and just focused on the music.

When the song finished, everyone stared at her, shaking their heads with wide eyes.

"Shit. There's no way we're not doing this." Thomas leaned on his guitar. "I'd haunt your ass too if you decided not to do it."

Koryn laughed. She found Dustin smiling at her from the corner of the room. Now if only they could perfect the song, then they might stand a chance.

Two weeks flew by between school, therapy, and band practice. It was hard to reconcile with Dustin being gone when he appeared every day, encouraging her, joking and teasing like he always did.

Every piece of Koryn dreaded the day when he'd truly be gone, and all she'd have was their memories.

With Christmas Eve in full swing, Boston was fully decorated. The Christmas tree had been delivered from Nova Scotia, the annual lighting ceremony had taken place, and now the city glowed warmly from the soft white lights. Each lamp post was wrapped in garland and lights, a big wreath with a bow hung from the top. It was beautiful, but tonight, Koryn didn't have time to take in the awe-inspiring beauty of Boston. Tonight she'd be in the House of Blues.

She'd seen dozens of bands play there, but not in a hundred years did she think she'd ever be the one playing.

Without the lights on, it didn't look as intimidating. Just an empty auditorium with rows of vacant seats. The floor in front of the stage stared up at her, causing butterflies to take flight in her belly. There would be hundreds of people standing, thrashing, and cheering—or booing.

She clutched the guitar case's strap the moment the notion struck her. Was it too late to back out now?

Thomas nudged her with his elbow, disrupting her intrusive thoughts. "Can you believe it? I've got goosebumps. Man, thank you for letting me step in, guys. This is surreal. No matter what happens tonight, we came this far."

Everyone turned to inspect the railing beside Tyler; or at least it *looked* like that to anyone watching them. Dustin lifted his brows, then, throwing horns, he stuck his pierced tongue out.

Koryn smiled. So many emotions clashed. Koryn was afraid that if she laughed, she'd either cry or throw up.

A month ago, Koryn had wanted nothing to do with music. Now here she was amidst the seats, shining lights, and soon-to-be crowd. If it hadn't been for Dustin coming back, where would she be? Stuck inside her head, crippled by her anxiety and self-doubt? He'd come back for her, encouraging her like he always did, and this time, she saw this would be her last gift to him.

Dustin pushed through Thomas and Tyler, then brushed a kiss against Koryn's forehead. "You've got this. Just stay out of your head, get into the music, and I'll be with you. All of you."

Thomas's jaw clenched. His eyes shimmered with the threat of tears. Not that Koryn had forgotten about how he must have felt—they all grieved for him—but sometimes she forgot Dustin was his cousin.

"Ready or not, here we go." Thomas nudged his arm into Koryn's side, opting to take the lead down the hall backstage.

Excitement galloped through Koryn's veins. Her hands shook from the combination of adrenaline and anxiety. She was cold and hot at once, felt like shivering, and altogether wanted to race out the door.

"But you're *not* going to run," Dustin broke through the silent torment.

Koryn glanced in his direction, biting her bottom lip. "Not this time."

Backstage, several other bands lined up, waiting for a sound check. The light technicians fiddled with the settings, changing the color from white to blue and red. Christmas lights hung from the balcony, blinking on and off in a soft white hue.

One by one, each band checked in and tested out their instruments and microphones.

When it came time for Koryn, she sang Audioslave's "I Am the Highway". Thomas adjusted his guitar, and Koryn did the same as she crooned into the mic. Tyler took it easy on the drums, almost too easy for his typical style. Hopefully he was saving it for show time and wasn't allowing nerves to creep in.

As the song ended, they left the stage, and Koryn took a moment to collect herself. Panic rose like a tidal wave, threatening to pull her under.

"I have to go to the bathroom. I'll be right back." She darted off the stage and headed down the hall to the restrooms. Her cheeks were flushed as she looked in the mirror. Thankfully, despite sweating, her makeup was still in place. For tonight, she'd opted to wear her hair in dual buns, but she regretted that now. She'd have to look out at the crowd and meet everyone's eyes instead of hiding behind a curtain of red and orange.

Koryn hoped the neon lights would blind her from the crowd, because there was nowhere to focus that didn't have someone in view. Even the Exit sign.

She sighed, willing herself to calm, to believe in herself and trust in her abilities.

"You can do it. I know you can," Dustin said next to her ear. His arms wrapped around her waist, tugging Koryn against his chest. To anyone looking, it must have appeared as if she'd stumbled backward, leaning awkwardly to catch herself.

She didn't care.

Koryn wished for the millionth time that he was truly there, that he could experience this with her. She bit her bottom lip to keep it from trembling.

"Take a moment, breathe, and then you're going to go out there and you're going to kick ass."

Koryn laughed, swiping at the fresh tears on her cheeks.

"For you, Dusty."

"For you too, Koryn."

One by one, the bands went on stage, performing their hearts out. Some were cringe-worthy as guitars whined, vocalists forgot their lyrics, or drummers dropped a stick. Koryn felt better about her nerves since everyone was on edge, but she prayed to God she didn't forget her lyrics. Wasn't it worse if you forgot your own song?

"Now, for our next act, Another Tempting August."

Behind the curtain, Koryn fidgeted, her eyes immediately seeking out her bandmates. Dustin wasn't there, though, which made her heart sink.

As soon as the curtains swept to the sides, the lights shifted, signaling for the music to begin. Immediately, Koryn's fingers ran along the strings in a melody that had become reflex more than anything.

Day after day, hours upon hours practicing this song.

Koryn's eyes closed as she felt the music, felt the pulse of it in her chest, and then she sang with all she had.

Dustin's smooth voice joined hers, and she knew without opening her eyes that he was beside her, singing his song.

The part of you that lives in me
Chases away the monsters inside
A wind that blows away the storms
And silences the mounting tide

The Spirit of You
Yeah, that's the part I love most
A strength that can bring me through
The Spirit of You

In my times of desperate need
You're always there, whispering in my ear
Like an angel who carries me along
I feel free whenever you're near

Koryn's guitar hummed against her body, joining the thrum of the crowd's mounting... what was that? An eruption of cheers filled the building. What she originally thought was discontent was the sound of their roar bouncing off the walls.

Tears filled her eyes. No matter what happened tonight, this was what made it all worth it.

Turning, she nodded to Thomas and Tyler. But where was Dustin? She frowned, looking around frantically.

"And there you have Another Tempting August. That

was the last of the bands, so I want you to remember all the bands you heard tonight, all the sweet jams you never knew you were missing. We're going to pull everyone up on stage in just a second so you can vote. All right?"

The crowd bellowed their praises, shaking Koryn to the core. If it wasn't for the support of the announcer, she might have collapsed to the ground.

"You okay?" the announcer mouthed to her.

She nodded, chancing a glance toward the other end of the stage. A flood of bands climbed the stairs, lifting their hands to garner more of a reaction from the crowd.

Thomas sidled up next to Koryn, and Tyler swiftly joined in the huddle. Smooshed between them, Koryn squeezed her eyes shut, sending up a silent prayer.

"Now, for the best part." The announcer paced the front of the stage, prolonging the inevitable voting portion of the evening. "Your time to decide who wins tonight's competition, and a chance at creating an album for Subliminal Records..." He started at the furthest band, then walked his way down.

Each response sounded muted, like Koryn was standing in a room across the building, not in front of hundreds of people. She found Thomas's hand, then Tyler's, squeezing them as the announcer stood before them.

"And these guys, remember them?" He lifted his hand to his ear, while the other motioned to Koryn.

The stage shifted as the thunderous applause came from the crowd. Whatever numbness still clung to her quickly faded as the cheers sliced through it all.

Tears pricked her eyes as she waited for the announcer to turn around, and when he did, he smiled at Koryn.

"Another Tempting August, you are the winner of tonight's competition. Congratulations!" The announcer rambled off a list of things, including the chance to perform for a Subliminal Records manager, but Koryn didn't hear it over the riotous sound of her heart in her ears.

"We won," she shouted, leaping at Thomas's side. Koryn bounced on the balls of her feet, batting at his shoulder in her excitement.

"We did!" Tyler hooted.

Amidst the glee, Koryn noticed Dustin's absence the most, and as she peered up at the guys, they seemed to notice too. But they only allowed themselves to be upset for a moment; soon, a trophy appeared before them, carried by one stage attendant, and then the photographer jumped in, snapping photos, leaving Koryn and the guys blinded.

The rest of the evening passed that way, until they escaped to Copley Plaza, where they'd stay for the night. Luckily, Koryn had a room to herself, so Thomas and Tyler wouldn't see her breakdown.

Koryn paced around her room. "Dustin?" No answer. "Dustin... we did it. Please come back to me." Nothing. Not even a subtle touch. The bliss she should've felt was dashed by the realization that maybe singing on stage had been the very last time she'd see him—hear him even.

SIX

Buzz. Buzz. Buzz.

It was a distant sound, a niggling, something that poked at Koryn's mind but couldn't rouse her. Not until the phone fell from the nightstand. With a groan, Koryn swiped her hand along the floor, blindly searching for the device.

She found it. Glancing down at the screen, she saw a missed call from Mrs. Serrano. Immediately, Koryn's heart froze.

"Dustin," she murmured, hoping beyond hope he'd returned.

In the corner of her eye, she saw him, but something was off. Instead of appearing solid, light passed through him. Not quite see-through, but not opaque either.

"Good morning, beautiful. Merry Christmas." He smiled, but this time it was half-watted. Crossing the room, he sat down next to her, staring at his hands. "I'm beyond proud and happy for you, Kor. You put your fears aside, and you kicked ass." Dustin looked over at her, grinning.

"I could never have done it without you."

"Oh, but you did." He leaned over, attempting to cup her cheek, but his hand passed through her.

Koryn yelped. "Dustin, what's happening to you?"

"My guess is that my time is up. Wait." He held his hand up, silencing Koryn's budding wail. "I want you to remember what you wrote for me, okay? I'll always be a part of you, Kor, but I don't want you to stop living life. I don't want you to forget to live. Promise me, okay?"

Koryn swiped at her eyes, nodding. "I promise."

"For you."

"For me, I promise."

Dustin leaned forward, placing a cold, featherlight kiss against her lips. "I love you."

"I will always love you."

"I know."

One moment he was there, the next he wasn't. The reality that she'd truly lost him set in, opening the festering wound again. Unfortunately, Mrs. Serrano would have to wait until she collected herself. It was time to go home and build a new life.

One week and two days after the competition, Koryn sat in an office with Thomas and Tyler. Their lawyer sat with a contract open in front of him. Across the table, a record company representative watched them pensively. The lawyer nodded to himself—or to the paperwork—then glanced up at Koryn.

"It's a simple contract, one that will protect you and your copyrights to the songs. I think you should sign it." The lawyer slid the paperwork over to Koryn.

The representative, Mr. Best, cleared his throat. "Remember, this doesn't mean you are signing with us. It's the opportunity to perform in front of us, without any red tape. No distractions, no sending in thumb drives hoping we listen. We *will* listen, and if we like your sample, we will meet here again and discuss more business opportunities."

Koryn swallowed roughly. She'd barely come to terms with winning the competition and what it meant for her and the guys. The loss of Dustin was still so fresh. It almost felt as though she were betraying him somehow, moving along so quickly without him. But he'd made her promise to live, and this was the only way she knew how: music.

"Okay. That sounds fair. Thank you for the opportunity, Mr. Best."

All she and the guys could do was try.

"For you, Dustin, and for me," she whispered, penning her name on the agreement.

The new year promised many things, but most importantly a new start and a chance at a dream come true. Without the spirit of Dustin aiding her, Koryn knew she wouldn't have made it this far. But she also knew she could make it from here on her own.

The Spirit of You

By Elle Beaumont

Elle was born and raised in Southeastern, Massachusetts in a little farm town by the harbor. She grew up fascinated with all things whimsical and a strong love for animals. As she grew so did her passion for reading and writing. Although she prefers devouring all genres she largely enjoys dark fantasy.

She is married to her best friend and has two lively sprites who inspire madness, love and a sense of humor in her. They also have a menagerie of animals, two dogs, three cats and a horse. In her downtime, Elle enjoys creating candles, crocheting, horseback riding and running.

The Hunter Series

Hunter's Truce

Royal's Vow

Assassin's Gambit

Queen's Edge

Baron Weaver Series

Game of Bezique

Secrets of Galathea Collection

Brotherhood

Bindings

Voice

King

Anthologies

Of the Deep: Mermaid Anthology

Blood From A Stone: Villains Anthology

Cirque de vol Mystique: A Circus Anthology

Something in the Shadows: A Halloween Anthology

Veiled Allurement

The Castle of Thorns (coming Soon)

The Dragon's Bride (coming soon)

www.ellebeaumontbooks.com

Facebook.com/ellebeaumontbooks

Instagram.com/ellebeaumontbooks

Twitter.com/ellebeaumont

facebook.com/groups/ElleBeaumontStreetTeam

bookbub.com/profile/elle-beaumont

ellebeaumontbooks.com/newsletter

wattpad.com/user/ElleBeaumont

pinterest.com/ellebeaumontbooks

I Saw Her Again

Lauren Emily Whalen

One

For Jason

I don't know why I dropped my phone through the grate.

There it is: my whole digital life, not to mention an absurd amount of money, hanging out with melted ice and cigarette butts in the alley behind the theater, five feet down. It wasn't an accident. This thing has a lavender rubber cover to prevent slippage *and* a hot pink PopSocket for maximum perfect selfie angles. We're talking effort here: peeling, unsticking and then meticulously fitting the thin piece of plutonium—or whatever—through metal slats and out of my hands forever.

My parents are going to kill me.

Tonight should have been amazing. Tomorrow kicks off holiday break, and the final semester will be cake. Before I left the house, my parents presented me with an early Christmas gift: their blessing in the form of a plane ticket to London, where lives the Royal Academy of Dramatic Arts. They've been so hardcore about me going to regular college next fall, I had to sit down from sheer shock. They also know that Christmas is a... challenging time for me, so the ticket was like a double whammy of kindness.

Once I got over that, I brought the house down with my final death scene. To play Hamlet as a female is a legacy I'm now part of, one I take very seriously. Never mind that this is high school: to paraphrase a dumb T-shirt I got years ago, "Life isn't a dress rehearsal." Sarah Bernhardt, Ruth Negga, and now I, Ronan O'Hara (such an actor name I'll never have to change it) have all taken the stage in what's considered one of the greatest roles of all time.

I'd been prepping since *Hamlet* was announced last year, beat out resident drama alpha male Chris Walker, and when I took my final bow, the lights blinded me. I felt luminescent, as if I could levitate above the boards. So much so that I could almost ignore the blurriness in my eyes when I looked over at Ophelia... and thought of who should have played that role but didn't.

Couldn't.

Maybe that's why I waited until everyone left, fellow actors drifting off one by one to the cast party at Gaby Morgan's, leaving trails of red-smudged makeup wipes in their wake. Sure, we deserve a celebration. But all I could do was sit in my chair and scroll through my phone. It was full of emails from conservatories wanting me to audition, Insta posts from every performer I try to emulate, and texts from classmates ranging from barely-masked jealousy to upfront lust, but I didn't really *see* anything.

And suddenly, I just... snapped. I hated these emails, pics, and texts. And I knew it was a slap in my parents' faces —they've worked so hard to ready me for a career with no guarantees, including buying me a phone that ensures constant communication to get me to my goals—but I was possessed. I found my way to the grate in the alley, the one I never stand on because back in '77 a junior supposedly fell through and got a concussion that prevented her from playing Juliet. Defiantly perching on top of the metal slats like an avenging angel, I fit my phone through with the precision of a brain surgeon and heard the *clunk* as it hit wet concrete.

Now I stare down until the phone lights up one more time with an innocent *where r u* from Gaby. Turning my back, I shove open the heavy door and flee to the dressing room like I'm being chased. I run my arm along my designated dressing table space and shove everything into my bag.

I gotta get out of here. Find my way to the car, then to Gaby's to drink terrible schnapps filched from her parents' liquor cabinet then collapse on the floor when the post-show crash inevitably overwhelms the tipsiness. I'll wake up tomorrow and drive home with a prepared, "I'm sorry, I'll pay for it, I'll never do it again," speech for Mom and Dad, polished as any soliloquy. They tend to go easier on me at Christmas, ever since...

Don't think.

Breathing deep and pulling on my vintage peacoat—that's really not appropriate for the deep freeze outside—I carefully walk down the stage steps and up the aisle to the heavy auditorium doors.

Locked.

Shit. I push again, hoping it's just my upper body, weary from intense stage combat, that failed me. The doors still don't give.

I cross to the other side of the auditorium and try *those* doors with all the force I have left. No luck.

Time for a self-pep talk.

Ronan, you just played Hamlet for two weekends and you kicked the most ass tonight. You're going to RADA next year. This whole time—auditions, rehearsals, that moment you blanked out while confronting Ophelia during final dress, tonight's curtain call—you only thought of her once, saw her again just for a second. You got out the door to the alley, you can do it again. Breathe: *in through the nose, out through the mouth, just like your yoga teacher mom has taught you to do since before your first* Christmas Carol *audition in kindergarten.*

Right then, all the lights go out.

Adrenaline is replaced by sheer panic. Why did no one wait for me? Chris, Gaby, that little freshman weasel who was clearly gunning for my role? Mr. Janvrin, our director and head of the drama department?

Right. I told Mr. Janvrin not to wait. Said I'd find my way out, fake-joked about needing a minute after turning in the single best performance this school has ever seen. He laughed right along with me, convinced. I don't just act on stage.

I did need a minute, but not for the reason I gave him. And that minute led to *The Dropping of the Phone*. Now I stand in the dark with no ability to contact the outside world and no way to make it to the alley to get my phone and my life back.

I am left with only myself and the infinite thoughts swirling around my head.

Focus, Ronan.

I could fumble down the long, dark, slanted aisle, but I'm almost sure something will end up twisted or broken. Old fears of the dark creep in, along with my love of horror movies. If there's one thing I know, it's that you want to have everything in working order when running from the bogeyman.

And even if I get to the stage, there are stairs to contend with, endless things to bump into.

Seat. Find a seat. And for god's sake, breathe. You might be here for a while.

In through the nose, out through the mouth. My exhalation bounces off the dark, empty walls, and I sound like the woman giving birth in that way-too-graphic movie shown in sophomore biology. One foot in front of the other. Never mind that I can't see my hand in front of my face.

There it is: I grip a reassuring handful of hard plastic and nubby velvet. The back row of the main floor. I've never been so relieved to touch something so germy during cold season.

Armrest... *here.* My hand closes around the polished wood, finding the engraved brass nameplate from some alumna or another. One tiny, tentative step forward and the soles of my Doc Martens meet the concrete under the seats. Triumph! I'm sweating as my fingers undo the buttons of my coat then unwrap my pashmina scarf. I shake out my hair from its trap inside my collar, and it's down to my waist now, so that takes a minute. Cool air meets my skin as I close my eyes and sit.

Psst.

My eyes fly open.

Psst. There it is again—the tiniest whisper of a sound, in a voice like bells, one I haven't heard in almost three years.

I jerk my head around, trying to find the source. I can make out the fronts of seats and the shimmering glass of the light booth at the very back of the auditorium now.

Psst. Now it's coming from audience right, stage left.

I open my mouth to say her name for the first time in I don't know how long. I can project like a mofo and making my voice big has never been an issue. But all that comes out is a small, terrified squeak.

The seat's velvet feels like it's poking through my jeans. I can feel a hot, itchy rash spreading over my neck and upper chest—my tell when I'm most nervous. People talk about their hearts pounding, but I can't hear mine at all.

Senses heightened to a sharp point, I listen as hard as I can. I remember the way she whispered in my ear and shove that memory down as far as it will go. Flash back to her soft lips brushing the delicate skin of my lobe, and the way they felt on mine when we first kissed behind the very stage curtain I can't see right now, and I bite my own bottom lip, hard.

"Hey, kiddo."

My shriek rings through the auditorium, pinging off the walls. He flinches.

"I'm so sorry!" I say. And then I start laughing. I don't know why, probably from the shock and relief of it all. Then my words rush out, one over the other, perfect diction be damned. "Oh my god, Mr. Janvrin, you have no idea how happy I am to see you."

Except, my drama teacher looks... *off*. His plaid button-down shirt is untucked, khakis rumpled. There's no sign of his traditional closing-night bow tie. Even the guy's perfectly gelled coif that we joke we could bounce a quarter off of backstage is mussed.

"You've noticed I'm not myself, I see," he says in the commanding baritone that's legendary throughout the drama department. "You never miss much, do you, Ronan?"

I laugh again, shaking my head. Mr. Janvrin knows me better than any teacher. I'd say he's like my dad, but I already have a dad, whom I love. No, Mr. Janvrin's more like a fun gay uncle who, for almost four years, has given me all the space I need to grow.

"I wonder if I gave you too much," he says.

"Crap!" I yelp, then clap a hand over my mouth—he hates swearing. "Did I say that out loud?"

"No. I can read your thoughts."

Please. He's a good teacher, but no one's *that* good. And why, exactly, aren't we rushing out of here? I can't see the clock on the back wall, but it's got to be late.

"Scooch over," my drama teacher says, and I oblige, moving down one seat so he can take the one closest to the aisle. His legs are a lot longer than mine. Once he's settled, Mr. Janvrin turns to me. "Wondering why you're here?"

I sigh. "I locked myself in. I have no idea how it happened. And before that I dropped my phone, uh, *by accident*" —he doesn't need to know—"so I had no way of telling anyone I was here."

He points at me the way he's done a thousand times since freshman year when he's about to say something important. "*You*, Ronan, are here." He then points at himself. "*I*, however, am not."

"But you're sitting next to me," I say slowly, just in case he swung by the cast party and got a little bombed. Not that I've ever known Mr. Janvrin to drink with his students.

My teacher shakes his head, running a hand through his hair and messing it up more. "Gonna ask you to suspend your disbelief, kiddo, for a minute." He pauses. "For a lot of minutes."

I have no idea how to respond to this. "Is this some sort of weird improv game, because we already did our final—"

"It's not," Mr. Janvrin cuts me off. "I'm a ghost."

I laugh again, this time more of a what-the-eff bark of disbelief. "Yeah, okay." I stand up. "I think it's time to call you a Lyft—"

"Sit down, Ronan." This is the don't-mess-with-me tone he uses during tech when we're all getting squirrelly and there are still a million light cues to get through. Without even thinking, I obey.

My teacher's eyes gleam behind his Buddy Holly specs. "I need you to listen."

I nod. There's nowhere else to go. And I trust Mr. Janvrin. Maybe it's weird that I'm sitting in the dark with my male drama teacher, but I'm not afraid of him. He's taught us about consent and body scans and boundaries in stage combat and kissing scenes and stuff, so we're never uncomfortable and we can take care of ourselves. I'm as tall as he is and could kick his ass anyway.

"'Ghost' is the wrong way to phrase it," he says slowly, crossing one leg over another. "That's usually reserved for people who've... *passed on*. That's not me. Mr. Janvrin, as you know him, is alive and well and streaming 30 *Rock* before he goes to sleep, while hoping the freshmen don't get too wasted."

"Wasted? Mr. Jan—" I start to protest, and he raises an eyebrow.

"I've been teaching as long as you've been alive."

Touché.

"I'm a spirit," he continues. "A facsimile of the teacher you know and trust. The one who's watched you grow up, distinguish your Shaw from your Chekhov, and turn in the performance of your life tonight. You were like no Hamlet I've ever seen, and I've seen a *lot* of Hamlets." He smiles, and I can't help but smile back.

"I've also watched you mess up. Get angry. Make mistakes, onstage and off." His smile fades. "We're human; we all do these things." He points at me again. "But you, Ronan, have to move on."

"From what?" I ask, but he holds up a hand. I roll my eyes but take the hint.

"An actor has to *live*," Mr. Janvrin says. "I've told all of you that since day one, right?"

I still have my freshman drama notebook with that creed inscribed on the very first page.

"And you can act like no one I've ever seen. But I'm not sure you've *lived*. You're stifled in the place it matters most, and sooner or later, that's going to severely hold you back as a performer and a person."

I have no idea what he's talking about.

"You will," he says. "We're going to help you."

"Who's we?" I ask, looking around the auditorium. Onstage, low lights have mysteriously turned on so I can see the fake gray bricks of the Elsinore castle backdrop that the set crew will strike tomorrow, quashing their hangovers with big cups of Dunkin' Donuts coffee while they work. Freshman year, I was required to help dismantle the spring musical, coming in after closing night, laughing and getting dust all over my sweatpants, sucking down a way-too-sweet latte with...

I shake my head. *No.*

"Yeah," Mr. Janvrin says. Before I can ask what he means, or moreover, yell at my beloved teacher to get out of my head, he starts talking again. "Tonight, you'll get three visits from those who have something to teach you." He grabs a leather jacket hanging on the back of the seat and shrugs it on. "Something you missed when they were a part of your life." He shoulders the worn-out black backpack he told us he's carried since 1997.

"And then what?" I still think this sounds nuts, but I might as well indulge him.

Mr. Janvrin smiles. "You'll know."

There's a chill in the air, a December breeze, like the door to the outside has opened, and I look away to the back of the auditorium to see if someone's here.

Mr. Janvrin is gone.

I wait for him to pop back in, throw on the lights with a "gotcha!" I'm pretty well-versed in drama department traditions by now, but maybe this is one I don't know about: surprise the senior lead on closing night. Granted, I'm not sure what I'm supposed to get out of a cryptic conversation with my teacher and director, but hey, I'll go with it. Especially if they bring cake.

"Okay, everybody," I call out. "You can come out now. Mr. Janvrin said he was a spirit and reminded me to live or whatever. I appreciate the send-off!"

Standing up, I whirl around and listen hard for laughter, for whispers, for anything.

It's quiet.

You'll get three visits from those who have something to teach you.

What if Mr. Janvrin—or whatever version of him I talked to—wasn't kidding around?

I feel the sudden urge to *move*, especially now that I can see better. Clinging to armrests for support, I maneuver down the slanted aisle to the stage—my home for the last three-and-a-half years. The fact that I just did my last winter show hits me like a ton of bricks, and any remaining sense of triumph dissipates into the ether so quickly it makes me shiver.

A huge chapter in my life just closed.

Sure, I'll take senior independent study next semester with Mr. Janvrin and direct a one-act for my final. There's also the monologue competition in February. But I don't do musicals, so the spring show has always been a nonstarter. When it comes to conquering the high school stage, tonight was pretty much it, and I'm not sure how to feel.

My heart sinks to my Docs, but at least I'm almost to the stage. I can sprawl there until morning comes. Take a nap—suddenly, I'm bone-tired.

I've just about reached the steps when I hear a mighty *thud*, the sound of a million sneakers stomping a concrete blacktop in unison.

Losing my footing, I stumble over the remaining bit of aisle, landing in a heap facedown in front of the covered orchestra pit.

"What the ffff—" I scream, lifting my head to push my now-tangled hair off my face and coming eye-to-toe with... shoes.

Cheerleading shoes. The laces are double knotted, and the thin soles ensure they won't hurt the hands of people lifting you up. Normally they'd gleam white, almost glowing in the dark, but these are speckled with... mud? Mr. Janvrin looked slightly off from his usual self too. Guess it's a spirit thing.

And above the shoes are a pair of brown and muscled legs, just as I remember them. They are the result of a thousand basket tosses and shoulder stands and whatever the hell else she does twice a day during season.

There's no need to look any further. I take a deep breath and say her name.

"Brandy."

"Stretch me out," is her response. She mounts the steps to the stage, sure-footed and sassy with a shake of her ass. The girl knows how to command a room, that's for sure. And spirit or no, those three words are more than my ex-girlfriend has spoken to me since October. I have no choice but to do what she says, the way I used to.

I never thought I'd date a cheerleader. Call me naïve—and OK, maybe a little judgmental—but until I met Brandy, I didn't realize there *were* queer cheerleaders. "Queer-leaders" is what she calls them. Brandy always made me laugh.

"Back or legs?" I ask, following her onstage.

Brandy turns to face me, dark curls bouncing. When we got together, she showed me how she curled her hair for competitions, wrapping it around the barrel of the iron, then gradually letting go. I liked helping her, turning the soft strands into something immovable and majestic.

I turn and place my back against hers, our shoulders perfectly fitting together. We're the exact same height—unusual when you're a tall girl, to find someone on your level in every way. Neither of us ever had to stand on tiptoe to kiss.

"Get your mind out of your pants," she scolds.

Great, can every *spirit read my thoughts?*

"Yes," Brandy snorts, rolling her eyes. "Less thinky, more stretchy." She always did get to the point.

I tip backward as she bends forward. "Too much?" I ask.

"Just enough," she says.

This spirit thing is odd in that I can literally *feel* the heat of my ex's body through her uniform, *hear* her breathing the deep way she does when she stretches, even *smell* her signature lavender lotion. As Brandy bends farther, my feet lift off the ground and I'm suspended, balancing on the middle of her back.

I wonder if she'll drop me. I definitely deserve it.

Instead, she gently rolls up and my soles hit the floor once again.

"Your turn," Brandy says. I bend like I used to do between cheerleading practice and homework, before we made out with her door open a crack (per her mom's rules).

"Soooo," I say, staring at my booted feet, trying not to enjoy this too much. "Did you see the show?"

She laughs, a short, brittle *ha!*

"Okay, dumb question. Here's a smarter one: why are you here?"

Now all I feel is cold air on my back. I turn around to find

Brandy, arms crossed over our school letters on her top, eyes glowing chocolate brown in the dark. Even the giant bow perched on top of her head looks extra pointy, as if it might cut me if I take another step.

I wait for the tongue-lashing, delivered in the precise, modulated yell that rivals mine. We have a lot in common. Brandy and I are singularly driven toward pursuits with very, *very* short careers. Others don't understand our intensity, but we get each other.

Instead of screaming at me, she simply says, "Hips." She plops down next to Elsinore's fake door.

Guess even spirits carry tension.

Brandy sits with her legs splayed in a V, huge eyes staring up at me expectantly. Scrambling to a position that mirrors hers—only with way worse form—I take her outstretched arms, gripping just above the elbows, and she does the same to me. Stretching someone out is almost more intimate than... the stuff you think of as intimate. There's a trust, a balance of high and low. You don't stretch with just anyone.

I pull her toward me, leaning back until her chest touches the floor and I'm staring at the ceiling. "You never answered my question," I say. "Why are you here?"

She snorts, lifting her face just enough to rest her chin on the floor. "I think you know. Pull harder."

I oblige, struggling to keep my balance as I lean even farther back. "You broke up with me over text. You didn't even yell at me." I tilt my head so I can see her. "I deserved it."

Her fingers dig into my forearms, feet flexing extra hard. "After what you pulled, I would have lost my voice. Besides, would you have listened?"

"Yes?" I volunteer. She raises an eyebrow at me, like

Really? I can barely see the rest of her body, so it's as if a disembodied head is skeptical of me. Or Yorick. Alas.

I sigh. "No. I messed up and I wasn't ready to acknowledge that."

Slowly, Brandy sits up from her pancake position, and I'm able to sit up myself. Her eyes are soft. We're still holding on to each other, and I wonder if she's going to drop my arms, scoot in, and kiss me.

Then I'm yanked forward. I have almost no flexibility, so my hamstrings are screaming. I swear I can see every granule of dust on this stage floor. If Brandy lets go, I'll smash into it face-first and break my nose.

"Relax," she says. "I'm not going to hurt you." She laughs again, but not in a funny ha-ha way. "I *am* surprised you admitted it."

"That I messed up?"

Her hands slide off my arms, but I catch myself, then roll up one vertebra at a time like I've done in every acting class I can remember. Brandy's eyes are still glowing, but this time with sadness. Regret?

"Yeah," she says. "That you, Ronan O'Hara, messed up."

I cheated on her at a party.

Last year, Brandy transferred here, asked to borrow a pen in geography, and I was a goner. Things were going great between us. We'd been together four months, which was the longest relationship I'd ever had after a string of hookups.

She taught me how to *really* kiss someone. I learned the ins and outs of cheer. Brandy developed a new appreciation for *Three Sisters* (I was cast as Irina—only lost out on Masha because it was Keri Floyd's senior year). We were the school's power couple: the queerleader and the rising star.

"I don't even know why I did it," I say, unable to look at

Brandy. And for the first time, I realize what sounds like a stupid excuse is actually true.

It says a lot—about me and the whole gross situation—that I don't even remember her name. All I remember is her adorable carrot-colored bob and freckles, the way she'd "accidentally" brushed my hand over the bowl of spiked punch. Brandy had immediately taken that hand in her own, lacing our fingers together and giving the girl her best "she's mine" look. But the minute Brandy went for a refill, I pulled the cute redhead into the nearest bedroom and we started playing a very competitive game of tonsil hockey. Neither of us were drunk. We could have been thirty seconds or thirty minutes into it when I saw Brandy's face in the frame of the door that I hadn't bothered to close behind me.

Confusion. Hurt. Her expression showed everything one would expect from a beautiful girl whose relationship was imploding in front of her. She found her own ride home.

The next morning when I stumbled out of bed, I had a text: *We're done.*

That was the last time Brandy ever spoke to me. The cheer squad was pissed, giving me epic glares in the hallway for the next month. I even heard a rumor that they made up a chant about my worst attributes, but I never heard any evidence.

Did I care? Nah. Onto the next.

It was Brandy's fault, I rationalized, for getting so involved with the theater department's most notorious player. I was bound to stray sometime, right? Only at night, when I was tossing and turning from yet another bout of insomnia, or when I was alone backstage with only dim light and my thoughts for company, did I allow myself to regret.

I look up and Brandy is staring at me. "You heard that whole inner monologue, huh?"

For a second, she lets a hint of a knowing smirk show. Then just as quickly, she's stone-faced. "Every word."

I pull my knees to my chest and take a deep breath.

"I'm sorry, Brandy," I say. "I screwed us up on purpose. We were getting too close, and I just... couldn't. And instead of talking to you like a normal human, I sabotaged us." *It's all I know how to do,* I think, and I know she's listening.

"Ro," Brandy says gently, resting her manicured hands between her still-splayed legs, spine stick-straight. "I know what happened to you. Everyone does. I never knew how to bring it up, and maybe that's on me. But then after I broke up with you, you didn't do *anything*. You didn't apologize. You didn't explain."

"You didn't want to talk to me!"

"You," Brandy says, raising her voice just enough, "didn't *try*."

She's right.

"In order to move on, you have to acknowledge where you screwed up." Brandy smiles at me sadly before jumping to her feet and brushing off her hands. "Apology accepted. Good luck, Ro."

And I swear to god, she starts *fading*. Like bad CGI except, well, not. Can this night get any weirder?

"It's about to," says another voice just behind me. I jerk around. Of course. My parade of exes wouldn't be complete without...

"Dorian," I say flatly, not making a move to get up. "The ghost of the guy I ghosted."

"Predictable, yeah?" He grins in the way that used to melt me, running a hand over the stubble on his shaved head. It's just long enough, and I know it's really soft. Not that I'm going to try to touch him. Oddly, Dorian isn't disheveled in any way. He looks just like I remember him, though I haven't seen him in a long time.

My legs still hurt from that brutal stretch, so I lie back and stare at the ceiling. I put my arms over my head, pointing and flexing my feet in their Docs. "Am I dreaming?"

"Nooooot even," Dorian drawls, lying down next to me. We're not touching, but it feels like we are. "Remember when we used to stargaze—"

"Yeah." I smile.

"—before you ripped my heart out?"

I roll over on my side to face him. "This is already getting old. Who's next, my prom date?"

"Maybe." The ring piercing his septum glints. "Depends on how quick you learn."

Maybe I can game the system. "Give me a spoiler and we'll get outta here?"

"Not a chance, O'Hara."

I shrug. "Worth a shot."

And just like with Brandy, Dorian and I are back in our old patterns. The back-and-forth dialogue sounds just like his favorite movies with Spencer Tracy and Katharine Hepburn. We spent whole Saturdays in his parents' basement watching them the spring of my sophomore year. I loved the quick intimacy that came from the sharp exchange of syllables, found myself shortening my own sentences in anticipation of his next quip. In an unparalleled move for two teens alone, we would make it through the whole movie before we started kissing.

Most of the time.

Dorian could kiss. Between him and Brandy, my skills improved a thousand percent. Everyone in my summer workshop six months ago owes him a thank-you note.

One night, when we were curled together on that ugly

brown '70s couch, he even whispered to me his deadname. Dorian was out as trans to everyone, but only his parents knew him as anything other than Dorian, for legal and medical reasons. I never told anyone. Never even uttered it aloud. I keep his confidence in my heart.

He'd been so open, so vulnerable, and it scared the shit out of me. Because next it would be my turn. Well, not if I could help it.

"Did you move because of me?" I ask Dorian.

He snorts. "Not everything's about you, ace. My dad got a new job."

Which I would have known if I hadn't blocked his texts. I even asked my parents to tell him I was sick when he stopped by one night. From my window on the second floor—lights out in my room so he couldn't see me—I watched him gaze up for the longest time before slinking off to the curb where his bike was parked and then pedaling away.

He didn't look back. He avoided me after that day and quit stage crew. Two months later, his family moved, and I never saw him again.

I know. I *know*. I was awful.

"Yeah you were," Dorian says. And now he's scooting farther away from me.

It was too soon after... I brush the thought away before the spirit of my ex-boyfriend can pick up on it.

But it's too late.

"She's coming," he whispers.

And then, just like Brandy before him, Dorian fades.

I wait in the thick silence. My eyes seem to un-adjust to the dark, and I'm staring up at pure black.

Hamlet was visited by his father. I'm visited by my exes. Now my hamstrings hurt *and* I want to watch a Katharine

Hepburn movie, both of which Hamlet never had to deal with.

I didn't even get to tell Dorian how sorry I am. And I still can't grasp why this is happening, or why I've been in this state of relationship inertia where I believe if I break enough hearts, I'll be okay.

She's coming. Dorian's words hang suspended in the air.

But I don't see how *she* will make things any better. If anything, the prospect of seeing, talking to, touching her ghost makes me want to double down on what's gotten me this far.

I'm not ready for what happens next. Shit, I can still smell Dorian's Old Spice on my sweater. Apparently, the spirit world doesn't care, because it begins anyway.

A whirlwind of smells assault me all at once: strawberry perfume, peppermint essential oil, good old-fashioned cis boy BO. Then snippets of every song I downloaded, every playlist I made for whomever I was wooing, but mostly for myself, start. A soundtrack of conquests. And then their faces. A tornado of visage and voice, whispering and shouting and purring my name. *Ronanronanronano'hara.*

My body startles as though I've just awoken from a nightmare, except I'm existing in one. I try lifting my hands to cover my ears, drown out the sound, but my hands stay rooted on the floor, as if they're bolted down. I want to squeeze my eyes shut so I can't see them: Marcel's pretty green eyes, Christina's kinky hair, Xiomara's voluptuous curves. Yet my eyes remain wide, held open by some invisible force, darting left and right and up and down and all around.

She's not here yet, but the rest of them very much are.

Brandy and Dorian, I almost let in. But they were far from the only ones I touched, kissed, flirted with.

Before, after, and during my boyfriend, then my girlfriend, I went hard at three things: school, theater, and messing around. I texted and posted and talked about it constantly. The only sports metaphor my drama-geek ass ever employed—there's no shame in playing the field—and I used that rationalization for all it was worth. And now, seeing all the cute smiles and the big eyes morph into tears and frowns, I know the way I play the field isn't right.

I never see conquests as people. Getting a message or a makeout feels the same as scoring an A on a test or landing a coveted role. And none of them, *none,* were her.

Surrounded by these spirits of my ex-flings, a cacophony of pretty faces and dulcet tones and favorite tunes, I'm still alone.

"Enough!"

And with those two syllables, everything stops. No fade to black, but a full blackout. That single angry command, the one that stopped the gruesome parade of everyone I hurt, came from me.

I can blink again. And even better, the low lights are back on. I lift my hands up and wave them in front of my face, see them clearly. I jump up and stomp downstage, the sound of my tread bouncing off the walls. No one's in the audience, but my delivery is as passionate as it's ever been.

"What do you *want*?" I scream at the empty seats. "What do you *want*? I did what I had to do, or I would have completely lost my shit!" I'm out of breath, so I take a brief moment. "Yes, I've *majorly* screwed up, but I don't see how trotting out all my mistakes is going to solve anything!"

I'm not even sure who I'm yelling at—God? The universe? The forces that took her away from me in the first place? Whomever, whatever they are, I am over it.

I may have been awful, but I don't deserve this. Not after all I went through. Not after losing her.

"And if she's coming," I shout, "where is she? *Where is she?*"

A flash of light and a deafening *BOOM* knock me on my ass. Blinded and too stunned to cry out, I rub my eyes just to make sure I'm not hallucinating.

She's here.

The one that got away is right in front of me. Silky black hair frizzes and curls around her face, like it always looked when she took down the French braids she loved so much. She would style my hair that way too. I'd close my eyes and savor the feeling of her fingers gently separating the strands. Sometimes she'd smooch the back of my neck and giggle, and I'd twist my head around so I could see her face, the way her nose scrunched up when she laughed before she admonished me to turn back, she wasn't finished yet!

That very giggle was the sound I heard earlier, right after I got locked in.

I try to say her name, but it comes out as a pathetic squeak. Gazing up at her, I swallow hard and try again.

"Sam?"

"Rony." There's that high, sweet voice. The way she says my name is the same—after our first date, later in Acting I, later still in her room after I'd kissed her silly. The diminutive only she's allowed to use.

"Sam," I say again. I'm too afraid to approach her, as if she's a bird who will fly away if I charge. I want to take her in my arms, ask a million questions, but I'm worried that the first spirit all night I'm actually excited to see will disappear with the rest.

Instead, I drink in the vision before me. Her freckles, so many I could never count them all, and I tried. I thought Brandy inspired me to grow my hair, but no, it was my Sam. Samantha, but she hates her full name.

Hated it.

She's wearing Ophelia's crown of flowers, the wreath Carl Bussel painstakingly crafted in the costume shop for weeks so they'd look real. Ophelia's torn, cream-colored, vintage lace dress from the mad scene looks like it was made specifically for Sam's body, which is very different from...

"I saw you tonight," Sam says, light in her soft dark eyes as she approaches.

Those are the first words she ever said to me.

Freshman year, I landed a tiny speaking role as the first fairy, the one who talks to Puck in *A Midsummer Night's Dream.* I don't know how it happened. Actually, yes, I do: the junior originally cast got a DWI the first night she had her license.

I couldn't feel my feet walking into my first rehearsal. The fear I didn't belong, that someone would call me out as an imposter, was powerful, spreading to my toes so I felt every step I took up to the stage and the judgmental faces of upper-class people. I hardly had the most lines in the play, but I was the first one off-book.

I was so obnoxious.

Sam approached me after opening night, the week before Christmas, almost exactly three years ago. She was a freshman too. Looking at Sam now, I see her face as it was back then: shy, tentative, biting her lip like she did when she was especially nervous.

She sits opposite me, criss-cross-applesauce like we're in kindergarten. "I remember when I saw you for the first time," Sam says.

"I was just thinking about that!" I squeal, then remember. "Oh, right. The mind reading. It's only happened a million times already." I always lost myself a little around Sam.

I don't even know what came over me that night after

Midsummer closing. Maybe end-of-play adrenaline. Maybe the way the audience applause increased just the slightest bit when I took my bow separately from the other fairies. Maybe it was just how mesmerized I was by her face, in a way I'd never been with anyone, any gender, anytime.

"Do you want to go to the cast party with me?" I'd blurted out. And when she smiled, I felt like I'd come home.

From then on, we were inseparable. As vomit-inducing as any first love. We held hands and giggled and stole kisses by our respective lockers. We were partners in Acting I and chose the balcony scene from *Romeo and Juliet* as our spring midterm. I was Romeo. Mr. Janvrin smirked when we told him our choice, but he let it go. The result was just goofy—two freshmen acting out what they then thought was the greatest love story of all time, while they were actually *in love*—but we got an A.

"Ugh, how annoying were we?" I say, burying my face in my hands and giggling.

When I look up, Sam's laughing too, her cheeks glowing pink. "Our final kiss!" she shrieks. "Oh god. Mr. Janvrin had to separate us!"

And I can't resist. Just like I used to, I hold out my arm so she can snuggle underneath. "C'mere."

She shakes her head. "I can't."

"Not even one last time?" I try not to let frustration creep into my voice, but I don't get it. Why can I touch everyone except the person I want to the most?

She fiddles with the lace on her dress, avoiding my eyes, and repeats, "I can't."

And that denial jerks me into a different memory. One much sadder.

Sam had the kind of depression that meant she couldn't function sometimes. Couldn't come to school, couldn't do anything but lie in bed, staring at the glow-in-the-dark stars on her ceiling that she'd arranged during a happier time. It's the kind of shit you see on TV only real, and really, really hard for me—her girlfriend—to understand.

It's not that I was unfamiliar. My dad's a psychiatrist, for god's sake, prescribing meds all the time for people managing ADHD or anxiety or whatever. And it's no big deal: you take medicine, and you feel better. Simple as that.

Only with Sam, it wasn't.

Her first depressive episode happened when she was four. Her parents understood and they cared. They took her to so many doctors, who prescribed every drug that was legal, plus exercise and meditation and every kind of therapy you can imagine. Nothing took. She may have had chronic fatigue syndrome as well, but they could never get a real diagnosis because the medical profession and invisible illnesses still aren't in sync.

I never knew when we could have fun—snuggle, kiss, watch dumb movies, just be with each other—or if I'd bound up the stairs to her room, dressed extra cute, and find her buried under the covers. Even worse was when she felt too guilty to call or text. Then *I* felt guilty for not being someone she felt comfortable coming to, then guiltier for feeling relieved, then guiltiest for making it about me. At one point, I realized that no matter how much I loved Sam, I had to choose between us.

And I chose me.

Sam didn't have mood swings. She was never mean or awful. And while she was pissed that her brain was wired this way—who wouldn't be, really?—she didn't take it out on the people who supported her. She was nothing but a loving girlfriend... when she could be.

If anything, she put me on a pedestal that my fourteen-year-old dumb-ass self found really, really precarious. It was inevitable I'd teeter too hard to one side and fall off.

I broke up with Sam just before the end-of-year showcase. What followed is what you'd expect from any barely-teenaged separation: long, sobbing phone calls on both ends, texts so numerous my parents threatened to cancel my data plan, one reconciliation that led to a re-breakup the very next day. More sobbing.

It was a very long summer and fall. I never thought the back-and-forth would end. Until one day, it did.

On the last day of school before winter break, Sam seemed... normal for the first time in forever. She was showered and dressed, wearing her favorite peachy-pink lip gloss, going to class and rehearsal. She even smiled at me in the hallway once.

Two days later on Christmas Eve, she sneaked out in the middle of the night, took her parents' car, and drove straight into a concrete wall in the middle of an intersection just outside of town.

Here's the thing: when your dad's a therapist, you are allowed to process. You are found a counselor through his many connections before your dead ex-girlfriend is lowered into the ground. You are escorted to the funeral, he and your mom on either side, just in case you need physical support as well as emotional.

You are watched, constantly, and it gets to a point where you welcome the surveillance because you're not sure what you'd do without it. Luckily, that desperation passes. But once it does, you immediately question whether you're "over it" too fast.

It's not that I blame myself. Another thing about having a therapist dad: I understood, before I was old enough to know the concept, that grief is a process. That suicide, while terrible and tragic, is something no one but the person who dies by it can fully unpack. The only part that ate at me was the timing. As a psychiatrist's kid, I knew the statistics about suicide, how many take place around the holidays, especially *the* holiday. In my darkest, most vulnerable moments, I wondered if I should have kept a better eye on her at Christmas.

Acting saved me—that's not an exaggeration. Mr. Janvrin let me borrow any play I wanted, pointed me to the classics and the new works, gave me extensive notes when I asked for them. Putting myself in others' shoes, I started to heal. I realized, through therapy and family and theater, that Sam had to have been in a terrible place to do what she did, and it wasn't my fault or anyone else's.

I know in my head and my heart that Sam's final choice was hers, and hers alone. She was too far gone to care how it would affect anyone else. She just wanted the mess in her brain to end. I was mad at her, until one day I woke up and wasn't. One day I was just... over her.

"Except you weren't, Rony," Sam whispers. "You think you got over me, but you didn't."

Oh, how dare she.

Jumping to my feet, I stomp to the other side of the stage. My cozy moment with Sam's spirit is over, and now I want to put as much distance between us as possible while still being locked in this stupid auditorium. How long have I been in here?

"I don't think you get to say that, *Samantha*," I hiss. Crossing my arms, I level her with a glare. "You did what you had to do, and so did I."

Sam uncrosses her legs and turns to face me, eyes burning. I can see the flash from across the stage. She's definitely no longer of this world. "Tell me, Ronan. What exactly did you do?" She toys with the hem of her ragged white dress. "I know about the therapy and all that. But how do you think you moved on?"

I throw up my hands. "I date! I date a *lot*. I am the freaking Casanova of the drama department, the whole damn high school, Sam."

She says nothing, just crosses her arms over her breasts. I remember exactly how her skin felt, how she exhaled a sweet little *ooo* every time we kissed, and I ball my hands into fists so I don't touch her. Or her ghost. Whatever.

"In fact, I date so much I'm missing the cast party because a ghost who looks like my drama teacher thinks I have to talk to *other* ghosts who look like my exes!"

Except they're all still alive. And Sam isn't.

I can handle the others, the spirits of those who still exist. I know where they are right now, probably. Mr. Janvrin has conked out while 30 *Rock* is still playing on his TV. Brandy is finishing her pre-bedtime push-ups, dreaming of human pyramids and shiny trophies. Dorian is in another town, watching *Woman of the Year* for the fiftieth time with a cutie by his side. The parade of hookups are doing whatever they like, whatever it is that gives them joy, that I didn't stick around long enough to find out about.

And here she is, my ex-girlfriend who's an *actual* ghost, guilt-tripping and quite possibly slut-shaming me.

"Oh my *god*." Sam rolls her eyes. "I am not *slut-shaming* you, Rony."

I laugh because it's kinda funny. She grins like she used to do, like she'd been looking for something and found it in me.

Suddenly I'm so overcome with missing Sam, having her here with me but not really, that my knees buckle and I'm falling fast...

"Hey."

I feel soft but strong arms around my waist. Her big brown eyes meet mine, looking up at me because I'm the taller one. Sam touches her forehead to mine.

"Don't leave me again." The plea escapes my mouth in a frenzied whisper, embedded with all the nights I've lain in bed, *wanting*. It didn't matter if I'd winked at, flirted with, even made out with someone earlier. They weren't Sam. She stands on her tiptoes, and I open my lips, ready for her to sweep me away.

But instead, Sam looks deep into my eyes and whispers the last five words I want to hear.

"You have to move on." She puts a hand on my cheek, and I always read about ghosts feeling cold, clammy, but she's so *warm*. The tears start to run down my face. "For real this time."

And maybe I'm picking up on the mind-reading trick, but I know exactly what she's talking about. Or more precisely, *who*.

Macy.

Macy, the nonbinary babe who moved here to start their junior year. Macy, who rocks a pink-tinged platinum blonde pixie cut like no other. (We're talking Mia Farrow levels of awesome. I told them that, and they said, "I love that you know who Mia Farrow is," as I tried to ignore the pitty-pat of my heart.) Macy, who blew everyone away at the *Hamlet* auditions so much that the role of Ophelia, which would usually go to a senior—and which absolutely would have gone to Sam—went to them.

Macy, who locked eyes with me tonight when we took our final bows. When I thought I'd see Sam, instead, all I could see was Macy.

Sam. Where is she?

I looked away for a millisecond, and she's left me too.

Alone again, I'm rooted to my spot stage left, next to the plywood castle wall that looks like it could collapse at any moment. As though it knows it's served its purpose and isn't long for this world, soon to be knocked down by a hungover-and-trying-to-hide-it sophomore, then recycled into the back-drop for *Bye Bye Birdie*.

All night, I've wanted my exes to leave me alone. Now I'm hoping for anyone or anything to distract me from the truth. I wait, watch, listen.

Nothing. Just me and the Hamlet that exists within, who I'll always carry around with me as I do with all my characters.

Hamlet puts on a play, forcing his mom and evil stepdad to confront their sinful selves, before losing his life in a fight with Ophelia's protective older brother, Laertes. Has my post-Sam existence been a play too? Was I really invested in Brandy and Dorian? Or was I putting on a show, proving to everyone, and mostly myself, that I was okay, that I would always be okay, that it didn't matter if my first love was so sad that she didn't want to live anymore?

I sink to my knees. The tears I shed for Sam have given way to full-on crying. I recall what happened hours ago, just before the lights went up.

Macy gave me flowers.

Early in the rehearsal process, Macy was having trouble with iambic pentameter. Despite their kickass audition, they'd never done full-length Shakespeare, and the language is tricky. Mr. Janvrin recruited me to tutor Macy.

No, wait. I volunteered. There was just... something about them. Their audition was captivating, their way of moving through the hallways even more so. But I was good. I didn't flirt. I kept it professional, actor to actor, at least at first.

Running lines, stumbling over syllables that soon became smooth and natural—Macy was a quick study—gave way to road tripping to the next town over because Macy loved a record shop there. We texted in the morning after we woke up and at night before we went to sleep. We grabbed lunch together in the cafeteria, ostensibly to talk character motivation, but ten seconds later, we'd be bitching about our upcoming tests and how were we ever going to get everything done and get off book in time?

I thought we were just friends.

No, Ronan. You didn't. Sam's voice is clear, as if she were still sitting beside me, flower crown perched on top of flowing curls, big brown eyes knowing. Judging.

Okay, Sam. I didn't. Are you happy now?

Tonight's flowers tipped me over the edge.

Macy tried to give me the bouquet right after I'd finished my makeup. At some point, I must have mentioned loving pink roses and white daisies. Where Macy found daisies in December, I'll never know. They smiled, round green eyes ringed with mascara and full of hope. I knew I'd gone too far with our friendship. No one other than my parents had ever given me flowers, and at *Christmas* too.

"I can't," I blurted, shaking my head. A couple of sophomores scurried out of the dressing room, undoubtedly to gossip in the hallway. The resident player was about to break another heart.

Reaching over to shut the door, I looked back at Macy, bouquet now dangling from their hand. I swear I could see the daisies wilting.

"I can't," I said again. "I just..."

"You had to know how I feel about you," they said. "I... I think we could really be something, Ronan." The way they said my name was so melodic, water bubbling over rocks. I wanted to pull them toward me and never let go.

But they just. Kept. Talking. "I know, Ronan," they said, stepping closer to me, hands full of bouquet, outstretched. "I asked around, right when we started hanging out. I know you can't... get close to anyone because of what happened with Sam—"

"Don't say her name," I commanded through clenched teeth. "You don't get to do that."

"I'm sorry," Macy said. "I'm so, so sorry for your loss, and I know you'll feel it the rest of your life." By now, I'd sunk into a chair, my legs no longer wanting to help me up. "But Ronan," they said, setting the flowers down next to my makeup kit in its worn, smeared cardboard box. "I just... I like you, okay?"

"You have to go," I said, looking up. "This, *us*, just isn't a thing. Okay?" I smiled tightly. No hard feelings, we had a show to do and we had to be onstage together. A lot. "Break a leg."

Without a word, Macy nodded and left the room. The sophomores flooded back in, chattering up a storm. I started doing my breathing exercises so they'd know nothing was wrong. Just another rejection to a wannabe lover. It's what Ronan O'Hara did best.

I didn't see Macy again until our first moment onstage. We played our parts perfectly, our chemistry even better than usual. Ophelia's mad scene was positively breathtaking. It was only during curtain call we broke character: we locked eyes, and I knew that gaze would be our last. Not long after, I dropped my phone through the grate in the alley. I didn't want to look at those old texts, full of happiness and flirting and obscure Bard quotes, ever again.

I'm on my side now, curled into a ball on the cold stage floor, tears drying, making my face itch.

I know why I'm here.

To say that truth hurts is an understatement. The truth sucks. I'm being stabbed with a thousand daggers, all tipped with cyanide, worse than anything Hamlet himself endured. And I *know* the spirits are right. Sam and Mr. Janvrin and Dorian and Brandy and the hookup parade.

My head knew I wasn't to blame for Sam's suicide. The rest of me was another story. Until Macy, my heart refused to open. And when it did start to bloom like one of those pink roses that's still in the dressing room, it scared the living hell out of me.

Hamlet was visited by a ghost for a reason. So was I.

My future might not include Macy. I've probably screwed that up forever. But as Mr. Janvrin said, I have to *live* as an actor and as a human. I must open my heart so it'll be ready for the next person who sticks around, holding a perfect bouquet.

I sit up. My face doesn't itch anymore. The tears evaporated along with the ghosts, leaving no discernible traces. Only memories.

I'm going to that cast party. I will try to talk to Macy, but if they don't want to, I will respect that. I just have to get out of the auditorium first.

And then I see it: way in the back, a crack of light.

I hear my name, water bubbling over rocks, a tentative cry accompanied by the *squeeeeeak* of the auditorium door.

"Ronan?"

"Macy," I call, standing up.

"Hey. You okay?"

"Macy?" I ask again. Is this really Macy, or another spirit?

But now that I think about it, the spirits weren't opening any doors. They just... appeared.

"Yeah." They wave, silhouetted against the light of the lobby. "I was worried when you didn't show up at the party..."

"Macy." Apparently, that's all I can say, but I don't care. Euphoria floods through me so hard, I'm emitting happy-waves. Following the light from the lobby, I carefully make my way down the stage stairs, then beeline up the aisle, just to make sure Macy isn't another figment of my screwed-up imagination.

It's them. Blonde pixie cut. The sweet breath of their favorite cinnamon Altoids. Even their purple glitter boots I covet. So real and beautiful and *human*. Right in front of me.

They were worried. They came back, just for me. Even after I'd hurt them.

"Macy." I want to kiss them. I want to hold them. I just *want*. But I stay, rooted to my spot just inches from them. They radiate warmth.

Macy smiles at me. "What are you doing in here, silly?" they ask softly. I can tell by their tentative expression that they're not quite over the flower incident. They're scared. I am too. "The door was unlocked."

Wait, what? "Uh, I tried it earlier," I say, looking behind me as if the ghosts will reappear and back me up on that. "I was completely locked in."

They grin incredulously, and who can blame them? "Ronan. I think you need a—"

"I'm sorry." The words burst forth. "About the flowers. They were, they *are*, they're still in the dressing room, just gorgeous. And so thoughtful. And"—I stop to suck in air before I pass out—"and you were right. About Sam. About me. I..." I inhale slowly, taking a moment. I want Macy to know I mean every syllable. "I think we could really be something too."

I stop talking. Because Macy is kissing me, their lips soft like the petals of those pink roses. Another Christmas gift, a way to reclaim the holiday after all I've lost. I cup their face in my hands as their arms slide around my waist, my heart bursting as I realize exactly what the spirits and Sam taught me.

The door was always unlocked.

I just had to open it.

I Saw Her Again
By Lauren Emily Whalen

Lauren Emily Whalen is an author and performer living in Chicago with her cat, Versace, and an apartment full of books.

Her debut YA novel *SATELLITE*, a coming-of-age tale about chosen family, classical ballet and rock 'n roll, was published in late 2017, and her YA nonfiction book *DEALING WITH DRAMA*, part of ABDO Publishing's *Strong, Healthy Girls* series, will be released in 2021.

Lauren writes for adults as Lauren Emily, and her work has appeared in *Playboy, GO, BUST,* and *SELF* magazines and the website bellesa.co, as well as two anthologies: *Best Women's Erotica vol. 5* (Cleis Press, 2019) and *Between the Covers* (Volumes, 2018).

An Equity Membership Candidate and professional actor, Lauren has appeared in theater throughout Chicago, including the Shakespeare plays *Romeo and Juliet, The Tempest, Love's Labour's Lost,* and *A Midsummer Night's Dream.* She's a very amateur and slow-learning aerialist.

Lauren's story "I Saw Her Again" was inspired by her love of *A Christmas Carol, High Fidelity, Hamlet,* and The Mamas and The Papas.

Satellite

Dealing With Drama (*coming in* 2021)

Connect with Lauren

www.laurenemilywrites.com

twitter.com/laurenemilywri

Facebook.com/laurenemilywrites

Instagram.com/laurenemilywrites

goodreads.com/maybeimamazed02

Yesterday's News

Leslie Rush

ONE

"You don't have to believe in ghosts to see one," explains the Zia Ghost Tour guide, her name badge— "Heather"—glinting in the lamplight. "Is everyone ready? Show me your wrist bands."

A dozen dutiful arms shoot up, and their luminescent bracelets wiggle like a conga line of glow worms. The last cold streaks of daylight are fading fast in the deep sapphire New Mexico sky.

"We're standing on Zia's most deadly corner," Heather continues. "There are over twenty documented shoot-outs right here at the corner of 3rd and Orchard."

"Now *there's* some lovely holiday spirit," I mutter, hitching my bag back up onto my shoulder. The camcorder inside smacks into my hip.

"Shh, we're supposed to blend in. You wanna get busted?"

Matt's right, of course. We can't afford the $30 apiece to learn about historic Zia Square's ten most famous ghosts. That's $3 per ghost, each! Even worse, shit rolls downhill, and when a cop's kids get caught breaking the law, it's an avalanche. So we're hanging back at the edge of the group, acting like we're in the vicinity only by coincidence.

The tour group crosses the Street of Death to a wooden sidewalk that stretches the length of the square. At the far end sits the small Spanish church and the former territorial courthouse that's now a restaurant/museum. A tumbled combination of original dilapidated buildings, original-but-restored buildings, and fake new-but-look-old buildings line the other three sides.

To keep our disguise intact, we stop and pore over the Ghost Tour flyer, which lists the buildings and their histories, waiting until the group gets ahead by a few yards. In a few minutes, it'll be dark, and no one will notice if there are two extra glow-in-the-dark bracelets making their way toward the hangouts of Pat Garrett and Billy the Kid.

We thought Black Friday would be the perfect day to hunt for ghosts, since there wouldn't be much of a crowd. Everyone goes Christmas shopping, right? And the ones who didn't are at home battling a turkey hangover. No one's going to get haunted at the Z-Mart, so here we are. We figured it would be the perfect time to capture footage of a real live ghost and win the $20,000 prize offered by the *Zia Sun*.

We were wrong. The square has been packed all afternoon with people shopping for Authentic New Mexico Tourist Crap, only thinning out as the sun set and shops began to close. The sweet shop and the souvenir stand will stay open until after the tour is over, hoping to scrape a final few dollars out of the ghost-lovers' wallets.

By then, we'll be long gone.

As the group shuffles down the wooden sidewalk, Heather sets the stage with colorful local stories woven with historical details. When they stop at the Billy the Kid bookstore, Heather details how The Kid was jailed here in Zia. Based on statewide claims, this legendary juvenile delinquent appeared in every town in New Mexico during the two years he was at large, but at least here in Zia, there's an actual record.

We duck into the doorway, put on our unauthorized fake bracelets, and then fall into step with everyone moving to the next stop.

"Besides the church and the courthouse, Number 47 Orchard Street is the oldest building on the square, and one of the oldest surviving in Zia," Heather announces as the long, sloped roof looms overhead, blocking the twilight stars. "It was built in 1902 by Alexander Frost, a wealthy rancher, for his young wife, Josephine Winters. It was a luxurious home for this area at the time, with oak floors and a stamped tin ceiling. The *real* luxury was a water pump in the kitchen and bath, and an actual flushing toilet."

"Can we go in?" asks a middle-aged woman amid appreciative murmurs from the crowd.

"Sorry, it's not open to the public right now. It's undergoing renovations, and we're working with the state to designate it as an historic landmark. This was Zia's first public library in the 1930s."

I wish we'd go inside *somewhere*. I've had a sore throat for a few days and this cold air isn't helping.

A couple in their mid-twenties cup their faces and peer through a gap in the boarded-up window. The man flicks a flashlight across the inside, grumbling that he can't see anything.

"There have been reports of paranormal activity here since the 1920s, when Josephine died," Heather continues, paraphrasing the flyer's paragraph about the house. "She experienced a great deal of tragedy in her life. She had four children and lost three of them in a scarlet fever outbreak during the spring of 1912. The oldest son, Alex Jr., survived, but he left home after a falling-out with his father, only to be killed in Pancho Villa's raid on Columbus in 1916."

"A falling-out with his father," I hiss. "See? That's the kind of thing that gets you killed in a bandit raid."

"Shut up, Abbie. It isn't funny." My brother's face settles into the stone mask he wears whenever anyone mentions the feud between him and Dad.

It's gotten so bad that when Dad left tonight, headed for his second job as security at the Z-Mart Supercenter, Matt didn't respond to his goodbye. He continued to play Warcraft without even so much as a blink, poking his middle finger in Dad's direction. Mom didn't see it, and neither did the twins. No one saw it but me.

Most kids wouldn't care, but when your dad's a cop, there's an unspoken rule: no leaving angry, no bitter words before doors get slammed, because sometimes cops leave for work and don't come home.

I saw the finger. I see a lot of things no one else notices. Like the exasperation in Dad's eyes, and the wary underlayer behind Matt's curtain of scorn and indifference.

"What kind of activity?" I can't resist asking, earning a sharp elbow in my ribs.

"People have heard someone weeping," Heather says, holding the battery-powered lantern at shoulder-level and peering across the group—hopefully not noticing the two tag-alongs at the back. "For several years it was an ice cream parlor, and the employees reported hearing small children. They apparently liked playing with the swinging door." Heather pauses for the group to buzz, and they happily oblige. "Okay, everyone, the sidewalk narrows for the next part of the block. Please walk in single file and watch your step."

She steps into the street to let us shuffle by one at a time. As the group moves down the wooden walkway, she acknowledges each person with a slight nod, as if she's counting.

"Shit, she's going to notice us," Matt mutters.

When we get to the window, he presses his face up to the hole in the boards covering the glass. I crouch in the recessed doorway to tie my shoe.

"*Abbie*." Matt stiffens and whispers urgently, "There's something—"

"Sir, let's keep moving, please." Heather's crisp, pleasant tone cuts him off.

Matt signals me to stay in the recessed doorway, out of her line of sight. She said *sir*, not *you two*.

"Oops, I'm sorry to keep you waiting. I just wanted a peek." He turns from the window, brandishing his video camera and conveniently blocking her view of my hiding place. I can practically hear him opening the drawer of charming tricks he's gathered over the years. "This is such a great job you have. Have you ever seen any ghosts yourself?"

Footsteps walk away from me, and I peek around the wall in time to see Matt following Heather. He turns, points sharply toward the house, and mouths, "Go in there."

How am I supposed to do that? I turn my palms up and dip my head to ask, and all I get back is the same gesture: *Figure it out*.

Okay then. I stand up and try to see something—anything—through the evening gloom and the soaped-up windows on the double door. A faded sign taped on the bottom gives me a feeble warning to KEEP OUT. I grasp the doorknob and give it a wiggle because even though it's surely locked, you never know. As an assistant-aspiring-prize-winning ghost hunter, I have to rule out the obvious.

The door is locked, but a wisp of air brushes my hand on the knob, raising the tiny hairs and sending a shiver up my arm. A closer look, lit by the faint glow of my fake tour bracelet, reveals the sign is not taped to the window completely. Peeling under the edge of the sign, I hit the jackpot.

There's a hole in the window. A big one.

I yank off the bracelet and stuff it in my pocket with the flyer before its unauthorized glow gives me away. Lifting the sign away, I snake my hand through the hole, careful not to slice my wrist on the glass. I can see the headline now: TRESPASSER BLEEDS OUT IN HISTORIC ZIA HOME. I flick the old latch open and turn the knob. With one last glance over my shoulder, I pull my hand out of the hole and slip inside 47 Orchard Street.

It's funny how the silence of a house where nobody's home is different from the silence of a house where nobody lives—and nobody's called this place home for an awfully long time. It has an atmosphere of its own, comprised of old wooden floors and long-ago lifetimes, that recedes to make room for me, then closes back in like the tide. I don't know what Matt thought he saw in here, but it's time to get down to business.

I set my backpack on the floor, get out my video camera, and switch on the digital voice recorder in my pocket while my eyes adjust to the gloom. There are newspapers all over the floor—a thin carpet of headlines to protect the wood, I guess.

"Friday, November 27, 2009. 6:47 p.m. I'm Abbie McLeod, inside the Frost home in Zia Square," I begin, panning the room slowly, lowering my voice to sound professional. Even if Matt doesn't get anything on video at the other haunts, I might capture the evidence that wins him the prize, and then Dad will have to see there's a future for Matt as a video journalist.

"Reports of paranormal activity inside the house include the sounds of a woman crying, children playing, and physical manifestations around the swinging door."

The main room is large, with deep sturdy shelves on all of the walls. From the library days, I guess. I zoom in on the heavy swinging door that I assume leads to the kitchen and inch my way toward it. Maybe I'll step into a cold spot. According to all the ghost hunting websites, one of the first signs of a place being haunted is cold spots. Actually, it's pretty cold in this whole place, and shivers are running across my neck and shoulders. This little adventure better not make me even more sick. Maybe there's a hot spot instead? That would be a shock to paranormal geeks everywhere.

The newspapers give way to a bare floor by the kitchen. No hot or cold spots. I push open the door, which catches on something on the floor—a hard rubber wedge. Perfect! I nudge the wedge into place with my toe, leaving the door just wide enough for me to back into the kitchen, camera still trained on the main room. Deep shadows are punctuated with dusty shafts of moonlight and looking through the camera lens makes it impossible to see much of anything. Then a spark, a glimmer, blinks at the far end of the room, making my heart jump. But it's just a momentary flicker of light from the square.

Which reminds me: according to the ghost hunting websites, you're supposed to alert the possible spirits to your presence. Even if you can't hear them answer, sometimes voices—EVP—show up in the recordings.

"Hello," I say softly, turning a slow three-sixty.

Josephine's kitchen is twice the size of ours, with a cast-iron sink and a mammoth wood-burning stove. "My name is Abbie. Is anyone here?" I count to twelve, then, "Josephine, are you here?"

As I complete the circle, a wisp of light crosses the open doorway. My chest tightens again as something in the air... shifts.

"Hello?"

But of course it's just the same light from outside. Or maybe from the window over the sink. I let out a breath and lower the camera—to the sound of a soft scrape over by the doorway, like a finger across a wooden table. Or across a piece of paper.

The ice cream door closes.

A chill slithers up my neck, twisting into my hair and rooting me to the spot. "It's okay," I whisper to myself—at least I *think* it's to myself—as I move one foot in the direction of the door. With the second step, my breath comes flooding back and anger replaces fear. I didn't get it on camera! Then it hits me—the wedge! That little wedge wasn't tight enough to hold the heavy door after all.

Duh, I scold myself. *Prop it open right this time, Abbie.*

I push the door wide open to the main room, looking down at the floor for that bit of hard rubber, but it's nowhere in sight. Where did it go? It's not on either side of the door.

"Okay." I turn the camera to my own face and continue my report, determined to un-spook myself. "The door seems to have slipped shut, gave me a scare for a second, but—"

A dull thump sounds at the other end of the main room where the hallway begins. Like the sound of a chunk of rubber.

Heart in my throat, I scan the main room and lock my eyes on the back hall. A small girl stands there, and even in the dim light I can see her clearly. She has two long braids with untamed curls framing her face. A drop-waist calico dress covers her from neck to knee, with heavy stockings and high-button shoes below.

She bends down and scoops the door wedge up from the floor, then tosses it into the air. This time she catches it, looking right at me and smiling. The faintest hint of evergreen tickles my nose, reminding me to breathe.

"I see you," I whisper. "Who are you?"

Even though I can't feel my feet and the blood is screaming in my ears, I walk toward her across the newspapers. When I get closer, she darts to the right, down the hall. The scent of Christmas evergreen is stronger here, with an undercurrent of clove and pipe tobacco. I follow, camera still rolling. With a quick peek back to see if I'm there, she slips through the first doorway on the left. I struggle to stop my hands from trembling and keep the camera trained on where she just was.

She's a ghost, I'm following a ghost—

Did I say that aloud? I have no idea, but the thought that maybe I should be afraid is barely registering, a moth flitting around the edges of my consciousness as I follow the newspaper trail into the room.

It's like looking into a tunnel of fog. At first, all I can see is the warm glow of an oil lamp at the center of the room. The girl's face is golden in the light as she turns to me, her eyes filling with tears. A wave of sorrow and desperation rolls out from her and engulfs me.

The lamp's glow wavers and expands like a lens, pushing the fog to the edge of my vision. Pinpricks of light emerge, becoming glass Christmas ornaments on a pine tree strung with popcorn garland and tiny paper snowflakes. Two faces materialize across a cherrywood desk, and then their bodies materialize in the growing light—two men in old-fashioned suits, dark hair parted in the middle. One is standing, young and agitated, while the other is seated. He's older, with streaks of gray in his thinning hair and his thick mustache, but they look like they're cast from the same mold. Father and son.

They're arguing, but I can't hear what they're saying—it's like being underwater while people are yelling up above. The father has the same hard look I've seen in Dad's eyes lately, the look that paralyzes my heart. The son is red-faced, angry, pointing his finger at his father. The older man rises and pounds a fist on the desk, then utters something sharp and quiet, a poisoned dagger that seems to pierce the younger man's heart. He goes very still, the blood draining from his face, then turns on his heel and walks away from his father into the fog. The father shouts at him to come back as the fog closes in and the light goes out, the muffled sound of his name roaring across a century: *Alex*.

The boy from the flyer. Alex, the son who left and never returned.

"*No!*" I shout helplessly. "Don't go! Don't let him go!" Shaken, I lower the camera.

A quiet sob shudders from where the Christmas tree was just a moment ago—or a century ago—and the ghost girl's shadow curls up on a small chair under the window, wracked with grief. She raises her head, her tear-streaked face imploring me to help. But how?

"Hello, umm, little girl?" I take a step toward her and the floor creaks, popping the sound bubble. The silence of an empty room returns, and there is no little girl, just moonlight shining on a vacant chair.

Even more newspaper crinkles under me as I set down the camera and sit on the chair with my face in my hands, trying to get my bearings. My head feels like a hot air balloon, not quite attached to my body, and I'm shivering. What did I just see? It was real, but somehow *not* real, like a memory or a dream. I rub my eyes and when I open them, the moonlit headlines between my feet come into focus. FLU CASES TRIPLE it says. CITY CLOSES CHURCHES, SCHOOLS. Whoa. They said this year would be bad, but closing the schools? This is real news. I peer closer: *The Philadelphia Inquirer*. Ha, lucky kids in Philly! But how did a Philly paper get so far from home? I pick it up; it's soft in my hands, crumbling like confetti. As it falls away, I see the date: October 20, 1918.

1918.

No wonder it fell apart in my hands. But a paper that old just lying around? Curious, I peer at the other ones at my feet. School board meetings, sports scores and weather reports, all from the last few months. But then one giant word peeks out from under the scattered words: MOON. I lean over and pull it out from the pile:

MEN WALK ON MOON. *New York Times, Monday July 21, 1969.*

What the hell is going on here? I drop to the floor and crawl around on my hands and knees, flipping through dozens of pages. Random days of normal news in no particular order, punctuated with major events: New Year's Day, 2000. President Nixon Resigns, 1974. VE Day, 1945. Stock Market Crash, 1929. How far do these go back? The Spanish Flu pandemic of 1918 at least. Earlier than that even? Matt needs to see all of this. *He's* the wannabe reporter.

The camera! It's still on. I grab it and look into the lens. "There are papers all over the floor here, from everywhere and every time. I don't know what it means or how it's connected to the ghost girl." Still on my knees, I pan the camera slowly across the headlines, then glance at the newspaper lying on the chair. Wondering what headline I was sitting on, I hold it up to the light of the camera. It's the *Zia Sun*. My father's face stares up at me from his official ZPD photo.

What the—my hand trembles as I lean closer to read.

OFFICER KILLED IN CONFRONTATION WITH SHOPLIFTER

A veteran police officer was shot and killed late Saturday night when he confronted a shoplifter in the parking lot of the Z-Mart Supercenter. Officer Thomas McLeod followed a man who had left the store with unknown items. When he confronted the suspect, the man pulled out a gun and fired one round into McLeod's chest. Witnesses say the officer returned fire, wounding the suspect before collapsing on the ground. Officer McLeod was pronounced dead shortly after arriving at Vista Hospital, where the suspect remains in critical condition. The suspect has been identified as—

Shock slams into me like a wall. *Officer Thomas McLeod.* The paper trembles in my hand and the camera falls to the floor. *Pronounced dead.* What the fuck, *what the actual fuck,* is going on here? I snatch the camera up, shine its light on the hideous headline again, and then I see the date. Monday, November 30, 2009.

Three days from now.

A cold sweat grips my body as a thousand questions flit through my mind. How can this be real—a headline from the future lying in the scattered remnants of the last century? Is this just a warning, or is this already written in stone, like a tombstone for my dad? How does the ghost girl fit into any of this? One thing's for sure: Matt needs to see it, all of it.

Clutching the camera, I stand up, tuck the paper under my arm, and bolt for the doorway. But as soon as I reach the hall, the room... slips. Newspapers slide out from under my feet, up into the air, fluttering down around me as I'm suddenly somehow back by the chair again.

Panic clutches my throat. I've got to get out of here! Okay, Abbie, no running, no skidding, just get this footage and the paper out of this house. Stepping carefully, I cross the room again. But when I reach the doorway, the same force tumbles me back to where I started, knocking the paper to the floor.

The ringing in my ears almost drowns out the pounding of my heart. *The room won't let me leave.* But maybe—

Maybe it's the paper. Maybe *I* can leave but the future headline can't. That makes sense in a bizarre time-travel-rules kind of way. Okay then. I don't need the paper. I have it on video, right?

"Third time's the charm," I whisper. I'm sweating now, not sure if it's fear or a fever or both. But a few quick steps is all it will take. I'm not even going to think about what I'll do if this doesn't work. Deep breath, one-two-three—braced for another impact, I stride across the room and stumble into the hall.

The chatter of tourists drifts in from outside, so I make my way to the front door and peek through the hazy window. The tour group is by the souvenir shop, meaning the ghost tour is already over. How long have I been in here? It can't have been more than ten minutes since I unlocked the door.

A sharp tap jolts me away from the door like a frightened rabbit.

"Abbie! Are you still in there? Come on!" Matt stage-whispers from the other side.

"Yes! Get in here! You have to see this, Matt—" My tongue feels sluggish, too big for my mouth.

"We gotta go. Everything's closing, security is walking around."

"'Kay." I grab my backpack. "Is it clear?"

"Yeah!"

I open the door and slip out in one adrenaline-fueled move, then poke my shaking hand behind the KEEP OUT sign to lock the door. Matt takes my backpack and slings it over his shoulder as we jog over to the parking lot.

"Abbie! We were in the courthouse, and I think I got something! What about you?"

"Oh my God, *Matt.* There was a girl! And all these papers, and the boy who was killed and his dad, and these *headlines* from everything, and *Matt,* the paper from Monday! It's Dad! He's-he's—we have to *do* something!" My heart is racing when we reach the car. Sweat rolls down my neck as I yank open the door.

"Did you get anything on camera? You were in there for an hour!"

"An hour? I-I don't know—it was on the whole time, but I haven't looked yet."

"Wait'll you see what I got!" Matt crows. "There's an old ink stand on the judge's bench at the courthouse, and I think —I'm pretty sure it *moved!*"

Scrunched together in the car, we hover over the video screen, watching the dark shapes of tourists filing through the dimly lit restaurant/museum. The heat is on in the car and my shirt is sticking to me under my jacket, but now I'm shivering.

"Man, I wish we had infrared," Matt says wistfully as the camera turns toward the judges' bench. "Can't hardly see anything. But check this out!"

Matt's voice floats up from the camera, echoing the same words I said in the house: "My name is Matt. Is anyone here?" There's a long pause as he waits for possible EVP, then, "Can you show yourself?"

Deep in the back, on the right-hand corner of the bench, there's a wobble. It's almost impossible to see what the thing actually is, but there's definitely movement.

"There!" Matt taps the screen in triumph. "That's the ink bottle! This is so *awesome!*" He plays the footage again. I can finally breathe normally, but what I saw, what I know, can't wait one second longer.

"Matt, that's fantastic, but look, *please*—you have to see this!"

"You got something too?" The screen lights up our faces as we peer at the shadowy footage of the Orchard Street kitchen. I hear myself say, "Is anyone there?" and a blip of light flashes at the edge of the picture. The light that came from outside the house.

"Wait, back it up and turn up the volume—there was this scraping sound, and the door closed. After that is when it all happened."

Sure enough, when Matt turns the volume up, we hear both the faint scraping sound and the heavy door swinging closed. The picture on the screen swings up and pushes through the door. I hear myself moving around, looking for the rubber wedge. My heart pounds, waiting to see the silhouette of the ghost girl in the hall. There's the thump—and static covers the viewer.

"WHAT? Give me that." I go to the beginning and start over. There's my intro, followed by shuffling noises... and then static.

"No!" My heart sinks. Not only do I not have the ghost footage, I have no proof of what I saw in the paper. "Matt, there was a girl. A little girl in a long dress. She dropped the doorstop—that's the thump you hear at the end. She went to one of the back rooms, and I followed her. She was crying and she showed me Mr. Frost and Alex, the one that got killed in Pancho Villa's raid! They were arguing, and Alex left."

Matt gives me a sharp look. "The guy that's on the flyer? Nice try, Abbie, but a little obvious. I know you hate seeing me and Dad argue but using a fake ghost story to try to make me back down? That's pretty lame."

"No, that's not all! There were newspapers all over the floor, some with headlines going back a hundred years. She left one on her chair. It was from Monday—THIS Monday—and it said Dad will get—he'll get—shot and *killed* Sunday night."

"What? Are you fucking kidding me? *Abbie*—"

"If you don't believe me, then let's go in and I'll show you. I couldn't bring the paper out. The house... wouldn't let me."

"It wouldn't *let* you? How did it 'not let you'?" Matt's scornful expression glows in the light of the static snowstorm and he switches the camera off.

"I know it sounds crazy, but I couldn't get out of the room until I left the paper there. Come on, let's go back in. We have to find a way to warn Dad!" My hands start shaking again. "Matt, please!"

"Okay, show me," he decides, adding, "*I'll* handle the camera this time." Like I somehow screwed it up. The prickle of annoyance is short though. We've got bigger things to think about.

There's no one in sight. We slip across the parking lot, up onto the walkway and into the deep shadows of the doorway. My fingers fumble with the latch, but we get in quickly.

It's even darker than before, with only the streetlight outside to penetrate the gloom.

"I started right here at the door." I call out to the house,

"Umm, this is Abbie again—and Matt. If you're still here, can you give us a sign?"

Matt follows me across the room to the swinging door. I push it open and we circle around the kitchen.

"Nothing so far," he observes. "Where's all the newspaper?"

"Right out there, all over the floor!" I push back out into the main room, anxious to show him the carpet of headlines from the past hundred years, but especially the one from Monday—and I freeze.

The floor is bare.

Dusty oak stretches from the kitchen across the front room all the way to the hall. Hundreds of pages, maybe thousands... vanished. There are no newspapers anywhere.

"They were here!" I stride across the room to the hall. "They were all over the floor!" The first room on the left is empty except for the chair. No fluttering pages, no moon landing or Spanish Flu. And no headline for November 30.

"Well, I don't know what you think you saw, but it's not here now, and you didn't get it on video. Maybe you just imagined it." Matt lowers the camera and looks at his watch. "But I've got enough to send to the *Zia Sun*! And we need to get home. No point pissing Dad off even more."

We trudge back to the car in silence and get in. My head is spinning as Matt backs out of the Zia Square parking lot. There's no way I just imagined that whole thing! How can I make him understand what happened? What words will make the warning real?

"I don't know who she was," I begin, trying not to hyperventilate. "She looked about ten, and she was crying. She showed me the two men arguing, and the son leaving. Then she left me the paper from Monday—*this coming* Monday. Matt, it said Dad will be shot and k-killed. Tomorrow night, at the Supercenter. I didn't hallucinate this, Matt. I read the article. I *saw* it."

Matt's somber face is focused on the road ahead. "So what exactly happened? What caused it?"

"A shoplifter. Dad followed him out to the parking lot. It said the guy pulled out a gun and shot him in the chest. He shot back, and the guy was in critical condition. I didn't read any more—I was trying to get out of there." The hard lump in my throat is too hard to swallow, and uncontrollable tears pour down my cheeks. "It's a warning. We have to tell him!"

"He isn't going to believe anything like that, Abbie. Honestly, if it wasn't you telling me, I'd be thinking this was bullshit." He puts up his hand to silence my protests before they begin. "Obviously you believe it. But it might not be what you think it is. We'll figure it out."

"The only thing we have to *figure out* is how to keep him from going to work tomorrow!" Then something occurs to me. "You're the one who insisted I go in the house. Just what was it you saw in the window, anyway?"

Matt turns onto our street, a street of new houses full of families getting ready for Christmas, no hauntings or tragedies. "I don't know. Nothing, really. It just seemed like something was moving in there."

"It was *her*. Maybe we can find out more about the girl."

"Knock yourself out." He shrugs and opens his door, trying to be chill about it, but his eyes gleam with excitement. "I was just hoping to have some fun and maybe get some footage. And I did! I'll have to enhance the video so people can see it better. Maybe I'll win the prize! Right now, though, I have actual homework."

He strides to the front door, leaving me sitting in the car with my mouth hanging open. How can he not *care?* How can he not believe me?

I climb out of the car, my head hot and pounding with confusion. Maybe I wanted to see something so badly I *did* imagine it. Or somehow fell asleep and dreamed it. It felt like only ten minutes, but he said I was in there for almost an hour. Maybe my worries about Dad and Matt got tangled up in my head with the tragic Frost family and wove themselves into some kind of freaky dream.

I lean in to grab my backpack and something falls out of my shirt pocket onto the seat. The digital voice recorder—and it's been on the whole time.

I get back in the car and close the door, where I can listen without any other noise or interference. It starts with my own familiar introduction.

"...reports of activity include the sounds of a woman crying, children playing, and physical manifestations around the swinging door." Pause, rustling... "Is anyone here?" More soft shuffling noises, like someone walking on newspapers, newspapers that were never really there, but one of those rustles sounds like—

Just me.

My heart thumps in my chest. *Just me, just me, just me.*

A thin, high-pitched hum begins, making it hard to hear anything. I think I detect the sound of the door closing, but I'm not sure.

"The door seems to have slipped shut, gave me a scare for a second, but—" The hum gets louder and I can barely hear myself speaking now. "I see you. Who are you?"

The hum rises to a squeal of rushing static, but I hear it: a wisp of sound swirling away in the rising tide of white noise:

Emily.

"What do you *mean* you don't hear her?"

"I just told you." Matt spells it out with exaggerated patience: "I. Don't. Hear. Her."

He taps his pencil with each word and turns the page in his physics book.

I've replayed the audio four times. And yeah, it's not crystal clear, you have to listen closely for it, and it *could* be just the static... but it's not.

"It's Emily. Emily Frost." I point to the flyer. "One of the kids who died of scarlet fever."

"If you say so. I mean, I can hear *something*, but it could be anything you want it to be." He shakes his head. "If I turn this in, it'll make my footage look weak. I'm sorry, but I just can't use it. And by the way, you look like shit. You're all red, like *you* have a fever."

The rest of the night is a blur. My body hurts, my head hurts, even my eyes hurt. This must be the flu or something. Mom orders me into my room so the four-year-old twins Randy and Josh won't catch it and brings me Tylenol and soup for dinner.

She sets the soup on my nightstand, then feels my forehead with her wrist. She pulls a digital thermometer from her pocket to get the actual number: 100.2. "Okay, you definitely have a fever."

I hesitate at first, hating to bring up the feud going on in our house, but lying here with nothing else to think about, my overheated brain has hatched a plan.

"Mom, I'm so sick of this fight between Dad and Matt.

Why are they even arguing? It's Matt's life, anyway. His choice. Dad should just sign the application."

"Your father just wants Matt to have a secure future, honey. Growing up the way he did, never knowing where the next meal was coming from—you know how he is." Yeah, I *do* know how he is. Taking every extra shift, just like this extra duty at the shopping center. Always putting money aside, preparing for the worst.

"I wish they'd find some kind of compromise. What's wrong with them? Matt will turn eighteen and apply to the journalism school anyway. They're just being hard-headed for no reason. And it's almost *Christmas*."

Mom's eyes brim with sympathy, and her voice is tired. "Abbie, those two are as stubborn as mules, but eventually, they'll figure it out. Some people just have to see for themselves instead of being told."

"Well, I think we need to *make* them listen. Like an intervention."

She laughs, but I'm serious. "Mom, can we at least try? Maybe if they see how much it's affecting everyone else around here they'll at least talk to each other." I prop myself up on one elbow. "We could do it tomorrow. We could maybe drive up to Ruidoso." Taking a drive up into the mountains is one of my family's favorite day trips.

"I'm pretty sure your dad is working tomorrow night. Let's get the Christmas tree up and see how it goes."

I *know* he's working tomorrow. That's what I have to prevent.

Saturday morning, I'm still sick. My throat is red, my

tongue is red, and every muscle in my body feels like limp spaghetti. Mom still has me under semi-quarantine, but my door's open. I hear boxes and tubs being dragged inside in preparation for decorating the Christmas tree, which Mom informs me will be brought home by Dad and Matt within the hour.

Hope blooms in my heart. If they're getting along, maybe I can talk my parents into some kind of family activity tonight —anything to keep Dad away from the Supercenter. Meanwhile, I have to try to find out more about Emily.

I unfold the ghost tour flyer and peer at the picture of the Frost family. Josephine is seated, holding an infant, while the dignified Alexander stands behind her, resting his hand on her shoulder. Three other children cluster around their mother: the solemn Alex Jr. who looks about twelve; a mischief-faced little boy in a sailor suit who looks the same age as Randy and Josh; and holding her mother's hand is Emily, the only daughter. Younger than Alex, her riotous curls are tamed with a big bow, and she's wearing her Sunday best. She's younger than she appeared last night, but with the same luminous eyes that seem to follow me. Googling the family on my phone, I find a few more old pictures of the house and this same photo.

I zoom in on Emily's face. Her sorrow draws me in, but it might also be like what Matt said about the voice on the recorder. I could just be reading emotions that aren't really there. She didn't actually *know*. She would never know the full extent of the tragedy coming to sweep her family away. By the time her brother stormed off for good, she'd been dead for four years.

But what if that's why? What if she *did* know? What if her spirit stood there, watching her brother and father destroy their relationship, powerless to stop it? How many times has she begged for help, unable to end this loop of terrible events —and nobody heard or saw?

Until now.

Until *another* girl with a brother and a father tearing each other apart comes into her house, another family heading for disaster. A disaster that Emily somehow sees and is able to warn me about in a way she couldn't warn her own family.

The sound of Dad's truck in the driveway jolts me out of bed. I'm jamming my arms into a hoodie before my feet hit the floor. Fever-dizzy, I make it to the doorway just as the front door pops open and Matt pushes through. His face is like stone, his eyes grim as they briefly meet mine before he sweeps past me to his room and closes the door.

"Matt?" My voice is dry and quivering.

So is my heart. The *click* when he locks it sounds so... final.

"Mandy, come hold the door?" Dad's voice pours in with the cold air from the front porch, where he balances a plump evergreen. Mom hurries from the kitchen to help, giving me a sidelong glance.

"Abbie, get out of this draft and back in bed!"

I take a step back, watching them wrestle the Christmas tree through the door. Randy and Josh are jumping up and down, shouting, "Tree! Tree!" The house is flooded with the smell of evergreen as Dad wrangles it to the traditional spot in front of the living room window and hoists it into the stand. He smiles at Mom while the twins shriek with delight. But his smile is tired and disappears completely when he sees me.

"Didn't your mother tell you to get back in bed?" His sharp tone slices through the twins' giggles.

"I-I am, Dad. I'm just watching for a minute." With perfect timing, my dry throat seizes up and I start coughing.

"Don't tell me 'I am.' You're standing *right there* coughing your germs all over the place. The last thing we need around here is for everyone in the goddamn house to get sick!"

His loud voice stabs into the weight I'm already carrying —Matt's anger, Emily's warning, and my spiking temperature. Hot tears spill from my eyes as I stumble back to my bed. So much for the "happy family" plan. I'm pretty sure Dad can't wait to get away from his hostile son and germ-spewing daughter. He'll probably go in early now just to get away from us.

I burrow under the covers, fever and despair making the bed spin. How can I keep him here tonight? Cheerful lunch sounds drift in from the kitchen, breaking my concentration. There has to be a way. Emily wouldn't have shown me if there wasn't. She's been waiting through moon landings and world wars, every day for a century, trying to get through. But why? Why me?

A tap at the door breaks my train of thought. I peek out from the covers, expecting Mom, but it's Dad. He's carrying a tray with some tomato soup and a grilled cheese sandwich.

"Hey, A-bee-bee. Brought you some lunch." He only uses my baby nickname when he's worried or acting silly. Not a trace of silliness appears as he sets the tray on my nightstand.

"You doing okay? I thought you just had a cold, but your mom says it's maybe a touch of the flu. And it's time for more Tylenol." He hesitates. Then, "I'm sorry I snapped at you. Sometimes things get a little—"

"Crazy?" I mumble.

"I was going to say busy, but you're right. Lately, it *has* been a little crazy around here." He feels my forehead. "You're pretty warm." He hands me the pills.

"Dad, do you believe in ghosts?" The words come out of nowhere, bursting from my mouth by themselves.

"No, not really. I believe there are things we don't understand, but somewhere there's an explanation for everything." He smiles quizzically. "Why? Did you see something on the ghost tour?"

"You know about that?" Did Matt tell him about the ink bottle? I'd better proceed with caution. Avoiding Dad's cop-gaze, the one that always sees everything I try to hide, I dip the sandwich in the soup and take a tiny bite.

"Matt said you guys were late yesterday because you went. I assume you didn't catch the prize-winning footage." His voice takes on the ironic tone he's adopted lately when he mentions my brother, but he's listening.

Could it be this easy?

"I *did* see something. It was about *you*." I take a breath, but the hideous thing refuses to be voiced. I can't say the words. "It was—you—please don't go to work tonight! Something bad is going to happen."

Dad pats my hand. "Aww honey, nothing bad is going to happen."

The lump in my throat swells and a wave of dizziness washes over me. "Please. Tell them you can't come. I *saw* it." It's choking me, coming out all garbled and wrong.

"What did you see?" He's humoring me now, like I'm five years old and telling him about a bad dream.

"The future. Headlines." I lean back on my pillow and close my aching eyes against the light. "We have to change the future."

"The only way to change the future is to change the present, A-bee-bee," he reminds me, standing up to leave. "You're just upset because you're sick. Finish your soup and get some rest. I promise, everything will be ok."

I pick at my lunch and lie there willing the Tylenol to kick in so I can think straight. *Change the present*, he says.

That's what I'm trying to do, but I'm just spinning my wheels, getting nowhere. The actual present that has to change—Matt and Dad—isn't cooperating. The only help I've gotten has come from one hundred years in the past.

Change the future by changing the present. The mantra spirals around me as I close my eyes and try to sleep. The sounds of boxes opening and the low murmur of voices drift in while I doze for a few minutes... *Change the present, change the present...* But how?

The thought hits me like a bolt of lightning, yanking me upright in my bed.

Change the future by changing the present... Change the present by changing the past.

Emily couldn't change her family's future because she was already dead when it happened. But what if I can change it *for* her? An idea is blooming in my mind, opening up one leaf at a time. If I can find a way show Alex and his father their future the way Emily did for me, maybe I can knock them out of the time loop that has trapped all of them for a century. I don't know exactly how that will change things for *my* family, but it will do something. It *has* to.

There's no noise coming from the rest of the house. I peek out the window. No cars are in the driveway, and the sun's rays are short and low. What time is it? I look at my alarm clock—oh my God, it's after four! I slept for three *hours*, not three minutes. I shove my feet into a pair of shoes, grab my backpack and a jacket, and head for the back door.

"Matt?" There's no answer, but there's a note on the kitchen table:

Abbie,
Went to see Santa, home before dinner.
If you are reading this, get back in bed!
Love, Mom

Good, no one's around to stop me. I drag my bike out of the backyard and pedal down the street towards Zia Square. The cold air is like a knife on my flushed cheeks, and my sore throat threatens to clamp shut. Crap, I should have brought more Tylenol. That lunchtime dose will be wearing off soon. It'll be okay though. I only have one stop to make on the way, and then I'll be inside, out of the wind. Changing the present by changing the past.

By the time I turn onto 7th Street, my ears are ringing, I'm sweating buckets, and the cold air is shredding my lungs like a cheese grater. The lights are on in the library, so I've made it before closing time. Now all I have to do is find proof for Alex and his father—proof that if Alex leaves home for Columbus, he'll be killed in Pancho Villa's raid a few months later. And Emily showed me just the kind of proof I'll need: a newspaper. There must be copies of the local papers of the time—maybe even the originals. They would have accounts of the battle, some photos, and most importantly, the list of people killed. I'll make copies of everything and take it all to 47 Orchard Street. Then, Emily will have physical proof, not just phantom headlines. It sounds crazy even to me, but I'm trying not to think too hard about all the holes in this idea—much less what will happen if I fail.

I drop my bike and yank on the library doors. Locked! It's not 5:00 yet; why are they closed? Gasping for air, I cup my hands around my eyes and lean on the glass door, trying to see in. There's not soul in sight. Then I notice a piece of goldenrod paper taped neatly to the glass just above where my forehead is mashed onto the door:

CLOSED THANKSGIVING WEEKEND

11/26-11/29

Noooooo. I lean my back against the door and slide down to the ground, my spirits sagging even lower than my overheated body. *Now what?* The wind picks up, sending a shiver through my spine. I get up off the cold ground. What if I ride three miles to the Supercenter and try to intercept Dad before he starts his shift? I can already picture how that will turn out: epic failure.

Maybe Matt can figure out a way to sidetrack Dad. I dig in my backpack for my phone, but it isn't there. In my rush to get out of the house, I must have left it on my bed. I pat down all my pockets to make sure but come up empty—except for the ghost tour flyer. I smooth it open on my leg, trying to squelch the rising tide of panic. My chest hurts, my heart aches with fear for my family and grief for Emily's. There they are, frozen in time. None of them know what's about to happen. They can't see what's written right *next* to them: *The Frost family had four children and tragically lost three of them in a scarlet fever outbreak during the spring of 1912. The oldest son, Alex Jr., survived, but he left home after a falling-out with his father, only to be killed in Pancho Villa's raid on Columbus in March 1916.*

Wait.

That's *it.*

I don't need a newspaper. It's all right here in black and white. With a picture!

Hope surges through my veins. I hop on my bike, pedaling furiously down the last few blocks to Historic Zia Square. Deep streaks of red slash the winter sky as the sun sinks behind the mountains, and by the time I get there, the square is deep in shadow. A few cars are in the tiny parking lot and tourists are sprinkled around the shops, but no one's near the house. I turn down a side street and come up the alley behind Number 47, then lean my bike against an old hitching post by the kitchen door. My head is throbbing and I can't catch my breath. I try the door, but of course, no miracle has unlocked it. I'm going to have to sneak around to the front and go in through the KEEP OUT sign.

No one sees me under the deep overhang of the doorway. I'm shivering uncontrollably now. Sweat trickles down my neck, and my hand shakes as I lift up the cardboard sign to pop the latch. *Careful, careful, don't slice your arm open —shit.* As I draw my trembling hand back out, a jagged edge slices into me just below my thumb. Now there's blood dripping on the sidewalk and the door. The clock is ticking and I can't look at it right now, so I clench the sleeve of my hoodie around my stinging palm and slip through the front door.

"Emily, I'm back. It's Abbie," I croak.

I don't know what I was expecting, but the only answer is a deep, cold well of silence. My head and hand are both throbbing and I can hardly see. There are no darts of light, no newspapers on the floor. Over by the kitchen, there's a slightly-less-dark rectangle in the gloom.

The swinging door is propped open. I *know* it wasn't open when Matt and I left yesterday. Someone must have opened it for me, someone who knew I'd be back. Emily.

The room sways a little when I crouch down in the doorway, looking for the rubber wedge.

"Okay, Emily. I know you're here," I wheeze. It feels like

steel bands are tightening around my chest, and a tremor of heat shakes my body. I peel off my jacket, sliding the sleeve gingerly over my wounded hand and tossing it on the floor. The cuff I've been clutching is dark with blood. I don't know if it's the blood or the fever that makes me woozy, but prickly black dots are circling my vision when—YES!—I find the wedge with my good hand.

The wedge that's holding the door open between past and present.

I lean against the door frame, sliding up with wobbly knees until I'm standing, facing the hallway at the other end of the room, which has stretched out to what seems like one hundred feet away. A high-pitched whine is growing in my ears, like the one on the voice recorder, when I see her in the hall. Her curly hair and old-fashioned dress are silhouetted by an eerie glow, dense and green, as if it's coming from a feeble lamp at the bottom of the ocean.

"Emily," I breathe, my heart hammering. I take a step towards her, and she immediately steps back. Her face becomes visible, and like before, her eyes shine with tears. I take another step, and she nods almost imperceptibly. The room shifts under my feet, and my head swims with the smell of evergreen and cloves, but I focus on her face and the light, staggering across the room with the wedge clutched in my bloody fist, digging into my back pocket with my free hand for the ghost tour flyer.

When I get to the hall, Emily darts into the study where the glow has turned to amber. I stand in the doorway, now shivering uncontrollably, my vision spinning with fever and the feeling of déjà vu. The room looks the same as last time: the oil lamp on the corner of the heavy wooden desk, the Christmas tree... but no Alexander Frost, and no Alex Jr.

Emily stands by her chair, but I can see the chair and the

silver ornaments shining through her. This is where she has dwelled for a hundred years, translucent, unable to act. Stranded in the wavering half-life between the tragic past and an inescapable present.

Until now. Shivering or not, I am a solid, flesh-and-blood person. The flyer is solid too and getting smeared with fresh blood as I unfold it. I reel toward the desk and slap it down on a neat stack of papers, fighting the cloud of buzzing black dots swarming into my vision, blotting everything out.

"Alex. Alexander Frost!" I shout. The sound echoes, joining the ringing in my ears. "Both of you! This is from Emily. She couldn't tell you then, but I'm here now, and I can: a hundred years of this is *enough*. We're all sick of it! It's *Christmas!* You and Dad—Alex—" I'm getting confused. My thoughts are squeezing through my brain like wet cement. "You and Matt, your father, you're—we're—a *family*." The walls ripple as I manage one last gasp. "You can't leave, or you'll *die*. You have to talk it out, find a way to be together and stay home, *you have to stay home*."

The room buckles, pitching me to the floor in a shuddering heap. My teeth are chattering and I struggle to sit up, fighting the darkness closing in. Emily is kneeling next to me now, her eyes wide with hope as Alexander Frost hurries in from the hall and stands over the desk, looking for something. His head tilts and a quizzical furrow appears between his brows. He picks up the flyer and reads it. The blood drains from his face, and he reads it again.

Alex! He yells, spinning wildly, looking around the room, and his eyes stop when they find me.

No, not me... Emily.

She stands, eyes locked with her father's, and in that moment, a gossamer thread spins out between them. Soft shadows shift behind him, and the ghostly faces of Josephine and the little boys emerge in the glow of the lamp, and the tiny strand of light surrounds them too. From the side door, a dark form takes shape, and Alex Jr. steps out of the night, his face uncertain.

Emily is as tense as a bow, and I hold my breath as Alex Sr. holds his hand out to his son, who hesitates, then steps into his father's arms. Both men's faces crumple with joy and relief as Alex Sr. whispers something and drops the blood-stained flyer to the floor.

Emily walks across the room, glowing like a Christmas angel. She joins her family, then turns to me, tears streaming down her face—but this time, they're tears of happiness. Reunited for their first Christmas together in a century, they're fading now, wavering in and out of focus. Emily smiles, then touches her palms together and holds them out as if to catch something.

I toss her the rubber wedge. She catches it with one hand and gives me a little wave with the other as the Frost family dissolves into sparks that circle each other and disappear into the Christmas tree behind them.

The wailing siren in my head rises to a roar, and the icy tide drags me under into inky darkness.

"Here, she's in here!"

"Abbie!"

"Careful, she's bleeding."

"Oh-two, eighty-six percent."

"Did you call Mom?"

"One-oh-four, BP ninety over sixty."

"Get the thermal, and oxygen, stat."

"See that rash? Scarlet fever."

Something jostles me. I'm cold, *so cold...* There's a thing on my face, and it won't come off when I move my head. A red flashing light spears my eyes. Loud voices, someone tucking a blanket around me. Straps.

"One, two, three!"

Is that Dad's voice? Something lifts me up and begins rolling.

"I'll ride with her, Matt. Go home and help your mom, okay?"

More jostling. Scraping sounds. Rumbling movement. I groan, scrunching my eyes against the bright light.

"Abbie, you're okay. I'm right here. You're in an ambulance."

"Dad?" I pry open my eyes. Above the oxygen mask strapped to my face, an EMT is watching spikey lines on a machine. Dad's leaning over me, in uniform. The radio on his shoulder squawks, and he silences it with a quick touch.

"Where... What happened?"

"I was hoping you'd tell *me.* Your mom and the boys got back from the mall around five, and you were gone. You left your phone, so she called all of your friends and nobody knew where you were. She was frantic! She called me, and I left the Supercenter to try and find you."

"I'm sorry." The feeling is returning to my feet, and my hand is throbbing inside thick layers of gauze. The other arm is hooked to an IV. "How did you find me?"

"Matt figured it out. He said you were obsessed with the house on the ghost tour, and—"

"*Me?* He's the one that wanted to go in there in the first place!"

"Well, he was convinced you were there, and after our conversation at lunch today, I thought he might be right.

When I saw your bike and all the blood..." He trails off and a shadow flickers across his face. "That's when I called the ambulance. You scared the crap out of me, Abbie. All of us."

"I'm sorry." I know exactly how scared he's been. *Exactly*. "Where's Matt?"

"He's taking your bike home in the truck. You know, he knew exactly how to get in there. I never figured either one of you for breaking and entering." Dad gives me his stern cop face.

"I entered, but I didn't break," I protest. "The window already had a hole."

"He was really worried, Abbie. He insisted on coming with me to look for you. You guys like to bicker a lot, but when it matters, Matt's all in for you."

"For *us*, Dad. We're a *family*." My eyes seek his. "We're supposed to talk things out and help each other, remember?"

He's quiet for a moment, looking at me thoughtfully. "You're right. Sometimes we forget, but we're all in this together."

The ambulance pulls up to the hospital, and when the doors open, Dad hops out. The EMT murmurs to him, but I only catch a few words: "...hypothermia ... antibiotics ... dehydration..."

"Dad!" Alarmed, I struggle against the blanket and the straps as they unfold the gurney and pull it onto the pavement with a jolt. I grab his arm with my good hand. "You're not leaving, are you? Please! You're not going back to work!"

"No, A-bee-bee. I took tonight off. They'll have to go without police security tonight. And I already gave the next two shifts to someone else."

He holds on to the gurney as we're ushered into the ER, his eyes never leaving my face. "They're saying you have scarlet fever. A good round of antibiotics and a few days' rest, and you'll be good as new." He shakes his head. "Leave it to you to get an old-fashioned disease like that. You know, that used to wipe out entire families."

"I know, Dad." Tears of exhaustion are blurring my vision. "I'm sorry I breathed on everyone. Just promise me you won't go."

He squeezes my hand. "I'll be here all night, Abbie. I promise. I'm going to go get some coffee, and I'll be right back." He clears his throat. "You know, this little prank of yours will probably make the paper. They've got nothing else to write about over there. I can't wait to read Monday's headline!"

I close my eyes. "Me too, Dad. Me too."

Yesterday's News

By Leslie Rush

Leslie Rush grew up near Philadelphia. She moved to El Paso and fell in love with the desert Southwest. When she's not writing or teaching History, Leslie can be found on the road with her husband, exploring the desert and the world of dreams.

More from the Author

Leslie Rush

The Secret of Santa

leslierushwritingbooks.wordpress.com

twitter.com/lesliedrush

instagram.com/leslierush_author

facebook.com/Leslie-Rush-is-Writing-Books

Paw Prints

Kristin Jacques

One

The snow fell thick and fast. Hadley smiled as she rang the doorbell. Chill flakes kissed her cheeks, quickly accumulating and soaking her shoulders. She couldn't remember the last time they'd had a white Christmas. Katie would be so excited by the snow. The door opened, and Hadley clutched the brown string handle of her bag of gifts. They were modest, sweet little gifts that felt inadequate on the stoop of such a grand house, but she kept the smile plastered on her face as her brother opened the door.

"Hey sis! So glad you could make it." It wasn't her brother's tested and patented charming smile but the blinking reindeer nose on his hideous holiday sweater that released the tension in her frame.

"Good to see you, Jake," she said. She kept the brown paper gift bag between them as she leaned in to kiss his cheek. "How's the rest of the fam?"

He hugged her tight as he spoke low in her ear. "Oh, you know, both working late, couldn't be bothered to drive out." Hadley bit back on her retort. Not so long ago, Jake was just like them, until the "incident." Their father and other brother didn't understand, but Hadley did. Hadley understood what transpired better than Jake would ever know.

"House smells great. What's Lauren cooking up this year?" Hadley pushed the subject change. Jake gave her shoulders another squeeze then pulled back, easing the gift bag out of her death grip.

"A roast! She's been working on it all day," he said. He glanced back over his shoulder, in the direction of the kitchen, and Hadley glimpsed the warmth in his expression right before a squealing little girl slammed into her gut.

"Auntie Hadley!"

"Hell—oh my gosh, you are getting so big," said Hadley as she hugged her niece.

"You say that every time you see me!" Katie's giggle was muffled by Hadley's snow-dampened coat.

"Well, you are."

"You saw me last week."

"Yes, and you've put on at least a foot, maybe two," insisted Hadley as she moved them out of the entryway in a three-legged shuffle, Katie glued to her side. Jake's wife, Lauren, waved at her with a dripping baster as they passed the kitchen. It still blew Hadley's mind that Jake had managed to marry a woman like Lauren. She was a finance department head, knew how to cook, and was totally out of his league, though only Jake and Hadley seemed to recognize that.

Hadley shook her head as she flopped down on the sofa with her niece. She managed to untangle herself from Katie long enough to shrug out of her coat and hand it off to Jake, who left the two of them alone.

"Santa bring anything good this year?"

Katie went full pre-teen and rolled her eyes. "Auntie Hadley, I know Santa's not real."

"Look at you, ten years old with such deep wisdom," said Hadley. She gently tweaked Katie's nose. "You'd be surprised by what *is* real."

Katie shrugged. "Maybe, but I did get something awesome!" She wiggled out of Hadley's arms and crawled on her knees to a nook under the massive Christmas tree taking up a third of the living room. Hadley frowned as Katie cooed and extracted a ball of white fluff from under the tree.

The kitten gave a plaintive meow over the disruption to its nap. It was very young, almost too young, as it squirmed in Katie's arms with stubby little legs. Hadley's heart tripped a beat. Her gaze shifted, focused on the deeper shadows beneath the Christmas tree, which lingered in spite of the bright blinking lights strung through the branches. She swallowed the lump in her throat and pasted on a bright smile as Katie plopped back down beside her with her "gift."

"His name's Sir Puffnstuff," said Katie. "Puff for short." She tickled under the kitten's chin, and he purred furiously.

"Adorable," murmured Hadley. She looked up as Jake ducked into the room.

"Lauren says another couple hours until dinner, if that's okay, Hads."

"That's fine," said Hadley, her tone tight as she squinted at Jake. "Nice Christmas gift. Big responsibility for Katie."

Jake's gaze shifted to his daughter, his expression solemn. "She knows. It's been a few months since Plato passed. We figured it was time."

Hadley gnawed the inside of her lip. At least he understood the gravity of the situation, though Hadley secretly hoped Katie never would. "Awfully young?"

Jake met her gaze. "Youngest at the shelter."

Understanding passed between them.

Hadley nodded and turned her attention back to her niece and the playful Puff, now batting at the little girl's fingers. She slid her arm around the girl's shoulders and kissed the top of her head. "He's beautiful," said Hadley.

"So fluffy," said Katie. "I wuv him."

Hadley watched the two play, thinking. Her gaze flickered to the shadows beneath the Christmas tree, where no shadows had any right to be. She knew the gift was not a flippant holiday gesture; Jake knew better. She also knew Katie would love that kitten with everything a little girl had to offer. Still, Hadley couldn't shake the sense of unease, the weight of unspoken rules and judgement unseen.

"Would you like to hear a story about cats?"

"Uh, duh. I love your stories, Auntie Hadley," said Katie.

Beneath the Christmas tree, the shadows deepened.

Hadley resolutely ignored them, dangling her fingers for the kitten to play with. "Sometimes, when a cat is in trouble, when they have a desperate wish, they send out a call."

Katie frowned. "Like a prayer?"

"Something like that," said Hadley.

"So that humans will answer?" Katie asked with a grin.

Hadley gazed down at her niece with solemn hazel eyes. "Someone does." She smoothed the girl's hair back. "Remember when I used to sing 'The Owl and Pussycat?'"

Two

The Owl and the Luci-Cat

The smack of the front door against the wall woke Violet from a dead sleep. She squinted at the invasion of light from the hallway, ears pricking forward as Luci's hand batted the wall for the light switch. The reason for her sightless flailing soon became apparent as she backed further into the apartment, arms wrapped around her paramour of the last three months. She managed to flick the light switch with her pointed-toe shoes, giggling as he lifted her up and carried her toward the bedroom. Violet's ears flattened against her skull, her chest-deep growl ignored as the two humans tangled themselves in one another, mindless of furniture and disapproving felines.

Luci often spoke about Oliver Kingsley. She would sit on the couch after a long day at work with a pint of ice cream that smelled like chocolate and cherries, stroking between Violet's ears as she talked to her about the charming Oliver. How he brought her flowers and sent her little love notes through the office mail clerks. How she was worried she would get in trouble for their romance because Oliver was the son of her boss. How she felt inadequate next to the other women Oliver had dated in the past. The gap of money and society between them, on and on, little human qualms that cats paid no heed to.

Cats were cats, whether they lived in luxury or on the streets. They cared little for the status and wealth of their chosen human. There was only one thing that mattered as far as Violet was concerned, and Luci provided it in spades.

But Oliver Kingsley troubled her. Violet could smell the oily scent of lies rolling off the human's skin. She could scent the feminine reek of other women that were not her Luci. Earlier, she'd watched Luci's painstaking preparations for the evening. Her human had paced the apartment in uncomfortable looking lace coverings, wringing her hands about the interactions she'd face at the holiday office party. Violet could smell her anxiety for weeks leading up to tonight. She'd crawl into Luci's lap and purr until the ozone smell of fizzing nerves began to dissipate, but not tonight.

Tonight, Luci didn't sit for Violet. Tonight, she came home entwined around the liar. She reeked of sour wine.

Violet was worried for her human. Her ears flicked back and forth long after the sounds of the bedroom faded to the deep breathing of slumber. Violet was only a cat. What could she do to save her human? She let out a plaintive meow that echoed through the living room, still lit by Luci's careless passage.

The lights flickered and went out. The night breathed around her. Violet turned and stared at the open window that led out to the fire escape, sensing the presence long before the faint outline appeared.

Every cat knew of the Malkin.

If human children had bedtime stories of Santa Claus and tooth fairies, mother cats whispered stories of the

Malkin to their kittens during the long hours of the night. He was not a deity or a divine spirit, for cats did not believe in such things, but he had walked the Earth when humans believed that cats could be gods, and their belief stuck like flies to honey. Beliefs tended to linger; they shifted form, to legend, to superstition, or to... something else entirely.

Violet rose from the couch and padded across the room, her tail twitching as she clambered out onto the fire escape. The day had been mild for the time of year, but the night air held the bite of winter that nipped and pulled at Violet's long fur. She settled on her paws to keep them warm and stared up into the Malkin's sharp chartreuse eyes.

'You called, little one?'

Violet shifted, settling into a more comfortable position. Had she called for the Malkin? Or had he come because no one else could answer? *'I worry for my human. Her heart is weak, and she courts a liar. I worry he will crush it.'*

The Malkin was silent for a moment before he lifted his great head and scented the air. His pupils thinned at the light of passing cars and lit up businesses below. He heaved a sneeze that caused the whole block to pop and go dark. Violet sighed; so very dramatic. She happened to like the play of neon lights on the glass windows, like great fireflies that lit up the night.

'What would you have me do to this liar?' The Malkin's words were a silky purr in her head, more tiger than housecat, but the Malkin answered to them all, great to small. *'I could eat him. Liars are delicious.'*

Violet's tail flicked with impatience. *'That is positively barbaric.'*

He gave her a feral grin, a reminder of days when humans had sacrificed their criminals to the Malkin for a good harvest or to end a prevalent illness. Violet sneezed, unimpressed.

'I want her to see his truth,' she said.

'Ah, so simple a favor,' said the Malkin. *'Let's hope it's not one you regret.'*

Violet's ears flattered at the warning. The Malkin stood and stretched, but instead of his body elongating with the movement, it contracted until he was merely twice her size. He shimmied his still considerable bulk through the open window and headed for Luci's room.

Curiosity tugged at her whiskers. Violet followed. After all, she was a cat, and some sayings held true. By the time she caught up to the Malkin, he'd jumped up onto the bed and sat upon Luci's chest.

Her human frowned in her sleep, but the Malkin's actions didn't wake her.

'Can't she feel you sitting on her?'

'No, little one. To a human, I weigh no more than a bad dream.' The Malkin opened his mouth and breathed a faint white fog that curled around Luci's face and sank into her skin. Her human whimpered.

The Malkin began to sing, his deep sinuous voice winding through the air. *'The Owl and the Pussycat went to sea, in a beautiful pea green boat.'*

'They took some honey, and plenty of money, wrapped up in a five-pound note.'

Violet lay down and listened. The salt and fish scent of the sea teased her nostrils, a memory buried in instinct and longing. A soft briny breeze stroked through her fur and stirred the scattered papers and receipts on the coffee table. In her mind, Violet could see the words gain form: the Liar in a coat of fine brown and white feathers, and her human in a fluffy robe that mimicked violet's own fur. The Owl carried the Pussycat to an elegant craft bobbing on the shore of a sparkling blue green sea.

The Owl held up an oddly shaped guitar, plucking the strings with long white talons.

"O lovely Pussy! O Pussy, my love, what a beautiful Pussy you are." And the Pussycat laughed at his antics, even as the Owl's eyes strayed to another feminine figure stretched out on the beach.

"You elegant fowl! How charmingly sweet you sing! O let us be married! Too long we have tarried: But what shall we do for a ring?"

The Pussycat smoothed her hands down the Owl's chest, but his gaze continued to wander, first to the swaying gait of a lady dove as she walked to the market, then to another pussycat stretched out to bathe in the sun. Pussycat's smile faded as she saw his distracted mien.

"Owl?"

"Pardon me, I'll be back, my sweet," he told her, stroking his talons along her sleek cheek. The Pussycat leaned into his touch, still smitten, still enamored. She settled into the boat and waited.

She waited as the sun slowly sank down to the horizon. She waited, shoulders drooped, as the sun set. Beneath the underbelly of the dusky night before moonrise, Pussycat sighed. Her head perked up at a sound.

The Malkin's voice intoned once more. '*And hand in hand, on the edge of the sand, they danced by the light of the moon, the moon, the moon, they danced by the light of the moon.*'

Pussycat rose, her face stark, as she watched Owl dance beneath the moonlight with another woman in his arms. Tears ran down Luci's face as she slept.

Violet startled at the buzz of a cellphone. The Malkin

dispersed with a Cheshire Cat grin into the swirling fog of the dream. Luci woke with a start. She peered at the glowing red numbers of the clock with a groan as she wiped the tears off her cheeks. She sniffled, lying awake and quiet in the bed, when the phone buzzed again. She frowned and picked it up. Not her phone. The liar's phone. Luci squinted at the lit-up screen and froze.

Violet watched her human's heart fracture to pieces.

Luci rolled from the bed and tossed the phone onto Oliver's chest. The man woke with a yelp. The shouts began. Violet wiggled under the bed as they rowed. Guilt gnawed at her at the sobs in Luci's voice. She stayed under the bed until the liar stalked from the apartment and slammed the door in his wake.

In the ensuing quiet, Violet slunk from beneath the bed. Luci sat on the edge of her mattress, her hands pressed against her face. Violet climbed up and crawled into her human's lap. Luci gathered her in her arms and pressed her wet face into Violet's fur.

The cat found she didn't mind. She purred and licked her human's face, but the scent of hurt was iron sharp on the air. Nothing Violet did for her human made it go away.

Katie tugged on her bottom lip. "Auntie Hadley, I don't understand."

"What don't you understand, sweet pea?" Hadley held the sleeping Puff in her lap now as Katie listened to her story.

"Why was Luci so angry with the liar?"

Blood rushed to Hadley's cheeks. "We'll expand on that conversation when you're older."

Katie snickered. "I'm kidding, Auntie Hadley, I get it." She rolled her shoulders. "I know the password to the Netflix."

"Lord save me from precocious ten-year-olds," Hadley muttered. "Do you want to hear more?"

Katie blinked and her eyes lit up. "There's more?"

Three

Cat on a Hot Rod Roof

Eric paused, wrench in hand. There was that noise again, a small desperate plea coming from beneath the hood of the old wagon. Carefully, holding his tool high like a weapon, he wedged the hood up higher and higher. Nothing jumped out at him. The sound went quiet. Eric made a face and used the hook to prop up the hood, a terrible suspicion forming as he took a step back. He crossed his arms and waited.

A few minutes of silence passed before he heard it again, louder this time, unmuffled by the car hood. He took a breath and slowly peeked his head over the lip of the hood to peer inside the engine block. There was the source of the noise, the terrified mewling of a kitten. Poor baby must have taken shelter there for the night before the wagon got towed to his shop. Eric held out his hand, trying to coax it forward with soft clucks, but the little gray face ducked back among the tangle of hoses and wires.

He headed to the back of the shop, fishing a can of tuna from the small kitchenette he kept stocked for busy lunch breaks. It didn't take long before the scent of fish lured the kitten out. Eric scooped it out of the engine and set it down on the floor where hunger won out over fear. The little gray kitten eagerly ate the offering of tuna while Eric looked it over. A lift of her tail told him it was a girl, her smoky fur streaked with grease. She was a scrawny little thing, far too young to be on her own. A chunk of her ear was missing, the price of living on unforgiving streets. Eric left her to eat. He poured hot water into a bowl, got a washcloth and mild soap. The van could wait. Not like it was going anywhere.

He caught the kitten before she could flee again, settling her on his lap as he patiently cleaned her fur, rubbing under her chin until her little body shook with purrs. Her fur was a gray so dark it was almost a smoky blue.

"Blue it is," he told her.

"Wait, Auntie Hadley, how does this connect with Luci and Violet?"

"Do you want to hear the story or not?"

"Yes—"

"Then shush."

He set up Blue as a shop cat. Within a week, she no longer hid under car hoods unless Eric was working under them. Blue would come up and butt her head against him while he worked until he relented and scratched her ears.

The week turned into weeks, and then months. Blue was no longer a kitten, but she stayed with Eric.

Soon there was a niche in the kitchenette just for her food, a place for her litter box in the hall, far from customers and cars. During the day, between changing oil and replacing hoses, he would stop and stroke Blue's soft head. Sometimes she would crawl on his shoulder while he did paperwork at the desk, wrapping herself around his neck like a living scarf. At night, he would bundle her up in the front seat of the car and take her home. Blue enjoyed the rumble and warmth from the inside of the car a great deal more than she had from the outside. Eric made her feel safe. She could feel the connection between them every time his calloused fingers scratched behind her ears.

One day, a sleek, shining car was towed into Eric's shop. Her human was excited to see the vehicle, though Blue saw nothing special about it. She curled up on the roof of the car as her human explored under the hood. She enjoyed the sounds of his delight, but she didn't like the humans who stared at him from across the street, lean and hungry as they peered into Eric's open garage doors. They reminded Blue of the older, meaner cats who had circled and bullied her when she was too small to fight back. A twinge of forgotten pain went through her scarred ear.

Blue shifted, uncomfortable with their attention on her human. She stared, unblinking, until they finally moved on, but their scent lingered on the air.

Her senses remained on high alert for the remainder of the day, waiting for the scent to fade. But as the day gave way to night, it remained, strong enough to sting her delicate nose.

She dropped down off the hood of the car and began to meow.

Eric wheeled out from out under the car. “Hey, little one, we’ll get going soon. Not every day I get to play with such a sweet machine.” He patted her on the head, deaf to her insistent meows.

Blue huffed and paced, her nose twitching as the ugly sour scent grew stronger and stronger. Eric did not shut the garage doors. The night was still warm from the day’s sun. The honks and purrs of traffic were distant to this secluded part of the neighborhood off the main street, with only the light of a lone streetlamp to keep the shadows at bay.

Blue watched as they emerged from the dark, her fur puffed up in response to the violence they oozed like sweat. She took a swipe at Eric’s bare arm. Her claws left bloody tracks. Her human yelped, angry until he saw the shadow-eyed humans stalking into his shop.

“Hey, man, I’m sorry but we’re closed for the day,” said Eric. The shadow-eyed humans looked at one another, a silent signal passing between them, before one of them stepped forward.

“That’s a’ight homes, we’re just looking for spare parts.”

Eric didn’t have a chance to react before one of them ducked behind him. Blue hissed at the dull thud of metal against flesh and bone. Her human dropped, a bloody lump at the back of his head where one of the shadow-eyed humans had struck him with one of his tools.

Blue’s claws scrambled across the cement floor of the garage as she ducked under the car. Her heart pounded against her ribs. The shadow-eyed men danced around her human like ghouls, gibbering and laughing. She feared they would kill him before they took what they wanted and left.

Blue didn’t want her human to die.

‘What would you give to save your human?’

Blue looked up into the luminous green eyes of the Malkin, wide as hubcaps. They were the only corporeal piece of him, the rest of him a swirling mass of dark vapors to fit his massive form in the narrow space.

She studied the Malkin. He smelled of wild dark places, of rot and ashes, of lightning and rain and the fresh spilt blood of a kill. He made her nervous, like those lean feral cats who had cornered her long ago and took their price in flesh.

Her attention shifted back to her human, who groaned with pain, shifting on the ground. One of the shadow-eyed humans kicked him in the stomach. Blue hissed.

'*I would give my life.*' She bowed her head to the Malkin, waiting for the snap of teeth.

The Malkin chuckled. '*One life will do. Save the rest for a rainy day.*'

Puzzled by his words, Blue looked up as a wide, coarse tongue swathed across her entire head. The lick left her tired and weak, but she was alert enough as the smoky mass of the Malkin slithered out from under the car.

He coalesced behind the shadow men and waited. They didn't notice him at first, until the tiny quailing prey part of their minds tuned in to the predator that waited behind them. One by one they froze, eyes wide as they remembered why humans lit fires against the dark of night.

The Malkin waited for their awareness to peak before he rose up and clamped his jaws on one of their heads. Blue was grateful her human was unconscious for this part. She ignored the ensuing chaos as the shadow men screamed and tried to run. The lone streetlamp snapped off, plunging the area into darkness. The shadow men dissolved into terror of their own imaginations as they listened to the sounds of the Malkin picking them off one by one, surrounded only by each other's choked off cries and the wet tear of flesh beneath claws. Cats, however, had excellent eyesight in the dark.

Blue wrinkled her nose in distaste. It was not her place to criticize the Malkin's methods. She curled up on her human's chest, listening to the steady beat of his heart. He was safe. That is what mattered.

The cries of the shadow men drew the human law, but by the time the flash of blue and red filled the shop, the streetlamp had snapped back on. There was not so much as a drop of blood to be found. Efficient, Blue thought, though she could smell the hint of truth in the air. Beyond the streetlamp, at the edge of the woods behind the garage, Blue saw the Malkin's tail as it disappeared. Eric groaned under her. Blue began to purr.

A young woman in an officer's uniform crouched beside Eric, shining a pen light in his eyes. "Sir, what happened here? Your neighbors called in a noise complaint."

Eric grew more alert. He sucked in a breath. "These guys jumped me. Said they wanted spare parts."

The officer glanced around and gave an appreciative whistle at the sight of the car behind Eric. "Probably wanted a piece of that hotrod."

Eric grunted as he sat up on his elbows. "Pretty, isn't she?" He noticed Blue sitting on his chest. "Oh, thank god," he said, picking her up.

"Loyal, that one. She was sitting on your chest when I came in, guarding you," said the officer. A look of concern crossed her face as she gently reached up and brushed Eric's bruised head. "Hey, you should get this looked at. Make sure you don't have a concussion. I'll call you an ambulance."

"No, I'll be okay. Some Tylenol—"

"Oh, that wasn't a suggestion. If you don't want the ambulance, I'll give you a ride," said the officer.

Eric smiled at her; his eyes were slightly glazed. "Mind if I bring my cat?"

"Is that the concussion talking?"

"I swear she's car trained," said Eric.

The officer bit back a grin. "Why am I not surprised? Let me call this in and I'll drive you to the ER, mister...?"

"Harris, Eric Harris," he said.

"I'm Officer Montoya," she said.

"What's your first name?" Blue watched the exchange with partially closed eyes. She purred at her human's rising pulse and the answering heat in the officer's scent.

"Anna-Marie," she said. "Though most everybody calls me Anna."

"Would you be up for a coffee later, Anna?"

The officer cleared her throat and blushed. "Why don't I get you to the hospital first, sir?" She gestured to her squad car. "I'll be right there."

Eric shifted Blue to his shoulder, humming as he headed to the officer's vehicle. Behind him, Blue watched the officer crouch down, a puzzled look on her face as she studied the enormous pawprint left in a puddle of oil on the garage floor.

Katie grinned. "Eric and Anna, sitting in a tree, k-i-s-s-i-n-g!"

Hadley bit back a snort. Of all the parts of the story for her niece to focus on, it *would* be the hint of romance between those two. Katie was silent for a moment as she rubbed her kitten's belly.

"The Malkin is kind of scary," she said, her voice quiet and small.

"Yes," said Hadley. "Yes, he is."

"Auntie Hadley?"

Hadley shifted her niece closer so that she could rest her chin on top of Katie's head. "I told you, you'd be surprised by what is real."

Four

Something About Cats and Old Books

Hadley pinched the bridge of her nose against the oncoming migraine. She'd been at the library since six in the morning, and here she was, still burning the midnight oil as the clock edged closer to one in the morning. She sighed. She had a paper due for class. When you were plugging away at a master's degree, sacrifices had to be made, and sleep was the first to go. At least Sampson was here for company.

The old tabby had wandered into the library one winter, and the staff hadn't had the heart to kick him out. Instead they pooled their resources to fix him up, get him shots, and keep him fed. There was even a chore wheel for litter box duty. It amused Hadley to no end that the library had its own cat mascot, but the patrons loved him, and the staff loved him, and Sampson never clawed the spines. Very important criteria in one's library cat.

She petted him as she walked by, pushing the cart full of her research material that needed to be re-shelved before she left. Her boss had had a hissy fit at all the books she left stacked by her desk. She didn't think anyone would miss the twenty or so books she had squirreled away, but her boss insisted she return her materials at the end of the night in case any patrons went looking for them.

At least the class was interesting enough. She had picked up the course on religious iconography to round out her history studies. When the paper topic first came up, she'd been sitting at her desk, mulling over what the heck to write about as Sampson rubbed against her leg, looking for attention. Her professor was surprisingly receptive to a paper on the role of felines in religion throughout the centuries, though she was certain it had cemented his opinion that she was an eccentric cat lady.

Hadley didn't care; the subject was fascinating, from their place of worship in ancient Egypt to the Dark Ages where they were considered carriers of the Black Death. She wondered what the ancient Egyptians would think of how people worshipped cats today, via YouTube videos and memes.

The thought made her chuckle as she heaved the thicker volumes back into place. The impact dislodged a slim volume that had slipped behind the others at the back of the stack. Hadley frowned as she picked it up and adjusted her glasses. Odd, there wasn't a call number on the book. She turned it over to read the cover.

The Malkin

The illustration on the front looked more like a sinister German fairytale than a reference book. She'd never heard of anything called the Malkin. Curious, she flipped open the book.

To her surprise, the pages weren't printed, but handwritten in elegant but legible script. The thin tome gave off a sense of time, from the delicate crinkle of worn pages and the musty scent of age to the faded ink and frayed binding. She wondered where the library had acquired it. Some of the older materials were donations from estate auctions, but they were kept in a collections room to preserve their condition. Had someone stuffed this behind the reference books with the intent to steal it later?

She could understand why as she flipped through the beautifully illustrated pages inked in styles that echoed the masters of centuries past, of idyllic natural settings and snapshots of people in everyday situations. The common factor between them all were the cats. They lurked in corners, nearly hidden and entirely missable but always there. Her gaze strayed to the script.

Hadley read aloud, her own voice comforting in the empty library. "No one knows the exact origins of the Malkin. He is an entity borne of human faith and worship from before the hearts of man turned away from feline deities. The Malkin is something darker, an avenging entity who preyed on evil men and punished the wicked. This also changed as time went on, and the Malkin slipped from human memory. It is said that, fed up with the ever-changing nature of human hearts, this feline entity now only answers the pleas of his descendants, the modern wildcat and the common housecat. If you ever find your cat companion staring at nothing in the room, there is a chance they are holding a private conversation with the Malkin, who can only be seen by those humans he chooses to appear to."

The meow made Hadley jump. She clutched the book to her chest as her pulse thundered. Sampson jumped onto her half-empty cart with another squeaking meow. His tail thrashed.

Hadley smiled and stroked his head. "Sorry, am I giving away state secrets here?"

Sampson stilled. His pupils contracted as his gaze locked on the space behind Hadley.

"Oh, very funny," she said. Still, the hair on the back of her neck stood on end.

'I do not find it amusing.'

Hadley shrieked and dropped to the floor. Her head shot up and she froze, her brain trying to process what she was seeing. Her mind had to wrap around the size first, its bulk somehow compressed into the narrow isle of the library, where the rules of reality seemed to lose focus and warp at the edges. A hairless cat, the wrinkled folds of its skin the shiny black of burnt charcoal. The cat peered down at her with imperious green eyes the exact shade of the absinthe she'd once seen at the hipster bar down the street from her apartment, and he was the size of an SUV. Hadley cringed and curled around the book still plastered to her chest as the massive cat creature leaned toward her, its mouth open to reveal teeth as long as her forearm.

'This knowledge is not meant for humans,' he said, his voice a booming baritone that should have made the windows rattle. The cat creature hadn't spoken out loud; his voice had wedged itself directly inside her head. His words continued to rattle around in her skull. *'Where did you find this book?'*

Hadley gaped at him, her thoughts careening into each other as she tried to pull herself together. "I—I found it behind the other books," she whispered, grateful she'd emptied her bladder earlier, or she'd be sitting in a puddle of urine right now. The muscles of her belly quivered, drawn tight, as the creature shimmied forward between the stacks. He extended his claws to grip the carpet and pull his body forward. Her gaze widened. This had to be the Malkin. There was no other conclusion her terrified brain could reach.

'How much did you read?' that booming voice snarled in her head. He sounded so very angry, and somehow, hurt. As if she'd intruded on something private.

Hadley clapped her hands over her ears and sobbed. "Please, I didn't mean any harm. Please!"

The Malkin roared. Hadley screamed and ducked her head, certain she was about to die.

An angry yowl answered. Hadley flinched at the brush of a tail against her nylons. She peeked out from between her fingers. Sampson stood in front of her, his tail snapping back and forth as he faced off with the Malkin. The library cat growled low; his fur fluffed, on end. The Malkin sat back on his haunches, considering the much smaller creature.

'Sampson says you are one of his humans. Is this true?'

One of his humans? Hadley managed to find her voice. "Ye-yes."

The Malkin's lip curled. He narrowed his eyes, bigger than serving platters, as he glanced around the stacks. His wide flat nose twitched as it scented the air.

'This building smells of dust and secrets. A wealth of knowledge at the tip of one's claws,' said the Malkin, a note of respect in his deep mental voice. *'He has free reign of this place?'*

"Sampson lives here," said Hadley. "Everyone loves him."

The huge creature sighed. *'Ah, to be worshipped again.'* There was a note of longing that echoed through her mind. Hadley swallowed hard, determined not to say anything that might jeopardize her precarious position, though she wondered what culture once worshipped such a nightmare.

Sampson nosed under Hadley's arm until she gave him enough wiggle room to crawl into her lap. She held him to her chest, unable to stop shaking. It only got worse as the Malkin turned his attention back to her.

'Be that as it may, this book no longer has a place in human hands,' he said.

Hadley swallowed and pushed the book across the floor. The Malkin laid a huge paw on it and slid it beneath him.

'Now, as for what you read—'

Sampson burst into a series of broken meows. The Malkin listened carefully. *'We have a deal.'*

Deal? What deal? Sampson seemed to have protected her so far, but she couldn't imagine what deal the cat would have made to save her from the Malkin's wrath. She yelped as the Malkin's face shoved far too close into her personal space. She caught the scent of long dead things mixed with sweet grass, musk, and wildflowers.

'There will always be a cat to roam these shelves, to soak in the knowledge, and to guard their secrets.'

Hadley thought about telling the Malkin this was a public library and that nothing was secret, but, like a regular housecat, he seemed the sort you didn't tell anything to. A larger concern was making sure a cat remained in the library. Sampson was an older male, at least seven years old already by the vet's tally, and cats did not live forever. Hadley hadn't even planned to work at the library beyond earning her master's degree.

'You will do this, or I will make my displeasure known.'

Hadley didn't have to ask if the Malkin meant her specifically or the staff in general; she could feel the impact of the word in her bones. Looking into those ancient, alien, predatory eyes, Hadley knew she never wanted to know the Malkin's displeasure.

"I will."

The lights flickered above her. The Malkin disappeared between one flicker and the next. Sampson stayed with the shaking Hadley until the other librarians arrived the next morning.

Hadley never forgot what Sampson did for her that night, though she tried to dismiss the encounter as a stress-induced fever dream. Sometimes she would wake up in the night, sweating, remembering the Malkin's insidious voice inside her head. Years later, when Sampson finally passed, Hadley went to the local animal shelter. None of the librarians argued about getting another cat. It just felt right.

Katie stared at Hadley, her lips parted in equal parts shock and disbelief. The little girl shook herself, clamping her mouth shut with an adorable scowl.

"No way. I'm not buying it," Katie hissed. She folded her arms, nearly dislodging the sleeping kitten on her lap. "There's no way that happened. The Malkin's not real."

Hadley glanced at the deep shadows under the Christmas tree. Maybe she *was* just imagining things. She leaned in close and spoke softly in her niece's ear. "If he's not, why are you whispering?"

The lower branches of the Christmas tree shivered as if some large, unseen entity had stifled a laugh. Hadley pursed her lips.

"We could stop now—"

"No!" Katie grabbed her arm. "What comes next? What happened to Violet and Blue? Does your library still have a cat?" In her lap, the kitten stirred and stretched.

"He's a kitten now, but one day, he'll get old, like your dad's cat, Plato," said Hadley. The kitten's ear twitched.

"Don't cats have nine lives?" Katie stroked the back of Puff's ear. "Maybe he can spend another one here."

Hadley didn't look at the shadows under the tree, but she could feel the weight of attention on her.

FIVE

THE MIDNIGHT TRADE

The Mistress was sneaking out again. Old Blue could hear her quiet steps as she crept through the house, past her sleeping parents' room. The Mistress closed the front door of the house with slow, practiced movements, then rushed down the front steps to meet her friends on their bikes.

Normally, Old Blue didn't bother none with the Mistress sneaking about. The girl was nearly ten years old now, and curious as any cat. She snuck out many nights to explore the quiet suburbs with her friends, riding her bike under the stars. Old Blue encouraged such antics, but tonight was different.

The Mistress had been to the old mill. Old Blue could smell it on her, the dark thing that lurked there, unseen in the revealing light of day. It was an old dark thing, long spoiled by malice, jealous of the living. It squatted in the old mill, stirring at night, snapping up any creature fool enough to wander into its range. The Mistress planned to go there tonight with her naïve friends, to scare themselves as children do by exploring a creepy old building that wouldn't really hurt them.

Except this one would. Old Blue paced. Could she risk the Mistress being scared enough not to venture inside? Scared children had a habit of being stupidly brave when they egged one another on.

She stalked past the room with the girl's sleeping parents, the familiar scent of grease and metal shavings giving her no comfort this night. Even if the girl's parents woke to find her gone, they wouldn't know where to find what was lost, not until it was too late.

Old Blue heaved herself up on the windowsill, the window thankfully open to the let in the cool spring air as she wiggled out through the gap. The children were long gone on their bikes, but their scent still hung heavy on the air, of sugar-sticky hands and cut grass. Urgency nipped at Old Blue's worn paws as she slipped through the opening and landed on the ground below. Every cat in a fifty-mile radius knew where the old mill was, and they knew to avoid it.

Age slowed her trotting gait, the ache of sixteen years in her bones, but the Mistress needed her, so Old Blue forced herself to go faster. She padded through the sleeping neighborhood, slipping between the pools of light from scattered porch lamps, through the quiet early morning streets of the main road. The shops were still shuttered against the night, until the tall, lean brick buildings gave way to boxier, squat structures with the scent of wood shavings and faint sharp sting of cleaning chemicals. Eventually those buildings, too, fell away to the long dark stretch of grass and grazing cows, dotted by towering lamps, few and far between, that whined throughout the night. Her scarred ear twitched as she drew closer to the old mill. The building seemed to breathe in the dark, crouching low on the pavement with the patience of an ambush predator. Old Blue slowed, sniffing for the Mistress. She slunk down, her hair standing on end.

The children were already inside.

Old Blue scuttled forward, her belly low to the ground, ears flat against her head. She could sense that wicked old thing moving in the dark, unseen by the Mistress and her innocent friends. It was closing in on them, too close, far too close. Old Blue yowled in the dark.

'What would you trade to me this time, little one?'

The Malkin's eyes glittered from the dark entrance of the mill. Old Blue stood up, her meow long, drawn, and sad.

She had been there when her humans, Eric and Anna-Marie, brought the Mistress home, a little squirming bundle of grunts and squawks and wrinkled pink skin. Old Blue had circled the rocking chair with that bundle for days, uncertain, until she got close enough to stare into those wide gray eyes, the same color as her fur. She'd nosed that soft little cheek as tiny fingers curled into her fur. That day, Old Blue gave the tiny human her heart.

She was there as the Mistress grew, through those first wobbly steps, through patient tugs and dolly outfits. She was there through sweet, tender cuddles, when the Mistress smelled like milk and cookies and the world held its breath while she slept. Old Blue was there for the day the Mistress lost her grandmother, listening to her chest-deep sobs and wishing more than anything that she could take her human's hurt away. She was there for broken bones, skinned knees, and stubbed toes. Now, as her human grew older and Old Blue's bones began to ache, her Mistress lifted her with such care, cradling her close for forehead kisses.

The dark something crept closer, and Old Blue felt her connection pulled taut.

'I will give you the rest of my lives,' she said.

The Malkin paused, his great head tilted, intrigued. '*All your lives, little one? You do not have many years left of this one.*'

Old Blue hated that he would tease her in a moment with danger so near the Mistress. She stared up into those endless green eyes without hesitation. '*Better one life, full of love, than seven more lives without the one I chose.*'

The Malkin held the stare for a breath longer. A cat could hold the stare of any being, in all of creation and beyond perceived reality, but Old Blue could not read the emotion in those ancient eyes.

'*Very well then.*' The Malkin bent over her and lathed the length of her body with his rough tongue. The after effect of seven lives stripped away made Old Blue slump to the ground, her head fuzzy. Inside the old mill, she heard the first child scream as the terrible wicked thing sprang at its prey.

The Malkin turned and stalked into the mill. A heavy silence rolled outward into the night, the bated breath of two predators sizing each other up. But where the dark something was old and touched by vile energies, the Malkin was ancient. The ghost of a god lived inside his skin, powered by the prayers of thousands of long dead humans.

Old Blue watched the doorway of the old mill as the Mistress and her friends ran out into the night, their faces pale with what they had and hadn't quite seen. There was a tear in the Mistress's sleeve and a long scratch down her arm but otherwise, she was healthy and whole. Old Blue's whiskers pushed forward with relief.

The three children stared at one another, their reactions delayed by the stillness, when sound erupted from the old mill. Unearthly shrieks and thunderous roars cracked the night like fireworks as the security light erupted in a shower of sparks. The children screamed and clung to each other, too scared to run, until finally, the terrible sounds ended, and the peaceful silence of the night resumed.

The children hustled to their bikes, stumbling and panting in the near pitch black as they scurried back to the safety of their beds. Old Blue waited for what they couldn't see. It did give her a small sense of relief when the Malkin padded, victorious, from the old mill.

He lay on the grass beside Old Blue and washed his paws. '*You're certain your human was worth the price?*'

'*Yes,*' said Old Blue, '*because she is mine. Now, I need to go.*'

The Malkin perked his head up. '*Are you certain? There's leftovers.*'

Old Blue sneezed, certain she didn't remotely share the same sense of taste with the Malkin, but there was something lonely in his question that deserved an honest answer.

'*She saw something tonight, my human,*' said Old Blue, staring off in the direction the children had fled. '*She will need my purrs and my softness when those memories scratch inside her mind during the long hours of the night.*'

'*You really love that human?*' The Malkin didn't sound incredulous, merely curious. It was their trademark trait.

'*Yes,*' said Old Blue.

She bid the Malkin farewell. The walk back was much longer than before. Her bones ached fiercely when she finally squeezed through the open window. Each step hurt as she crept past the sleeping parents and made one last painful leap onto the Mistress's bed. The little girl stiffened at first, still wide awake, as she fingered the band-aid on her arm. At the sight of Old Blue, her chin trembled before the Mistress pulled her close and buried her face in fur.

Old Blue sighed. This was where she belonged, for however long it lasted.

Katie failed to cover her sniffle. She looked down and away, lifting Puff to press her face into his fur. The little kitten nudged his face against her cheek.

"I'm sorry, that one was a little sad," said Hadley. The sight of the two of them made her smile.

"It was wonderful," said Katie. She glanced at Hadley with Puff tucked under her chin. "Do you think Plato ever saved Daddy like that?"

Hadley coughed to hide her grimace. "Well, now that you mention it," she said, with a quick look around the room to make sure her brother wasn't listening, "did your daddy ever tell you the story of how he got Plato?"

SIX

A Cat May Look At Kinglsey

Jacob Kingsley was in a foul mood. His father had been on his ass all day about something or other, questioning every decision he made until Jacob began to doubt his own business acumen. His mother was in a tizzy that he'd declined an invite to the family Christmas party. The last thing he wanted was to spend an evening pandering to his father's rich friends for favors he didn't care about. But the cherry on top of his day had been Oliver, storming into his office at two in the morning to rant about the poor secretary he'd gone off with at the office party. Really, did he think he was remotely discreet? But his brother liked the quiet ones, and he'd set his sights on that little mousy girl the day she got hired.

He sighed as his brother changed clothes, still ranting from their office bathroom. He couldn't very well go home to Angelica with that shade of lipstick on his collar. At least the secretary had had the sense to throw his ass out of her house when she'd realized she was the other woman. Jacob should send her a fruit basket or something.

"Ollie, it's beyond late, and I've had a long day. I'm heading out," called Jacob.

"Hey, Merry Christmas, big bro," called Ollie. It didn't matter that he didn't say it back.

He just didn't see much point in mistletoe and holiday cheer anymore. Barely thirty and he was already a hardened cynic. Jacob made his way through the lobby, calling an obligatory farewell to the building's janitorial staff. At least he knew they worked hard for their paycheck. He stepped out of the building and inhaled a deep breath of late night city air. There was a freshness to the air in the early morning hours, before it clogged up with grease, street food, and exhaust. There were barely any people out at this hour to fill the sidewalks or the street. It was honestly his favorite time of day.

A stray cat rubbed against his pant leg. Jacob kicked it away in disgust. A mangy gray tiger stumbled and fell from the blow; damn thing probably had all sorts of parasites. Jacob sneered at the animal. Damn cats bred worse than rabbits in the city. He'd have to call animal control tomorrow to catch the damn thing. Oh, that's right, he'd have to call animal control the day after tomorrow, since tomorrow was an actual holiday.

At least he could sleep. Jacob walked through the empty car garage, ticking off the tasks he could accomplish on his day off, when the creepy crawly sensation of being followed slithered along his spine. He stopped and turned around, his spine ramrod straight as he searched the empty garage. The lights in the far back corner flickered on and off.

Jacob shook his head. The long day had gotten to him. His car was in sight, only thirty feet or so away. His pace quickened ever so slightly. A gust of warm damp air ruffled his hair, teasing his nose with the smell of carrion and wet fur. Sweat flushed his skin. Jacob broke into a run. He didn't know why, but his tired brain decided to ignore all sense until he was ensconced in the safety of his car. He ran so hard, he slammed into the side of the Lexus, fumbling with the key fob before finally jumping in and slamming the door shut behind him. Jacob clutched the steering wheel, his heart thundering in his chest until the absurdity of the situation caught up to him and he burst out laughing.

The lights in the garage went dark. Jacob closed his mouth with a click of his teeth and pushed the ignition button. The car stuttered as the engine turned over and failed to catch.

"You've got to be kidding me," he muttered. He flicked the headlights on. Massive green eyes stared at him through his windshield. Jacob barely had time to suck in a shocked breath before a huge paw ripped his car door off. Jacob's scream dried up in his throat as the creature shoved its face in through to door with a snarl.

'Has your time on this Earth taught you nothing, cretin?'

The voice boomed everywhere and nowhere. It filled his head and spilled out, vibrating the leather seat beneath him. A trickle of urine soaked through his pants.

One of the sewer-cap-sized paws suddenly pushed down on his chest, claws the size of butcher's knives sliding free to prick at his two-thousand-dollar, now piss-stained, suit. Jacob finally found his voice and let out a hoarse scream. The creature sneered at him

'Don't fuck with cats.'

"Auntie Hadley!" Katie tried and failed to look properly scandalized. "That's a dollar in the swear jar."

"Oops. Don't tell your dad, and I'll put in five. Deal?"

Her niece's smile was a little too smug. "Deal."

The monster opened its maw. Jacob flinched back, bracing himself for pain. Instead, a white fog emerged. It wrapped around his head, thick with the scent of sandalwood and sage. It sank into his skin. Jacob's eyes rolled up into his head.

His awareness slowly prickled. Jacob groaned.

The sound was wrong in his throat, as if his vocal chords were wrapped in steel wool. The sound rumbled in his chest. He opened his eyes. The world looked wrong, far too large, the edges sharper, the colors strange and surreal. Jacob lifted his hand to wipe his eyes—or he tried to. His body pitched sideways as paws went out from under him.

Paws? Jacob peered down at his body with a growing sense of horror. He scrabbled back, fur dragging over the pavement as his paws slid over the cold, snow-slick stones. Thoughts collided, his mind spinning in useless circles as he looked over his gray tiger-striped body, his short fur matted and dirty from the street. Jacob mewled, shuffling back and forth as he tried to make unfamiliar muscles do what he wanted them to do. It took him several minutes to stand up on his shaky legs.

Slowly, he got a rough sense of his surroundings, deep in a trash-strewn alley. He stumbled toward the sidewalk, appalled by the weakness in his limbs. His belly ached for food. He'd never felt hunger like this, nor the terrible sensation of fleas that crawled under his matted fur. He could feel the things moving on his skin, biting him, but no matter how he scratched at himself, he couldn't get rid of them.

Jacob walked out onto the sidewalk. He needed help. Somebody had to help him.

A woman in high heels walked by.

'Help me, please, help me, I'm human,' he called to her, but she held a hand over her nose and walked faster. This behavior quickly became a pattern as people rushed past or outright ignored him. Why did nobody see him? Why did nobody hear him?

A little girl tried to pet him until her mother yelped and nudged him away with her boot. "Don't touch him, honey, he's gross."

But worse still was the dog. Jacob barely registered the snarl and warning call from the dog's owner before the slobbering beast charged at him. Jacob scrambled back with a frightened hiss, the dog nipping and chasing him until he dove back into the alley, wedging his body between two trash cans as the dog's idiotic owner finally wrestled him back on his leash. Even after they were gone, Jacob stayed where he was, too scared to move. How had this happened to him? Why had this happened to him? He wasn't a bad person. Compared to the rest of his family, he was nearly a saint.

Memory stirred of the monstrous beast who had ripped off his car door. What *was* that thing? His human mind didn't have a freaking clue, but the cat mind, the mind he didn't know quite what to make of, had an answer.

The Malkin. He shivered without really knowing why.

Jacob wondered if he was stuck like this. The temperature began to drop, fresh snowflakes falling between buildings to soak into the wet newspaper strewn across the alley. Jacob wandered from his hiding place, shivering against the cold as he searched for somewhere even remotely warm.

"Hey, little fella. Where did you come from?"

Jacob jumped at the voice. There was merely a chuckle in response. "I won't bite. You're welcome to share my spot. It's gonna be a cold one tonight. I think I might have a tuna pouch in here."

He followed the voice to a lean to against the alley wall. A middle-aged man in ratty flannel and fingerless gloves dug through an equally worn backpack. The man's clothes were as filthy as Jacob, clearly one of the city's many homeless residents. Despite his appearance, the scent of soap tickled Jacob's sensitive nose. The man's fingernails were clean, his long hair brushed and pulled back into a ponytail.

Then a new scent teased Jacob's nose. He forgot all about scrutinizing the man's appearance and all sense of discretion as the heavenly scent of tuna filled the air. He rushed forward, led by the growl in his belly, as the man dumped a heap of tuna on a broken plate and set it down. Normally, Jacob would balk at eating in these conditions, but his hunger was too great to care. He'd never felt such desperation in his life and hoped he never would again.

He'd devoured half of the tuna in seconds when the man's fingers came down and stroked between his pointed ears. Jacob froze, a strange sensation stealing over him at the contact. It wasn't just the pleasant fizz that washed through his veins, or when he began to purr, much to his mortification. It was the realization that he couldn't remember the last time anyone had touched him, especially with such hapless affection. Jacob leaned into the touch, shocked at the sense of connection and care he felt from an absolute stranger.

"Poor little guy, you've been through the wringer, huh?" The man murmured. His fingers began to work the clumps from Jacob's fur. "I know how you feel, little guy. Grizzled old fella like me, I used to work in one of these big glossy office buildings. I was good at what I did too, but layoffs got me. Then nobody was hiring. And the bills piled up. It's amazing how quickly things crumble out from underneath you."

Jacob glanced up at the man, that craggy, far away face lined with sadness. But his fingers kept moving, kept giving affection. Eventually, the man shifted, making room for Jacob in his sleeping bag despite the fleas that crawled beneath his fur.

He settled in next to the man, whose hand slowly dropped off as he fell asleep. Jacob went quiet inside. This man had nothing, absolutely nothing, but he'd freely given up his food. He'd offered warmth against the cold to a small creature who could give him nothing in return but fleas.

A deep shame washed over Jacob. It occurred to him he might not be the best of humans after all.

'*Ah, but will the lesson stick,*' said a horribly familiar voice from deeper in the alley. '*Will it be enough?*'

Jacob peered into the deeper gloom of the alley to find the Malkin watching him.

'*What was the point of this?*' he asked, not really expecting an answer. But the Malkin understood him in this form as easily as any other.

Those enormous eyes peered down the length of his muzzle at Jacob. He could feel the weight of age behind them, judging him and finding him wanting. Jacob wanted to bury his face in his paws.

'*I've lived a rather thoughtless life,*' he admitted.

The Malkin stalked forward, his head tilted as he considered Jacob's diminutive form. '*It's a start.*' Again, Jacob found himself looking into the great maw of the beast. Silvery white fog wrapped around him.

Jacob coughed. He blinked, and the world that resolved

around him was much smaller. He was surrounded by that fresh car smell. The leather squeaked under his very human butt. Had it been a dream?

A brush of chill air hit his side. Jacob turned to find his car door gone. Deep claw marks marred the edges of the frame. He swallowed. His insurance was going to have a field day with this claim.

Jacob crawled from the car, finding himself very much in need a fresh air. He walked from the garage, shocked to find the world still quiet, steeped in the early hours before dawn. The snow was falling thicker now. Jacob strolled down the sidewalk. He paused at the mouth of a nearby alley. A small gray tiger-striped cat watched him from the shallow shadows. The two stared at one another for a long moment before Jacob squatted down and held out his hand. The cat was slow to creep forward, body hunched to the ground in a belly crawl, but Jacob waited until it drew close enough for him to scratch between its ears.

The purr rumbled through its chest a second later. Such a small sound, but it made Jacob feel better. He glanced further into the alley at a familiar lean-to. If he listened carefully, he could hear the loaded silence of someone trying to make no noise at all. Jacob scooped the cat up in his arms and approached the man.

"Hello, sir. What's your name?"

The homeless man seemed too shocked at being addressed to lie. "William," he stuttered.

Jacob took a breath, tucking the cat in the crook of his elbow. A flea dip and bath were needed first, then tuna, lots of tuna. He turned his attention back to the man. "How would you like a job, William?"

In the deep shadows of the alley, the Malkin settled in to wash his paws. It was a start. It was enough.

"William?" Katie's face scrunched up in concentration.

Hadley nudged her with her shoulder. "Didn't Mr. Bill come to Thanksgiving?"

Katie gasped in recognition. "Daddy's P.A.?"

"One in the same," said Hadley with a wink.

Katie went quiet for a long moment. Hadley wondered what thoughts were turning in her niece's keen mind. Then, "Maybe Uncle Ollie needs a kitten."

Hadley's heart broke a little at the comment. "It might make him a little softer around the edges," she admitted. Neither her father nor her younger brother had spoken much to Hadley once she dropped out of the family business to pursue her own passions. Jake continued to work hard for the company, but his priorities were clear, and she hated that he'd been ostracized by his family for it. In Katie's lap, the kitten kneaded his paws against her legs. He'd stayed there the whole time, dozing on his new lady's lap.

"Hey, sweet pea," said Hadley. "I've got one more story for you."

Seven

Cats Choose Us

It had been a hard Christmas for Luci. She was more than a little heartbroken at what an absolute tool Ollie had turned out to be. How could she have been so blind to his flaws? The whole office knew he was a womanizer. She sighed and pushed it out of her mind. She needed to clear her head and move on. The Christmas day phone call to her parents helped. She wished she could have gone home this year instead of staying in town for that jerk.

Luci put in for the next three days off after Christmas, putting her racked up PTO to good use in a much needed stay-cation. No parties, no late nights drinking, just some peaceful time to herself with a good book and some Violet snuggles. Luci dropped by the library to stock up, grabbing a selection of genre fiction to keep her in spaceships and bodice rippers all weekend long.

She stopped by the checkout desk to pet the library's patron cat, a massive tabby with his own well-worn bed perched on the desk. "Hey Sampson, long time no see." She rubbed between his ears, loving how his whiskers pointed forward. "Keep guarding the books."

"Oh, he will," said the lady behind the desk.

Luci gave her a bemused smile and stuffed her haul into her tote bag. She grabbed a couple pints of Ben & Jerry's at the corner CVS, and when she finally shut the front door of her apartment, she heaved a sigh of relief to be home.

She'd burnt sage to get rid of the smell of his cologne. The sheets had been washed twice. Her heart still hurt. Her eyes welled up as she leaned against the door, until Violet rubbed against her legs with a meow.

Luci gave a teary laugh and scooped her fluff ball up in her arms. "You always know, don't you, Vi-vi?" She sniffled, tucking the purring cat under her chin as she settled on the couch and snuggled.

"You remind me of the cat I had as a kid," she said as she absently ran her fingers through Violet's soft fur. "She was a beautiful cat, all smoky gray fur and big yellow eyes. My dad said he found her as a kitten in the engine of an abandoned car. She always knew when I had a nightmare. Just snuggled in next to me and purred and purred until I fell asleep again. We had her until I was thirteen."

Luci rubbed her cheek against Violet's head as she spoke. "I love you, Vi-vi." The tears started to flow thick and fast then. It hurt trying to hold them in. It hurt letting them out. Luci cried until she was too exhausted to keep her eyes open. Violet stayed in her arms, purring like an idling engine. Her presence soothed Luci, but the hurt didn't go away. She curled up on the couch, far from the bed she'd shared with him. It was easier that way.

Violet nosed her sleeping human's hair. Her heart ached for her Luci-girl. She didn't want to bring her sweet Mistress this much pain.

Violet stilled, her tail twitching. She'd never thought of Luci as "Mistress" before, but the word felt *right.*

A shadow slid across the living room floor. Violet huffed and leapt down. It was cold enough that Luci now shut the window, but it was loose enough for Violet to paw at the crack until she could join the Malkin on the fire escape. Snow was falling on the city. The true bite of winter was in the air, but it didn't seem to bother the furless Malkin.

'*Beautiful isn't it?*'

'*Yes,*' said Violet. She hung her head. '*You were right. I regret my request.*'

The Malkin was silent for a long moment. '*Human hearts are stronger than you give them credit for,*' he said. '*Give her time. She will heal. And you will be there, in the long hours of the night, to soothe her broken heart.*'

Violet stared up at the Malkin. '*I thought you took all eight of my lives. That I would never find her again.*'

The Malkin shifted his bulk on the fire escape, a strange look on his face. Violet could almost call it longing. '*A love like that deserves at least one more lifetime.*'

Violet said nothing. She rubbed her cheek against the Malkin's wide flat nose. The great beast froze, startled. A rumbling purr rattled through his chest, vibrating the fire escape beneath them. The two settled side by side, warming the metal as they watched the snow fall.

There was a watery smile on her niece's face as she ran her fingers through Puff's fur. "Thank you, Auntie Hadley."

Hadley hugged the girl's shoulders. "By the way, I think Sir Puffnstuff is a perfect name."

"Dinner time, ladies."

Hadley looked up to find her brother and sister-in-law leaning into one another in the doorway.

There was a small smile on Jake's face that made her wonder how long they'd been there. Maybe her glance around the room hadn't been as thorough as she hoped.

"Why don't you go wash up, Katie-cat," said Lauren. She winked at Hadley. "Consider yourself our new official babysitter."

"I'm too old for a sitter," said Katie, who flinched as she set her kitten on the floor. "Though I'd take Auntie-and-me time."

"You got it, lady," said Hadley.

Katie stopped mid-step and leaned down to whisper in Hadley's ear. "I don't think the Malkin was that bad. Maybe lonely."

Hadley watched her race off to the sink, bemused. "I'm starving. I can't wait to try your roast, Lauren."

Puff watched his Lady race away for dinner. He caught Auntie Hadley glancing back at him as she followed the others out of the room. His legs were still unsteady as he trotted over to the pool of shadows under the Christmas tree. Unfortunately, Puff was not very good at stopping yet, and he tripped and sprawled over the Malkin's wide paws.

'Puff? Honestly?' The Malkin heaved a sigh that nearly

blew off the low-hanging ornaments. Puff batted at one as it swung on the branch.

'I like it.' It was a soft, like his Lady. He lifted his chin, whiskers pointed forward. *'Thank you. I'm not scared anymore.'*

The Malkin watched him with enormous green eyes. *'It was a plea worth answering.'*

Puff thought about the stories he'd heard, and what the Lady said before she left to eat. He flopped down over the Malkin's paws. *'Just the same, would you stay a little longer?'*

The Malkin huffed, but there was an up-tilt at the corner of his mouth as he eased his head down. As Puff curled against his cheek, he swore he heard the great beast purr.

Paw Prints
By Kristin Jacques

Kristin Jacques is speculative fiction author and content creator from New England. She holds a B.A. in Creative Writing from Wells College.

She has written for Warner Bros, National Geographic, and has participated in several contests. Her flash fiction *'Skirt'* was a winning entry in Hulu's *#myhandmaidstale,* selected by Margaret Atwood. Her stories, *Marrow Charm* and *Edgewise,* won two consecutive Wattys in 2015 and 2016 for excellence in digital storytelling.

Her award-winning dark fantasy *Marrow Charm* was released from Parliament House Press in October 2019. In September 2020, Marrow Charm won the Gold Medal for Young Adult Fantasy General in the Readers' Favorite Annual Book Award. In 2020, she signed a four-book deal with City Owl Press for the paranormal series *Midnight Guardians.*

When not writing, she is juggling two rambunctious boys, spoiling her cats, and catching up on a massive TBR pile. She is currently working on projects full of magic, mystery, and delight.

More from the Author
Kristin Jacques

The Gate Cycle Series

Marrow Charm

Skin Curse

Ikepela Ives

Ragnarök Unwound

Connect with Kristin

www.kristinjacques.com

twitter.com/Krazydiamond07

facebook.com/krazydiamondwrites

instagram.com/krazydiamond_writes

bookbub.com/profile/kristin-jacques

Coffee Talk

M. Dalto

ONE

Angela wrapped her winter jacket tighter around herself as she glanced up at the sign above the door of the shop. She let out a dramatic sigh.

Café Cuervo Negro. The Black Crow Café.

She couldn't help but shake her head. It was likely the most non-festive location in town during the holiday season, though she did give the owners credit for their attempts to make the dismal décor festive. Santa hats on their taxidermized crows and rows of multicolored lights gave the otherwise red and black interior a somewhat jolly glow. The heavy metal covers of seasonal favorites piping through the speakers was an added perk.

Angela shook her head as she stood in line to order her drink. If nothing else, Delilah had always been one for theatrics, and shame on Angela for agreeing to meet her confidante at her bistro of choice. She was more than happy remaining home, sipping on a steaming mug of home-brewed loose-leaf of her own design while watching the snowfall from the comfort of her own living room. But no, not this time. It was Delilah's weekend. Therefore, Angela had no choice but to swallow her pride—and extremely overpriced beverages—and meet her colleague in her own domain.

Searching around the small café, she sought out her colleague. There she was, sitting in a corner table dressed for the club rather than a casual friendly encounter. Delilah's black corset accentuated her already perfect form, worn over tight black leggings and red stiletto heels. Her dark hair, a harsh comparison to Angela's lighter features, was piled atop her head in a haphazard mound of curls and combs.

She smiled lightly as her arrival finally caught Delilah's attention. "*That's* what you decided to wear? I thought you weren't working today," Angela muttered by way of greeting as she placed her steaming mug on the table before shrugging off her heavy coat and draping it on the back of her chair.

"Angela, my dear, I am *always* working." Delilah grinned with lips as dark as the coffee shop's motif.

With another sigh, Angela took a seat across from her acquaintance, straightening her white pencil skirt and brushing her straight, blonde hair over her shoulder. A casual glance at her surroundings showed that they were not alone in the café despite the snow outside—not by a long shot, and she knew Delilah would be in a mood tonight because of it.

"That one," Delilah started as soon as Angela was in her seat. Following her friend's gaze, she lay her eyes on a rather attractive young man in a three-piece suit, leg crossed over his knee as he sipped on an espresso while he read the daily paper.

"I don't think so," Angela challenged, but Delilah's eyes were already on fire.

"Three people: his wife and two co-workers."

"How?" Angela whispered, her eyes wide. She hated the way Delilah could always surprise her, no matter how many times they played this game of hers. Somehow, some way, she was always able to determine the darkness in someone's soul merely by the coffee they drank. She found it amusing, but Angela felt it was somewhat morbid, especially when most of the targets, by her estimation at least, were blatantly murderers living like there was nothing wrong with them. For once, she would have preferred Delilah's depictions of these strangers to involve petty theft or forgery, but no—it was as if Delilah chose these places knowing the people who would frequent them.

"Cyanide." The tone of her response made it seem like it should have been obvious.

Even so, Angela's jaw dropped. "Why?"

"I'll let you know once I ask," Delilah mused, grinning devilishly. "After I take him home to Daddy."

Angela rolled her eyes, though the unease lingered. She never did ask Delilah what happened to her targets once she brought them to her father, and sometimes ignorance truly was bliss. Playing off the discomfort, she dragged her attention to a pair of young girls, no older than fifteen, sitting in the opposite corner, giggling over their large mugs of white chocolate mocha. "What about them?"

"They convinced their friend to hang herself over some ridiculous urban legend," Delilah said as she watched them, the answer as casual as if Angela had merely asked her about the weather.

"Why would they do something like that?" she whispered incredulously. "They're practically children... and it's the holidays!"

"Why do any mortals choose to sin?" Delilah countered, folding her hands in front of her. "Because they want to. Because they can. Regardless of the season."

"They don't have to," Angela insisted. "There is good in

most of them. Just look around you! The lights and the decorations and the music and—"

"And they also don't have to spend a ridiculous amount of money on overpriced, excessively strong coffee either, and yet here we are." Delilah smirked.

Angela groaned as she looked into her cup of tea as if hoping some unknown answer would show itself through the tea leaves at the bottom. "So, you assume there's always a correlation between life's choices and espresso?"

"And then some. I've told you, it gets worse the stronger the drink."

"So if I went up to that counter and ordered a tall skinny soy-milk caramel swirl latte with extra ice—"

"They would immediately see you for the angel that you truly are."

"And this is why I stick with tea," Angela murmured, delicately sipping from her cup.

"And when it's your weekend, we can go to that fu-fu bookstore you adore so much, but this weekend is mine, and so we play *my* games."

Angela glared at her friend before focusing her attention back on the delicious herbal concoction that sang to her taste buds. How anyone could prefer bitter, burnt beans to this she would never understand. And to believe that someone's choice of beverage could allude to their moral wellbeing—

"Test it out," Delilah mused, watching her from across the table.

"Excuse me?" Angela inquired, raising a well-manicured brow.

Delilah waved a hand toward the rest of the café. "Pick one—anyone. I can probably tell you the exact drink they have in front of them based on the sin alone."

She was often this pretentious, especially in her line of

business, but Angela would give her friend the benefit of the doubt. It was the holiday season, after all—the season of giving, even if that meant inflating Delilah's ego.

Angela turned in her chair and surveyed the small store. It appeared like any other coffee shop set in any other town trying its best to lure busy consumers in the midst of choosing their seasonal purchases. Its customers came and went as they would, unaware of the silent assessment being made of their current circumstances, what it meant, and who was watching them as they did so.

If she was honest with herself, Angela would never judge another for their actions, past, present, or future, if not for Delilah's company. She was certain Delilah could say the same when she ventured out with Angela. Gray areas did not exist where Delilah was concerned.

Black and white, good and evil—one cannot survive without the other, and so the cycle continued.

Whether Angela wanted it to or not.

She worried at her bottom lip, wondering who would be the easiest to assess based on Delilah's request. The two young girls were giggling as they made their way out of the coffee shop, and the man they had noticed earlier had put his paper down to furiously type away on his phone. No one else lingered enough to grasp Angela's attention...

Until *he* walked through the door.

His brown hair was tousled from the winter wind, and his blue eyes surveyed the shop as if he, too, was looking for something.

Or someone.

His frosty stare met Angela's, and she felt the chill run through her veins, right to her core. A shiver climbed up her spine, and she wished she'd worn a warmer sweater or a scarf, both of which the stranger currently wore as he brushed the snow off his jacket.

"What about him?" Angela asked, turning back to Delilah, but her companion was already staring at him with a less-than-favorable look.

"Not him."

As she looked between the two of them, Delilah's glaring at the stranger while the stranger continued to watch her, Angela asked, "Do you know him?"

"No," she responded curtly. "And neither should you."

"What are you talking about?"

"We should go."

"Go where?" Angela scoffed. "You wanted to come here, remember? You wanted to play your game and—"

"And now I've changed my mind." Delilah stood from her chair. "Let's go."

"Hello," came a deep male voice, pulling Angela's attention away from her friend.

The dark-haired stranger stood above her, a slight smile on his face as his blue eyes once again looked her over.

"Hello," Angela responded, her voice smaller than she'd intended.

"I apologize for staring," he said quickly, "but you looked like someone I know. Have we met before?"

A bashful smile came to Angela's lips as her cheeks reddened. "No, I don't believe so. Unless you're often at The White Page bookstore?"

"No, unfortunately, I don't believe that's it. I can't say I'm one for books—that's usually my..." He seemed to hesitate as if looking for the correct word. "...friend's preference."

She barely knew this person, so why did it bother her that he was already being so guarded? Not that she didn't have her own demons she'd rather hide. "I know that feeling well enough. I also have a friend who would rather do anything but read," Angela mused with a glance toward Delilah, but her friend's attention remained on the stranger. Her nails dug into the tabletop, and Angela feared they would break if she tried to grip the wood any harder.

Delilah's distaste glanced off the stranger as he continued, "I was wondering if I could possibly join you?"

"No," Delilah hissed.

"Yes," Angela countered with a scowl in her friend's direction.

He gave Angela a grateful smile. "Thank you."

She watched as the man retreated, heading to the counter to place his drink order. There was something curious about him, something almost intriguing that Angela couldn't quite decipher. She wondered if it had something to do with Delilah's initial reaction to his presence.

Remembering Delilah's earlier challenge, Angela considered the stranger a moment longer before saying, "I bet you he's getting a green tea matcha."

She turned to Delilah with a smile, wondering how close she was...

But Delilah was gone.

Frowning, she stared at the empty chair where her friend had sat and continued to stare until the man returned to the table with a mug in his hand. Startled out of her trance, she watched him as he placed his drink on the table, then removed his jacket and slung it on the back of the chair, rubbing his hands together as if to warm them. Finally, he returned his attention to her.

"Thank you again for allowing me to sit with you," he said softly. "My name is Seth."

"I'm Angela," she replied.

He smiled, and it was contagious—she returned the smile as he sipped from his mug.

"What are you drinking?"

He swallowed before responding. "Oh, it's just coffee. Black."

She had to wonder what Delilah would interpret from that.

Talking with Seth was surprisingly easy. In the short time they spent in the café, she discovered he was a graduate student working toward his master's degree, living in the city but looking forward to taking the train home for the holidays. Angela disclosed as much about herself as he did, explaining that she had moved to the city soon after graduating college, was now working at The White Page bookstore, and had no plans to return home for Christmas.

Before Seth could ask why, forcing Angela to make up an excuse about her personal reservations about returning to her family during the holidays, she realized that the café was closing.

"I guess it's time for me to start my walk home," Angela mused as she stood from her chair, gathering her empty teacups to clear the table.

"Do you have far to go?" he asked as he joined her on her walk to the dish return.

"It's just a few blocks down the street." She offered him a reassuring smile. It was a walk she had made many times, through all types of weather and times of the day. She had no worries about making it home safe.

And neither did he, it seemed. "Let me at least get your phone number before you go."

Angela nodded her assent and took her phone out of her coat pocket, exchanging numbers with the mysterious man she had only just met hours ago.

"If it's all right with you," he said as he put his phone back into his pocket, "I'd like to see you again. At least once before I have to leave for the holidays."

Something tugged at her gut, but she ignored it as she nodded once again. "I would like that a lot, actually."

It wasn't a lie. There was something about Seth that attracted Angela to him. Maybe it was because she had been entertained solely by Delilah's attention for so long that having someone new to interact with was exactly what she needed.

The smile he gave as he put on his jacket her made the tugging at her gut move lower, and she bit her lip. She quickly threw her own coat over her shoulders to distract from the illicit thoughts trying to invade her mind.

Maybe *that* was why Delilah disapproved. She often seemed to know Angela better than she knew herself, but in this, Angela wasn't so certain. She wanted to defy Delilah's initial reaction to him. Sure, she may have generally been right about most people when she read them like she did, but she couldn't get a perfect read all the time. Delilah took that for a negative, but maybe Angela needed to take it as a positive. Perhaps she could prove to Delilah that the world was more than coffee shops and murderers.

They walked each other to the door, and Seth held it open to allow Angela to pass. The evening turned colder, and the snow still hadn't stopped, so she wrapped her arms around herself just a little tighter to not only keep herself warm but to keep her body in check as they stood on the sidewalk.

"Well," he started.

"Well," she responded.

His attention was solely on her, and she had nowhere to go, even if she was ready to leave. She bit her lip, trying to think of something to say—anything that would break the palpable silence between them. But the winter wind swept past them, and it made his blue eyes glisten.

Her face heated as she remained under his watchful gaze and she couldn't pull herself away, as if Seth was a magnet and there was something more attractive than his pretty face that kept her near.

Another gust was enough to cause her to shiver, and he blinked for what felt like the first time in an hour.

"I should go," he said, almost apologetically, as if he knew he'd kept her there in the middle of the city sidewalk because she was afraid if she left she'd never see him again.

But she would. She had his number after all. He would be just a call away.

And she would call him.

Even if Delilah was skeptical, after the time spent with him, for the first time Angela was uncertain of her friend's game.

Angela's apartment was located a few blocks away from the city's center, which was always appealing to her. She was never too far away from the coffee shops or the bookstores or just the people of the city in general. Their location always made Delilah content to people-watch, and sometimes Angela wondered if that was where her desire to be around others came from. Like Delilah's influence on her interpersonal relationships was directly correlated to her need to be near others.

But then that would mean Delilah had more control over her daily life than she ever wanted to admit. To anyone.

It's what had brought them to the city, after all.

Frowning at the memory, Angela made her way to three-family-house-made-apartment-building where her cozy, second floor, one-bedroom apartment awaited. No sooner had she hung her coat on the rack and removed her shoes than did a soft, familiar chuckle ring out from the living room.

"I was wondering if you were ever going to come back," Delilah mused from her seat by the window. The dim lights from the Christmas tree shadowed her features, making her presence appear far darker than it already was.

"No one told you to leave," Angela countered, taking a seat on the sofa across from her.

"You're right—I chose to leave, which you should also have done hours ago. But now, here you are, and something tells me you didn't spend the time buying last-minute presents or getting lost on your way home."

"Seth is a very interesting person."

"So he has a name." Delilah rolled her eyes.

"And he drinks his coffee black."

Delilah's countenance darkened. "Does he now?"

"He does. So what does that mean?"

Her friend's frown deepened before her attention returned to the falling snow outside the window. "I don't know."

Angela felt her stomach flip at the admission. "You don't know?"

"Which is all the more reason you need to steer clear of

him." Delilah turned toward her once again. "No one should be able to hide their sins from me."

"Maybe he doesn't have any."

"Impossible. All mortals sin, from the day they're born."

"Then maybe you're reading him wrong?"

Delilah sputtered at the insinuation. "Or maybe he's the type of person I'm supposed to protect you from."

"Ah, yes—knowing the sins of everyone we pass on a daily basis is far safer than not knowing the sins of one man."

"Yes." The look on her face was more serious than Angela had expected.

She groaned in frustration. "You're insufferable. All because one person crossed your path and you couldn't get a good enough read off of him."

"I couldn't get *any* read off of him, and that's more than enough for me to keep my distance, which means you should as well."

"You can't read everyone, Delilah."

"Yes, I can." Delilah let out a breath. "Or I should be able to. And the ones I can't, I know well enough to stay away from."

Angela peered at her friend, trying to look beyond the dark leather and red lipstick. "I think you're jealous"

Delilah rolled her eyes and turned away, blatantly ignoring the glare Angela shot her way. "I don't get jealous. People get jealous of *me*."

"Good, then you won't mind if I call him tomorrow to get together and run some errands."

Turning back to her, Delilah abruptly stood from where she sat before the window. "That's a bad idea."

"Because having him help me choose presents for the rest of the people on my list is such a dangerous concept?"

Delilah took a step closer. "Because letting someone too

close—especially someone with too many sins to be deciphered—is a bad idea."

Angela scoffed. "I told you, you're wrong."

"We'll see how wrong I am when he breaks your heart. Or worse."

Angela had heard enough. Pushing off the sofa, she moved to stand face to face with Delilah, meeting her friend's gaze head on. "You *are* jealous. No one is breaking anyone's anything. It's Christmas! And you're just bothered by the fact that, for once, you may know no more than the rest of us."

The look of Delilah's face was one of both arrogance and resentment. "Remember you said that," Delilah hissed. "Especially when his sins come back to haunt you, you remember I warned you."

But Angela was done with the conversation. She didn't want Delilah telling her what she could or could not do. She wasn't a child to be protected. Instead of responding, she turned on her heel and marched out of the living room and down the hallway, slamming the door to her bedroom without further acknowledgement of Delilah's taunts.

There was no sign of Delilah the following morning—not in the living room where she'd last seen her, not in the bathroom taking a longer-than-necessary bath, not in the kitchen complaining about the lack of available coffee.

With a sigh, Angela returned to her bedroom to contemplate the previous day's events. It wasn't the first time she and Delilah had been at odds—it was just the first time it had been over someone else. When she was younger, she'd heeded Delilah's warning-laden advice, and often her friend's judgment had been correct. But never before had there been someone Delilah couldn't read. That alone should have been enough for Angela to want to avoid Seth at all costs... But there was something about him that made her want to know more. There had to be a reason Delilah couldn't see through him, and if nothing else, Angela wanted to get close enough to figure out why.

The phone on her bedside table buzzed and Angela picked it up.

Delilah was still nowhere to be seen while Angela confirmed plans to meet with Seth via text, nor while she showered and dressed simply in a light pink skirt and a white button-down blouse.

There was no sign of her, either, as Angela ate a quick breakfast of her favorite sugary cereal paired with a cup of tea. Perhaps it was for the better. With the way Delilah had acted the night before, some time alone with Seth without Delilah's constant objections and interruptions would be refreshing. It would also give her the time to figure out more about him without Delilah's assumptions overshadowing their meeting. Not to mention it had been far too long since she'd really spent time with another living mortal being, and there was no better time than the holidays to reacclimate oneself with the spirit of the season.

She slipped on her boots, wrapped herself in her winter jacket, and headed out into the wintery afternoon. The sidewalks were still white from the new-fallen snow. It all looked so pure. So peaceful. So innocent.

She could almost hear Delilah's snide remarks about how quickly it would all turn to shit, and Angela instinctively glanced over her shoulder just to be certain her companion wasn't behind her.

But there was still on sign of her.

Should she be more concerned that Delilah couldn't read him for the sinner he may or may not be? Was her friend's continued absence a sign of how deep-rooted her beliefs were?

Perhaps.

But that was Delilah's dilemma, not hers.

The White Page bookstore was nestled in the middle of the city's main thoroughfare, with constant traffic moving in and around the store. Probably one of the longest-running independent bookstores in the area, Angela loved the smell of old parchment and new books as it mingled with the scents wafting from small café's baked goods. Various breads and muffins, fresh from the ovens, waited behind the glass display case, just begging to be devoured. Aside from her own apartment, it was her favorite place to be. Which was all the more reason she'd invited Seth to meet her there—not that she wasn't comfortable being with him, but she felt better being on neutral ground in a comfortable and familiar atmosphere. If Delilah was there, she'd at least have to applaud her for meeting him somewhere she knew was safe.

To her surprise, he had beat her there. He sat at one of the café's small tables writing in what appeared to be a small, leather-bound notebook. She paused, watching his elegant fingers as they dragged the pen over the page, admiring how his brow creased in concentration as he wrote. His thick, wavy brown hair fell into his face as he focused on the journal before him. His tongue poked through his teeth as if he was in deep thought, and a small smile graced his generous lips as he worked.

The knot she'd felt in her stomach when she was with him the day before began to loosen as she watched him. As much as she didn't want to interrupt, she wanted to be nearer to him, to ask him what he was writing, to have him look at her with those blue eyes the way he was looking at the journal in front of him. She continued her fond internal debate until she was unceremoniously bumped from behind by a holiday shopper too busy on their phone to even notice the intrusion. The unexpected jostle caused her to let out a yelp of surprise, which was enough for Seth to look up from his task toward the sound. Just like the magnetic attraction from the day before, his eyes immediately found hers. The low knot reformed, but this time, it was a pleasant tightness, and one she wanted him to unravel. The thoughtful smile that had been on his face turned into a welcoming grin, and he gave Angela a small wave, motioning for her to join him.

Remembering she was standing in the middle of the café, she hurried over to him. "I hope you weren't waiting long," she said as she moved to the seat across from him, paying extra attention to situating her chair rather than acknowledging her embarrassment.

"Not at all," he confirmed. "I actually arrived early to have some time to myself."

"For your writing?" she asked, nodding to the notebook between them.

Seth quickly closed it and kept a hand on its cover, almost protectively. "Yes. I don't have much freedom to do it at home, so I find that coming here helps."

"Nosy roommates?"

"Something like that."

Angela smirked. "I know the feeling," she said, considering her own roommate. Another glance over her shoulder confirmed her companion remained nowhere to be seen. Where in Hell was she?

"Are you expecting someone?" Seth asked.

She returned her attention to Seth, who studied her with a perked brow. She gave him a reassuring smile. "No. I was just wondering if anyone I knew was working today."

"And are they?"

She shrugged. "It doesn't matter." She pointed to the notebook again. "Do you want to tell me what you're writing about?"

For the first time since their paths had crossed, Seth looked taken aback and almost speechless. "I... uh..."

"It's okay," she assured him, feeling slightly guilty. "It's probably none of my business anyway."

His expression changed almost to a scowl and he paused, not looking at her but at his journal. She was again going to insist that it wasn't for her to know, but he quickly opened it and turned it toward her. "I'm just making a list," he explained, "of who I still need to buy Christmas presents for."

"Oh..." Now she really felt guilty as she looked at the list. She didn't think Christmas lists were enough to give someone pause but to Seth, it seemed personal. She glanced down the list and saw names of people she didn't know—most likely family, friends, his nosy roommate. She was going to apologize again for causing him whatever grief sharing the list created until a certain name caught her attention.

"Do you know another Angela?" she asked carefully, looking back up to him.

"No." That smile was back on his lips. "None since yesterday."

Her cheeks flushed at the admission. "You do *not* need to get me anything."

"I know," he said, taking the book back and closing it, this time slipping it into the pocket of his jacket. "But isn't that what the holiday spirit is all about? The season of giving and all that."

"I suppose."

He looked as if he was assessing her. "Do you have anyone to buy for?"

Angela shrugged slightly. "I generally don't exchange presents with many people."

Seth frowned. "Do you not have anyone to spend the holidays with?"

"Oh, that's not true at all. I have—" She paused. "My roommate."

"And *she* doesn't have anyone else to spend the holidays with?"

"Well, she has her father, but Christmas is the furthest from something they'd celebrate together."

"Ah," he said, nodding as if he understood. Angela was sure he didn't, but she was going to let him continue to think he did, which would save her from having to explain any more.

"And I'm sure your returning home will give you a break from your nosy roommate," she offered quickly to change the subject.

"My... roommate... He's almost too much into the holiday spirit. He'd be here now if I let him be."

"You could have invited him." Though having another person was the last thing she wanted. Angela silently thanked Delilah for her unaccustomed absence.

"No. He's too much of a distraction, especially when I want to spend my time focused on you."

Angela blinked, uncertain she heard him correctly at first. The way Seth's cheeks reddened, however, told her she had heard exactly what he had said.

Clearing his throat, he stood from his chair and avoided her stunned gaze. "Maybe we should get going? I heard the temperature is going to drop tonight, and the last thing we want is to be out in the bitter cold."

Angela smiled and nodded. "Let's start crossing some of those names off your list."

The remainder of the day was spent walking up and down the city's main strip, visiting its small shops and admiring the holiday display windows. Seth's Christmas list dictated their itinerary, and Angela offered her advice as best as she could. Not knowing the personalities of the people he was buying for made it somewhat difficult, but she did the best she could with what she had. Seth seemed appreciative, especially as she helped him carry the shopping bags between stores. Balancing the parcels distracted her enough that she didn't see Seth reach out to take her hand until his warm fingers wrapped around hers.

Hand in hand, they walked through the city's center. Festive lights were lit despite the afternoon sunlight shining off the mounds of fallen snow. Church bells rang, and the sound of choirs could be heard singing Christmas carols to entertain shoppers as they passed by. Street vendors offered all sorts of pastries, cookies, and cakes, ready for sampling or boxed to take home.

She wanted to eat it all.

They decided on a cart that sold molten hot chocolate. It resided near a manmade skating rink, already bustling with skaters laughing and hollering on the ice.

"Two please," Seth said to the man at the cart, finally

releasing her hand as he shuffled his packages, reaching into his pockets.

"You don't need to do that" Angela protested. "You've already spent so much money today."

"I insist," he insisted as he finally found his leather wallet. "Besides, your name still remains on my list. Consider this part of your gift."

She felt almost guilty to be the source of another expenditure, but his logic was sound, and she refrained from arguing after that.

They settled on a bench situated on the outskirts of the skating rink, each with a cup of steaming hot chocolate between their gloved hands. Angela took a small sip, and the sweet drink coated her tongue with a menagerie of festive saccharine flavors.

A twig snapped behind her, and she turned. Delilah leaned against a tree not too far behind them. Angela had been wondering about her friend's whereabouts throughout the day and knew she wouldn't be able to stay away forever, but now that she and Seth had finished their day's errands and finally had a chance to sit and talk, she hoped Delilah would maintain her safe distance rather than interrupting with her tidings of doom and gloom.

"Do you ever just stop and... watch people?" Seth asked, pulling her attention back to him. She tried to read him—in her own way, not Delilah's—to figure out where such a sudden question would have come from, but his focus remained on the activity in the skating rink.

"You mean like how we're watching them right now?" she offered.

"No, I mean... *really* watch them. Like, try to see if you can tell the kind of person they are. For better or for worse."

Angela almost choked on her hot chocolate, the liquid

burning her throat as she coughed. "No... I can't say I have," she lied. She glanced over her shoulder to where Delilah remained leaning against the nearby tree and wondered if she could hear their conversation. Or sense her lie.

"It's fascinating, really," Seth continued. "We're surrounded by so many people on a daily basis who don't even realize it."

"Realize what?"

He turned and looked at her. "That they're being judged."

Angela could only blink in response.

He turned back to the skaters making their way around the frozen rink. "As children, we're told to be good or Santa is going to give us coal in our stockings. As teens, religion tries to teach us to repent for our innate sins or else we're going to Hell."

"And as adults?"

"As adults, we realize it's all bullshit."

Her jaw dropped slightly as she tried to find the words to challenge him or to counter him or to ask where this philosophical stance derived from. Instead, she could only focus on Delilah behind her, like a presence breathing down her neck, making her skin prickle.

"What do you think?" he asked softly, turning back to her.

"I... I think anyone could be anyone they want to be, and no one should make assumptions about a person without knowing them first."

Seth scoffed and looked down at his hot chocolate. "I have a... friend. My roommate. Who thinks that there's good in each of us if we only just look."

"That's funny," she mused, doing all she could to not

glance in Delilah's direction. "I have a friend who believes everyone is born inherently evil."

"Sounds like we should get them together sometime."

Angela shook her head. "Something tells me if that ever happened, it would cause the Apocalypse."

Seth snorted, nudging her slightly, playfully, as if she had told the punchline to an amusing joke. Maybe she had, but again—he'd never met Delilah.

The thought of her companion had Angela turning around once again, looking back to the tree. Delilah made sure she had her complete attention as she motioned to her wrist, mimicking a watch or some other timepiece. It was enough to tell Angela that she was ready to be done and home, but Angela was nowhere near ready to finish the evening as of yet.

She wasn't ready to leave Seth yet either, especially when the presence of his body next to hers kept her warm even in the coldest winter breeze, and their cups of hot chocolate remained between their hands unfinished. For far too long, Delilah had dictated what Angela did and when she did it, but she wasn't going to allow it now.

After her moment of consideration, Angela turned back toward Seth. Delilah be damned. "Would you like to come back to my apartment?"

Seth coughed on the sip of hot chocolate he had just taken and looked to her, eyes wide, as he wiped at his mouth. Rather than saying anything in response, his gaze drifted back toward the skaters on the pond.

Had she read the signals incorrectly? She thought they were enjoying themselves well enough—she didn't think it was something that needed that much deliberation. Then again, it had taken her this long to decide to invite him back to her apartment in the first place.

"I don't know if I should stay the night," he admitted.

Now it was Angela's turn to sputter. "Oh... oh! God, no, I didn't say that! No, no, no, I didn't mean it like that!" Angela said quickly. "I just meant to get out of the cold, have dinner, drinks, warm up. I mean—you could stay longer if you wanted to, but—"

Seth chuckled. "It's all right. I'd love to accompany you home and warm up before heading back to my apartment."

"Great." Angela smiled, letting out an exasperated breath before standing up and helping Seth with his packages.

She turned back to see if Delilah was still watching them, a satisfied look plastered across her face, but Delilah had disappeared once again.

Angela half expected Delilah to be sitting on her window perch the moment they entered, but the apartment was empty. The lights from the Christmas tree were on, decorating the room in a colorful hue, but Angela couldn't remember if she had turned them on before she'd left that morning.

"You can put your bags by the coat rack," Angela instructed, placing down the ones she held in her own hands before removing her jacket.

Seth followed, adding his parcels to hers as directed and hanging up his own jacket before stepping deeper into the apartment. "I thought you said you had a roommate?"

"She's... out."

"Very fortunate and convenient." He gave her a knowing smile before looking down the hallway. "Do you have a bathroom I can use?"

"Oh, of course," she said, startling herself into action. "It's right down the hallway, first door on the right."

"Thanks." He gave her a nod before excusing himself.

Angela watched as he maneuvered his way through her apartment, her all-too-familiar stomach knot tightening, not only from anticipation, but also the unknown. She'd never had anyone to her apartment before. The possibilities for their evening seemed endless, so long as—

"What is he doing here?" Delilah asked.

So long as Delilah stayed away.

Angela turned around slowly. Her friend's sudden appearance on the sofa was the last thing she wanted at that moment. "I invited him," she said curtly.

"What did we discuss?"

"No, it was what *you decided*. You were the one with issues from the beginning, all because you couldn't read him."

"I was the one with issues because he can't be read! What part of this doesn't make sense to you, Angela? I can't tell a mortal by his sins. That's something that should cause concern!"

"Not everyone needs to live their lives according to some damn vision! I've listened to you too many times when you felt someone was off or wrong or you didn't think their coffee choice was relevant enough. How many more good people need to pass me by for you to be satisfied?"

"Has it ever occurred to you how many times that damn vision may have saved you from imminent disaster? Remember David? That train wreck was a catastrophe waiting to happen, and you would have been right in the middle of it if it wasn't for me."

"Leave David and his train wreck out of this. The only 'imminent disaster' is what's going to happen if you don't mind your own business and let me and Seth have a decent evening in peace."

Delilah leaned back on the couch as if leaving was the last thing she had in mind. "If you think anything decent is going to happen with someone like him—"

"Enough!"

"Who are you talking to?" Seth asked as he returned to the living room.

Angela whipped around, turning her back to Delilah "No one." Seth had emerged from the bathroom much quicker than she expected.

"Now I'm no one?" Delilah mused.

Angela glared over her shoulder. Her patience was running thin, and she was so close to writing them all off and hide in her bedroom for the rest of eternity, if only to crawl away from the uncertainty her current situation.

"I'm sorry, did I do something wrong? I can leave if you want," Seth offered, but Angela was already beyond aggravated. This was not what she'd had in mind when she considered bringing Seth back to her apartment, and not what she needed right now, with him standing right before her. The stress of the situation and fear of having to further explain herself caused her head to pound; the pressure grew as if her skull was stuck a vice.

"Just... stop," she hissed, rubbing her temples.

Delilah lounged back, leering, while Seth, oblivious to Delilah, looked stricken.

"Angela, what's going on?" He stepped toward her, and she recoiled.

"I'm fine," she said too quickly, moving toward the small kitchen off the living room. She needed space, and her apartment was starting to feel very small.

"Can I help you get something ready for dinner?"

The pounding in her head increased to searing pain and she had to grip the kitchen counter until the nauseating wave passed. "I'll figure it out," she said through clenched teeth.

"If it's easier, we can order out? I won't even mind going to get it."

"Make sure you get enough for three," Delilah called from the living room.

Angela wanted to scream.

"Hey."

The unexpected hand on her arm startled Angela and the jumped, spinning around so she faced Seth straight-on.

"What's wrong?"

Her breaths were deep as she met his gaze. Was that pity she saw in his eyes? Too many people had pitied her over the course of her life, and she wasn't about to add one more to the list.

"Tell me, let me help."

"Sometimes, Seth," she said on an exhale, "there are some things that you don't have to concern yourself with."

He peered at her. "Where is this coming from?"

"I'm not like those people out on the skating rink," she continued. "Don't think you can look at me and see what's good or bad."

"I wasn't." He took a step back. "I mean... yesterday at the coffee shop, I may have, but today, I knew exactly who you were. That you were someone I wanted to be with. Someone I wanted to know better, to know more about—"

"Well, look harder. Maybe look somewhere else. Some things don't need to be explained and some questions don't need to be answered."

He didn't deserve the lashing she was giving him, but Angela had moved beyond caring and was running out of options. Delilah was suffocating her, and Seth was taking the remaining air from her lungs. She should have known better —should have realized this time would be no different. That Seth would be just like everyone else.

"Look, we all have our... thing. I'm not trying to judge you—"

They always judged. Everyone different, everyone special. Everyone with their "something extra" that kept them from being normal like everyone else. "Why don't you just leave and find someone else to judge."

"That's my girl," Delilah murmured.

She marched out of the kitchen to see Delilah lounging on the couch, the smugness written all over her expression. "No one asked you!" Angela's voice cracked and tears stung her eyes.

"Angela, there's no one there." Seth came up from behind her, gently placing his hands on her shoulders and spinning her around so he could look her over. Something hopeful flashed in his eyes as his gaze returned to hers. "Are you sure you're okay? Do you want to sit down? Is there someone I can call?"

Angela's fists clenched as her temper rose, and she tried to center herself as the world began to spin around her. "You think I'm crazy too, don't you?"

"Whoa," he said, stepping back, his hands out in front of him defensively. "That is not what I said."

"Remember your parents," Delilah purred from the sofa. "Remember the last time they tried to convince you that you were insane? Try to remember the last time you had a conversation with them that didn't turn into a psychiatric evaluation."

And there it was again, the memory that wouldn't leave her alone. The first time her parents caught her talking with Delilah, she had been able to use practicing dialogue for a play at school as an excuse for their conversation. But the conversations had become more emotional, more frequent, and Delilah refused to stop when Angela needed her to the most. Screaming at the top of her lungs in the middle of the night had been when her parents realized that there was something going on, and instead of asking Angela, they assumed it would be better for a therapist to get to the bottom of her problems. There were too many therapists to name, too many appointments, too many tests. Too many terms and diagnoses that didn't even come close to explaining her relationship with Delilah. Eventually Angela's parents gave up trying to help her, and Angela moved out as soon as she turned eighteen to avoid being just another problem for them to solve.

Thoughts of the past made Angela want to cry and scream and run. Instead, she closed her eyes and took a single, centering breath. "You know, I thought you were different than..."

"Who?" he asked carefully.

"Everyone," she hissed. "Everyone who thinks they're better than me."

"I never thought I was better than you. In fact..."

She opened her eyes and met Seth's gaze. "In fact, maybe you're just better at hiding it than the rest of them."

Something in Seth seemed to darken, and the look of betrayal changed to one of rage. Baring his teeth and releasing his own growl of frustration, his fists clenched as his sides. "You want to talk about people who hide what they really are? Ever since I met you, you've been avoiding telling me anything about you, and I've been trying to figure out why. At first, I thought it was just because you wanted to wait until we got to know each other better, but now I think I know the real reason."

"And what would that be?" she snapped.

"You're afraid of letting anyone get close to you. Like their very presence will taint the precious equilibrium of a life you seem to have created for yourself."

"If it works—"

"It doesn't." He threw his hands into the air, clearly exasperated.

Angela clenched her jaw and stood her ground. "Like you said, you know nothing about me, so don't even begin to assume you do," she gritted out.

"And maybe that's why you're here—alone."

"I am not alone."

"Then why is there only one bedroom? So much for your roommate... or is there something else going on you don't want to tell me about? Too afraid to hurt my feelings, to let me down, to let me know you're already in a relationship?"

She wanted to deny it but stopped herself because he was right. She didn't need to explain herself to anyone, especially this stranger. He was nothing to her. "Were you snooping around my apartment?"

"This is exactly what David did before we booted him, too," Delilah reminded her, remaining where she sat on the couch and watching their exchange like it was a boxing match. "And that bastard actually had the nerve to call your parents!"

"Just like David," Angela agreed out loud.

"David, huh?" Seth shook his head. "Here I was, trying to get a better understanding of the woman who invited me back to her apartment, but it seems as though I just saved myself from a whole lot of headache."

"Then maybe you should go."

"Then maybe I will."

"No one's stopping you."

"Fine."

"Fine."

Seth hesitated only a moment before he moved, muttering as he threw on his jacket. "And here I thought Michael was right for once. But when you actually allow yourself to think there's good in someone, it just comes back and bites you in the ass."

"Well tell Michael or whoever he is that the only good people are the ones who stop judging people over what they don't know!"

"Oh, I know enough. More than enough." Wrapping his arms around the bags on the floor, Seth lifted his packages before shuffling through her apartment door. He didn't even have the decency to close the door behind him, so Angela did it for him, slamming it so hard the framed pictures on the wall rattled with the reverb and her favorite photograph of Boston came crashing to the ground.

She let out a cry of frustration as she leaned against the door, closing her eyes as tears finally escaped down her cheeks.

"Now that that's out of the way," Delilah mused, standing up from the sofa and stretching as if she'd just had the workout of her life. "Want to go get some coffee?"

Angela's rage had reached its breaking point. She stormed over to her companion and glared, her left eye jumping.

"Go to Hell!"

With a frown, Delilah closed her eyes and was gone as quickly as she had appeared, leaving Angela alone in her apartment in the shadows of the Christmas tree lights.

Angela wasn't much for alcohol, but waking up had her feeling like she'd spent the night drinking her cares away and was suffering for it now. For once, Delilah listened to her and was not in the apartment when she emerged from her bedroom. Good; let her stay away. Let them all stay away. They were better off that way anyway.

With a pounding headache, she readied herself for another day of retail at Christmastime, yet deep down, she half-hoped that she'd walk into The White Page and see Seth sitting at that same table, focused on writing in the same journal.

When she arrived, his table was occupied by an elderly woman and her granddaughter sharing a red and green sugar cookie.

She let out a breath and turned away from the café to begin her shift. She wouldn't have even known what to say if he'd been there anyway.

The next week went by as uneventfully as one could expect from the holiday season. Angela felt as though she was merely going through the motions—waking up and going to work, coming home and going to sleep. Wash, rinse, repeat. Even the mad rush of Christmastime retail couldn't distract her from the monotony that plagued her. It was just one busy day after the other until they all blurred into one and Angela lost track of time, regardless of it being the holiday season.

One night after another busy and mind-numbing day, she laid on her couch with the lights from her almost-dead Christmas tree providing the only light source. It wasn't much different than how Delilah had lounged last time

Angela had seen her. But it wasn't like she could just call her friend when she needed her. And her phone remained eerily silent. No text messages, no calls—nothing from anyone. Playing devil's advocate, she scanned through her texts, noting that the last one she had received from Seth was his confirmation on time and place the last time they saw each other. Her fingers hovered over the keyboard, but she stopped herself.

Just then, her phone rang. Startled, she dropped it to the ground. By the time she rolled over to pick it up and see who it was, the caller had hung up. The caller ID revealed the culprits: her parents.

Delilah knew well enough to leave her alone.

She did go so far as to leave a note on the kitchen counter in an attempt to communicate. Angela found it the day after her parents tried to call her and she refused to call them back. It asked if she wanted to get coffee in Delilah's familiar elegant script. Angela crumpled it up and tossed it into the kitchen trash barrel before she left for work.

The morning after, Angela found another note in the same spot on the counter, this one asking if she could meet at The White Page after work. Again, the note was thrown away.

With both requests ignored, Delilah didn't ask again.

Before Angela realized it, it was Christmas Eve. The

bookstore had closed early to give its employees the opportunity to return home and begin celebrating with their loved ones. To Angela, all it meant was a long walk home in the cold to an even colder apartment, leaving her alone to contemplate the life choices she had made up until that point, or rather, the choices that may have been made for her, as if she was no more than a puppet following along on pulled strings.

Between Delilah and Seth, perhaps that's all she was: a toy to be played with, a marionette to be strung along for a greater purpose... but what? To prove a point? Another person whose to be judged? No, she didn't want to be either of those.

And she didn't want to go home. Instead, she decided to walk the length of the city's main street before she reached the almost empty ice-skating rink at the center of town. There were only a few couples skating their laps, as if trying to get in some final quality time before the holiday madness fell upon them. Angela couldn't blame them.

The winter wind gusted through the square, and she hugged herself as she took a seat on what she realized was the same bench she and Seth had occupied the last time they were together, on their date. She wondered how it would have turned out if things had gone differently. If Delilah hadn't shown up, or if she hadn't asked Seth to come back to her apartment at all. Maybe she wouldn't be so alone—

No, she would always be alone.

"It's quite cold out for Christmas Eve, don't you think?"

Angela hadn't noticed the man sitting next to her a moment ago, but she had been so lost in her own thoughts it wouldn't have surprised her if ten people had tried talking to her between the bookstore and the skating rink. The man was bundled in a woolen trench coat with a plaid scarf wrapped around his neck and a small pair of wire-rimmed glasses on his nose. He was alone, but Angela made a quick sweep of the surrounding area to ensure he was, in fact, talking to her.

"I'm sorry, was this seat taken?"

"Oh, not at all," he responded with the lilt of a British accent. "In fact, you're right on time."

"For what?"

"For that."

The man pointed a gloved finger in the direction of the church across the square, and with what appeared to be a snap of his fingers, the evergreen tree standing tall before it was alit with the glow of hundreds of sparkling white lights.

Angela was in awe. She never remembered seeing such a display there before, but with the state she had been in lately, her tunnel vision focusing only on what she had to do rather than everything else happening in the world around her, it wouldn't have surprised her if it came and went without her giving it a second thought.

"It's my favorite part of the season," the man said as he watched the lights, their twinkling reflected in his glasses.

Angela had to agree. "It's beautiful."

The man turned to her with a sparkle in his eye that matched the lights on the tree. "Did you know that holiday lights are the symbol of the light, hope, and good in the world?"

"I can't say I did," Angela responded, not wanting to appear rude, but also not looking for a lesson.

"And the Christmas lights serve to remind us to provide light to others during the holiday season and throughout the rest of the year. Sometimes it's hard to remain on our path, and the light shows us the way, even in the darkest of times."

"And what if your life is all one big darkest time?"

"Then you need to surround yourself with more light." The man winked.

"I don't see that happening any time soon."

"And why do you say that?"

"My track record doesn't seem to be ideal when it comes to spreading light, or whatever it is I need to do."

"Well, I don't believe that, and I've only just met you."

"Stick around for a bit and I'm sure you'll see what I mean."

As the man continued to watch her, she hugged herself tighter, uncertain if she wanted to be the center of someone's assessment.

"So why are you out walking alone on Christmas Eve? Don't you have a family to visit or friends to celebrate with?"

"Not as of late," she admitted, looking anywhere but at the man.

"Hmm," he said. "I'd offer to have you join me in my ventures, but I'm depending on my compatriot this holiday season, and it wouldn't be proper for me to invite you when I haven't asked them if the invitation would be allowable."

"It's quite all right," Angela assured him with a small smile. "I'm not exactly the best company for anyone at the moment."

"You seem well enough company now."

"That's because you've just met me."

"Yes, we've gone over that already." He smiled.

Angela could only shake her head—this was not what she imagined her Christmas Eve would be like. But the more she considered it, the less sure she was of what she *wanted* her Christmas Eve to be like. Any other year, it would have been just her and Delilah, and that was fine... until she'd met Seth. And then, for a short moment, she'd considered what it would be like to have a holiday with someone else—someone new—and she had been so close until she blew it.

But there *was* someone new, and chances were she wasn't going to be seeing him ever again, and she so desperately needed someone to talk to—someone potentially impartial—to tell her, for once, that she wasn't crazy.

"In the spirit of the holiday," she started, turning toward the man, but he seemed as though he was already expecting the conversation. Angela continued, "Do you believe in the good—or bad—in people? Or that there's a way to truly absolve yourself from sins or judgment during your time in this world?"

The man gave her a warm smile. "That seems like quite the inquiry from a stranger on the day before Christmas."

"I know," she conceded. "But I hate feeling I've made a ridiculous mistake because I didn't know any better."

"Do you feel as though you've incorrectly assumed the worst about someone?"

"Or he's incorrectly assumed the best in me. Either way, could we both be wrong and right at the same time? Are we allowed to judge someone for what we see without knowing who they are?"

"The power to judge another, for better or for worse, is dangerous to behold. Some believe they have that ability, while those that truly do aren't so quick to admit it out of fear of the power they possess."

"But there's so much in this world that deserves to be judged—so much that's wrong, and it doesn't just go away because there's snow on the ground and lights on a tree."

A change in the season didn't change a person's true nature. There were so many who saw the holidays as a way to absolve themselves of their past—her own parents were a prime example. They only called during Christmas. Only tried to call, anyway...

"No, but it's a good place to start. Just like those lights, there's hope—hope for a new start, a new beginning, and the hope that our past wrongdoings can be forgiven, and we can move on."

"And if we can't?" Her parents, Delilah, Seth... would new beginnings with any of them ever be a possibility?

His smile widened. "Are you familiar with Luke?"

"Can't say I've ever met him."

He chuckled softly. "'*And there were in the same country shepherds abiding in the field, keeping watch over their flock by night. And, lo, the angel of the Lord came upon them, and the glory of the Lord shone round about them: and they were sore afraid.*' So it just goes to show, even in the brightest of times, with the greatest hope, we are still allowed to be scared."

She shook her head. "Your Lord isn't going to do anything for me. This is going to have to be something I figure out on my own. For too long, I've allowed other people to tell me what's good and what's bad, who deserves to be judged and who remains without sin. But what if no one deserves that treatment? What if none of us deserve that hope? What if those who judge are no better than the sinners they hold in judgment?"

"We are allowed hope. We are allowed to judge. But we need to be cognizant of it and realize that there are others who may be doing the same to us."

"So, in the end, none of us are good enough."

"We all have the power to be good, Angela. We just need to make the effort to see it."

She whipped her head toward him. "What did you just say?"

But the man didn't pay her any attention. Instead, he pulled out a gold pocket watch and flipped it open. "It's almost 8:06..."

Her heart pounded against her ribcage. "I didn't tell you my name."

He put his pocket watch back into his coat. "I do believe the train will be leaving soon."

"Train?" Angela asked, but stilled as the memory swept over her like the chilled winter wind.

I'm looking forward to taking the train home for the holidays...

"Train..."

She stood and moved before her brain could catch up with her.

Train.

Seth said he was leaving on a train to return to his family for Christmas. If she left now, she'd just about make it to the train station in time, before Seth left for the holidays, and if she could just see him one more time, maybe she could begin to explain to him...

Suddenly remembering her manners, she turned back toward the man on the bench. "Thank you very much for listening—"

The bench was empty.

"Wait!" Angela yelled as she ran down the train platform.

The snow had started falling again by the time she reached the station. There were only so many trains leaving at 8:06 P.M. and she hoped she had made the right choice. At first, she didn't think it was enough—not loud enough, not soon enough. She stopped to catch her breath, and just as she was about to give up hope, Seth reemerged from the train, eyes wide with surprise.

She let out a desperate groan. Forcing her sore muscles and aching lungs to move, she pushed herself forward again. She stopped only when he was within her reach and she wrapped her arms around his neck.

He held her tight; he was warm. Like the hot chocolate they'd shared, like a roaring fire on the coldest night. He was comfort in the dark, the light of hope.

They stood like that only a moment longer before Seth took a step away to assess her. "Angela? What are you doing—"

"Shut up and let me talk." She panted once more before she met his gaze. "I can't let you leave without knowing the truth about me."

"I've been trying to figure that out since the day I met you at Cuervo Negro."

"I know, and I know I've been less than forthcoming, and there's a reason for it."

"Does it have anything to do with David?"

Angela blinked. "What? No. I mean, not exactly."

Seth raised a brow in question.

"But David's not the point," Angela continued. "It's more about what's happened since we met, and why I don't want what happened to David to happen to you too."

The booming voice of the announcement system broke into their conversation.

"The 8:06 train will be departing from Platform Three in two minutes.

Time was running short, apparent by the pleading look on Seth's face.

"The point is... regardless of what coffee you drink or how you dress or whether my friend likes you or not, none of that matters. All that matters is what I think of you—the good I see in you. And I know that it's something I'm willing to chance, and forget all the rest."

"Angela—"

"And I'm sorry. There's so much I need to tell you, but I know there's no time to tell it to you now, even though I want to bare my soul, regardless of the ramifications."

"You don't need to do that."

"I know. But I want to. Just like I want to do this."

She didn't allow him the chance to counter her. She didn't think, didn't pause to consider her actions. Instead, she leaned into him and, with her arms tight around his neck, brought her lips to his.

Kissing Seth was sweeter than she ever could have imagined, and she closed her eyes to cherish the moment. The sound of the trains pulling in and out of the station around them was drowned out by the rushing of blood through her body. The Christmas snow falling around them melted against her heated cheeks. She smiled against his lips. Kissing Seth just felt... *good.*

"How about I meet you for coffee as soon as I get back," he said softly when their lips finally parted. His hand remained on her face, his thumb gently caressing her cheek as their eyes met in such a way that Angela's stomach tightened and her toes curled in her boots.

"I would like that very much," she whispered, as if afraid talking too loud would frighten him away for good.

He smiled. "I'll try to be home for New Year's."

"I'll keep the champagne chilled."

His smile broadened as he leaned in to kiss her brow. The announcement that the train was departing sounded once more, and there was no more time to delay. Seth gave her one more kiss, gave her hands one more squeeze, and she watched as he disappeared through the train car's door.

Seth let out a huff as he sat down in the plush seat of the train car, his attention remaining on Angela where she stood on the platform until the train rolled on and she disappeared out of sight.

"I told you she was good. I knew you'd like her. You really do need to pay attention to me more often."

Seth pulled his attention from the window and toward the prim and proper British gentleman now sitting in the seat across from him. His three-piece suit was impeccable, as always, and the wire-rimmed reading glasses resting on the end of his nose completed the pompous get-up.

Shaking his head, but unable to remove the smile from his face, Seth turned his attention to the passing landscape outside the window.

"When you're right, you're right," Seth agreed with his friend. "Happy Holidays to you too, Michael."

Coffee Talk

By M. Dalto

M. Dalto is a bestselling Young Adult and New Adult author of adventurous romantic fantasy stories. Her bestselling debut novel, *Two Thousand Years*, was one of Wattpad.com's 2016 Watty Award winners for excellence in digital storytelling. She has since released two sequel novels and and three companion novellas.

She was recruited to participate in Wattpad Paid Stories program for serialized authors in March 2019 and has since been invited into the Wattpad Stars program. She continues to volunteer her time as both as a freelance editor and as a mentor, where she hopes to engage, assist, and inspire new writers through their literary journey.

She spends her days working as a full-time real estate paralegal, leaving her evenings to pursue her own writing agenda. When she's not typing furiously at her computer, she enjoys reading fantasy novels, playing video games, and drinking coffee. She currently lives in Massachusetts with her husband, their daughter, and their corgi named Loki.

The Empire Saga

Two Thousand Years

Mark of the Empress

Beginning's End

The Empire Saga Novella Series

Reylor's Lament

Treyan's Promise

Saryana's Fate

Arms of the Ocean

Escaping the Grey

Masks Anthology

authormdalto.wordpress.com

twitter.com/MDalto421

facebook.com/MDalto

instagram.com/author.mdalto

Bound by What

Jess Moore

ONE

Anne, 2019

Everything always seemed so dire—urgent. And now? Now, I can't feel time passing. I see it. I watch the world moving forward and progressing toward—well, no spoilers—but from a floaty, faraway, magical distance. A place that keeps me as only an observer. Limbo. Purgatory. Ever Land, where moments unwind from a constantly changing spool of fate. The poor, shimmering thread doesn't seem to even know its own shape until it's too late. And then it snaps.

Jesse Hudson, co-founder and CEO of one of the most successful direct sales marketing companies in the United States, stands before me. I would've recognized her tight ass anywhere. And it is currently filling out an elegantly-tailored scarlet-red business suit as she paces along the edge of a stage.

Beyond her, cast in a dusky shadow under dimmed chandeliers, are hundreds of listeners. Microphone in hand, Jesse spews out meaningless "inspirational" quotes about being one's best self and leading without fear and letting vulnerability rule the day. I recognize them all because I was there when we collected them from the internet. We spent long nights drinking way too much wine and laughing about all the memes we were going to turn into sales motivation. I never really thought people would fall for it, but I'd been wrong.

Jesse's speech falters as if she forgot her next line. Someone in the audience coughs, and Jesse takes her time unscrewing the cap on her bottled water. As she sips, a stream of sweat trickles down her temple, taking with it layers of Candied primer, foundation, and powder. She is melting.

She taps her laptop and the next slide appears on the projection screen behind us. For a second, I think I've caught her eye. Lord, can she actually *see* me? But it was only a fleeting moment and within seconds, I recognize it as the coincidence it probably was. Jesse points to the big screen to reiterate her next point.

"You can choose to make things better for yourself." She smiles at the crowd. The Bing cherry-colored Candied lip stain highlights her perfect blue-white teeth. "This is America, people." Jesse stops again, whether for dramatic effect or because something is wrong I can't be sure. She clears her throat. "You have a God-given right to your dream, and..." Jesse step-stumbles backward. Her hip grazes the table where her laptop and water are situated. The water topples to the floor and, since she still has the cap in her hand, spills. There is some scrambling off stage.

"Jesse!" A man frantically stage-whispers from the wings. "Jesse, are you all right?"

She seems dazed, as if she just woke up in front of an audience hanging on her every word. The man calls her name again. She glances in his direction and shakes her head. Minions rush around backstage, prodding her to keep going.

"Excuse me," is all she says, and then the click-clacking of her heels fill the lecture hall as she marches herself off stage.

I never make a conscious decision to follow her, but there I am being yanked behind her as she snakes her way through the maze of what I assume is a convention center. The place is decked out with holiday decorations and Candied marketing materials: life-size posters of models wearing Santa hats and makeup trends for the new year, booths filled with free samples, pamphlets, and enamel pins shaped like a piece of hard candy that say, "Always treat yourself. XOXO, Candied." Instinctively, I know what all of this is—our annual Twelve Days of Candied sales conference—because it was my idea. It seemed brilliant at the time. What mom wouldn't want to get away for a few days after bustling her kids back to school?

The chaos of the holidays is over, now indulge with Candied. For only $299 (sell four Luscious Look kits), you can partake in the luxury that is being your own #girlboss!

*Accommodations not included.

Jesse practically runs through all the hoopla, seemingly ignoring the people calling out her name as she races by. Soon enough, we are out in the open and Jesse is doubled over, taking big, gulping breaths. And me? I'm trying to remember what cool air felt like on my skin. It's then that I look down and notice the manacles around my wrists and the chain connecting me to a shackle around Jesse's ankle. With the realization comes the feeling; the metal, hard and icy-hot, sends waves of tingling pressure through my whole being. It's unpleasant in that it is unwavering, reliable like the ocean tides. My ties to her are repetitive and terrible.

Jesse is trembling as she reaches into the pocket of her blazer and pulls out a pack of Parliament Lights—our brand since high school. She lights her cigarette, her fingers still shaking, and inhales deeply, then blows a long stream of smoke into my face. I should be able to smell it, but nothing registers except for the longing of it.

"What the fuck?" Jesse asks, her voice barely more than a whisper.

I look around, trying to place who she's speaking to. The only people on the sidewalk keep their heads down and their shoulders hunched in their warm, puffy winter coats. Traffic creeps by while a slushy mix of rain and snow collects on the road. The lamp posts are still decorated with the limp, wet boughs of some evergreen.

Jesse's teeth are just starting to chatter when a young, nerdy-looking guy wearing a sweater vest and a headset emerges from the building carrying a creamy-white wool coat. He holds it out for her, and she slips into it without so much as a word, her cigarette clamped between her lips.

"Thanks, Billy."

"It's what I'm here for," he says and rubs his arms against a cold that I cannot feel. "Are you okay?"

"I'm fine." Jesse blows another long trail of smoke from between her pursed lips. I desperately want to stand in front of her and suck it all in, feel that heavy, burning sensation deep in my lungs, but I don't even try because it wouldn't work. I'd just end up being more frustrated when it ends up tasting like nothing but a big ol' void.

"Then what happened back there?"

"I don't know. I got spooked."

"Well, it's very common to experience stage fright—"

"It wasn't fucking stage fright, Billy. I've been doing these things for years."

"Then what was it?"

"Overwhelm. I was overwhelmed."

"That's to be expected, ma'am. Your schedule has been—"

"Don't call me ma'am, you little prick. Who's finishing the presentation?"

"Tara."

"Good." Jesse drops her cigarette and steps on it, the toe of her pointed, neutral pump snuffing out the lit end. "And after that are the workshops, yes?"

"Yes, ma—Ms. Hudson."

"That's better. I'll be in my hotel room should anyone need me."

"What about the Vision Belle Coordinators?" When no answer comes, Billy continues, "You're the featured presenter for that workshop."

Jesse rubs a circular pattern in the space between her eyes. Her fingernails look newly manicured and match her suit. "Patch me through on my laptop. I'll meet with them that way."

"Are you sure? They paid extra for access—"

"I can't, Billy. I can't be in a room of needy people right now. Okay?"

"All right. Should I offer them a refund?"

"What the fuck for? I'll still be there, sitting through an hour and a half of their whining. I'll just be doing it from the comfort of my own room."

"Yes, Ms. Hudson. I'll set it up."

"Thank you." Jesse pulls the collar of her coat closer around her neck and walks to the nearest crosswalk. I trail behind her. If she feels the drag of the shackle on her ankle as it wrenches me along, she doesn't let on.

"Damn," she curses under her breath as we approach the other side of the street. A man dressed in a tattered flannel shirt with a long beard, his bottom half covered by a torn and dirty sleeping bag, holds up a sign. He asks for change and naturally I know Jesse has some. I can't feel the chill bite of the wind as it whips her hair off her shoulders, but I sense her fingers grip a few coins in her coat pocket as if they are my own. She looks away from the man. Even though it is dead cold and she has so much to give, she looks away. Disgust wells in her mind and heart, simultaneously blooming in my own.

We pass a line of cars waiting near a valet station under a canopy of twinkling lights. Jesse pushes through a revolving door and we enter an extravagant hotel lobby. White stone pillars frame the seating area. Comfortable-looking chairs and couches form a perimeter around a marble fireplace, crackling with actual logs and flame. I long to hold my hands near it and feel something as simple as heat, versus the burning sparks that pulse through our rattling chains, but Jesse doesn't slow down. She clip-clops her way past the front desk and waits near the elevator doors. Her movements are spastic with anxiety. It's an old tic. When Jesse's feelings run high, her body has trouble remaining still.

The elevator is empty, and Jesse braces herself once the doors close.

"Breathe," she says. For an instant, I think she's commanding me, directing my stagnant lungs to draw in oxygen. Now that would have been a luxury, something I would have paid any price for. Instead I listen as Jesse pulls air through her nose and blows it out through her mouth.

What opulence! How grand that must be! The chains send another throb of stabbing pain, and I absorb it.

Jesse looks at the ceiling, her lips parted and trembling. I wonder what spooked her so and almost ask, then remember I have a voice that no one hears. Jesse blinks rapidly, her fake eyelashes fluttering like insect wings. Tears form and she dabs at the corners of her eyes.

"Stop it. Stop it. Stop it," she mutters.

The elevator dings and the doors open. A man dressed in a cozy camel-colored sweater stands just beyond the threshold and asks if we were going down.

"Up!" Jesse shouts. "Look at the lights. I'm going up, dumbass!"

"Um, okay." The man's brow crinkles over a set of startingly ice-blue eyes, obviously confused as to why he is being yelled at.

Jesse steps forward and frantically presses the Close button until the elevator doors slide shut once more.

I laugh at the scene. I'd forgotten this about her. She's almost always responding in ways that are inappropriate. She says what she thinks with little to no filter. I loved this quality about her because it meant I never had to play the guess-it game. If I wanted to know what she thought, I merely had to ask. It was wonderfully refreshing, and it's what made her a great boss. People who worked closely with her considered her both a straight-shooter and a bitch.

When the doors open again, we're at the floor number she selected, and we plod toward her room. The hall carpet is dark green and plush, like a freshly mowed lawn in the summertime. I imagine what it might feel like against bare feet—soft, tickling, that slight dip with each step—and the shackles light me up with another crashing stab of pain.

Jesse swipes a key card across the door's scanner and a

pinprick of green light appears as the lock clicks. She opens the door and tears her coat off, throwing it across a satiny love seat. She kicks off her heels, losing several inches in the process, and paces in front of a wall of windows that show off the city's skyline. The sky begins to change, blue fades to gray, and little pockets of square lights pop on within the surrounding buildings, each one representing something—someone—like stars.

But Jesse doesn't notice any of these things. She's too busy rummaging through the mini-fridge and cracking the seal on a tiny shot of alcohol. After swallowing half of it, she unloads her laptop from its bag and sets it up on the desk. Her phone dings excessively with notifications, and she clicks on one. Her assistant's face fills the screen, and he asks if she is all set up for the class he mentioned earlier. She says she isn't, and he tells her to pull up the video conferencing app and that he'll patch her through. Jesse clicks her phone off and takes a few deep breaths. She does as he said and then crosses over to the line of windows and watches as I did, the individual lights flickering on in every building, every room, representing a life, movement, someone's forward motion, time passing.

"Why are you here?" she whispers, her face so close to the glass that it fogs with her words.

Can she see me?!

Her computer bleeps, and she rushes toward it, plopping herself in front of the tiny camera and primping just a bit before clicking Accept. But not even the interruption is enough to stop the rush of joy spreading through my whole being. When I'd been, well, wherever I was before all of this, I'd felt nothing for what seemed like forever. It had been an abyss; I'd been alone and that's all there was. But now someone—my Jesse, of course it would be her—sees me, and a spark of something burns around the place where my heart had been.

Had been.

I used to be like one of those lights flickering against the coming, inevitable dark, but now, here I am, only a ghost.

Okay, so yeah, I'd been a bit cognizant of it. There had been some inkling that my body wasn't really a body back in that Ever Land space. And then there were the burning chains, the lack of any other feeling, the stagnancy of my own lungs, the ability to just *be* wherever Jesse is without any real purposeful movement on my part... Sure, those all seem like big ghost vibes, looking back. But through either denial or a glitch in my memories, the realization that I'm an apparition, a shadow of myself... well, it's just not the most natural of conclusions. And if I am getting technical—which was something I always did when I was alive—I had to come here to actually *be* the ghost, *to do* the haunting.

"Hiii-eeee!" Jesse drawls and waves at the screen of her computer. "I'm so happy to be with all of you this evening. Look at you all!"

I hover behind her, staring at a window screen into a room of about fifty people, all wearing Candied's pink-and-white striped neckerchiefs around their necks, which means they have conned seven of their closest friends into salesmanship. They smile and wave at Jesse as she instructs her assistant to walk his laptop around the room. She personally greets each of them. The mask she uses to welcome people sparkles with sincerity. It is nearly impossible to think this woman, with her mom-next-door demeanor and polished look, is conning the shit out of them all.

Each face the camera pans over is happy and smiling, but I know what comes next. Story time. It's part of the schtick. We ask questions—*What's holding you back from having all the success you want?*—and that's all it ever took. The Vision Belles open up about their lives, and it bonds them to each other, and to the company by proxy, in inexplicable ways. Ways that are almost predatory, definitely exploitive, but no one ever complains. They leave our conferences with a sense of community, and who are we to judge?

"I'd love to hear about you, especially since I can't be there. I know this class was advertised as having access to me and my winning sales strategies, and we'll get to that. But I need to know about you in order to help. So yes, I see you in the back. Go ahead."

A woman with a thick ponytail stands up and introduces herself: Maria, thirty-one, from here. Her mother got sick last fall and needs full-time care, but Maria can't afford it. Medicare only covers so much. They sold off her mother's condo and belongings and they can just manage—for now. Maria's hope is that selling Candied products will absorb some of the financial burden. She has a day job but plans to quit and be her mother's primary caregiver once her business takes off.

It will never work. I know it; Jesse knows it. Maria wipes tears from her cheeks and someone next to her hands her a strategically placed box of Candied-brand tissue infused with aloe vera and coconut oil.

Jesse clutches her chest. "Oh, Maria. Your story... Well, that's the kind of thing we always hoped Candied would be able to do for people. And if you work the system, you'll build your own success. I know you can do that for yourself and your mom."

On the surface, it sounds wonderful. We help people. Direct sales seems like a way for people to break the chains of the system and become their own boss. Their success is theirs; they just have to reach out and take it. Or at least, that's what we keep telling them.

More people stand to take their turn. They share stories about wanting to take their kids to Disney World and spouses working multiple jobs and the loneliness that comes along with becoming a new parent. In short, they are all just wanting to get a step ahead, a boost, or some connection, and Candied came along at just the right time. They pass out tissues and pat each other's arms. Several hugs are given. This is what Candied was built on: these people and their needs becoming our profit, not theirs.

Throughout the workshop, Jesse barely flinches for the camera. Her expression never wavers with boredom or loses its look of compassion and love. She is their matriarch and they must think she cares. She learned that from me.

For years, we were a tag team. She was the unfeeling, hard-edged one, and I was the soft place for people to fall, the listener. Together though, we were perfect—a powerful force. She taught me how to be bold, and I tried to teach her how to give a shit. I don't know if Jesse was a bad student, or if I was a crap teacher, but her ability to empathize was never truly authentic. She harbors the same feelings for these people that she had for the man on the street, a secret disgust for their neediness, as if it were contagious. Eventually, I stopped trying to change her. We used to break for the night, open an expensive bottle of wine, and never speak of them. Never touched on their narratives again. Never asked ourselves if what we were doing was right. Because the wine always tasted better than the truth.

"Ladies, I see great things for all of you. Your goals are within your grasp." She sips some water and launches into act two, the origin story. How Candied came to be: a tale of two young college grads tending bar while obsessively researching how to make makeup that reminded them of the candy-flavored lip glosses and eye shadows we played with as kids. After a shit-ton of experimentation, the research became a legit side hustle, and after a while, we were making enough money to quit the bar. We hired more staff to keep up with demand, secured a loan, and steadily grew the company. Then, and this was all spin, we decided to help other women get the same shot by implementing a direct sales business model. What really happened: we got greedy. Like miserly, Ebenezer Scrooge levels of money-grubbing.

Wait.

Ebenezer Scrooge?

No.

It can't be.

But...

Is that what this is all about? Am I some kind of stand in for Jacob-fucking-Marley? It must be a joke. No way did THE Victorian era writer, Dickens Himself, tap into some universal truth about spirituality and the realm after death. It isn't possible. Is it? And if it is real... I'm linked to Jesse Hudson for, what? Eternity? Bound by what, exactly? I see the chains, I feel the chains, but by what power do they hold me here?

Jesse drones on and on, platitude after platitude. *Doubt is the dream killer. Happiness equals choice plus action. You can't lose if you don't ever give up.* Lies disguised as motivation. What does it really mean? Stay longer. Try harder. Spend more. Buy in.

How am I supposed to teach Jesse a lesson? On a good day, she's stubborn as hell and singularly focused on expanding Candied because that's the only way any of this works. What the hell happens to my spirit when she inevitably says, "Thanks, but no thanks"?

As if in answer to my questions, the shackles around my wrists give another tug of searing pain. A blinding silver light fills the room, but I don't look away. I can't. It grows ever larger, devouring every shadow, spotlighting every high point, until there is nothing but the gleaming chrome finish of a mirror. For an instant, I see myself reflected in the surface. I am there, but only in the way one reads about in ghost stories —a faint specter of my former self. My hair, what is left of it, is stringy and hangs limp around my shoulders. Wraith-me, translucent and blue, with valleys of indigo under my eyes and in the hollows of my cheeks, hovers directly behind Jesse. And oh my god, the contrast! Her vibrancy stirs a devouring sensation in my core.

And just as suddenly as the mass of reflection appeared, covering every surface of the room, it starts to collapse in on itself. The mercury-like substance oozes away from the corners and back out from under the loveseat until it coagulates into a mass of undulating silver.

Pop!

A cat with fluffy silver-blue fur primps itself in the place where the blob had been.

"Have you begun?" The cat meticulously drags its paw over one of its ears.

"Excuse me?"

"You heard me." Its voice is sonorous, with a fullness like warm milk and chocolate.

"I'm sorry. I have no idea what I'm supposed to be doing here. I've just figured out that this might be some kind of Scrooge-like scenario."

The cat blinks and runs its tongue over its teeth. "No one's been in contact with you?"

"Uh, no. I've been alone for... well, I don't know how long, until today, when I just kind of showed up here."

"Oh, for fuck's sake," the cat grumbles. "So you have no idea what's going on?"

"Not a clue."

"Typical." The cat leaps onto the coffee table and seems to be speaking to itself. I manage to pick out the words *management* and *incompetence.*

"Dunning-Kruger effect?" I ask, remembering that smart-ass part of my personality.

The cat laughs, a jarring purr of a ha-ha. "Yes, maybe. So you mentioned Scrooge; are you familiar with the story?"

"I mean, sure." A little green frog puppet wearing a newsboy cap and a crutch comes to mind.

"Then you get the gist. You have to change this life."

As the cat references Jesse, her voice returns to the room, its tone warm and inviting, cheerful and encouraging. "Candied products can change your life, but you have to take the first steps. Believe in what Candied can do for you and your friends and family. Don't be afraid to ask that clerk at the gas station about her skin care regimen. People want to talk." Jesse pauses and adds a little rehearsed laughter. "I mean, look at us! We've opened up about all kinds of things here today. And really, the bottom line is, you're helping people. Teaching them how to feel better about the way they look by using products that are proven to work."

Translation: give me all your money.

"And who are you supposed to be? The Ghost of Christmas Past or something?" I ask.

"Uh, no. That's not a thing. There's only me and a series of higher ups that claim to be in charge of this whole thing, but from what I can tell..." The cat suddenly gags and makes that awful, horrible retching sound cats make right before coughing up a hairball. "Sorry." The disgusting wad of matted fur and glowing bits of silver light puddle on the carpet. "They can be a vindictive bunch."

"Who?"

The cat raises its paw and extends a claw toward the ceiling. I look, but the only thing there is a boxy, oatmeal-colored hotel ceiling with recessed lighting.

"I'm sorry..." I pause, not knowing if the cat has a name.

"I don't have a name in the Earthly sense."

"What do I call you then?"

"Past. Present. Future. Time."

"Time," I repeated. "You're a Time Cat. None of this makes much sense."

"Has it ever?"

The question seems like a riddle, but the swelling in my chest, the part of me that just instinctively knows the answers to things, thinks, *No.*

Time Cat continues as if it's heard my thought. "Right. So, the way she's feeding herself from too many plates, that is what must change." An almost imperceptible sneer raises the cat's jowl and shows the sharpest point of a fang.

"Okay, calm down. I'll try." A little startled, I step closer to where Jesse sits, still chatting away at the computer. My mouth close to her ear, I whisper her name. She flinches and her shoulder raises, passing through the bottom part of what would've been my face, then continues with her practiced speech.

"She won't listen. I know her; it's a waste of time."

"Did time seem to matter where you just came from?"

"No."

"Well then, try again."

I turn back to my old friend as she clicks out of the conferencing app and closes her computer, but before I say a word to her, I have a question for the cat. "Why didn't anyone do this for me?"

"How do you know someone didn't try?"

"I never experienced any interactions like this."

The cat's tail flicks, patting against a coffee table leg. "Oh, there's no use hiding it. You're right. No one was chained to you. I mean, if this one"—Time Cat nods toward Jesse, who is now rummaging through her luggage on the bed—"would've died first, then maybe she'd be the one talking with me. But as is, you showed up first."

"So if I do this, what happens to me?"

"*Hshsh!*" Time Cat hisses; its back arches and the fur spikes on end. "You... people." It spits the word just like the hairball. "You never learn anything. You're dead. What does it matter what happens to you? Either help her or not, but I'm not revealing what's in it for you."

"Will there be other ghosts?"

"No. Just you." Time Cat licks its paw and nibbles at the end of one claw. "And me."

"And what are you exactly?"

"A demigod."

"Really?"

"Yes. No. Kind of. It's what you understand. Can we get on with this, please?"

"I thought she could see me earlier. Can she?"

"She might be able to detect your presence. There are some people that have the ability to sense those kinds of things. But no, she can't actually see you yet."

"She spoke to me though. Over by the window."

"Might she have been speaking to herself?"

What had she said? *Why are you here?* I assumed it was meant for me, but maybe it hadn't been. Given that twist, her words ring desperate. Is my old friend okay? I can't be sure.

Time Cat waves one of its front paws and a veil of sparkling particles snow from the ceiling, delicately covering the heavily patterned, stain-resistant hospitality carpet. I step forward, disturbing the other-worldly layer of shine.

Jesse had gone into the bathroom; our tether pulled tight between us. There comes a flush and the splashing of water, then the chains connecting us pool as she reenters the room. To her credit, she doesn't start at my ghastly appearance. She drops the hand towel she carries and gapes, but she doesn't scream or hide, which are all viable reactions to finding your dead friend standing in your hotel room.

"Anne?"

I nod, unsure whether my voice can be trusted.

"What's happened to you?" She shakes her head as if she's asked the wrong question, surely grappling and disbelieving what stands in front of her. "Why—How are you here?"

I hold up my wrists and the chains rattle with the movement, filling the air with their terrible clanging. Jesse's eyes widen as her gaze follows the metal links to her own ankle. She gasps.

"You haven't been with me all this time, have you?" Jesse steps closer, the manacle causing a slight hitch in her stride. This close, I can see what the makeup can't get rid of: her eyelids sag a little and there are fine lines at the corners of her eyes. She holds up her hand, fingers set to graze my cheek, but pulls away at the last moment. "The accident... It was nearly fifteen years ago."

So that's how long I'd spent floating in that Ever Land. Fifteen years had seemed like hours. But maybe that's what happens to time when you stop being able to count it. It folds in on itself. Or maybe that's all the afterlife is anyway: a bodyless, timeless consciousness. The idea is somewhat freeing, more freeing than anything I'd been attached to here on Earth, except this friendship, this relationship with Jesse.

"I..." The sound, my voice, is scratchy. I try to swallow but there is nothing. "I have to warn you." My words come out with a moaning undercurrent to them, and I try not to roll my eyes. I wish to talk normally to my friend, but apparently this whole ghost encounter thing has standards to maintain.

"Warn me? About what?" Jesse crosses her arms, the material of her red blazer pulling tight around her shoulders.

"Candied."

"What about it? We're crushing our bottom line. It's a huge success."

"At a huge cost."

"Jesus Christ. I can't believe you're still going on about this. It's business, Anne."

"You know this is different." There is a surging in my chest, combined with the very real feeling that we've had this argument before. Years ago. Fifteen years ago, to be exact. Right before... I fell. The realization comes with a ringing sound that fills my whole head. My best friend had grabbed me and then pushed.

"You-you killed me?" I didn't mean for it to come out sounding like a question, but it did.

"That's not how it happened!" Jesse is pacing now, as much as she can with that manacle around her ankle. "Fuck! I can't believe this is happening."

"Well, it is. You pushed me that night." I could still feel her fingers gripping my arms, the spittle hitting my cheek as she yelled, screaming wildly about change and money and nothing being personal. I yanked my arm from her grasp, but there'd been a little shove that came with it. I stumbled backward and our eyes met. We'd both known what was going to happen right before it did. Her face was at the railing and she screamed my name.

I knew in that moment she hadn't meant for me to fall. I'd threatened the business, told her I planned on going public about what our company really is: a pyramid scheme. And she lost it. Had the fight happened inside, I'd probably still be alive, but it hadn't. I sprang the news on a rooftop terrace in the Caribbean. And then I tore my gaze away from hers to get one final look at the ocean, its turquoise waters calm and alluringly green before it all went black.

Time Cat saunters into view. "Reunion shows are always so messy."

Jesse jumps, her eyes wide and staring at the walking, talking, seemingly all-knowing cat.

"Oh, screw you," I say.

"I will ignore that. While in the grand scheme time may be as immaterial as the soul, it actually does have limits here. And you're running out of it." Time Cat leaps onto the bed, leaving a trail of silvery dust floating in the air behind it. Somewhere in the middle distance, bells tinkle and ring—a gentle alarm.

"To do what?" Jessie and I ask in unison.

"Convince her to change her ways." Time Cat's nose wrinkles.

"Why would I do that?" I ask. "She killed me last time."

"You know that's not true." Jesse crosses her arms defensively.

I give her a withering look.

She shrugs. "What? It was an accident."

"You don't feel guilty for what you're doing? What you've done?" I ask.

"Honestly?" She rolls her cherry-red lips together, the gloss still slick and wet-looking even after the all-day wear because we designed it that way. Together. "I feel bad about us and the way our relationship... ended. But no. I don't feel bad about the company. Candied does help people."

"It helps, like, twenty people! Not the people you just met over the computer. You heard their stories. You know they'll spend more money on product than they'll ever be able to sell. And they'll probably lose half their *actual* support system along the way because they're constantly trying to sell shit to their friends. You know this!"

"First of all, it's not shit." Jessie gestures with one finger, then two. "And secondly, why me? People have been ripping other people off for lifetimes. Candied is just our turn. Our time."

I'd heard similar words all those years ago on that rooftop. While the warm tropical breeze blew, the scent of sunscreen and piña coladas wafting in the wind, I could never convince her that it wasn't about what other people do, but what *we* do. Her response always boiled down to one question; why must we be the ones adhering to a higher standard? I said as much to the cat. "This is the same argument we've always had."

"And you will continue to have it until she sees." Time Cat licks its paw and rubs it over its ear repeatedly.

But why? I fall back into old patterns, agreeing with Jesse's logic because it's so easy. I turn to my old friend, giving her a certain look and hoping she can still read my expressions the way she used to. She winks. Tag team, just like the old days.

Jesse clears her throat. "Excuse me, Mr...? Mrs...?"

"It's Time Cat," I offer.

Jesse's eyebrows draw together for a moment, but she continues, "Uh, Time Cat."

"Yes." Time Cat yawns, licking its teeth and muzzle in a drawn-out process.

"We're curious as to what the selection process looks like in this little... shall we call it an experiment?"

"We?" Time Cat asks.

"Yes." I take over for Jesse, just like I used to in the boardroom. "What are the requirements for these winter-holiday-themed hauntings?"

Time Cat steps backward, leaving a trail of divots in the comforter, and arches its back. "You"—Time Cat points a paw directly at me—"are supposed to convince her to stop hurting people. It's the way it's always gone. I have no say in who gets chosen."

"See, that's where I'm having some trouble around this whole *thing*." Jesse crosses her arms. "Why us? Do you even know who the president is right now? Are you aware of the current state of this country? Of the world?"

"Who is it?" I ask.

"Clumwine."

"What? That creepy old actor?"

"Among other things, yes." Jesse nods. "So if that dirtbag gets to be president, why can't I make a couple cool million off some hard-working Americans? Huh? Answer me that."

"She's right, Time Cat. Why is she the one that has to be better while other people get ahead doing whatever they want? It's not fair." What the hell do I care about the state of the world? I'm not a part of it anymore.

"Why do I have to show up in cat form every now and again to make sure some humans don't screw hordes of other humans? You think I wouldn't rather be with my family? I don't know why I'm not in this Clumwine person's hotel room right now. But I'm here talking to you, trying to make sure you both do the right thing."

"And if we don't?" I ask.

"I don't know. That's never happened before." Time Cat

treads a circular pattern and then sits down again. "Look, you *must* agree that changing your ways will be one more step toward a universal balance."

"Good and evil shouldn't be balanced. There should always be more good than evil, and when there's not, well, fuck it all." I plop down on a plush armchair, defeated and half expecting to pass through the cushion. But I don't; the chair supports my essence, and the chains give a rattle.

"So what now? You two are just giving up. You're not going to *do* anything?" A seemingly angry urgency clips Time Cat's speech as its silvery fur bristles along its spine.

"I think that's the gist of it." Jesse hands me a flute of sparkling wine with two maraschino cherries nestled at the bottom of the glass, bubbles gathering along the skin. It's been our signature drink since our bar days.

"You do realize you're making more work for me?" Time Cat asks.

We clink our glasses and sip, the bubbles fizzing and popping on my lips and all the way down. And finally, I can taste it.

Jesse, 1997

Anne stands in front of me, but no longer is she the translucent wisp of her former self. Her billowing jeans hang low on her hips, exposing an inch of her back, more when she reaches for something, which is what she's doing now.

"Bobby said there was one more back here." Her voice is muffled, and her arm disappears into the mini fridge, then reemerges with a curvy green bottle in hand. Turning back to me, Anne's face is full and young and glows all on its own. We are celebrating something. She pops the cork and it shoots up toward the low drop-ceiling tiles, each individually painted to form a mural of Van Gogh's *Starry Night*.

It's the bar, our bar... from 1997? No.

"Hey. Are you okay?" she asks. "You look like you've seen a ghost." The body glitter sprinkled on her chest shines pink and pearly white.

"Um..." I scratch along my jaw. "I might have."

"Seriously?" She pours the sparkling wine into two glasses and drops a handful of cherries into each one. I don't have time to answer before she says, "Cheers." She holds her glass by the stem and waits for the *clink* of mine. I oblige but am too afraid to drink. The last thing I remember is being in a fancy hotel room dressed in a red business suit—*ew!*—toasting a dead-version of my friend with this very same drink. What happens if a take a sip now?

The date. The date. I need to know for sure, so I clear my throat and ask, "Is there a newspaper around here?"

A look of concern crosses Anne's face. "I think I saw one in the back. You want me to grab it?"

"Yeah, thanks."

She disappears through a doorway lined with twinkling, multi-colored holiday lights. I pour my drink down the bar sink, then scoop the cherries out of the drain and throw them in the trash. I'm not taking another chance. Future-me was cold, uncaring, her heart hardened by, what? Money. Grief. Guilt. Privilege. I don't want to be *her*; I won't let myself turn into *that*.

The bar is devoid of customers, but a few co-workers are smoking and flipping chairs onto the tables to clean the floors. One of them turns on a boom box and Mariah Carey's voice escalates through her upper range. Anne comes back around the corner, her wavy hair breezing over her shoulders, her face without a crease or line, that smile wide and quick and forgiving—always so forgiving. She still has her nose piercing—the one she'll lose at a Halloween party making out with some rando three years from now—and it glints under the bar lights as she slaps the newspaper in front of me.

"Here you go, J. Ugh, what are they listening to?" Anne goes to her backpack and pops a mixed CD from her Discman. "Tiffany, play this."

I scan the print for today's date and there it is: January 5, 1997—Twelfth Night. I've gone back in time, but how? Anne doesn't seem to have a clue that this has already happened, that we lived a whole life already. I turn, rotating around the bar stool until I face her and the others in the dining area. She twirls and dances with one of the guys. A sad little Christmas tree is propped up in the corner next to them, all lit up with white lights and red-checkered bows. Stockings with all our names written in glittery puff paint hang above the stage.

"Come on, Jesse! We're supposed to be celebrating!"

"Celebrating what?" The guy takes Anne by the waist and brings her toward him until his forehead touches hers. I should've held on to her like that. I ache as that last awful moment from another time—where she slips from my grasp and falls—materializes. It happened in slow motion, cynically so. The yelling led to the stumbling. The canopy smacked her back. And then she was suspended mid-air for a beat, as if time hesitated. I lost her then. The whole world lost her then.

She spins away and pulls something from her front pocket. "This." She holds up one of the little metal cannisters of lip gloss we make and sell at a flea market downtown. We finally made our money back and then some.

I don't even realize the scene has paused until the

jangling of bells ring above the door and no one moves, except for me. I hop up instinctively and shout, "We're closed!"

But no one is there. The room is filled with an eerie quiet. I should hear the spray of water over dirty dishes, the music, the cacophony of several conversations going on at once, but it's all stopped. And a gray cat saunters up to the bar. It leaps on to the stool next to mine.

"You again?"

"That's right."

"What now?"

"You already know."

"I have to leave her."

"Yep. Get me a drink, will ya?"

I walk behind the bar and ask the cat what kind.

"White Russian."

I mix the ingredients over ice and place a tumbler full in front of Time Cat, whose little paws press onto the bar top. The *lap-lap-lapping* of Time Cat's tongue in the cocktail is the only sound.

"Why do I have to leave?"

"Future-you won't change her mind." Time Cat laps more of its drink. But seemingly knowing I'm not convinced or that I need more information, it continues, "I'll level with you. You two are terrible for each other. Candied was never supposed to succeed and Anne wasn't scheduled to die when she did."

I cringe. I will never get over it. The look in her eyes when she understood that her life was over—the end. I spent the rest of my then-life hoping she knew that I hadn't meant for any of that to happen. I didn't leave my sandals there for her to trip over on purpose, and I certainly didn't cause the cabana tent to shift with the wind and smack into her. But I did grab her. I did shove her. I did argue with her over a stupid business model. And I am absolutely a piece of shit.

"Accidents happen." Time Cat taps a matchbook with its claw. "Management's been scrambling a bit ever since. Things got a little out of control."

"Ya think?"

"It's wild how one life affects so many things... Anyway, when I realized the two of you weren't going to change, I did a little dial adjustment and brought you back here. Figured I'd appeal to the younger you, the person that still loves her more than they love being rich."

Ouch.

"Can't I just talk her out of it? Convince her of a different plan? Do I really have to abandon her?"

"Look, that might work. But I can't just go around unspooling time *all* the time. One shot. That's all you get. If you won't do this for the thousands of people Candied ends up ripping off, then do it for her. Do it so she doesn't fly off that roof in the Caribbean, okay? She's the one that's supposed to help people. Not *Candied*." Time Cat pronounces *Candied* with a heavy dollop of sarcasm.

"I can just pull the plug on Candied. Make it so it never gets off the ground."

"Sabotage it?"

"Exactly."

Time Cat stares at me, its chartreuse eyes narrow and unblinking. If I felt confident in my ability to read a cat's facial expressions, I would say it was smirking.

"What?" I ask.

Time Cat places its paw on my hand. "Honey, you think I don't know about the other schemes?"

"I-I..." don't know what to say for myself. Anne and I ran some cons, but mostly they were coincidental. Or at least they started that way. Like, when we forgot to turn in the donation money after Trick-or-Treating for UNICEF and I convinced Anne we should put the funds toward pedicures instead. It's awful, but it's easy. So we kept at it. We made up fake organizations—Coalition for the Homeless, Friends to End Hunger, Pals of the Pound—and continued to go door to door. Nobody ever seemed all that interested in the charity details; they just gave us a few dollars to get us off their front porches.

"It's not just fake charities," Time Cat said. "You bring out the worst in each other."

"That's not true!" I protested. But a memory flash of portraits enters my mind, a long and winding gallery hall of people we hurt in one way or another: a teacher, we terrorized until she quit; that roommate freshman year, who we made fun of for crying in her bunk every night; that elderly neighbor who went on vacation and we forgot to feed her parakeet... Anne always felt guilty, but not me. I was just annoyed over the pep talks Anne required afterward.

So, I get it. I hear what Time Cat's not exactly saying, and it's me. The absence of me will make Anne great.

"Fine, I'll go." I don't even head to the back room to get my coat. At the door, I pause, giving my friend one final glance. She's frozen in time, happy and free, unaware that in the next moment I'll be out of her life forever. I didn't have feelings for all the people we screwed with, but I do feel something for her. I look at Time Cat and say, "You should've taken me farther back in time. Stopped us from ever meeting. Because letting me have half of this is cruel."

Time Cat shrugs. "Shit happens." Time Cat turns back to its drink, its delicate pink tongue licking the ice.

I walk out of that bar and never look back, quick stepping toward a different end.

Jesse, 2019

I click off the car radio, and the annoying laughter from the morning show fades to a soothing quiet. I-70 stretches before me. The sky overhead is as big and far-reaching as the dry and hollowed corn fields below it.

I've spent this whole lifetime hoping and wondering about her, all limbo-like. What happened after I left the bar? When Time Cat restarted the scene and Anne noticed I was gone, did she call out for me? Had she run outside, checking the sidewalks to see which way I'd gone? Did she find my tiny little Nokia phone that I left in my work cubby?

Answers I'll never know.

Online searches don't net much. I can only assume she got married and changed her name. Because only a thousand other Anne's in Ohio ever show up.

This life has been typical, a little boring. I got married, had two children, then divorced. I own a bar—called it Time Out, 'cause that's what this whole thing feels like—in the rural Indiana town where I ended up settling.

Now, I love love love my children. Loved my husband too, even though I don't always like to admit it. But the thrill of making millions, of having everything? All that carefree living? Well, that shit was fun as hell. It's hard to believe I lived a whole life without ever worrying about a hospital trip bankrupting me or the corn drowning in too much rain or a car being on its last leg. I guess that's a big ol' dollop of karma though, given my last life.

Anne's second chance had to be more than a little Midwestern life like mine. But I guess I'll never know.

I crack the window and let the cold of the plains chill both my skin and my thoughts. The holidays are over, and the kids went back to school a few days ago—one back to the freshman dorm at Purdue, the other finishing up the latter half of their junior year of high school. And I randomly realize that it's the twelfth day of Christmas: January 5, 2019. Twenty-two years have passed again. My hands are weathered and dry, skin cracking as I grip the steering wheel. I keep my nails clean and short, but never again red.

The parking lot gravel pops under my tires as I pull into my usual spot. It's almost 11 o'clock, so some of the overnight shift at the prison are bound to show up for a drink or two before heading on home. My fingers are burning from the cold by the time I get the key in the lock and open the door.

Jon and I still co-own this place, been trading off day and night shifts to cover the kids' schedule for years. But that's almost done now that they're 'bout grown up themselves. He worked last night, leaving his nasty ashtray full on the office desk and a used condom in the trash can for me to find. What an asshole. Who knows what bar fly he fucked this time; I haven't cared in years. I unpeel my banana and toss it over top of his spent self. The banana is overly ripe, a little mealy, and too sweet in my mouth. I go to make some coffee and grab some Lysol wipes for the desk.

Out front, but behind the bar, I scoop some dry grounds from a big blue can and spill them into the filter, then turn on the television. Clicking past all the sports channels, I stop on a chirpy morning news show. The hosts' laughter and chatter fill the empty space as I flip the chairs and scoot them underneath the tables. Quickly, the cozy, hazelnut smell of the coffee covers up the yeasty, cheap beer and Pine-Sol overtones.

A local walks in, bringing the mid-morning light with him before the door swishes closed once more.

"Hiya, Jesse."

"How ya doin', Carl?"

"Can't complain. Brought in your paper."

"Thanks. Coffee or beer?" I ask, placing the last chair on the floor.

"I'll take coffee if you've got it."

"You know I do." I pour Carl and myself a mugful, then pass his across the bar.

He nods a thank you and stares up at the television screen. It's an election year, and things are ramping up in some of the neighboring swing states, but not really in this part of Indiana where almost every vote goes red, no matter what new atrocious thing a candidate says or does.

"You keepin' up with this stuff?" he asks.

"You already know what I think of your dumb hat, Carl."

I unfold the newspaper, skimming past the "Celebrating Students" section and flipping right to the 911 call logs.

"I like this one," Carl says.

"What?"

"Her. Media's taken to callin' her a 'dark horse.' Think she might cause an upset come November."

Preparing for some overly-coiffed business/lawyer type, I look up and see my old friend. Anne. Anne Johnson, the screen declares. Her hair is pulled back in a low ponytail and her lips are painted a moist, cherry-red. There are lines around her eyes and forehead, and a wild streak of gray hair in her hair that had never been there before. And if I hadn't known it by the look of her, as soon as she speaks, my heart jumps at her familiar alto smoothness. It is definitely her, only with a new last name.

The button on the lapel of her scarlet-red jacket reads,

Vote! And she is busy talking about an organization she started—House Ohio—that provides services for people experiencing homelessness throughout the state.

"So what's the answer?" the interviewer asks.

Anne smiles before continuing, "It's multi-faceted, Kelly. First, we must look inward as a society and decide that when we say, 'We're all in this together!' we truly mean it. Then we dig in and do the work. We examine the systems in place—or lack thereof—and we change them. We make new plans. As governor, I'm ready to do the hard work."

To think, I snuffed all of this out of her, steering her one way and one way only.

And Carl is nodding along.

"You like her?" I ask.

"Yeah. I do. She talks like she means it."

I could've hugged him, but I've never been the hugging type.

I Google her on my phone and up comes her whole life: college, marriage, kids, and now this campaign for governor. In that other 2019, it seemed like nothing could stump the red tide, especially in Ohio. Another four years had been practically laid at the GOP's feet while billionaires and companies—like Candied—experienced success after success. The economy is healthy, they said. And from my hilltop vantage point, yes, that was true. But that was when the distance between my situation and any actual struggle were on opposite points of my timeline.

But Anne? Without me, she's been busy getting services available for some of the most vulnerable among us. And if guys like Carl can see it, maybe others could too.

I click on the Donate button and give twenty-five bucks. A thank-you dings in my email. I open the message and read more about her plans and other ways people can help her win. I sign up to make some phone calls. *Why the hell not*?

Anne might change the world. And for the first time in a long time, I feel something. A sparking twinge lights up around my ankle, starting right at the spot once shackled to her spirit. It doesn't take too long for me to realize what it is —hope.

Bound by What

By Jess Moore

Jess Moore originally hails from the Midwest, so you can always expect an "ope" from one of her characters. She moved to historic gold-country California ages ago and generally feels nostalgic about Ohio in the fall, when the leaves are wild with color and it's Cincinnati chili season.

She spent many years working in both teaching and social work, but for now, she writes in the very early morning while her family sometimes sleeps.

The Evolution of Jeremy Warsh

Love on Main – "Jane & Austen's"

Connect with Jess

itwasjess.wordpress.com

instagram.com/itwasjess

Charing Cross

Pam S. Dunn

ONE

After allowing the detective entrance, the frightened maid knocked on and then opened one of the doors in the long passage.

"Please ma'am, it's a police officer from Scotland Yard come to inquire after Mr. Lawton. He is wanted!"

The detective removed his hat and straightened his blue uniform. The house had none of the colorful baubles and adornments associated of late with the cheerful holiday. Barren of a Christmas tree, it was quite drab and uninviting, in an unsettled state that suggested the residents had not been there long and, indeed, did not intend to reside there permanently.

After introducing himself as Detective Bambridge, he handed the woman the letter from his superior and having dutifully wiped his muddy boots in the foyer, accepted her invitation to enter the sitting room, where a small coal fire burned in a grate. They were joined by her two daughters, both dressed like their mother in patterned woolen dresses. The taller of the young ladies was exceedingly pale and consumptive looking, while the shorter, younger one was energetic, with a rosy complexion.

The detective inspected the flowered wallpaper, which had swelled due to dampness, avoiding gazing at the mother, who crumpled her skirt's fabric in her fist as she read, her prematurely lined face filled with both sorrow and humiliation. Afterward, she said only, "That's all," and looked at the letter again as if she expected more.

"All that's known, ma'am," the detective said.

On the whole, the situation was most distressful, given it was nearly Christmas and all.

The girl's mother sat down heavily on the rosewood sofa, and the daughters arranged themselves on either side of her. "My Henry, suspected of murder. And now he has killed himself. We're ruined," the mother said, and the younger daughter quickly snatched the letter and read the contents.

"He was summoned for questioning, ma'am. He would have been considered innocent until guilt was proven." He stood beside a round table which held a colorful Tiffany lamp that provided little light. One hand clutched his hat and the other remained tucked behind him. "When did you see him last?"

"It has been several weeks," the woman said, and then called to the maid to bring tea. "He left to attend to some business and never returned. We reported him missing to the authorities, but they never sent anyone."

"People disappear here, ma'am. Never a trace of them found. Or the remains we find are unidentifiable. As there is a body in this case, there will be an inquest."

The older daughter clasped both hands over her mouth and repeatedly exclaimed, "No, no," in choking sobs.

The mother pressed her daughter's hand. "Henry changed so from the man I married after his father died. I met his brother Francis only once at our wedding. They were close once, but later became estranged over the inheritance. Afterward, Henry insisted on separating himself from his family."

"Do you think Father was murdered?" the younger daughter asked.

"That's for the coroner to discover." Despite its unattractiveness, the room had the clean aura of womenfolk. The bit of perfume wafting in through the air made him think of his sisters safe at home, and he found it impossible at that moment to mention that most suicides occurred during the holiday season.

"His body floated a long way before it was found," the daughter remarked.

"Indeed." The detective could have said more about the rag-clad urchins working the river banks with hooks and nets, hauling all manner of garbage, chunks of wood, and dead things to shore, salvaging anything they could sell, but in the presence of refined females, he kept that knowledge to himself. He produced a handkerchief, although none was needed as all the ladies' eyes remained dry. "Are there unique characteristics? Something that would help us to identify the remains. A photograph would be helpful," he drove on. "If the person found is your husband, the body will need to be dealt with."

The wife, now perhaps a widow, would need to answer two questions. She lifted her gaze. "We have a solicitor. I'll see he gets word of the situation. My husband used a cane, sir. His right leg was badly broken in a riding accident when he was a lad and never healed correctly."

The detective jotted the details down and accepted the cup of tea the maid offered. The weather was getting worse, and he'd taken a cab from Whitehall, Scotland Yard. He was aware the drying mud, which had caked the sides of his boots, was now falling in small chunks onto the Aubusson rug. He was still wearing his gloves, which were somewhat wet and soiled and left marks on the teacup. Several uncomfortable minutes of silence followed in which the detective finished his tea and pondered offering his humble assistance to the capsized women. "That will be all for the present," he said finally. "We'll be in contact."

"Then, good day, sir," the wife said, and roused herself to show him personally to the door.

Emily slid next to her sister, put her head on Racine's shoulder, and listened to her fragile heartbeat as the front door was opened and then shut against London's inclement weather, the foyer temporarily blasted with cold and silt from the coal fires.

Their mother stared out the paned window for some time, then finally looked at the clock. "I'd best see to dinner. I'm afraid it will be potatoes again."

Emily bit her lower lip. She never thought a tragedy would be connected with her parents, especially not one that involved eating potatoes every night. The house was leased. She was not certain how much money their mother had, or if it would even pay the rent for a few months.

When their mother was out of earshot, Racine said, "I will never believe Father was guilty of any wrongdoing as Mother does, but he should never have brought us to this horrible city." She coughed raggedly, and Emily found a shawl to settle around her shoulders.

"There, there," Emily said. "Be at ease." She more or less

agreed, although she did not have such faith in her father. He had been acting strangely for several months, disrupting all their lives, taking them from their home in Sussex, and she blamed him bitterly.

Her sister used a handkerchief she'd hand-embroidered to blow her nose. She was looking feverish again. "The men from the auction house are coming to collect the piano this afternoon. How will we live without it?"

"I expect we'll manage. But it does seem strange to have spent a fortune moving all the furniture only to sell it at half its value." The furniture was all that remained of her mother's dowry; they had little else now. She hugged her sister and got up to retrieve her coat and hat. "I'm going out for some air. I'll bring back fresh rolls."

Winters were mild in Sussex, but in London, the wind off the river was cutting and stank. On leaving her building, Emily had only to turn to the right and walk two blocks to find the bakery's four Ionic columns with the arched doorway in the center. But that afternoon, walking was far from pleasant. Rainwater and slush filled the cobblestone roadway, and passing carriages splattered mud in every direction, soiling her skirt. To make things worse, the bakery was closed, despite an inviting Christmas display in the windows, all goods having been sold.

Emily sighed. The bookstore was only one block further. *Mother and Racine are waiting for me*, she told herself, but still she continued walking.

From the heights of Highgate, a smoke-laden vista of steeples rose above a landscape of gray brick. She paused to secure her hat. On a clear day, she might have denoted the community of Cheapside, St. Paul's Cathedral and the Tower to the east, and Fleet Street and the Strand and Westminster Abbey to the west, the Thames linking all. But that day, a sooty fog enveloped the city, and she could not even discern outlines.

When Emily entered the bookshop, the dim daylight was replaced with an even dimmer gaslight. The shop owner was elderly, and the shop suffered from lack of order. Old books and new books were stacked on the floor in front of the shelves, fine leather-bound volumes mixed in with penny dreadfuls.

"Oh, Miss Emily, I'm surprised you're out today. I was just ready to close the shop." The shopkeeper, an elderly man dressed in a worn brown waistcoat, a frayed silk shirt, and wrinkled trousers, emerged from a room behind the counter. He had apparently been enjoying a smoking break judging by the strong smell of pipe tobacco about him and the smoke drifting from the storeroom's entrance. "I secured the copy of *North and South* you wanted. And at a good price, too."

Emily took off her gloves and loosened her hat. "Excellent. I intend to curl up with it and a hot cup of tea over the holidays."

"Any news of your father?"

"No good news," she sighed. "The police have found a body. But the identity is not confirmed."

"It's in the hands of God then. I'm sorry to hear it." The shopkeeper removed his spectacles and brushed a stray strand of thinning hair behind his ear. He polished the glass lenses with a handkerchief, put them back on, and began searching the shelves underneath the counter. "Ah, here it is." He sat the book on the counter. "It's used but in excellent condition."

The door's clock-inspired sign said "Back at 9:00" but the bookstore appeared to be open. The young detective held onto his hat and made the final plunge against the wind. Tomorrow would be a day of idleness unknown to a policeman, a brief respite after working several weeks without a day off. There was more crime, not less, during the holidays, the city at the mercy of cutthroats and pickpockets. As the newest member of the recently-formed Criminal Investigations Unit, he'd been assigned a caseload of unsolved crimes. And with lung conditions rampant among the force, the station had fewer men than usual to send out. But there, in the well-tended shop, for an hour, he was free to roam the shelves looking for reading materials, doing nothing at all but what brought him pleasure.

He was examining the row just beyond the front window when the store owner said, "You look like a Wilke Collins fan."

"I was hoping for something different. I've just finished the *Woman in White.*" He continued to scan the bookshelves, as if the book he wanted would magically appear somehow in the chaos. In truth, to be left alone to browse and not have to talk to anyone was all he wanted.

"Any updates on the Staunton murder?" the store owner asked.

Everyone asked the same question about the fortune-hunting husband and his relatives who had allegedly starved his wife and child to death. "I'm afraid not, sir. I'm not assigned to that case." He trained his gaze on the bookshelf before him.

"Miss Emily, there, she follows the modern writers. You must ask her for a recommendation."

The detective immediately recognized the young lady and tipped his hat.

"Oh, we already know each other, Mr. McKinsey. He's from Scotland Yard."

The detective hid his feelings behind a calm resolution; as much as he might want to, he could not tell her what she most wanted to know.

She asked casually about his family, and he explained that his two sisters and he were alone, both parents having died some years earlier. He managed to say he felt terrible about her family's situation, something he should have said earlier.

"Mr. McKinsey has asked if I might consider taking employment. Mother nearly swooned when I mentioned it."

"Many young women have jobs in London," the detective said. "One of my sisters works as a bookkeeper. So, what would you recommend?"

"Have you read *The Trail of the Serpent* or *Aurora Floyd*?" she asked, and he noted that the enthusiasm in her eyes, missing earlier, made her most attractive. "Both are by a woman writer, Mary Elizabeth Braddon. I remember seeing both books here somewhere," she said. "If you're interested, I'll help you look for them."

"Lead on," he said. "If she is willing to take the job, you should definitely hire her," he added to Mr. McKinsey

On Tuesday, Emily had just stepped out when she spotted a man walking away from the house. Shrouded in heavy fog, his features were blurred, but his bearing was much like her father's, as was his limping gait. In the thick fog, it was unclear if he was carrying a cane or an umbrella. She began to follow the ghostly figure. Three days had passed since the detective's visit, and she still held hope that the drowned man wasn't her father. Perhaps the watch and identification papers noted in the letter had been stolen, and this was her real father, still living.

She was a strong walker and easily kept the man's figure in sight as he headed downhill into Central London. In the haze, the city became a confusing maze of streets that all resembled each other, filled with labyrinthine alleys connecting hastily-erected tenements, all stacked one upon the other. The street her family lived on was one such universal street, in a better tradesman's area, but still indistinguishable from others just like it. People drifted in and out of eyesight. The sound of carriage wheels and horse hooves approached, a vague outline appeared, and then the carriage moved on.

At least an hour had passed by the time Emily found herself in a district she didn't know at all. She passed boot shiners, women in thick shawls clustered outside of poor tenements, fishmongers, and flower sellers. The line of brick houses was broken by a large gap containing an open arch. An old theater house stood on the other side. Two rows of gas lamps flooded its entryway with light. After casting a look behind him, the ghostly man disappeared through the columns. She followed him to the theater's entrance, alit with more flaring gas-jets.

A short man with greasy ringlets, almost dwarfish in stature, stood outside the entrance handing out playbills, wearing a sequined waistcoat so dazzling it hurt the eyes. "Have a box, my lady?" he asked, doffing his hat while holding out a ticket.

The prospect seemed enticing, and Emily wished she could afford a guinea for the stage-box. "I haven't brought enough money I'm afraid," she said and turned to go.

After looking to the left and the right, the dwarf caught her by the elbow and said in a low voice, "Usually we're so packed with people coming to see the hypnotist we have to shut the doors. But in this weather, we've got empty seats. You can go in if you're interested in clairvoyance. The hypnotist has already performed."

"Thank you, sir."

He made an overly elaborate bow to which she giggled and returned a curtsy. "You'll want a box seat. There are some rough lads in the common section. You'll have a fine view, miss. It often happens that those nearest the medium get the best chance, and you'll see her with a bird's eyes."

The theater's ceilings and pillars were adorned with cupids and cornucopias made of cheap plaster. Going up and down the aisles, vendors hawked oranges and ginger-beer and packages of nuts. The gallery and pit were fairly full, but most of the upper boxes were empty. She found her way to a secluded seat. From there, she could view the young men shouting to each other across the theater while sharing their oranges with the poorly dressed girls who sat beside them. A group of women laughed shrilly in the pit; Emily suspected they were drunk.

The arrangement suited her well. She could see everything while remaining sheltered. In secret, she was well-read on the subject of spiritualism, although her mother was wholly against it.

"The Devil has his foul hands in such things," her mother had said, "deceiving poor innocents, using their grief to cheat them out of an honest dollar."

Considering herself a modern woman, Emily was absolutely enthralled when the show began.

The front rows crowded with people hoping to get a reading. From the balcony, she could see line after line of faces, mostly women—small tradesfolk, shop walkers, artisans, lower middle-class women worn with poverty and toil—all of them, she supposed, hoping to receive some message from a departed loved one.

"We have with us tonight," the announcer cried, "Mrs. Darby, the well-known clairvoyant from Lincolnshire. Mrs. Darby has, as many of you know, been given the gift to speak with the spirits walking among us. A favorable atmosphere is critical, and Mrs. Darby will ask for your good wishes and prayers while she endeavors to communicate with the other side."

Very plump, wearing a green velvet cape and gold-rimmed glasses, Mrs. Darby accepted the audience's applause before seating herself in a chair facing them. "Vibrations!" she said to the audience. "I must have helpful vibrations."

The droning of a harmonium filled the vast chamber as she sat with her head bowed. Minutes ticked away. In the dim gaslight, shadowy shapes flickered in the corners of the theater. The medium began to moan softly and then to rock to and fro in her chair. Slowly, she raised her arms. The audience sat in astonished silence as if she might suddenly levitate and fly over their heads. Even the rowdy males grew quiet. The medium continued to concentrate, head bowed, as if tuning into a celestial harmony no one else could hear. Then she raised her hand and the music stopped.

"Stop crowding! No, not all of you! You can't all speak at once." The woman appeared to be addressing invisible people. "We must go one at a time, and only those with a loved one present." Then she said to the audience, "I don't feel that the conditions are very good tonight for embodiment. We may not be able to see, but I will speak for them."

After a moment, she pointed her ungloved hand at a

woman in the second row. "You! Yes, you, with the red hat. No, not you. The stout lady in front. Yes, you! There is a spirit hovering behind you. A man. He is tall—six foot, possibly. High forehead, eyes grey or blue, a long brown moustache, lines on his face. Do you recognize him?"

The woman shook her head.

"Well, I can provide a little more. He died after a long illness. I feel chest pain..."

The woman continued to deny knowing the spirit. The medium engaged in a silent communication. "Why didn't you say so in the first place?" She directed her finger and then shifted it to the right, as if it were a divining rod. "You! The woman two seats away."

The woman jumped to her feet, and the bird nested in her hat bobbed up and down. "I'm not certain. But I believe it's my husband, ma'am. Dead this year and left me a pauper."

"Yes, that's right. He moves to you now. He wants to say he's sorry for his temper. Forgive him, that is all he asks. I have a message for you. It is: 'Proceed, and my blessing go with you.' Does that mean anything to you?"

The woman looked pleased and nodded. "I plan to marry again."

The audience tittered.

Her next attempt was a failure. A portly man wearing thick glasses refused to have anything to do with a spirit who claimed to be his relative. The medium kept consulting with the spirit, adding further details, but nothing jarred his memory.

"Think it over. I do feel sorry for the spirit who longs to communicate. But we have others waiting."

"I don't know what to make of it," Emily muttered.

"I believe it is half guess-work and a case of confederates," said the man who sat down next to her. She startled, turned, and recognized the detective. "It is all clever quackery and bluff," he added.

"I'm surprised to see you here." She started to extend her hand, but he seemed so ill-at-ease, she let it drop. Out of uniform, he appeared to be much younger than she'd believed him to be, and his clothing was of the sturdy wool favored by the professional class.

"Occasionally I check into these events," he said. "I often look up at the boxes, watching for any sign the audience is being swindled such as signals passed to the stage from a hidden associate, but so far I haven't been able to catch this group at anything dishonest."

Mrs. Darby gave two more descriptions to the audience, both of them rather vague and both recognized with some hesitancy. It was a curious fact that while she could not see at the eye colors or facial details of the audience, she was remarkably accurate in describing them. In her next attempt, a man at the back of the hall claimed the spirit was his deceased wife. "She is worried about the children," the medium said.

"Yes, she was a good mother before the Lord took her," the man responded. "God bless her."

The detective seemed just about to say something when the woman's voice sounded louder, and Emily found the woman's glasses flashing in her direction.

"There is a presence behind the young woman in the balcony. The gentleman who sits next to the young lady. Yes, sir, behind you. He is a man of middle size, rather inclined to shortness. He is over forty with graying hair, stern features, and a small mustache. He is a relation to the young woman, I gather. Does that suggest anyone to you, sir?"

"That could describe almost anyone." The detective fixed his gaze on the stage and the clairvoyant.

"We will try to see a little closer," the medium said. "Ah... A mole over his left eyebrow. His face is deeply lined from pain or sorrow. I should say he was an unhappy, troubled man in his life. He bears a cane. Well, he seems very anxious, so we must help him if we can. He holds up a book. It is a schoolbook. He opens it, and I see maps in it. Perhaps he wrote it—or perhaps he taught from it. Yes, he is nodding. He taught from it. He was a teacher. Does that help you?"

Emily rose quickly. "You are describing my father. Please, we are most anxious to hear from him!"

The woman's head swiveled from Emily to the audience and back again. "Your father has a message: 'Accounts will square up and all will be well. Remain steadfast, and you will be happier here than ever you were in Sussex.'"

Emily gasped in amazement. "How could she know I'm from Sussex?" she asked.

"Rot! Perfect rot!" the detective muttered.

The woman bowed her head again. "I don't know that I can help him anymore. The channel between us is severed. Ah! There is one thing. I see danger."

Emily jerked as if stabbed, and the entire audience gasped. All eyes turned to her.

"That is all." A moment later, the medium was describing someone else. But she had left a badly-shaken Emily in the balcony above her.

"Perfect rubbish," the detective muttered. "I suggest you leave immediately." He stood up and offered his arm to her as a courtesy; his suggestion had really been an order.

On the way out, Emily and the detective conversed in undertones. "Perhaps you'd better tell me as much as you know," he said.

And so she found herself in the street once more, inhaling the evening air to clear her confusion. A moment later, the detective hailed a cab to carry them back to Highgate.

It was well after dark when she'd arrived home, and her sister and mother were frantic. Her mother forbade her to do anything similar again. Her sister clamped her lips tight and would not speak to Emily that night. But neither detoured her plans. Someone had to look after the family.

That night, after falling into a deep sleep, Emily dreamed she was in a bed covered with tapestry curtains and talking to a spirit. The unhappy spirit manifested itself here and there, coalescing and then fading into shadow. It appeared much distressed.

"In life, I was your father," the spirit said. "I will find no rest until I am forgiven." The ghost continued to metamorphize, losing legs and arms and torso until only its head was visible.

"How can I forgive you?" she asked. "You left us."

Fading into transparency, the ghost's voice became but a whisper. "Not intended... better life..."

"How could this be a better life for us if you're no longer in it?" she demanded. The ghost began to wail loudly, its form slowly tearing apart into tissue-like fragments. Emily awoke with a jolt to a freezing cold room and darkness.

The next day, at a breakfast consisting of stale toast and porridge, her sister badgered her for details. She especially wanted to know about the detective. How old he was. If he was married. Normally, Racine was quiet and mousy, not an annoying chatterbox. Emily reminded herself of how different her sister's daily existence was from her own. Racine lived a secluded life that excluded most of the things Emily took for granted. She wanted to tell Racine about the medium, but she dared not; she might slip and say the word the woman had used: danger. She also did not tell either her mother or her sister the detective's parting words: "For your sake, young miss, I suggest you leave this mystery to the police and have nothing further to do with it."

She wanted dreadfully to go out again, at least as far as the bookstore, but the streets were deserted, and blasts of whirling snow assaulted the windowpanes, so she spent the day exploring her father's desk. He had taught in Sussex at a private boys' boarding school, where they had lived in one of the cottages available for families of the faculty—a too small space filled with ornate and oversized furniture. The desk was usually full of ungraded papers. But the papers were gone now, as were all of his lecture notes. If her father had left a suicide letter, she would find it there. She gathered all of the letters that might contain clues as to her father's disappearance and set them aside. Her parents had taught her well enough to read and cipher and keep simple accounts, but no matter how diligently she pored over the legal documents, they remained frustratingly obscure.

When she opened the middle drawer, an envelope fell out; inside were five tickets to a London showing of Dickens' *A Christmas Carol*. This was not the act of someone contemplating suicide or a murderer, that she could swear to. The tickets covered his family and one other person, but whoever he'd intended to invite was a mystery.

As a little girl, she had been terrified when Marley made his appearance, howling and dragging his chains. She had shrieked and hidden her eyes when his jaw dropped, unhinged upon his chest, and he shouted: "I wear the chains I forged in life." She thought unhappily of her father and the nature of his business, which might have been the same as Marley's. She worried that in her short life, she might have begun her own iron links, being uncharitable, mean to her sister, or rude to her parents.

Her father was an unhappy man. Her mother said it had something to do with his childhood but refused to go into details. As Emily had explained to the detective, their lives had changed entirely after a former collegemate of their father's arrived for a visit. The two men had secluded themselves for several days, discussing some business, she assumed. Shortly after, her father informed the family they would be moving to London. He had never offered an explanation. And then, he'd vanished with no word. Once again, the anger rose inside of her. She had been forced to leave a fair country where the snow, when it came, was merely a thin blanket, for London, with its atrocious weather. No more than a month had passed when her sister's condition grew worse, and she needed medicine they couldn't afford.

The headquarters of the new London police force were in Whitehall, with an entrance onto Great Scotland Yard, upon which had once stood a medieval palace that housed visiting Scottish royalty. Recently tarnished by scandal, the unit had been reorganized, the central unit strengthened by adding a new investigative branch. The young detective had only recently joined the Criminal Investigation Department, hence his duties at the moment both required plain clothes and uniforms that must, as his father had said, look "all about the business at hand."

The young man returned from Highgate to the station house, where Inspector Murphy, who had sent him on an errand, was waiting for his report. Murphy, a red-faced, black-haired man of Irish descent, had a cheerful, fatherly way with the young officers on his staff. He sat behind his desk, his many cases strewn in front of him.

"Well, what luck?" he asked.

"I retrieved the papers from the family this morning," said Detective Bambridge. "I haven't read them thoroughly, but some are legal documents that are meant to be filed against the estate of one Francis Lawton. There's also a photograph."

The Inspector browsed a written list on the case. "You ran it on the general lines that I suggested?"

"Yes. I said we needed the papers for evidence."

"And what about this college chum?"

"You'll find a batch of correspondence between them concerning the family estate and properties. The women have little to tell us about this man, having seen him only once."

"The missing corpse appears to be part of the game. These villains will be sorry when we are through with them."

"Do you think we will catch them, sir?"

"Oh, to be sure. They are getting sloppy. First, a dead body appears that has in its possession both identification and a watch belonging to the missing suspect. Then, the body is stolen before it can be autopsied and a definite identity established. Then we have this ghost, which leads the young lady to a theater where it attempts to communicate with her. If the woman is here, let's bring her in."

The woman in question, Mrs. Darby, was high-strung and already aware that a warrant could have been served instead of a summons. In that case, without legal counsel, she would have been placed in a cell for several days, ending with a swift conviction on the Vagrancy Act.

Inspector Murphy made a show of bad humor as he glanced at the charge sheet and surveyed the accused. He rubbed his fingers against his furrowed brow, indicating an intense headache. "You charlatans are increasing in number, preying on bereaved parents and widows, and it is high time that charges should be filed against all of you to encourage your sort to find a more honest trade. You must know, Mrs. Darby, the law of this country considers the business of fortunetelling, spiritualism, and palmistry a crime where payment is involved."

"Oh, no harm is intended, sir." The woman's pear-shaped body filled the chair, making it difficult to shift her position to look from officer to officer. "The people pay to see a show, just as they might to see a play enacted, and if we help some of them in the process, well..." She paused a moment, as if collecting her thoughts. "One woman was saved from suicide by what I told her. Another man who had lost all belief in God now believes in the afterlife. And the spirits, sir... I do believe it helps them find peace in their new existence..."

The inspector interrupted. "The supposed ghost that spoke to the young lady in the balcony, what form did the communication take? Were you told by someone what to say to the girl to convince her the spirit was her father?"

The woman paled. "I assure you no trickery was used. He pushed his way through the other spirits and demanded to speak."

Inspector Murphy jumped up from his chair, his face as red as a Christmas bauble. "Now look here, woman. This man is wanted by the authorities! He is obviously trying to avoid a hanging. Save yourself a charge of accomplice to a murder and tell us what you know." He slapped a photograph on the desktop. "This is the man we're looking for. Now spill it."

The medium's shaking hands took the picture, and she studied it for a time. "Yes, I know this man. He came to me over a month ago and asked me to contact his brother. The brother had recently died, and I was able to find his unhappy spirit still bound to the earth. Some money was in question. An inheritance? 'Beware... Thomas...' the spirit said. 'He killed me.' Well, sirs, that jarred me right out of the trance. I didn't know if the living man before me was Thomas or the killer. He came several times more, up until two weeks ago. And I saw him not again until his poor spirit asked to speak to his daughter."

"Rubbish!" young Bambridge shouted. "You swindler! What did you charge that poor man?"

The woman turned ghostly white. "My standard fee, sir, for inquiries. Not a penny more. I assure you, all transactions are closely regulated and overseen by herself."

"And who is herself?" the inspector asked. "Answer the question. And no fainting. We know that ploy."

"Madam Chow. He might... well... I send them on, you see, to her, when I'm unable to help them."

The woman was released later with a warning, after admitting to nothing other than being clairvoyant. Detective Bambridge had violated his role of the calm, helpful observer, but Inspector Murphy did not take him to task afterward.

"I have to say, I find it most troubling," Detective Bambridge said. "I've never heard the like."

"Indeed, it is a strange affair," the inspector said, "unless you're Irish, and accustomed to the dear departed joining you at dinner."

The young detective laughed.

The police, being human, were inclined to varying beliefs themselves. In all honesty, Detective Bambridge and his sisters often shared the palmistry column in the paper. For the most part, it was harmless fancy. No society event or carnival was complete without its fortune-teller or palmist. Even Inspector Murphy, Catholic in upbringing, thought it was a waste of time to pursue charges. After all, there were frauds in every profession.

"After our meeting this afternoon, we shall apply for the summons," Inspector Murphy said. "The son, Thomas Lawton, is clearly mixed up with this business. He has a number of misdemeanor offences on his record. I believe he'll confess to his part when he realizes we intend to have him hanged."

Later, at the appointed time, Detective Bambridge called upon Inspector Murphy and they sat in consultation over the documents with August Jones, a solicitor who specialized in wills. The man studied each document carefully through his thick eyeglasses.

He placed a yellowed document before them. "This appears to be the original will executed by the father, Edwin Lawton." He opened the first document and then a second to the signature page. "If you look closely, the will that was used during probate and legally entered clearly contains a forgery of the original signature and is also of later origin." He spread yet a third document out. "And here is a copy of a will supposedly penned by the brother that would have deprived Henry Lawton of his rightful share in favor of the stepson. Do we have the original?"

"No, we don't know what has been done with it," the inspector admitted.

"We need to find it."

"Issuing a warrant might cause him to destroy the original document. We'll bring Thomas in for questioning, and while he is in our custody, we'll search his residence," Inspector Murphy said.

That afternoon, Detective Bambridge went back to his desk and filled out the summons.

To Thomas Lawton of 40 Downshire Hill, Hampstead:

An information was laid this 17th day of December by Patrick Murphy, Inspector of Police, that you are involved in the disappearance and possible murder of one Henry Lawton on or near the 20th day of November. Charges have been made that you intended to alter the true will of the now deceased Francis Lawton in order to inherit an estate to which you have no legal recourse. You are, therefore, summoned to appear before the Magistrate on Wednesday, the 20th of December, at the hour of 11 in the forenoon to answer to the said information.
Dated the 17th day of December.
(signed) B.J. Bambridge.

He wrote out an additional summons for a Christopher Farley of Oxford, the college classmate who might have been the last person to see Henry before he died.

"And now we must keep careful watch," the inspector said when everything was signed and in order.

A well-dressed woman arrived unannounced at the Lawtons' house early Christmas week, claiming to be their father's older sister, Petunia. The woman left her elegant widow's veil and overwrap in the hall on the tree. Emily left the room to change into her best dress and joined the other women in the sitting room for tea.

Petunias were usually vividly colored flowers, but their aunt's appearance was that of a shriveled prune. Enthroned in the family's best rosewood chair, she wore a large gold locket on a thick gold chain and was dressed all in black. Her gloves were black, close fitting, and finely stitched. Offered tea, she removed the gloves, placing them in her lap. "I see you have not begun mourning for my brother yet."

"My husband has not been officially listed as deceased. And the expense... In our present circumstances, I can hardly afford the cost of new clothing." Emily's mother hated admitting to poverty; she had come from a titled family. She sat the china cup aside, retrieved a handkerchief, and then pressed it against her wet cheeks.

"I should have come to you sooner, my dear sister, or sent our parish minister. I see you are under duress. Suicide breaks God's eternal law and must be punished. I fear Henry is now burning in Hell."

Racine gasped, her china cup rattling in her trembling hand.

"I don't believe it," Emily said. "I refuse to believe it."

Her mother looked aghast. "Emily, mind your manners."

The woman set her teacup aside. "I never approved of Henry raising his daughters at a boy's school. I imagine neither has attended a proper ladies' academy. Well, what's done is done, finances being as they are. I am a widow, as you see. I feel I must inform you that I am not asking for anything. My dear husband left me with enough to see to my needs..."

"Forgive me, but I fail to understand what you are implying." Their mother's hand moved to touch her bun.

"But Henry is the sole heir now, surely you know that. Francis assured me. Oh, those people... They'll try to claim otherwise, but they are related only through marriage. Francis never adopted the boy. Thomas was nearly five when Francis married his mother, and he has no right to take what rightfully belongs to our family. I fear that man is up to evil. Even with the death duties, it would still be a tidy sum. My poor dear brother... You said Henry left papers."

Emily could barely contain herself. "The inspector working the case came to retrieve them only this morning." She had placed great faith in the detective and hoped it was not unwarranted.

"Involving the police, Clarisse, was it wise? Just recently, four of the senior constables were fired. Could you not have taken the matter to Henry's solicitor? And who was this friend Henry claimed to know from his college days? He mentioned the man in his last letter. Might he not be in on the evil machinations?"

"I knew so little of Henry's past. He did not suffer inquiries." Her mother's hands made little convulsive movements. Emily rose and found the smelling salts.

The woman looked discomfited as she handed their mother a daguerreotype. From Emily's viewpoint, it appeared to be of two young boys dressed in vests and waistcoats, both very serious looking. The taller, older one must be Francis. He had placed his arm around his younger brother's shoulder.

"Henry was a charming lad, somewhat of a show-off, but Francis was always Father's favorite. Our father had a proud heart and a stern mind which would not soften toward his youngest son, whom he believed to be too frivolous. It was that harridan of a wife who led Francis into darkness. Many of us believed Father's will to be a clever forgery, but the lawyers upheld it."

"Everything is against us," their mother said. "I wish Henry had taken me into his confidence. I wish we had stayed in Sussex."

"There, there." Their aunt patted their mother's lap. "I see how difficult it has been for you. You must come to our house for Christmas. And if nothing can be done, perhaps I can find a place for you in our household. I hate dealing with the servants and could use you in that capacity. Perhaps our minister can locate a benevolent charity that runs a sanitarium for your oldest girl. Racine, isn't it? And your daughter Emily would make an admirable governess to my daughter's children."

Emily had not often seen her mother angry. In truth, Clarisse Lawton usually did whatever was required of her, but that day she was furious. As soon as their aunt left, she shouted, "Oh, she was always longwinded—sending those dreadful missives on living a good Christian life. How dare she! To presume we are nothing but poor relatives to be ordered. No, Racine will never go to a sanitarium, not while I am living! The gall! A Boughton does not serve—we are served!" And she began to pace back and forth across the Aubusson rug. Things were getting serious.

It was past eleven o'clock on a cold, frosty day when the two detectives reached their destination. The station was almost deserted, but a plump man in the ticket office provided directions to the nearby inn where they stopped for sandwiches and coffee, paid for by the force.

The inn had a timber framework, gas lamps provided lighting. After conferring with the proprietor, they sat near a warm fire at one of the trestle tables.

Inspector Murphy eased off his coat. "Have you discovered anything about this Madam Chow?"

"No, nothing." The detective stretched his long legs. "These people... they're like gypsies. They have their own laws. People who become involved with them are haunted by spirits, supposedly due to some past transgression. Others believe themselves victims of malign entities. For whatever reason, they are unable to find peace in their lives." Bambridge looked up as the innkeeper arrived with their meal. "Presuming these spirits were malicious in life, they would become even worse in death. Could such a malignant spirit be forced to do no more harm?"

"When I was a boy in Ireland, a priest came to our village to perform an exorcism," Inspector Murphy said, attending to his meal. "There was a house there which had a poltergeist, a very irksome one. There is an official exorcism in the Church, you know, so the priest thought that he was well-armed with his Bible, holy water, and cross. He held the ceremony in the sitting room, which was the center of the disturbances, with all the family on their knees beside him, and he read the service. What do you think happened?"

"I couldn't guess."

Murphy's pale face broke into a smile. "Just when the creature should have vacated the premises, the hearthrug rose and threw itself around the priest. He was out of that house and down the road in two leaps."

Bambridge laughed. "It sounds like the poltergeist was somewhat of a prankster."

"Or an offended fairy," Inspector Murphy said, throwing in some folklore for the young policeman to consider.

"Do you think it would be rude to leave a card at the young ladies' house?" Detective Bambridge asked. "My sisters and I... We would like to invite the family to Christmas dinner."

"I think that is a splendid idea," the inspector said.

They took a carriage to the Lawton manor. Located half a mile from the town, the house sat on the slope of a low hill. A barren moor stretched behind it, filled with overgrown heath and bracken. Overall, the place was gloomy and ominous. The stately gardens were a tangle of untrimmed roses and bushes, which in some places crowded the roadway. They waited some time at the gate for the groundskeeper, who directed them to the manor, a Georgian house with many tall thin windows. A dormered mansard roof covered the attic and lower two stories.

An aging butler answered the door, and Inspector Murphy presented the search warrant. The man seemed to be oddly relieved. "I expect you'll want to have a look around, sirs. It's a lonely house, not well tended these past years. A warning... It has become possessed of late, sirs, by a spirit that makes the blood run cold. The servants will no longer come, not for any money. I can only assume it is the ghost of our deceased employer, Francis. After his wife died, he lived here as a hermit with no one for company except myself and the servants." He paused by a winding staircase. "On these very stairs, it was, he fell to his death, or according to the maids' gossip, was pushed."

The policemen were currently considering two possibilities: the first, that Henry had killed his brother—less and less likely as events unfolded—and the second, that Thomas, the stepson, had killed either Henry or Francis or both.

"Do you know anything about his relationship with his younger brother?" Bambridge asked.

"I have served the family for many years, sir. I can only tell you what I've overheard. Before he died, the master called for his solicitor, intending to right a past wrongdoing involving his brother. But Thomas heard about it, and there was a great row between them. Thomas did threaten his life, I believe."

Detective Bambridge thought about Dicken's *A Christmas Carol*, and Marley, who must spend the rest of his existence wearing the chains he forged in life. Perhaps Francis Lawton had been trying to avoid an eternal afterlife in which he would relive old crimes of forgery and deception.

"This is Master Francis, sir." The butler pointed to a large portrait. Pausing at the foyer table, he retrieved a photograph and handed it to them. "Mrs. Lawton and her son. The son was most wayward. He was accused of ruining a local girl, but Francis Lawton was a powerful man, and no one dared prosecute the lad. The family sent him away to an academy for young men. It wasn't long before Thomas arrived back home in disgrace. Trouble with gambling and wantonness and cruelty to the other boys..."

He led them to a sitting room, where a coal fire burned in the grate and there were chairs and a table. He left promptly after promising to bring tea. A large oil lamp lit the cold room. Detective Bambridge stood by the fire while Inspector Murphy completed his preparations. From his case, he extracted a strong lantern and his revolver, setting both on the table. Then he produced a packet of candles for his young apprentice.

The butler served tea and left as hastily as he could manage.

"This place is depressing," Bambridge said when the tea failed to revive him. He felt he might have run away had it not been for his superior.

"I feel it too. A sinking of the heart. As if terrible deeds were enacted here. Believe me, young Bambridge, it is murder we are facing today."

Bambridge pulled out a cigar. "I believe I'll smoke before we start."

Inspector Murphy took out his briar pipe and lit the end. Pipe and cigar smoke clouded the chilly air. "Where do you think the elder Mr. Lawton might have hidden the will?"

"Some place his son would not think to look."

"We will have a look round, then, and see what we can find."

On opening the door, he flashed a light down the dark passage. There were doors on either side of the long corridor. The first door on the right led into a large, cheerless room containing scattered books and papers. Its disarray suggested it had already been searched by someone who was either in a hurry or in great distress. They checked the desk, looking for hidden compartments, but found nothing. A thorough investigation of the other downstairs rooms also failed to provide anything helpful.

At the top of the stairs, the upper passage led both to the left and right. On the right were three large, bare, dusty rooms. The cracked walls needed repair. On the left was a large room that appeared to be the master's bedchamber and one other chamber, perhaps designated for the wife. Adjoining them was the bathroom. Blotches of red covered the zinc tub, and though the marks proved to be only rust stains, they were terrifying.

Bambridge's own face, reflected in the mirror, was ghastly white.

Inside the master's chambers, a carriage clock on the marble mantel ticked slowly on from one to two. No human sound could be heard except for the distinct creak of footsteps on the stairwell.

"It could be the butler," Bambridge said, his voice a whisper.

The creaking continued, followed by first one furtive footstep and then another, as if something was attempting to sneak up on them. Then the noise stopped, indicating that something or someone had reached the top of the stairs. A strange mist uncurled beneath the half-open door and began to fill the chamber. The creaks began again. *Creak! Creak!* Murphy grasped his gun. Bambridge retrieved his cudgel. The door slowly began to open. Both were aware of a sense that they were not alone, that they were being observed. It seemed suddenly colder, and Detective Bambridge began shivering.

"Who's out there? Show yourself!" Murphy demanded.

An instant later, the steps retreated.

They both sat down in shock, looking at each other. Murphy's face was pale but firm. "Stay here, young Bambridge! I'll call if I need help. If that thing, whatever it was, comes again, it will have to pass me."

The two candles on the table cast circles of light, and the stair was darkened by heavy shadows. Murphy sat down halfway up the stair, revolver in hand. He put his finger to his lips and impatiently waved his companion back to the room.

Bambridge added the fireplace poker to his arsenal. Minutes passed, and then, suddenly, it came. There was a sound of rushing feet, the reverberation of a shot fired, a scuffle, and a heavy fall with a loud cry for help. Shaking with horror, Bambridge rushed into the hall. Murphy was lying on his face amid broken plaster. He seemed half dazed as Bambridge raised him and was bleeding from cuts on his face and hands. Looking up the stair, it seemed that the shadows were even thicker.

"I'll see if there are towels in the bathroom," Bambridge offered.

"I'm all right," said Murphy. "Just before I was attacked, I felt something touch me. It stank of rotting flesh. The next thing, I was knocked aside and fired, instinctively, it appears, bringing a shower of plaster down. That's as much as I can tell you. But something is there above us." He pointed toward the stairs that continued on to the attic. "I'm going up."

"You shan't go alone," said Bambridge.

"I think our help is needed, even desired by whatever resides here," Murphy said. "The entity, or whatever it is, did not truly harm me."

"If it continues helping us, I fear we will want a doctor before we get through."

Murphy managed a laugh. He had his hand on the balustrade and his foot on the upper step. Suddenly, it became intensely cold. Their breaths coalesced in front of their faces.

What was it? They could not tell themselves. They only knew that the black shadows at the top of the staircase took on a definite shape. A man's shape, but no living man. Ill-defined, with a dreadful face and twisted limbs, and smelling of Death. A document was hurled at Murphy's feet. He grabbed it up. And, shouting, they bolted downward. Both men blundered for the door. Bambridge caught the handle and threw it open. They dashed outside, and the door shut behind them.

Outside, they gathered themselves together, both of them badly shaken and bruised, and Murphy began dusting himself off. He had lost his lantern. Bambridge lit his remaining candle and was able to make out the final will and testament of Francis Lawton.

"That's enough," said Murphy, at last.

"More than enough," said Bambridge. "I wouldn't enter that house again for anything Scotland Yard could offer. Are you hurt?"

"Shamed, perhaps. Befouled! The horrible reek of the thing!"

Three days before Christmas, a man appeared at the women's door claiming to represent their father's solicitor. He wore a top hat and a tattered greatcoat and worn boots. Long, bushy red sideburns merged into a short red beard, cloaking his features. He claimed to have documents for her mother that must be signed. There was money involved. Money the family was desperate for. Emily couldn't say for certain why, but she didn't like the look of the stranger. The word she came up with was "shifty." There was something threatening about him that left her feeling unsettled. But she feared her mother would give into his demands.

Emily caught her mother by the arm. "Please, mother. You must listen. I don't believe he's from the solicitor. Sign nothing. We don't know for certain Father is dead."

Her mother appeared to startle from many long years of complacency. She nodded her assent. "I'll send him away, at least until we hear from the police."

Quickly grabbing her coat, Emily left without her mother's permission and trailed the man into the heart of Westminster, to the Charing Cross railway station, where stood the ornate Queen Eleanor Memorial Cross. All points of the city seemed to lead there: the east side of Trafalgar Square leading to St Martin's Place and then Charing Cross Road; the Strand; Northumberland Avenue; Whitehall.

The man met with two other men on the platform. Steam from the train's engine billowed around them. One of the men appeared to be gesturing toward the London embankment. Part of the London sewage system, the long, gray curve of the Embankment ran beside the river. She could just make out the spires of several sailing vessels from that distance. It was a dangerous place to go, as the river had long been the end of the road for victims of crime and suicides.

She continued following the man, walking now toward the Thames, thick that day with river fog and brown smoke. Emily began to cough, her eyes reddened by the thick, foul tasting air. It seemed hours had passed as she stumbled along in the flickering daylight. The man was clearly headed for the Charing Cross Bridge, the place where the police believed her father had likely died.

At the edge of the bridge, he vanished into the thick river mist. The day was fast fading, and the way back to Highgate was unclear in Emily's mind. She turned and headed back the way she had come, cursing herself for not paying more attention to the roads she had taken. As she struggled through the crowd, pushed unwillingly toward an undesirable section of the city, she felt as if she had entered Dickens's play. The air was filled with strange music, wailing, and loud shouts, the area containing no identifiable landmarks. All around her, hundreds of merchant stalls lined the road, illuminated by gas lamps, and in the poorer stalls burned old-fashioned grease lamps. In some booths, crimson flames emitted from small braziers upon which the merchants grilled meat, vegetables, and nuts. From others, the smell of potatoes and frying fish and whiffs of spices filled the air.

Firecrackers tossed by young boys crackled and sparked beneath the hooves of passing horses. Ground globes spun in the shops of exotic tea vendors, and the butcher's gas lights steamed and fluttered and flickered like flags, pouring forth such light it was like gazing upon a city set aflame. The din of hawkers filled the air, their voices loud and nonsensical. Merchants and buyers argued, shouted. Drunken men sang lurid songs on the street corners. Over all, a stench hung.

Soon, it seemed to Emily that she had walked a very long way down a dark highway. The streets were filled with black-shadowed archways and decaying houses from which emerged shrieks and oaths. As a child, she had feared the darkness, full of ghosts and monsters. Now, all those childish fears were frighteningly real. Drunkards reeled past her, cursing and chattering to themselves. Bawdy women in cheaply dyed dresses gathered on the street corners. She could see neither crest nor livery on the many carriages, nor could she have told a lord from a peasant. Eventide had caught her without an escort, except for a group of filthy children tagging just behind her. She began to walk faster. In the cloak of ashy gray air, she could not tell if they were still following. She clutched her purse tighter.

Now it was no longer just children following her; two men had taken their place. She stepped into a puddle, soiling the bottom of her dress and wetting her boots. The smell of the street-soil made her head spin. Poor fish mongers in rags held together with string illuminated their wares with candles mounted in small pumpkins and turnips, the wax dripping and the flame guttering.

A candle maker! Finally, some luck. She made her way toward the stall where tallow drip candles hung from every beam. Other thicker candles stood in stacked rows. The air smelled of paraffin, and it was the most wonderful smell in the world. Emily bought a thick candle from the merchant and asked how to get back to her street. The French woman inside the booth didn't seem to speak English, pointing first one way and then another.

Holding the candle before her, Emily kept walking, stepping over puddles of mire, caught in a waking nightmare. Her feet were cold and aching, her hands and face were numb. She had acted like a silly child playing a game and would now probably die here. A tattered hackney passed, its wheels showering turds and muck. Emily tried to flag the coachman down, but the shadowy carriage drove on. She clutched her light and her purse, her ears deafened by gruff shouts, and was nearly knocked down by several tangle-haired urchins bearing shovels.

A ghostly figure appeared out of the mist and called to her. "You certainly need looking after, child. This part of London is no place for the likes of yourself." She was almost certain the tiny man making his way to her was the dwarf from the theater, although in the candlelight, she couldn't say for sure. "Follow me, miss. I will see you safely home."

She had little recourse but to trust him. He began moving forward, walking quickly for having such short legs, and she made haste to stay within the range of his lantern light, which illuminated only a few feet around it. For a while, it seemed the light traveled through a darkness so deep, the world she knew no longer existed. Then slowly, the darkness fell away. At the corner of a long block of tenements, a stamping horse and carriage waited for her to board. She gave the cabby her address and stepped inside. When she turned to thank the dwarf, he was gone. As the carriage moved forward, she allowed herself to breathe. Ahead of her, a lighted street became visible. When the carriage stopped, she found herself outside her home in Highgate.

"Apparently, yesterday, a man appeared at the Lawton house with documents he wanted the widow to sign," Detective Bambridge told Inspector Murphy as he joined the other officer in the stakeout. "The young lady trailed him and said he met with two other men. They appeared to be discussing the embankment."

"Well, yet another player has appeared. Did you get a description?"

"It would easily fit many of the lower-class scoundrels who will do anything for hire. Red whiskers, red beard. I assume red hair."

"Young, old?"

"Middle-aged."

"It could be a disguise. Thomas Lawton has given us the slip before. We have to hope our informant was right about the hideout."

Under interrogation, the college chum had quickly confessed, naming Thomas as the murderer. His role had been to gain Henry's confidence by producing copies of the will Thomas had manufactured, which cut Henry off forever. By posing as a friend, he'd offered to assist Henry in filing legal documents. But Henry would need to be nearby, in London, making it easy to frame him for Francis's murder.

"Ah... There's our suspect now. The chase will be on soon, and we have a few good men at our back."

Both men, holding their revolvers, quickly moved forward. But by the time they reached the stairs, their culprit had entered the warehouse and closed the door behind him. As two other policemen rushed in from surrounding hideaways, they heard a loud clang upon the other side. The man had barred the door.

Murphy sent one of the officers to the nearby precinct to obtain an axe and wedge so they could break in. The other officer he left guarding the front. He motioned to Bambridge to follow him, and they headed for the back entrance.

From inside came a guttural, menacing voice. Whatever the voice said was instantly answered by Thomas Lawton, his tone edged with anger. Murphy and Bambridge crouched by the window, trying to hear the conversation.

"She would not sign!" proclaimed the gruffer voice.

"You worthless coward! You let a frightened woman get the better of you!" shouted Thomas in return. The discussion continued, full of shouts and disagreement, although little could be deciphered. A loud gunshot sounded. A moment later, the light went out in the left-hand window, the rear door was opened, and Thomas Lawton emerged. His face looked ghastly in the moonlight.

"I believe I know where he is going," Detective Bambridge said.

"He won't give us the slip again!" the inspector replied, and then aside to his man at the door, he added, "I believe you will find one of Henry Lawton's killers inside, possibly a red-headed gent, and the unfortunate corpse as well."

The officers boarded the waiting carriage, and the inspector gave the address in Highgate. By the end of the affair, Detective Bambridge had begun to question everything he thought he knew about the afterlife. The clergy had led him to believe once you were dead, you were dead, that the body was dissolved at death, and the spirit which survived made its way either to heaven or hell. But after recent events, the philosophy seemed a bit outdated.

Bambridge looked out the carriage window, urging the horse to move faster. There was little time if they were to catch their culprit before he did more harm. But worrying would not help. He settled his mind on a subject of interest.

"What was it we actually saw? The authorities I have read are all agreed that ghosts are composed of something called ectoplasm, and that this ectoplasm is siphoned from the human body. That when a human goes cold and his hair stands on end, he is sensing the drain of his own life force by the spirit, which may be enough to make him weak or even to kill him. It is human in origin then, is it not?"

"The spirit, or whatever it was, felt most inhuman to me," Murphy answered.

"Perhaps the spirit was drawing on me in the master's bedroom. And on both of us later on the stairs in order to manifest a strong appearance."

"We have taken on a bigger case than at first was presented," said Murphy. "We must hope the guardian angels look after us and arrange our chess pieces accordingly."

The policemen had barely left the carriage when Inspector Murphy shouted, "Thomas Lawton, you are under arrest for the murders of Francis and Henry Lawton. Put your hands up where we can see them."

Just at the door of the Lawton home, Thomas Lawton drew his gun. He turned, took a wild shot in the darkness, and then ran into the alleyway. Both policemen went on the chase, their bootsteps ringing on the cobblestones. Another shot rang out from an entryway. Inspector Murphy returned fire, and the two men darted behind the wall of a building.

"Stay here," the inspector said. He continued on alone, making enough racket for two men.

What happened next remained vague to the young detective. He saw a whitish figure skirting the wall, headed back the way they had come. He began to follow. The figure paused at the back entrance to the Lawton residence and reached for the doorknob. It was clear the culprit intended harm to the women. That was all Bambridge needed. He rushed the man, reaching for his weapon. A loud crack went off. Despite the blooming pain in his shoulder, Bambridge wrestled the man to the ground.

The maid stared at the two policemen in amazement when, in the chill of the winter evening, they presented themselves at Mrs. Lawton's home.

"Come in, come in," Emily said, peering around the maid. "We heard something that sounded like a gunshot. I wanted to take a look, but Mother..."

"What a night! Good Lord, what a night!" Detective Bambridge gasped and could barely stand. Blood clotted on his arm, staining both his uniform and his coat.

"Poor chap! He looks pretty bad!" said Inspector Murphy as Emily led the white-faced, haggard young man to the settle, calling loudly for first aid supplies and water. "The killer led us on a merry chase, but we got him in the end."

"Just outside your residence," Detective Bambridge gasped. "He saw us and pulled a gun."

"And young Bambridge here was shot while tackling him," Inspector Murphy added as the mother and other daughter appeared. "It's bloody but appears to be just a graze."

"Scotland Yard proved strongest in the end," Emily said, voicing her approval while helping the young man remove his torn coat and shirt.

"Yes. But I feel we were but the instrument of the higher forces." Inspector Murphy warmed his hands at the fire which the maid had just rekindled, while Emily cleaned Detective Bambridge's wound and bandaged it.

"We will get a cup of hot tea into him," Emily answered. "And something to eat."

"We shall be none the worse for some ourselves," the mother said, pulling on her shawl. "Henry's dead, isn't he?"

Inspector Murphy's expression told her what she expected to hear. "Yes. Francis had written a new will that excluded his stepson and left your husband as sole heir. The schoolmate, who worked in Francis's solicitor's office, saw the paperwork and contacted Thomas. For a goodly sum, he agreed to help frame Henry for his brother's murder. But mistakes were made. Francis's original will is now in the hands of the Probate, which should rule in your favor. Thomas will be hanged. We've caught our suspects, and we've survived several of your daughter's ghosts. But I will not tell all the details now. Perhaps later, after we've recovered."

Busy administering to the detective, Emily barely heard the conversation. She was professing the young man a hero, and he didn't seem to mind.

The neighborhood surrounding the pub was full of buildings with tall windows and front columns ridged with scrollwork, odd eroded animals, and the grotesque faces of gargoyles, their front steps spreading outward, cast in marble. The dwarf turned and took a little-known stairway which led underneath the Charing Cross station into the underground.

The London weather, dreadful as always, flogged him as he struggled with the heavy oak door. The wreath's center bell rang dolefully as he staggered inside, soggy, hair plastered against his forehead, stomping his feet on the mat. The dank smell of a cellar rose around him, and he entered a haze of tobacco smoke. The walls were formed of thick wood and blackened ceiling beams ran overhead.

At the bar, several men were singing songs of Christmas cheer and toasting to each other's good health. But there were others there, deep in the cups and not in good humor; the holiday brought no joy to their troubled lives. They glanced at the door, their lips set in bitter lines.

Amongst that crowd, he could always find a soul or two willing to part with good coin for a throw or two of the dice. However, for the moment, his work in London was finished. His company was leaving the city with its pestilence and its strife; not soon enough, in his opinion. But he knew in his heart they would likely encounter a worse place.

The barkeep had a good fire going, the heat causing the dwarf's woolen clothing to issue forth a good amount of steam. He took off his gloves and hat and heavy overcoat, gestured for his usual ale, and headed for the rear table where he conducted business and where a middle-aged man now waited for him.

"I see you had no problem finding the place," the dwarf said.

The air of lost prestige still clung to the man like leaves

on a dying tree. He merely nodded, probably regretting ever having encountered the company at the theater. Well, thought the dwarf, Madam Chow is Madam Chow. A person of last resort one could seek out when other mediums failed. A person who could summon apparitions and spirits and all manner of magical thingamajigs. For a price.

The overweight middle-aged barkeep approached the table. The dwarf could smell the mothball scent of the man's woolen vest, the pungent odor of sweat. The barkeep set the dwarf's mug on the table, wiped his thick hands on his apron, and waited for their order. The dwarf ordered a round of beer and fish and chips for both. "You're paying, I hope," the dwarf said to the man. "Or we could throw dice for it." He dug around in his vest pocket and set a pair of dice on the table.

"Not another game." The man leaned over the table as if he'd already had too much to drink, his head propped on his left elbow. "I've already bargained away more years than I have left to me."

"I've yet to figure out what you might contribute to our little company," the dwarf said. "You can't juggle or walk a tightrope or tell fortunes or spin a ball on your nose. And you have a rather bad limp. But Madam Chow was most insistent you join us."

The man remained silent. Clearly, he had no intention of easing his own suffering with conversation.

The dwarf quaffed his ale, studying the fire. Despite throw after throw, each one representing a year of the man's life in servitude, the dice presented the same outcome. The man would die, and his body would wash up somewhere along the Thames. He would leave his family in poverty. In the last throw left to him, he'd accepted a different outcome—his wife and daughters safe and taken care of.

The dwarf had his own part to play in the game, and yet it brought him no satisfaction. Rather, it made him appear to be one of those creatures of ill-fortune, a mischief-maker and a meddler in the affairs of humans, behaviors often associated with his kind. "We've met the terms of our agreement," the dwarf said. "All wrapped up in a Christmas bow. The culprits arrested. Family members rescued. The inheritance secured."

"I have one last thing to ask of you," the man said. "Could I see them one last time?"

The dwarf swung his short legs, downed a drink of warm beer. "That will cost you." From his pocket, he took out a gold watch and for a moment, he let it dangle like a hypnotist's tool. (He could never resist showing off.) Popping it open exposed both a clock and a mirror. The dwarf muttered his usual hocus pocus while shining the mirror's surface with his woolen shirt sleeve. The clock's wheels began to spin, and the hands moved swiftly around the dial. The mirror, a magical contrivance of some sort, cast forth a shimmering window that looked into a large setting room.

A Christmas tree hung with homemade ornaments and garlands of popcorn and nuts, clusters of sweet candies and cornucopias sat in the corner of the well-appointed space. In the dining room, a huge feast was being set out, servants going back and forth carrying trays of Yorkshire pudding, potatoes, and mince pie. On the table sat a large stuffed goose and rib of beef, and the sideboard overflowed with all manner of cakes and tarts. The image was so real, the man could smell the aroma.

Light was everywhere, shining brightly from glass globes and candelabras. And there were his daughters, laughing gayly with two other young women, while his wife looked on. A young man stood next to the fireplace, looking over the festivities with a content expression. Indeed, it was as happy a family picture as anyone could wish.

The man could not take his eyes from the vision; tears glittered in them. "Truly, the end is better than I could have imagined. I almost let everything important to me be destroyed. I already had more than any man deserves, but I couldn't see it."

"So be it," said the dwarf. But as he reached for the watch to put it away, the youngest girl looked directly into the mirror, saw her father, and called out to him.

"Emily," the man called back, despairingly.

The dwarf snapped the watch shut and stuck it in his pocket. "Oh, she is talented. We could do something with her."

"Never," her father said. "She will never suffer my fate."

"Come now, we're not such a bad lot," the dwarf said. "You could have done worse. Ah, here's the fish and chips." A large platter of food arrived along with additional mugs of ale. "Let us set to this hearty meal with good Christmas cheer. Tomorrow, a long journey awaits."

Charing Cross

By Pam S. Dunn

Pam S. Dunn lives in Angels Camp, in California's gold country, a town where nothing of note has happened since Mark Twain wrote the Celebrated Jumping Frog of Calaveras County and the definition of a road is "something passable by two mules going in either direction," but she wouldn't live elsewhere.

Born in Ohio to a family of native Kentuckians, her characters in novels and short stories face any number of personal and social challenges.

Pam is married, and she and her husband have two daughters and some grandkids. She loves the ocean, redwoods, and the mountains and can become easily lost in historical research on one thing or another.

Her most recent writing is included in Shifting Sands Anthology. Her other works include: "Retirement," *Out of the Fire Anthology*; "Sunflowers," *Suisun Valley Review #32*; and "Who Reads Anymore," *A Taste of Literary Elegance: Wine, Cheese, and Chocolate.* She is currently revising two novels.

A Taste of Literary Elegance: Wine, Cheese & Chocolate – "Who Reads Anymore"

Suisun Valley Review Vol. 32 – "Sunflowers"

Shifting Sands – "Artificial Intelligence"

Out of the Fire – "Retirement"

Connect with Pam

www.pamsdunn.com

twitter.com/pamsdunn

The Recipe for Cornbread

E. Lonzale Lewis

My fifth attempt at my Grandma Mary Alice's cornbread wasn't any better than the last four. Steam rose off the golden loaf, scenting the air with the delicious corn and butter smell. I'd decided, even though the recipe didn't call for it, to add butter to this last attempt. Brown around the edges, the middle sagged as if some key ingredient had been left out. Or, in this case, added.

The stained notecard my Aunt Anne had scrawled the recipe on sat in a smear of flour on the yellow-tiled counter. Moving in close, still holding the cast-iron skillet in my mitten-covered hand, I once again went over the ingredients: cornmeal, flour, baking powder, salt, milk, and lard (I'd used vegetable oil instead). While the original recipe had been written in black ink, someone (most likely my Aunt Betina) had added the precise measurements later in blue.

My grandma and my Aunt Anne never used measuring cups when they cooked. My mom, Gwen, had taken her set when she moved out six months ago, after my Aunt Desiree had passed away in her sleep. I'd had to purchase a set when I bought the food for the Christmas meal. I'd never developed the same culinary skills that my aunt and grandma possessed. I did okay in the kitchen, though I always had to follow a recipe. But now, staring at the almost empty egg carton—pissed that I'd have to go to the store for more eggs for breakfast in the morning—I knew I'd gotten in over my head.

I'd like to say the deposits of flour all over the counter were the final straw, but that would be a lie. Careful not to slam it down—I couldn't afford to replace the tiles—I set the cast-iron skillet on the towel I had resting on the countertop and blew out a breath of frustration. A single tear slipped down my sweaty cheek. My cousin Beatrice and her partner Raphael would be here in an hour to help, and the rest of the family would follow soon after that. Although I'd made most of the holiday meal (honey glazed ham, potato salad, greens, macaroni and cheese, a pound cake, and two pecan pies), I still had a few more dishes to fix. Including the cornbread. Thankfully, Beatrice was bringing the turkey and dressing.

Sweat slid down my back, and I pushed a lock of damp hair behind my ear as I snatched off the oven mitt and tossed it across the room, scattering the measuring cups. Only a few rooms in the house had air conditioning, and the kitchen wasn't one of them. My flip-flops smacked the heels of my feet, the sting adding to the rising fury within me, as I walked over to the bay window and shoved it open. Warm humid air rushed inside, bringing in the briny scent of the bayou not far off from our estate. The breeze, although warm, felt good on my face.

Smoke from the oven—filtering out of the vent on the side of the house—circled in the air outside the house. The smoke seemed to morph into a familiar silhouette of a man wearing a bowler hat, his face a ghostly outline. It tugged at the memory of the Christmas after my Grandma Mary Alice had died. I shuddered remembering Mr. Manning. I could still hear that slippery-slimy voice as it slithered all over me. Taunting me. I'd been five at the time. Too young to fight such a malevolent spirit. But somehow, I had found the strength.

It was too bad I didn't have any of that strength now. Pulling myself from the past, I turned and glared at the old-fashioned stove. "Why didn't my mother replace that damn stove?"

"You managed everything else just fine on that stove, little Charlotte. It ain't the problem and you know it," Grandma Mary Alice said. "No shame in asking for help."

She was right. The stove wasn't the problem. It was just an easy target for me to blame my mood on. It couldn't fight back.

I turned to the rocking chair sitting in the corner of the room. My grandma's favorite spot in the kitchen. She'd sit there, humming to herself, sweat coating her skin, while food simmered on the stove. Sometimes she'd have a radio playing. But mostly she'd just hum, occasionally wiping the sweat away with a towel she kept thrown over her shoulder. That's where she was now. Sunlight bathed her skin. Despite being a spirit, she appeared solid, looking the same as she always did. She even wore her favorite pale green flowered dress, the towel still thrown over her shoulder.

Her mother had been Cherokee and her father Creole. Her features were a nice mix from both of them. She had long black hair I used to love to help her braid. Of course, my braids were never much more than twists. She'd always fix it when I was done. But how I loved to play with it every summer when I came to visit. Even after her death, when her spirit came to see me, she'd let me braid her hair.

She stared at me, her dark brown eyes waiting. She had a patience I would never have.

"I can manage," I said, trying to infuse determination into my voice.

It would have been nice to just give up. We didn't need a big lavish meal anyway. I could fix Jerry and Kaylee peanut butter and jelly for all they cared. It was the presents (I finally had to hide them) they were more concerned with. But sadly, I had foolishly volunteered to make the Christmas meal. My determination had been rooted in the pain and embarrassment of Robert leaving me with two kids and only enough money for us to live on for the next few months. The divorce papers had arrived yesterday. Ten years of marriage reduced to thirty pages of cold legalese, dividing what little property we had left. While he asked for visitation rights, I knew he didn't want to see them.

I wasn't shocked by the papers arriving. What shocked me was the fact that he had known where to send them. I'd never told him about the horrors that had taken place here when I was five, but he knew it was something terrible. Every time we'd visit, I'd be uneasy. Yet, after clearing out our bank accounts and not paying the mortgage for the past six months, he'd abandoned his wife and children, forcing me to move back home to a place he knew I had issues with.

A loud bang carried into the kitchen and I closed my eyes, trying to push down my frustration. My kids had been at it since five this morning. I didn't have the energy to yell at them once again. There were only so many times you could say, "Stop it, or you're getting a spanking" before having to follow through with said spanking. I'd never hit my kids. And, truthfully, I never wanted to. Eventually, they'd figure out my threats weren't real.

"They need something to help settle them down some. Let them go outside," my grandma said.

I glanced out the window. Maybe it was the leftover fear

of Mr. Manning that was making me keep them cooped up. They had played outside by themselves in our small yard when we lived in California and had been good about staying in the front.

"The estate is too big for me to let them play outside alone," I said, as my eyes landed on the whiskey for the fruit cake sitting on the island in the middle of the kitchen. I'd never been much of a drinker. Robert usually drank enough for both of us. Not a drunk really, just, in my opinion, one too many on occasion.

He didn't start out that way. His drinking came when we brought Jeremiah home from the hospital. He said he wanted to celebrate. Looking back at it now, I believe he wanted to hide the fact that he really didn't want kids.

"We should remain young and free," he'd told me after Kaylee was born. I'd laughed, because he was always saying things like that. It was when he started saying it every day that I realized he was serious. I should have left then. But I foolishly believed he would come around and grow to love the life we had started. That he would, after a while, grow out of his impulsive behavior (I can admit I used to love that about him) and finally settle into our new life.

I reached for the whiskey bottle, hand trembling, then paused. This wasn't me. I wasn't going to be this person. Robert was not going to change me. Besides, once I started, it would be too easy to justify the next drink and the next.

The kitchen door slammed open, banging into the wall. My seven-year-old Jeremiah (he preferred Jerry, the name his father gave him) barreled into the kitchen and four-year-old Kaylee followed behind him.

"What did I tell you about slamming doors?" I asked, leaning against the counter.

I should have taken him to get a haircut yesterday. But

time had gotten away from me. Now his hairline was crooked. Something Robert hated. I shook myself. *Something Robert hated.* I had to stop thinking like that. Robert no longer mattered.

"She touched me!" Jeremiah yelled, his chest heaving up and down.

I glanced over at Kaylee. She stood just inside the doorway, her favorite doll smashed against her chest. Her bright hazel eyes fixated on the rocking chair. Could she see Grandma Mary Alice?

"Kaylee?" She slowly turned to me. "What are you looking at?"

She smiled. "Mama, he won't let me hug. I want hug." She set her doll on the table and started toward her brother. "Hug, Jerry."

I caught Jeremiah's arm before he could push her away. "Enough you two." I knelt down so that Jeremiah and I were eye to eye. "Why won't you hug your sister?"

He stared at me out of Robert's dark brown eyes. The familiarity caught me off guard and I had to fight my sudden urge to yell. To unleash all the anger that I'd had to suppress since Robert walked out on us. My children didn't need to see that in me.

"Did you hear, Jerry? Why won't you hug your sister?"

He shrugged. Another one of Robert's annoying traits. I hated that my son had picked up on that indecisive gesture. For Robert, it had always been a way for him to avoid answering a question. Now it seemed Jeremiah was going to use the same tactic.

"I'm losing my patience with you." Another shrug. I stood before I could react. In reality, I couldn't force him to hug his sister. That wouldn't be right. But at the same time, I didn't want him treating her bad because she wanted to show him some affection. Parenting didn't come with a manual, and it was times like this I really wish it did.

Opening my arms, I smiled at Kaylee. She wasted no time running into them. I inhaled deeply, pulling in her soft scent.

"Are the two of you ready for a snack?" I asked as I shifted Kaylee to the side so that I could look at Jerry. His face scrunched up as he stared at us. Again, I was walking a delicate rope with him. His temper could be explosive. And lately, it had been worse. He had started throwing things and slamming doors. Because of Robert's indifference, Jerry had always tried hard to impress him. Tried to create that bond. No small wonder that Robert's leaving had hit him the hardest.

Kaylee grabbed my face. "I want tiny apples." She meant cherries. I gave a lock of her hair a gentle tug and stood.

"I sure do miss you tugging on my hair, little Charlotte. Every time your mama brought you to visit, you'd climb up in my lap and grin from ear to ear."

Kaylee turned to Grandma Mary Alice. "I can tug," she said.

"She's talking to herself again!" Jerry shouted.

"Jerry. Stop yelling." I watched Kaylee as she hesitantly made her way to Grandma Mary Alice. A small smile started, growing as she got closer. This was the first time I'd seen her react to a spirit. It scared the hell out of me. But I couldn't show any fear. No, I had to be strong, and soon, teach her about the ones she needed to protect herself against. Teach them both the recipe that sent Mr. Manning away.

"Make her stop talking to herself!" Jerry knocked over a chair. The sound was like nails drilling into my eardrums.

"Stop it!" I yelled before I could stop myself. Kaylee, possibly believing I was talking to her, froze. My heart sunk as the first tear slid down her sweet face. I reached for her, but she ran out of the room.

"Jerry," I started. "What has gotten into you?" I leaned back against the counter, my hands gripping the tile and making my knuckles turn white.

He shrugged.

"Don't shrug at me," I gritted out. "You have behaved badly these past few days, and I won't tolerate it anymore."

He studied me for a minute. I knew that look well. He was trying to figure out just how much further he could push me.

"Don't," I said, my eyes narrowing. "If you say or do one more thing, I will spank you." This time I was serious. At least I thought I was. Truthfully, I didn't know how I felt. Robert and I had agreed we would try other ways to discipline our kids. While Kaylee just needed a firm 'no,' Jerry was becoming much more difficult to handle. Nothing worked all the time.

I closed my eyes and waited, gathering patience into me like it was a physical thing.

"I'm hungry," Jerry said.

I nodded and then opened my eyes. "Go get your sister and I will make you both a snack."

He hesitated. Then ran over, wrapped his arms around my waist in a brief hug, and dashed out the room. I relished these brief moments of affection that he showed. It reminded me that no matter what, my son was still in there. Buried under all that anger and frustration. And one day soon, my sweet boy would heal enough to let me in again.

"He's a handful," Grandma said. "Little Charlotte, you gonna have to help Kaylee. She's too wide-eyed about the spirits. Not all of them will be kind."

I wiped a stray tear from my cheek and straightened. "Yes, Grandma. I know. He's still gone, right?"

She nodded as her eyes went distant. "Mmm... Yes, little Charlotte. He's gone." She glanced out the window. "But others are out there. Lurking. Trying to find a way in." She turned back to me. "Might be good for you to teach them the recipe. Especially Jerry. His anger is like a doorway for Mr. Manning. He might end up letting him in."

"I wish he could see."

"Maybe just knowing his sister ain't really talkin' to herself will be enough. He might even protect her when she needs it."

I pulled the bread out of the breadbasket and thought about what she said. It wouldn't hurt. Or would it? Would he be angry he couldn't see ghosts? By the time they both returned to the kitchen, I had placed half a peanut butter and jelly sandwich and "tiny apples" on the table for each of them. I'd made myself some tea as well.

Kaylee pulled her chair out, watching Grandma the whole time. Jerry attacked his sandwich, barely giving himself time to chew, as soon as he was seated.

I sat down with my cinnamon tea and watched my children eat for a while. How would I make this suitable for them? I couldn't tell them the real story. They were not ready for that. Even I, at five years old, wasn't ready for Mr. Manning and the darkness he had infested my family with. It had almost destroyed them.

I took a sip of my tea as I filtered through my thoughts. In the end, I settled on turning the nursery rhyme into a song. One I hoped would keep them safe.

"So, who wants to learn a song?"

"Me," Kaylee said, raising her hand. She climbed out of her chair, grabbed her doll, and climbed into my lap.

Jerry shook his head, but I could see the interest on his face as he tried to hide his joy. I smiled at that. He did love music.

"Do you know that I can see ghosts?"

Jerry's eyes bugged out and he straightened in his chair. I had gained his attention. My heart warmed as his dark brown gaze bore into me, waiting.

Kaylee leaned in and whispered, her breath tickling my ear, "I can too, Mommy."

I tugged her hair and smiled. "I know, baby. I know."

While I told them the edited version, I allowed myself to remember it all. After all, there was strength in what had happened that Christmas. And strength was something I desperately needed right now.

Two
Coming Home Again

Silverwood was unseasonably warm in December of 1993. It was three months after my grandma had died, and we were headed back to the Silverwood estate to spend time with the family. My mother wasn't happy about it. She took to muttering under her breath as we got closer to Georgia. And when we finally drove into Silverwood, she started cursing out loud, forgetting entirely that I was in the car with her. I didn't understand her anger. Yes, things were tense. Even at five I understood that. But why the animosity?

After the funeral, my Aunt Betina had moved back into the house to settle everything while Mama and the rest of the family went back to their own lives. She called every day complaining about one thing or another; the insurance that had to be divided, the land trust that needed all of their signatures when money had to be withdrawn to make repairs to the house, final bills, and even concern over Aunt Desiree who was getting up in years and would soon need full-time care.

She resented that the rest of the family wasn't doing their

share. But, as my mama told her, she had a life and responsibilities and couldn't pick up and move back home. She loved teaching and didn't want to give it up. But my aunt figured if she could leave someone in charge of her beauty salon in Jackson, then my mama could get a substitute to teach her class.

My dad had to replace the telephone ten times because my mama would throw it when she finally hung up. The last time he replaced the phone, she'd told him the real reason she was hesitant to go back home. She said the house felt empty without her mother, and the pain was too much for her to bare.

Now, as we drove through the town (or city, to some) making our way toward the bridge that led to our estate, I wondered what would happen when she saw her sister again.

Our estate sat on a five-acre patch of land adjacent to Silverwood that most folks referred to as Across the Bayou. It was true; there are some resemblances to an actual bayou. Brackish water sat between the two land masses with patches of marsh-grass. But it was just a small deposit of water from Tulare River that had collected in a dip in the land.

I hung out the window. The ride was slow enough for me to get glimpses of the rare plants floating in the water—visible through the opening in the slats.

Once across the bridge, our estate was the first one on the left. My mama stopped the car to wave at Mae Declouette. She often sat on her porch, which was directly across from our family estate, giving out pecans and wisdom to those who would sit with her for a spell.

My grandma and Mae Declouette had gone to school together and, for a brief time, liked the same boy. Jefferson Daniels. Dark as night and smelling of sweet grass and cocoa butter, he charmed not only my grandma and Mae, but a few other women (white women included) until he was finally run out of Silverwood by a mob of men. A few rumors had started back in them days about his run-in with my Grandpa Jake Baptiste and Lester Declouette and how Jefferson hadn't got away but ended up buried in the swamp.

Down from Declouette's was the Boisseau family. Across from them, hidden behind a thick patch of trees, was the Arceneaux family. My Aunt Desiree and Evangeline were good friends for a while, until Evangeline got married and moved away. My aunt was torn up about it and had stopped talking to everyone for a short time.

Next to us was the LaRue family, where my cousin Beatrice lived.

Car tires crunched on the seashells that covered the driveway as we made our way to the house. The estate home rose from a moss-covered ground like a giant soul. Its windows were the eyes. And they seemed to be watching me. Five acres of land stretched out with a large sixty-five hundred square foot house—white with black shutters. Around the back of the house, a large boulder stood in the middle of the space where the slave houses used to be. All the names of those who had lived and died on the land were etched into the blue granite.

We got out of the car and stepped onto a bed of seashells. I stomped my foot, enjoying the sound of their crunching. My mother took my hand, unknowingly gripping it too tight. Squeezing my tiny bones. Only when I yelped and tried to pull away did she release it. I remember staring up at her, the sunlight cocooning her body, making it difficult to see her face. Or maybe it wasn't the sun but the tears that had started falling when we were in the car.

We took our time as we walked on those seashells toward the front door. When we reached the porch, my mother took my hand again and placed her other one on her swollen belly. A sound I will never forget burst from my mother's mouth, filled with pure anguish. I flinched, unsure of how I should react. I squeezed her hand.

My Grandma Mary Alice stood on the porch wearing the flower-print sundress they had buried her in. My mother had said it was her favorite dress. And even though it hadn't been buried with her, a yellow towel lay draped over her shoulder. She stared at my mother out of bright hazel eyes, while tears slipped silently down her face.

"My mommy's sad too," I said to her.

She looked down at me then. Her face stretched into a beautiful smile. "That she is, little Charlotte. But I know one day, she'll be all right. Just don't ever let go of her hand."

At that age, I believed she meant that literally. It was only later that year, when my mother became concerned about my need to always hold her hand, that I learned the sentiment was an emotional one. And showing my mother love was the best way to help her.

"We're all sad, sweetheart," my mother said, crouching down and pulling me to her. "Are you ready to go inside?"

I nodded and then looked back at my grandma standing there. "Are you coming?"

She reached out and ran her hand down my head, giving my braid a little tug like she used to do. I giggled, remembering us pulling playfully at each other's hair. "I will always be there, little Charlotte. But I can't come in with you right now. I want to see all my children as they finally come home." She knelt down, and my face was bathed with a cool, feathery air. "Grandma is going to need your help real soon."

"I'll help Grandma," I said and tugged at her braid.

"Charlotte, honey, don't," my mama said. "I know you

miss her, but it will be hard for everyone if you continue talking as if she's still here."

I glanced at my mother, confused. "But she is, Mommy. She is."

My mother paused, staring at the space next to me. Her eyes got that far-off look they sometimes got when she was thinking. Like she had to look farther than she could really see to find the answer. My grandma touched my mother's cheek. My mom closed her eyes. "Oh, Mama. Why didn't you just hold on?"

"I tried to, sweet girl. Mama tried. But I had to let go. If I didn't, he would have took all my will away from me. It had already spoiled you kids. My babies. Now, I just need you to remember."

My mother shook her head and wiped her wet cheek. "Let's go inside, Charlotte."

"Grandma..."

"Stop it, Charlotte. Stop it, please. Your grandma is dead. She's not here." Her voice came out strained, pain infusing each word.

"But she was just..."

My mother shook her head. Her mouth drew into a tight line. "Just once, pretend you don't see anything. Please," she said, her voice a mere whisper.

I looked over at my grandma. She stood, staring at my mother. I had believed my mother could see her. Even believed they were talking to one another. It was only years later, when I mentioned this day, my mother told me that while she hadn't heard her, she did feel grandma's hand on her cheek.

The house opened up to a large parlor area. Twin cherry wood staircases wound their way up to the second floor. Portraits hung on the wood paneled walls, and white marble flooring stretched back to the parlor behind the staircase. A large crystal chandelier dropped down from the ceiling, reminding me of snowflakes.

Raised voices traveled from the back room. The heated words made me cringe. I'd always hated loud, angry voices. My mother sighed as she walked reluctantly toward the sitting room. I'd almost believed she'd forgotten me, until she stretched her hand back, signaling for me to follow. I took her hand and walked with her.

The first person we saw was Aunt Betina, standing in the middle of the room with her arms crossed over her chest. My great Aunt Desiree sat in her favorite chair by the large window. The smell of burnt sugar hung heavy in the air. I rubbed my nose, trying to dislodge the foul odor.

"What's burning?" my mother asked, letting go of my hand. I reached for her again. "Not now, Charlotte."

"Is that the way you greet family?" Aunt Betina asked, rounding on her. "Accusing them of burning something?"

My mother scoffed. "You must be feeling guilty. *Family*. Cause all I asked is what's burning."

It was at that moment I saw my first tendril: a strange black thread that wavered in and out of the room. It circled around both my mother and aunt, sinking into their chests. When I reached out to touch it, it disappeared. And as I searched for it, they continued to argue. But I had stopped listening. I was too focused on finding that thread again.

"Little Charlotte," Aunt Desiree said, stopping me in my search. "What you lookin' for, sweet girl?"

"Shiny black thread."

The room grew silent.

"What did you say, little Charlotte?" Aunt Betina asked. She looked at Mama with accusation in her eyes.

"I'm looking for the shiny black thread."

She knelt down and looked at me. "Where did you see it?" I touched her heart and she shook her head. "Figures you'd teach her about Mr. Manning. You were always so devious. Always trying to scare us into believing."

"She doesn't know anything about him. I haven't uttered that nursey rhyme in years."

My aunt pulled me in for a hug. There was no warmth in it, and I pulled away quickly. Her face dropped. "Well, that's all right." She stood up. "I know when I'm not wanted." She walked out of the room.

"Go after her," Aunt Desiree said. "Let Charlotte stay in here with me."

While my aunt made it seem as if she didn't believe in Mr. Manning, her first question had let me know she really did, piquing my own curiosity

Where did you see it?

Aunt Desiree opened her arms, and I ran over to her. She scooped me up onto her lap. "Now that's Auntie's big girl." She smelled like caramel and sweat.

"I saw grandma."

"Charlotte!" my mother yelled.

"Now, Gwen, don't yell at her. Go on in the kitchen with your sister see if you can straighten out that mess she made with the sweet cakes." She shifted me on her lap. "Little Charlotte and I will sit here a spell." She poked my belly and I giggled. "Ain't that right?"

My chin struck my breastbone as I bobbed my head up and down. I always liked talking with my Aunt Desiree. Plus, she always gave me one of the Werther's she kept at the bottom of her purse—a small black bag with a gold buckle.

"She needs to stop believing she can see spirits," my mother choked out.

"Like you did?"

My mother gasped, but I didn't turn to look. I was too busy searching for a piece of candy at the bottom of my Aunt Desiree's purse.

"It wasn't real," my mother said, finally. "And the sooner she realizes that, the better. Now," my mother reached for me, "I will take her with me."

My aunt pulled me closer. "Stop, Gwen." There was something more behind that simple request. So much more that even I could feel it, and I stopped my search and turned to look at them. My mother's eyes had gone distant again while my aunt held perfectly still. Waiting, it seemed.

Once again, my mother shook herself from the... what? Memory? Knowledge? I never knew. All I did know was that she stopped looking for whatever it was my aunt's command had sent her in search of.

"Fine," she whispered and then looked at me. "You make sure you mind your aunt. You hear me?"

"Yes, Mommy."

She paused. Staring at me. Almost searching. Or waiting. I couldn't figure out what. Until finally, she turned and left.

When I turned back to my aunt, she held out a gold-wrapped piece of Werther's. "Now, why don't you tell Auntie what you saw?"

Not really understanding the significance of her request, I unwrapped the candy and popped it in my mouth. She waited until I had had my fill of the sweet caramel. Finally, I told her.

"A black string between Mama and Auntie Tina."

"Just as I figured." She gathered me closer to her. "Well, little Charlotte. Looks like we done run out of time."

"For what?" I asked.

She pulled two more candies from her purse and unwrapped one for each of us. Her fingers shook as she slipped hers into her mouth. "Now. You have to remember the order of things. You think you're smart enough to do that, little Charlotte?"

"What does order mean?" I asked around the candy in my mouth.

"It's how things go. Like you're first and then your little brother will be second when he's born."

"He's in Mama's belly."

She smiled and nodded. "That he is."

My hand wandered up and squeezed the skin on her cheek. I always loved to play with those soft folds of skin. She smiled as she stared deep into my eyes, as if reading something inside of me.

"You really are a bright light, little Charlotte."

I smiled at her, loving how the words made me feel special. Treasured even. "Squishy," I said, squeezing her skin a little harder.

She laughed. Her whole body shook. "One day, you'll have some squishy of your own."

That is when her mood shifted—a change so sudden it frightened me. I stopped my exploration of her skin and wrapped my arms around myself. I wanted to get up and leave but didn't have the strength to move. It was as if something had anchored me to her.

My aunt started to hum, the sound coming from deep within her. Her small frame shook with each note. There was pain in the melody. I do remember that. The more she hummed, the more it felt as if a weight had been placed on me. I looked at her, seeing the shift in her features like something buried deep was waking up. It both scared and confused me how her hazel eyes had changed color, deepening almost to black. Then words, whispered, slipped out of her open mouth.

Lay the shells so you can hear him coming
Plant the rosemary to keep him out

An engine revved out in the driveway, pulling me out of the trance she had put me in. My aunt shuddered, and she blinked a few times like she was trying to pull me back into focus. It was almost as if she had forgotten I was there. "Oh, sweet little Charlotte. Auntie didn't mean to scare you." She placed me on the floor and pulled in a deep breath as she closed her eyes. "Go on now. See who's outside. Let Auntie pull herself together. But wait 'til I get there before you go outside."

I ran toward the door, stopping just inside the frame, and watched my Uncle Anthony climb out of his bright red Corvette. The sunlight glinted off the hood, sending a ray of light toward the shadows on the porch. Dust motes danced in the beam as it bathed my grandma in light. It was then I noticed that she was no longer alone. A man wearing worn, blue overalls and a straw hat stood with her, staring at me.

I pushed open the screen and made my way over to them.

"Little Charlotte, this is my great-great granddaddy, Zachariah Washington," she said.

I smiled up at him. He appeared solid, just like Grandma. His skin was darker than the rest of my family's, a blue-black color that almost shinned. I later learned he had been brought to America when he was only seven years old and died at the age of seventy. Two years after slavery had been abolished.

"Well." He bent down in front of me, and a smile stretched across his heavily lined face and his dark brown eyes lit up. "It sure is nice to meet ya."

I touched his face, squeezing at the folds. I've often wondered why nobody ever told me how offensive this could be. But they gave me allowances for things my cousins would always get in trouble for. Maybe it was because I was always talking to the spirits that no one else could see. I was teased relentlessly for it. And that, in their eyes, made me a little special. It also explained them constantly referring to me as "little Charlotte." As a child, I loved it. It made me feel like a princess. As an adult, it got on my damn nerves. But not when my grandma said it.

"She's got the sight, too," Zachariah said, straightening. "That's good. You gonna need her help bringing the family back together again."

My grandma sighed. "I was a little afraid of that."

Raised voices pulled at my attention, and I glanced over at my uncle's car. His wife, my Aunt Trisha, and their two sons, James and Darius, climbed out of the vehicle. The car was so small; I wondered how they had all fit inside.

James was the oldest. Nine years old and going on four, my mama used to say. Skinny as a rail, he was the same height as my Aunt Trisha. Darius was a year younger than him and followed his brother's lead as if he never had a mind of his own. I tried to steer clear of both of them.

"I told you we should have taken the Buick, Tony. This car is too small for me and the boys," my Aunt Trisha said. Her white sleeveless sundress was sticking to her as if it had been molded to her skin. "All they did was kick my damn seat the entire way here. James, Darius, you two get the hell back over here. I don't want you running around this damn yard. Act like you both got some sense."

Neither one of them had any sense. Even today, as men in their thirties, they continue to act like juveniles.

"Trish, baby, don't start," my uncle said, shutting the car door and making the mistake of rubbing some dirt off the roof. He loved that car.

"Don't start?" She rounded on him as James and Darius

took off toward the back of the house. "I suppose you could sell this stupid car and pay for whatever damage they cause. Is that it? You want them to break something?"

"What are they going to break outside?"

"Them boys?" Grandma said to Zachariah. "They could break dirt if it was breakable. Lord, I told him he needed to take them boys in hand. Trisha all talk, and Tony act like he scared to wup them." She shook her head. "Mmm..."

"Oh, I can't with you," Aunt Trisha said to my uncle. "Not in this damn heat!" She stormed toward the porch, dust flying up from her heavy footfalls. "Come here, little Charlotte. Give Auntie a hug."

Despite the fury that she seemed to wear like a second skin, she was always so sweet to me. I wrapped my arms around her waist, feeling the bulge she hadn't had a few months ago at my grandma's funeral. I smiled up at her. "Baby?"

She harrumphed and shook her head. "Yeah." She bent down and kissed my cheek. "Maybe this one will be as sweet as you."

"Lord, Trisha I could hear you coming from deep inside the house. You gonna wake the dead with that loud-ass mouth of yours!" Aunt Desiree pushed open the screen door. "What you out here fussin' about?"

"That damn nephew of yours crammed me and the boys in his ego of a car. And the air-conditioning don't work. Them boys was kicking my seat the whole way here. If not for this baby taking up so much room, I'd have pulled off my shoe and smacked the hell out of both their legs."

"Well, maybe a run around the yard will tire them out."

Aunt Trisha scoffed as she rubbed her belly. "How are you holding up, Aunt D? And why is it so damn hot in December?"

"Fair to middlin'." She looked up at the sky. "Ain't gettin' up as easy as I used to. I do appreciate the heat, though. Give my old tired bones some rest."

"Hell, Aunt D. You going to outlive us all." She crinkled her nose. "And who on earth burnt sugar?"

"Betina in there tryin' to cook."

"Why didn't you stop her?"

"I'm too old to go running after folks. Besides, she was wearing me out with questions about what we goin' to do about the house. Figure she could pack me off to a home and sell it. I'm not havin' none of that mess." She pulled open the screen door. "Gwen! Your brother's here." The wooden screen door shut behind them as both my aunts continued their trek into the house, fussing the whole way.

Grandma placed her hand on my head as she stared out at Uncle Anthony. He studied the house behind his shades. I didn't understand why he didn't come forward. Why he stood there as if something was keeping him in place. A breeze ruffled his thin, baby blue button-down shirt. As he rubbed his arms, the sun hit his gold watch. He was the only man I'd ever seen wear so much gold jewelry. A chain around his neck and a gold chain-linked bracelet around his wrist. Flashy. That's what my mama always called him. He liked to show off his wealth. They owned two convenience stores in Dayton.

My uncle finally pulled off his shades and slipped them into the front of his shirt. "Hey, little Charlotte." It was funny that he had just now noticed me.

The screen door creaked open and I turned. Mama stepped onto the porch and glanced down at me. "You all right, baby?"

I smiled and nodded, my head bobbing up and down.

"I see you still have the convertible, Tony," she said, putting her hands on her hips.

"See you still don't know how to speak before you start in on someone, baby sister."

My mother sighed and walked down the steps, her hand rubbing at her back as she walked. She had been doing that a lot lately. She'd say the baby was anxious to get out. My daddy wanted a boy. And I wanted a baby sister so I could do her hair. My mama just wanted to stop peeing on herself when she laughed. Of course, Daddy always made her laugh, so she changed her underwear often.

"Shut up and give me a hug," she said as she stared up at him.

My uncle pulled her in tight and rested his chin on her head. Out of all the sisters and brothers, they were the closest. It had been the two of them for five years before my Aunt Lenora was born.

"Betina burned the sweet cakes," Mama said, stepping away from him.

He shook his head. "Why she in the kitchen in the first place? She knows she can't cook."

"Why'd you drive down from Dayton in this car? You know Trisha can't stand riding in it."

He winked. "She used to."

Mama smacked his arm. "Shut up."

They both laughed, and Uncle Tony pulled her back in for another hug. "Where is that husband of yours?"

My uncle never called my daddy by his first name, always referring to him as my mama's husband. I never did understand that. They got along. At least that was my impression. Then my daddy left my mama when I was seventeen, and Uncle Tony started calling him Jackass.

"He'll be in tomorrow for Christmas. He sends his love."

"I'm sure he does." Uncle Tony looked over at me, arm still around my mama. "Little Charlotte. Come give your uncle a hug."

"Did you bring me a present?"

He laughed. "Damn if she not just like you, Gwen. Always wanting someone to buy her presents." He made his way over, chuckling the whole way, and picked me up. "You can open presents with your cousins tomorrow." He kissed my cheek. "Same as everyone else."

The screen door creaked open and my Aunt Desiree stepped back outside. "Get that damn car off the grass, Tony." She put her hands on her hips and glared at him.

He laughed so hard his eyes started to water. "Nice to see you too, Auntie."

"Mmm..." she grunted, but I could see the smile playing around her mouth. "Now, I know you like folks to marvel at your bright red car, but do you need to destroy the lawn to show it off?"

Glass shattered, and we all turned toward the side of the house. My aunt turned and glared at my uncle. "Where them boys of yours?"

"They over there playing."

"With what?"

"They're just playing, Aunt D."

"Sounds like they breakin' shit." She never held her tongue. Even around us kids.

"I'll go get them."

She flapped her hand at him, then reached for my hand. "Start by moving your car. Once you're done, you and your sister go on in the kitchen to help keep the peace. Charlotte can stay with me."

"I'm not in the mood to fuss with Betina," he grumbled.

"Don't care nothing about your mood. Y'all ain't gonna

ruin my Christmas with your resentments and petty bickering. This will be the first Christmas my sister won't be here. She did everything in her power to bring y'all back together. And dammit..." She sucked in a deep breath as if to calm herself. Tears welled up in her eyes.

Uncle Tony reached for her, his face suddenly solemn and filled with regret. "I'm sorry, Auntie. I'll take care of it."

She nodded, tears streaming down her face. She pulled a tissue from her pocket and wiped at her eyes. "Go on now."

"Yes, ma'am." He stepped down off the porch and turned toward the side of the house. "James! Darius! Y'all get over here right the hell now!" They came running.

As my uncle scolded them, I stood next to my grandma watching the whole display. It was then that I noticed the black thread again. Only this time, it seemed to have grown, filling out and forming a thin chain of links between my mama and my uncle and my cousins.

"He got his hooks in them good," Zachariah said, coming to stand next to me.

I took one step off the porch and stopped. The link had started growing, pulsing even. I followed its trail back toward the front gate. A man stood there wearing a long black coat, a crisp white shirt and bow tie, and carrying a slender black cane in his hand. His long black hair hung loose around his face. He watched my mama and uncle with an unrestrained hunger in his eyes. I yelped when I realized he'd crept closer. He stood staring, his attention suddenly on me, just outside the ring of seashells covering the driveway.

Lay the shells so you can hear him coming.

When he stepped on them, my mother jerked, and her face drained of color as she turned toward the sound. Did she see him too? Uncle Tony pushed her behind him, and the boys stood with one foot on the steps. Their reaction suggested they heard him. But they didn't look at him. Instead, they searched the yard.

"Only we can see Mr. Manning, Charlotte. But they can feel him. He can't get past the seashells. Not yet," my grandma said.

"The rosemary might not stop him," Zachariah said, staring down at the dried-out bushes.

Plant the rosemary to keep him out.

"It'll keep for now."

After a while, they all went inside, and I stayed on the porch with my grandma, aunt, and Grandpa Zachariah. Despite knowing that my aunt couldn't see my grandma or Zachariah, my grandma still carried on talking as if Aunt Desiree could hear her. And every once in a while, my aunt would nod as if she could.

Next to arrive was my Uncle Ronald and Aunt Francine along with their three children. Marilyn was four and still liked to suck her thumb. Connie was two and didn't want to walk on the ground. My uncle always carried her. And my cousin Fredrick was six and bossy as hell.

Finally, near lunch time, my Aunt Anne arrived with her husband, Harold, and their fourteen-year-old son Lawrence. He didn't like hanging out with the rest of us and often went off on his own. I'd heard my aunts talking about a girl named Sherry that lived in town that he would meet up with. They unloaded the car, each of them carrying several dishes into the house, and we all went inside to eat.

Aunt Lenora and her husband, Uncle Francois, arrived after lunch. My aunt lived in Paris and was a famous dress designer. I always thought she was so glamorous. Despite this, she had a down-to-earth way about her that I really liked. She'd tried teaching me French a few times, but I never picked up the language. My cousins, Michelle and Martine (twins) were both twelve and acted like we were all beneath them. They were James and Darius's favorite targets.

Finally, toward the late afternoon, my Uncle Walter and his wife, Nancy, arrived along with my cousins, Carl and Raymond. Carl was three and Raymond was five like me. With them was Aunt Nancy's brother Greg, his wife Vanessa, and my favorite cousin Beatrice. Despite being two years older than me, she rarely hung out with my other cousins and instead stayed by my side as if she was trying to protect me.

While the adults stayed inside, talking and fussing, my cousins had started playing in the yard, yelling and running. I remember studying them from the front porch, sitting next to Beatrice.

"You want to play?" she asked.

I spotted Mr. Manning in the yard and shook my head. I wasn't going out there with the black chain circling the yard, connecting to all of my cousins.

Every once in a while, though, I would check both Beatrice and me for the black chain. I, in my young mind, believed if we just stayed on the porch, then we would be safe.

The fighting started as the sun went down. James had shoved Fredrick down, and Raymond jumped on his back. I was used to seeing the boys roughhouse, but somehow, this behavior was a little different. Almost as if it were being fueled by the black chains pulsating within them. Even inside the house, my family's voices were raised.

Both Beatrice and I moved closer to one another.

The rosemary, usually so fragrant, lost some of its potent smell.

I glanced over at it and watched the green turn brown, wilting as if acid had been poured on it.

Mr. Manning moved closer to the house. His hungry eyes

fixated on me and Beatrice while his chain wrapped around the yard, infecting my cousins. Connecting them to him.

I felt her presence before she spoke. She had been in the house, watching her children's anger blossom into a fury that no one seemed able to tame.

"Charlotte! Get inside!" my grandma yelled. I glanced up at her face. It was frozen in fear. I looked down to where she was staring. Mr. Manning had passed the last line of seashells and was now at the bottom of the porch steps, staring up at us.

His face looked slippery, like a rubber mask stretched over bone. Almost as if he was wearing someone else's body.

"Miss. I could see your beacon a mile off." He took off his hat and bowed toward me, scenting the air with ash and rot. Like someone had left a pile of meat out in the heat to spoil.

"Mama," I said, my voice small. My grandma laid a cool hand on my shoulder.

"What's wrong, Charlotte?" Beatrice asked, searching the area around us as I stared, horrified, at Mr. Manning.

"Mary Alice," he went on as if Beatrice hadn't even spoken. But then again, she couldn't see him. And he was so fixated on me. "She reminds me of you. So young and full of power." He turned. "Old Zachariah." I hadn't realized that he was standing on the porch as well. "Still haven't moved on I see. Care to watch me devour the last of your family?"

"They stronger than you," Zachariah said, his voice shaking with rage. "We defeated you once. My family will do it again."

Mr. Manning cupped a hand behind his ear. "No peace to be found here. Only pain." He smiled at that, showing rotten teeth, and then drew breath in and closed his eyes. "The meal will be so sweet." He opened his eyes and stared at me. "Tell me, little one. Who do you think will strike first?"

"Ain't none of my children gonna kill anyone. They still have love in their hearts," my grandma said, moving closer to him, blocking me from his view.

He laughed and took another defiant step forward.

I clawed at Beatrice, and tears ran down my face. She pulled me up, only for me to suddenly buckle under an invisible weight. The chains reached for me, seeking a home inside my chest. I started swatting at them, my hand going through them as if they weren't even there. Terror seized my heart, and I screamed, still waving madly. Even though those chains were insubstantial, I could feel the coldness of them.

A bitter taste of sea salt coated my tongue, and I heard the ocean crashing against something solid. In my young mind, I had no point of reference to draw on to figure out what the sound was. But later, I realized it was a ship I was hearing, beating against the waves of the ocean. The moans of men and women joined in the chorus.

Slaves. Mr. Manning's first victims.

"Charlotte, baby. What's wrong?" my mama asked, rushing outside. Beatrice must have gone to get her.

When she stopped, her body merged with Mr. Manning's. I didn't realize he had gotten so close. A loud chink sounded, like a lock being jammed into place. Mama's eyes fluttered for a moment. I reached for her, and my grandma pulled me back. A piece of the chain connecting her to Mr. Manning slithered out, reaching for me again.

I screamed, and everything went black.

Three

Fear

I came to on the couch in the parlor. Sweat molded my white undershirt to my clammy skin. The ceiling fan pushed warm air and the stench of the bayou around the room. Aunt Desiree shuffled over to me carrying a sweating glass of sweet tea.

"Here, little Charlotte. Sit up and drink this."

I pushed up from my prone position and took the glass from her. Her hand hovered near it as I took a few small sips. She had a damp towel in her hand, and after I finished the tea, she pressed the cool cloth to my forehead.

"Is he gone?" I asked.

Aunt Desiree sighed as she sat down heavily on the couch next to me. I shifted over and crawled into her lap. Her skin was just as clammy as mine. Thunder rumbled outside, though the sky remained clear. I pressed myself closer to her. I always hated thunderstorms.

"Don't suppose that dried-up rosemary kept him out. I can't see him." She pressed a knuckle into her chest. "But I feel him. Hovering around here. Trying to link me in his chain."

I rubbed my chest, remembering the chain reaching out for me. I shuddered, and my aunt rubbed my back.

"You hungry?"

I nodded, feeling tears well up in my eyes. I was scared and didn't know what I could do to protect myself. The adults were too consumed in their own anger to really pay attention. Voices from outside carried into the house. I slid off my aunt's lap and ran to the window. All my cousins were there now, playing in the dark. Completely unaware of the turmoil going on inside the house. Why couldn't they see Mr. Manning too? What made me so special?

"How come they can't see him?" I asked, pressing my face to the screen. Dirt tickled my nose and I sneezed.

My aunt grunted as she got up and joined me at the window. "There's something special about you and your grandma. That kind of power takes a certain sort of vessel to hold. It takes strength that not all people possess. Sight and strength combined. I can see the power that creates it, but not the spirits."

"Why didn't Mama get the sight?"

"I believe she did, little Charlotte, but it scared her so much that she let it slip away. Refused to believe what was in front of her." She looked down at me. "Don't you let go of that power."

"I won't. But Auntie. It scares me."

"Good. That fear will keep you safe. Now, let's go in and get you something to eat." She started off toward the kitchen. It was only then that I heard the adults' raised voices carrying into the room. There was so much anger in them.

"Why are they mad?" I asked.

"Because, little Charlotte. Hatred and anger fuels him, and he needs to feed."

I didn't understand what she meant. But now, at least I knew that she was talking about Mr. Manning. He needed to feed off the anger. He needed to divide my family even further.

My aunt shuffled into the kitchen, and they all stopped. My mama glanced over at me standing just inside the doorway. "You feelin' better, baby?"

I didn't respond. I was too fixated on the thick chains circling the room. Diving into each of them. Pulsing black with a bright, angry red sheen coating it. Thin tendrils were making their way outside to my cousins, catching them in Mr. Manning's web.

After dinner, they had set up a space in the parlor for all the kids to sleep. Blankets piled on the floor, and snacks had been spread out, and everyone was talking at once. Even as a child, I had craved my solitude. Their voices were too loud, and I wanted to run to my mama's room and sleep with her. But I knew if I had, they would make fun of me. So I sat there, in the middle of all that chaos, holding a piece of Werther's in my hand.

My cousin Beatrice sidled up close and wrapped her arm around me. "My mom said you fainted." I looked over at her and nodded. I didn't dare say anything out loud. My cousin James would likely hear and choose that moment to suddenly notice me.

I'd always liked Beatrice. She constantly defended me

when the teasing got bad. But she also carried this sadness with her that I could never figure out.

Darius, James' brother, plopped down next to us, and I cringed, preparing myself for the inevitable. Beatrice squeezed my shoulder. At that moment, I believed my Aunt Desiree couldn't have been talking about me. I had no strength. Not really.

"So, are you babies going to go in the attic with us?"

"Who you calling a baby, butt face?" Beatrice asked, staring daggers at him.

He opened his mouth then shut it. "Never mind," he said and got up. "They're scared. The rest of us can go."

Beatrice leaned in toward me and whispered, "Did you want to go in the attic?" I didn't miss the excitement in her voice, and I wanted to say yes, to be a part of that excitement, but couldn't.

All of them left the room, and it was only when I saw the tiny black chain trailing behind them that I got up and joined them. Maybe I could figure out a way to warn them. Besides, I hadn't seen my grandma's or Zachariah's spirits since I fainted on the porch. Had Mr. Manning got them somehow? And if he did, what did he do to them? All I knew was it was up to me to figure it out and save my family. So, I had to use the strength my Aunt Desiree believed I had.

The attic stretched across the entire span of the house. Rows and rows of old things covered the entire space. Perspiration covered my back as I made my way slowly across the dust-covered floor. Only a few lightbulbs were secured to the ceiling, making the light minimal and creating shadows all over the place. Boxes of clothing and toys and larger pieces of wooden furniture lay scattered, some under white sheets and some exposed to the dust and debris floating around in the enormous space.

In the center of the room stood a wooden chest. If I had been asked back then why I chose that chest to explore, I wouldn't have been able to explain it. But something had pulled me to that wooden box. Something that occupied my thoughts so heavily I didn't realize Beatrice was no longer next to me.

I ran my hand over the polished wood. Only a thin layer of dust coated it. Four gold metal bands, more decorative than anything, wrapped around the chest. A simple latch kept it shut. I went to my knees in front of it and tried to pry it open. It wouldn't budge. Since there wasn't a keyhole for the lock, I assumed I just didn't have enough strength to open it. I looked up and searched for my cousins. While I could hear them chattering at one another, their voices echoing, I couldn't find them.

"Beatrice?" I called out.

A hand rested on my shoulder, causing me to jump. I turned and found Grandma standing next to me. I jumped up and wrapped my arms around her, my whole body shaking with not only fear but happiness that she had returned.

"Where did you go?" I asked, my voice muffled as I pressed into her.

"Had to find a way to keep him out." She pulled me away from her and stared down into my face. I could barely make out her features in the muted light. "I'm gonna need your help, little Charlotte. You and your cousins are going to have to take the chest downstairs." She wiped at some dust that had settled on my face. "Think you can manage that for me?"

My chin struck my breastbone as I nodded vigorously. I wanted to help so bad.

"Who are you talking to?" Beatrice asked, walking up holding a baseball bat in her hand. As silly as it was, a stray thought entered my head when I saw her holding that bat. Like why a girl would want that and not a doll. I learned later why, and it had nothing to do with a desire to play baseball. She needed to protect herself.

"My grandma," I said. "She wants us to take this downstairs." I rested my hand on the wood. "Only, I can't carry it by myself."

Beatrice looked around the room, her hands tightening on the bat. "Is she here now?" she asked, a quiver in her voice.

I rushed over and placed my hand over hers. I wasn't going to let her hit my grandma. "Grandma is good. She won't hurt us."

Beatrice nodded. There was a haunted look in her eyes that said she didn't fully believe me. But still, she let the bat slide down her hand and rest by her side. "Well, we can get the rest of them to help too."

I shook my head. "They won't believe me."

She smiled. "We don't have to tell them why." She put her arm around me. "Follow my lead." I didn't know what she meant but I did understand enough to know she was going to help, and that's all that mattered.

"Hey, butt face? Are you still trying on dresses?"

"Screw you!" Darius yelled.

It was funny how he had responded to the nickname. It wasn't like she had said, "Hey Darius, you butt face." We both chuckled as footsteps pounded our way.

Darius came around the corner with his brother James and four of my other cousins. The younger ones were in the room with their parents.

Beatrice put her hands on her hips. "I bet the six of you can't carry this chest downstairs."

"Why should we?"

"So we can use a crowbar to open it, dummy."

James scrunched his face up in contemplation. He must have known something was going on. He just couldn't figure out what.

Finally, the boys circled around James as he whispered to them. Even I, at five, knew they could just go downstairs and get the crowbar. But Beatrice teasing them left them no room for negotiation. In the end, all six of them hefted the chest up and carried it downstairs.

When Darius smashed his thumb after Fredrick let his end slip going down the stairs, I had to cover my mouth to hide the snickers. It helped that grandma had placed her hand on my shoulder in a silent reprimand.

As kids, we never really understood that sound carries. Even the most careful footsteps could elicit sounds that adults always heard. And this was why, when we made it back to the parlor, all of our parents were waiting for us. Uncle Walter was even holding a belt.

"What in the hell are you all doing?" Uncle Ronald asked.

"Beatrice. Get over here now," her dad, Uncle Greg, gritted out. Beatrice flinched. She had brought the bat down with her. Her knuckles turned white as she gripped it. Her mother placed a hand on Greg's arm; he shook it off. "I'm going back home. You two can stay here," he said, and stormed off.

Aunt Desiree pushed through them and came to stand next to me. "Betina, go find your mama's key to the chest."

"Why?" she said, pulling her robe closed.

"Because I said so."

Aunt Desiree stared down at me. "Did your grandma tell you to bring this down?"

"No. Stupid Beatrice dared us..." James started.

"Shut up, James," Aunt Trisha said. "No one was talking

to you."

"Yes, she did," I said.

My mama came over and crouched down in front of me. "Baby. What did I tell you about talking about your grandma that way? She's gone. You have to stop."

"Gwen," Aunt Desiree said. "You and your brothers and sisters all know that if Charlotte said she can see your mama, then she can. You may have denied your gift, but you will not make little Charlotte deny hers." She sighed and then moved over to the couch, sitting down heavily. "Mr. Manning is back. And ya'll know it." She turned to Aunt Betina. "Now, go get the key. It's time ya'll remember the recipe to keep him out."

"Little Charlotte, do you see the chain?" she asked, rubbing at her chest.

"Yes, Auntie."

"Where?"

I pointed at all the adults, all my cousins, except for Beatrice and her mom.

Aunt Desiree nodded. "Shouldn't have let the rosemary go. We needed more than just rain to keep it thriving." She looked at Aunt Betina. "You knew that."

"You're scaring the children, Aunt Desiree," Aunt Lenora said, as she put her arms around her daughters. Her husband looked at her with questions in his eyes.

Aunt Betina returned with a key that fit into a hidden lock on the side of the chest. Once she opened the trunk, Aunt Desiree got up and walked over to it. She reached inside and pulled out a worn leather journal secured with a string. It had belonged to Zachariah, with a "Z" etched on the front.

"It's time ya'll remember the story of Mr. Manning," she said, and opened the journal.

The story of Mr. Manning, as dictated to me by Felicia LaRue.
Zachariah Washington
February 12, 1868

At the age of seventeen, Jesse Manning, developed a taste for killing. His favorite victims were the slaves his family owned. His father, angered by the loss of money, turned him over to the law.

Jesse was headed for the noose. To escape that fate, he made a deal with Papa Sin and traded his soul to exact revenge. It was Christmas Eve when he escaped jail and went home armed with a chain he'd stolen along the way. After tying the family up, he hung his twelve-year-old sister, while the entire family—tied to chairs positioned around the tree, watched. Next was his five-year-old brother, followed by his mother. They begged ole' Jessie to stop. But he just laughed. Finally, after taking his mother down, he put the chain around his father's neck and tied him to a tree. They found the family the next morning, along with the ten slaves who hadn't escaped his shotgun.

Eventually Jesse's soul came due. Papa Sin opened his coat to collect what was his. But when that coat was opened, a clever and evil spirit managed to escape the void and possess Jesse's body—trapping them both inside the human shell. Like Jesse, the thing that now inhabited him thrived on hate, anger, and pain. After driving three families in Silverwood to kill one another, Papa Sin knew he had to do something to stop him. Because the balance between good and evil had shifted when Jesse escaped his fate.

Papa Sin enlisted the help of their champion Felicia LaRue to set the balance right. For now, the spirit that inhabited Jesse could no longer be killed. Mama Root created a recipe that would keep him out. But it was up to the families to figure out the last ingredient. Only then could they defeat Mr. Manning.

Felicia LaRue, after warding her own home, passed the knowledge to the Baptiste family, the slaves that escaped the massacre the night Jesse killed his family.

Lay the seashells so you can hear him coming.
Plant the rosemary to keep him out.
Use the Aloe vera to repel his hate.
Sprinkle some cayenne pepper to make him ill.
Wear the obsidian to show him his soul.
Hang the mistletoe to freeze him in place.

FIVE

THE LINKS UNDONE

Silence settled over all of us. Even the kids felt the weight of the story Aunt Desiree told. One by one, they started to rub their chests as if they could feel the chain linking them to Mr. Manning. What worries me now, but confused me back then, was that Mr. Manning couldn't be killed. We could protect ourselves from him by using the ingredients that Mama Root had suggested, but where would he go?

I remember looking around at everyone and my gaze settling on Aunt Vanessa. She and Beatrice stood off to the side. The chain hadn't linked them to the rest of the family, but the looks on their faces in that moment were forever imprinted in my mind. It was as if the both of them had seen a ghost. I never asked why they were so scared. Of course, at that age, I wouldn't have. But I did learn, later, that Felicia LaRue was Beatrice's great-great grandma. The one who had given Zachariah the recipe to defeat Mr. Manning.

My mama was the first to move. She reached into the chest and pulled out a worn paperback book. *Little Women.* "Mama first told me about Mr. Manning when she bought me this book." She ran her hand over the cover, looking off like she often did, always seeking the answer. She pulled a piece of rosemary from between the pages. "She told me to always keep the rosemary alive. Said it would keep him out."

Aunt Lenora fingered the necklace around her neck. A piece of obsidian rested in a gold casing. "She told me to always keep this near." Tears welled up in her eyes, and Uncle Francois wrapped his arm around her and pulled her close. "I never did. But still..." she rubbed her chest again. "How did..." She looked up at her husband. "It is foolish to believe these things."

He wrapped his hands around hers. "Non, mon amour. I heard you all those years ago. Teaching Martine and Michelle about him."

She chuckled, but there wasn't any humor in it. Only pain. "I meant to scare them."

"Or keep them safe," he countered.

She nodded and turned back to the family.

Uncle Tony pulled a bright green toy bucket and shovel from the chest and smiled. "Boy, I thought I was in trouble when she made me and Ronald pile up all those seashells in the yard."

Uncle Ronald stepped up and pulled a red set from the chest. "I was cussing my head off with every single one of those scoops." He looked over at Uncle Tony. "How long did it end up taking us to build that driveway?"

Aunt Desiree laughed. "It took you two an entire week. Mary and I stood in the door watching you take your time. Fussin' and playin' around. You two were just like James and Darius. Up to no good." Her body shook as she continued to laugh at the memory.

Uncle Tony extended the bucket to his son. "Go get some seashells from the yard and bring them in."

"Why?" James asked.

Aunt Trisha snatched the bucket from Uncle Tony and thrust it into James' chest. "Were you listening? Go get the seashells."

He took the bucket—he really didn't have a choice—and stormed off toward the yard. Darius followed with Uncle Ronald's bucket. Mr. Manning's eyes flicked to them briefly as they walked by. And then focused back on me.

"And turn on the porch light before you go outside," Uncle Tony yelled after them.

"I can't believe she kept this," Aunt Betina said, pulling a green and gold fabric bag from the chest. She reached in and pulled out a hairbrush and a small black jar. "Aloe vera oil." She smiled. It was the first time I'd seen her really smile since we'd arrived. Her whole face lit up. "Mama taught me how to do my hair."

"You burnt mine a time or two with that hot comb of yours," Aunt Anne said.

A tear slipped down Aunt Betina's cheek. "I was so jealous of how well you cooked. I begged Mama to teach me something." She wiped at the tear. "Now, I love what I do. But still..." She rubbed her chest. "I still wish I could have shared that joy the two of you had."

"Are you kidding me? Sister," Aunt Anne walked over to her, "I just wanted Mama to brush my hair like she did yours. You should have seen her face as she rubbed your head. I burnt my fingers more times than I can count just trying to be good enough."

Aunt Betina wrapped her arms around her sister. "You are more than good enough."

Uncle Walter pulled a hammer from the trunk. "She gave this to me when I was seven, along with some mistletoe, and told me to hang it up over the door." He ran his hand over the metal. "She had to help me. Even kissed my cheek when I got it up. Said, 'That should keep him out.'" He turned to Aunt Desiree. "How did he get in?"

She turned to me then. And the rest followed suit. All their eyes were on me, as if I had the answers. "Ask her, little Charlotte."

I looked up at grandma, and she smiled down at me. "Tell them to remember their love."

I repeated what she said. At that moment, my cousins returned with buckets full of seashells. Everything moved so fast after that. My Aunt Anne pulled a jar of cayenne pepper from the chest. My mama went outside with a pot from the kitchen and brought in some rosemary. Uncle Walter found the mistletoe in the chest as well. I remembered wondering just how much stuff was in there.

After the mistletoe was hung, the shells laid out on the floor, and the other items sat next to them, the adults all stood around in a circle, putting the kids into the middle.

"The last ingredient?" my mama asked.

Aunt Desiree stepped up and took her hand. "It's love."

"And how do we show that?" Aunt Betina asked, signaling for Aunt Vanessa to take her hand.

"Well," Uncle Tony started, as he pulled his harmonica from his pocket. "Best I remember. Daddy used to have us sing. Never felt so much love as when we were all singing."

And so, we sang. All night. Starting with gospel songs that lead to some songs my Mama had sang when she was younger. Mostly Smokey Robinson or the Jackson Five. Aunt Betina insisted on singing a few Christmas songs as well. With her being the best singer, no one denied her requests. And I loved the way she sang The Little Drummer Boy. The whole time, I kept my eye on Mr. Manning. He stood just inside the doorway, well away from the mistletoe, anger radiating off him. As he twisted and turned, one by one, those chains connecting my family to him broke. His face stretched into a cartoonish mask as he cried out silently.

When dawn broke, flooding the parlor with light, my grandma placed her hand on my shoulder and smiled down at me. "You did it, baby. You made them remember."

But it wasn't just me. It was all of them. Remembering their love for one another.

SIX

LOVE

Kaylee climbed down off my lap. "Mommy, I want to get seashells."

"Me too," Jerry said.

"All right. You two sit here while I go get the bucket."

I went into the parlor and stood in front of the chest, where it had been ever since that day. My hand trembled a little as I pushed open the lid and peered inside. All the items we'd need to keep Mr. Manning away. Each Christmas, we'd all vowed to come together and sing the songs, lay the ingredients, and fill this house with enough love so that he could never penetrate these walls again.

I took the buckets back to the kitchen, making a mental note to get my kids their own. "Now, Jerry, you help your sister with her bucket once they're filled."

Jerry hesitated before walking over to Kaylee and giving her a one-armed hug. "I will take care of her."

I smiled down at them. My babies. The only thing good to come out of my relationship with Robert. I would protect them until my dying breath.

"Now, go on out. Your cousins will be here soon," I said, swiping at the tear that had slipped down my face. I'd worried that Jerry wouldn't be okay. But seeing him hug his sister without prompting, let me know that he would be. I just needed to give him time. Give us all some time to get over the pain of Robert's betrayal.

Kaylee followed her brother out, only to come running back in again. She went over to Grandma Mary Alice. "I see you."

Grandma tapped her nose. "I see you too, sweet girl." Kaylee leaned in and wrapped her arms around Grandma in a quick hug, then ran out of the kitchen.

I went over to the window and watched them for a while. Something was bothering me. And it wasn't until Jerry started putting the seashells in his bucket that it came to me. "How did he get in in the first place?" I didn't need to say his name. She knew who I was talking about.

Grandma sighed and pushed up from her chair. "I never told you or my children what happened to your Aunt Desiree. I swore I'd take that to my grave." She chuckled. "I suppose I did."

I turned and looked at her. She didn't make eye contact.

"Everyone knows the story of Jefferson Daniels and his many exploits. But what folks don't know is that he had set his sights on your aunt. She didn't look at him that way. She didn't look at any man that way. But he wasn't taking no for an answer."

My stomach dropped as I steeled myself for what she was about to say.

"Your aunt loved to walk in the woods near the Arceneaux family property. She had a bit of a crush on Evangeline Arceneaux." Grandma shook her head. "I believe they both felt the same way. Just never were able to act on it." She sucked in a deep breath. I wondered why: she didn't need to breathe. Maybe it was just a way to physically prepare herself for the story's pain. "Well, one night, Jefferson followed her. And when she turned him down, he took what he wanted. Your Grandpa Jake and Lester Declouette found him as he was putting on his pants. My sister lay on the ground, naked and bloody. They didn't think. They just went after him. And what was left wasn't enough to bury. So, they found an old tarp and wrapped Jefferson's body up with some bricks. And then sunk him down in the bayou."

"Oh, Grandma. Why didn't she tell anyone?"

"In those times, they would have accused her of leading him on. He had a reputation, and no one resisted his charm. Once it was done. Nothing was the same again. Every year, it ate at your grandpa. He took that anger out on the kids. I didn't stop him. I was angry too. Oh, he didn't beat them. Worse. He just stopped showing them love. It was enough to allow Mr. Manning to get his chains in."

"She never found anyone to love?"

Grandma touched the side of my face. "She loved you all. And that was enough."

I wanted to believe her. But I knew that being denied the love of someone close to you could cause soul-crushing pain. But she never showed it. I wish I had learned this before she passed away.

"Are we safe here?" I asked my Grandma.

"No malicious spirits can set foot on the property, but they're out there, and Kaylee needs to build up her strength to fight them. With Mr. Manning, we had the recipe. With the others, she will have to find out for herself just what will drive them away," my Grandma said.

I looked over at the stove. "I might need help making this cornbread."

“I’m glad you asked.” She pulled me into a hug, and I rested my head on her shoulder.

“I might need help later too. How long can you stay, Grandma?”

“Me and Zachariah with be here as long as our family is here.” She pulled away. “Now, let’s get started on that bread. First things first, get rid of them damn measuring cups. The key to any recipe is knowing in your heart just how much you need to make it turn out all right.”

The Recipe For Cornbread
By C. Vonzale Lewis

Carla & her Mom, May 1975

My name is Carla Vonzale Lewis and I like my martinis shaken... never stirred.

Carla was born in Georgia, but please don't mistake her for a Georgia peach. She's more like a prickly pear. Speaking of being born, someone asked her recently if she remembered her birth. And she had to say, "Yes, I do remember that handsy doctor pulling me out into the cold. Right Bastard!!!"

Despite being born in the South, she grew up in California. Every once in a great while she gets to experience all four seasons. But mostly, it's just heat.

She started writing her first novel in 2014, and 30 days later, she had a collection of scenes that needed some serious revision. Over the course of several years, her novel went through final draft after final draft until she finally came to... you guessed it, the final draft.

When not writing, Carla enjoys reading, binge watching shows on Netflix, and trying to convince my husband that getting a dog is a wonderful idea.

And one day, she will discover how many licks it actually takes to get to the center of a Tootsie Pop.

The Blood and Sacrifice Chronicles
Lineage
Zealot

Masks Anthology– "The Sin Exchange (Ginger Root)"

Love on Main Anthology – "Chasing the Story: The Adventures of Victoria Miller"

Flicker Anthology: Stories of Inner Flame – "Monsters"

www.cvonzalelewis.com

facebook.com/CVLauthor

instagram.com/carlavlewis

bookbub.com/profile/c-vonzale-lewis

pinterest.com/carlamc30/boards

A Note To The Reader

Dear readers,

Thank you for taking the time to reading Midnight Tide's second anthology. Link by Link holds a special place in our hearts!

A special thank you goes out to Meg Dailey, who compiled and edited this wonderful anthology. We appreciate you more than you know. You are our Bob Cratchit.

We wish you all the Merriest of Holidays.

—authors of Link by Link

If you enjoyed this story, please consider leaving a review!

Then check out more books from Midnight Tide Publishing!

The P.A.N. by Jenny Hickman

Since her parents were killed, Vivienne has always felt ungrounded, shuffled through the foster care system. Just when liberation finally seems possible—days before her eighteenth birthday—Vivienne is hospitalized with symptoms no one can explain.

The doctors may be puzzled, but Deacon, her mysterious new friend, claims she has an active Nevergene. His far-fetched diagnosis comes with a warning: she is about to become an involuntary test subject for Humanitarian Organization for Order and Knowledge—or HOOK. Vivienne can either escape to Neverland's Kensington Academy and learn to fly (Did he really just say fly?) or risk sticking around to become a human lab rat. But accepting a place among The PAN means Vivienne must abandon her life and foster family to safeguard their secrets and hide in Neverland's shadows... forever.

Available Now

The Curse of Thorn by Melanie Gilbert

The only thing Abigail Donovan wants in life is to escape her grandmother and magic. Is that too much to ask? When Abby inherits a house from a great aunt she never knew, she takes the opportunity and runs with it.

However, Abby's attempt to escape magic and all things witches doesn't take her far. Not only is the house plagued with magical residue, but Abby's not the only witch in town. Oh, and there's a ghost in her new house. His name is Thorn Alexander.

As Abby's friendship with Thorn grows and evil comes knocking at her door, Abby is torn. If she wants to save Thorn, she'll have to use magic. If Abby uses magic, she'll tie herself to a new coven. Only one of them can be free in the end.

Magic, curses, and a love beyond time all contained in one haunted house Abby never expected to inherit.

Available Now

The Girl in the Clockwork Tower by Lou Wilham

A tale of espionage, lavender hair, and pineapples.

Welcome to Daiwynn where magic is dangerous, but hope is more dangerous still.

For Persinette—a lavender-haired, 24-year-old seer dreaming of adventure and freedom—the steam-powered kingdom of Daiwynn is home. As an Enchanted asset for MOTHER, she aids in Collecting Enchanted and sending them to MOTHER's labor camps.

But when her handler, Gothel, informs Persi that she will be going out into the field for a Collection, she decides it's time to take a stand. Now she must fight her fears and find a way to hide her attempts to aid the Enchanted or risk being sent to the camps herself.

Manu Kelii, Captain of the airship The Defiant Duchess, is 26-years-old and hasn't seen enough excitement—thank you very much. His charismatic smile and flamboyant sense of style earned him a place amongst the Uprising, but his fickle and irresponsible nature has seen to it that their leader doesn't trust him.

Desperate to prove himself, Manu will stop at nothing to aid their mission to overthrow MOTHER and the queen of Daiwynn. So, when the Uprising Leader deposits a small unit of agents on his ship, and tasks him with working side by side with MOTHER asset Persinette to hinder the Collection effort, he finds himself in over his head.

The stakes are high for this unlikely duo. They have only two options; stop MOTHER or thousands more will die—including themselves.

Available

9.23.20